# THE SILKEN NET

For some years now Melvyn Bragg has been recognised as one of Britain's most talented younger novelists and the critics have acclaimed THE SILKEN NET as his best novel yet. Set in the Cumberland he knows and describes so well, it is the story of Rosemary Lewis, a half French, half English girl who grows up in the small town of Thurston between the wars. Through the passions and problems of her own life Rosemary grows at last to a calm maturity.

'Melvyn Bragg, who writes about love and marriage with keen insight, probes the same subjects in this moving novel on a more ambitious scale than before ... both perceptive and wise.'

*Publishers Weekly*

'A novel so rich with insight, so powerful, that it leaves you giddy and mesmerised, as though from a surfeit of sun or champagne.'

*Over 21*

**Also by the same author,
and available in Coronet Books:**

A Place in England
Josh Lawton
The Nerve

# The Silken Net

---

# Melvyn Bragg

**CORONET BOOKS**
Hodder and Stoughton

To Jay, Carol, Caroline and Joan

*He caught me in his silken net,*
*And shut me in his gilded cage.*

*He loves to sit and hear me sing,*
*Then, laughing, sports and plays with me;*
*Then stretches out my golden wing,*
*And mocks my loss of liberty.*

from 'The Prince of Love'
by William Blake

# I.   ONE FLESH

# Prologue

The people in the village left them alone. It was a remote part of Provence, the villagers were untravelled, unsophisticated, suspicious of strangers. The woman was too grand for them; the man too shy and, moreover, a painter; as for the child, she was outrageous. Licence was given her which shocked the hearts of the village women who had entered the twentieth century with a reproving sniff, not to be taken in by it. Even Félicité, their maid, was an outsider, coming from a neighbouring valley, unused to the ways of this place—asking for bread baked in the shape of a heart indeed! Overtures had been made of course by those who considered it their duty to embrace new arrivals, especially such interesting guests as these promised to be: but the woman's pride and the man's foreign politeness had repelled even the sturdiest social creepers. They were left alone and, the village noticed with some satisfaction, they appeared to suffer from the isolation.

Certainly there was no harmony in the picture which presented itself on this morning as on so many: Monsieur in front with his canvas and his easel; Madame—or rather—well, who?—clearly she had a title but firmly she shut out her adopted home from all knowledge of it—she, whoever she might be, trailing behind, parasol, lilac dress almost sweeping the dust, a beautiful woman but bold, you could tell, and restless; then Félicité plodding yet more paces in the rear looking forward to her mistress fearfully and backward to her charge furiously: the little girl dallied on, dabbled at what took her fancy, tired out the women by the playfulness which delighted her father. The four of them, in a line against the sky. Like Indians, said M. de Dumas, the apothecary, who had travelled; *tout à fait comme les noirs!*

And indeed the hill which they climbed every morning could have been a mountain jungle, so wearily did they appear to hack their way through the thin air, trying to keep in touch. Finally, at the summit, where an old castle was in a pleasant state of ruin, they would gather to a halt: he would set up his easel; she would

3

look out for a cool place and take out her novel; and Félicité would be told to amuse the child. The mother kissed her now and then but preferred not to be involved; she liked her daughter to be about her, she maintained, though not too close or too often—if only she had not detested solitude so much she could have returned to the house they had taken, bare and ugly though it was, and been rid of all the inconvenience of these dependents. It was fear which brought her out *en famille*.

The child would play nearby, loving to watch her father so grandly sitting there and her mother dozing in the shade. Then, having secured them, she would begin to tease Félicité, only half aware how much she tormented the old peasant woman by her games.

The lavender was coming out. The child grew wild at the smell of it. She wanted to hurl herself into those fields, to smother the lean-stalked flowers into her face: she wanted to bedeck her life in the sensations which came from this wonderful magic smell. The real world rolled into the little girl's mind on the back of this dreamy, potent scent. She dodged away from Félicité and wandered about the fields entranced. The olive trees gave her occasional shade. Lavender as far as she could see; she thought it went on forever—to the snow-topped Alps on the horizon, then beyond to foreign lands, to where her father came from; to heaven itself, this beautiful aroma.

On that day she went so far that she lost herself and was alone and began to cry. They found her late in the afternoon, exhausted, asleep, beside a river. She was feverish for some days afterwards. Félicité was dismissed. And in the spring they moved to another, similar, village.

# Chapter One

Like many others, Rosemary Lewis was conceived in the hope of restoring a great love and born to destroy it forever.

Her arrival blotted up all the remaining passion between husband and wife and they could only hope that affection at least would be sustained by their daughter's growth. They lived in France, in the South, where his landscapes—English, exact, appealing—and her small inheritance combined to provide them with a sufficient living but a restrained style. She was disappointed. She had married a painter in order to live like an artist and an Englishman to escape the European *haute bourgeoisie*. But once the fever of rebellion had passed she found herself with a provincial life and a man whose habits and compositions were as predictable and neat as the hours and ledgers of a conscientious bank clerk.

The Great War came just in time for them all. Rosemary was then six and perturbed by the strain and mystery: her mother was in despair at the deceits she forced herself to practise daily, and her father was relieved to have such an honourable line of retreat. He went to London to join the Artists' Rifles, bringing his daughter with him to England, for safety, they agreed.

She was taken to the far north, to Thurston, a small market town on the northern edge of the Lake District. There, cold, isolated and foreign, she was placed in the house of his relatives, Lawrence and Sarah Armstrong, a brother and sister who lived together, bachelor and spinster, Lawrence a clock-maker and local antiquarian, Sarah, his elder, his housekeeper, and a buttress of the Anglican church.

News of her father's death did not reach Rosemary until months after its actual date. It came from her mother, already remarried, and, judging from the crested notepaper, once more back in her class—though a well-informed look at the ornate flourishes on the emblem might have suspected the security of the title-holder. Written in a mixture of schoolgirl English and

5

elaborate French, it began a six months' correspondence between Thurston and Forcalquier—the village in Provence where she was newly settled—and at the end of that period, Lawrence Armstrong could draw only one conclusion. Rosemary was not wanted by her own mother. He discussed this awful fact with his sister, swearing her to eternal secrecy. The clock-maker was already fond of Rosemary and the realization of such an injustice stirred his feelings deeply. Though dismayed a little at the prospect before her, Sarah, *not* as fond of the strange child, girded up her Charity and determined to demonstrate that certain people knew what was what. Their joint and solemn letter made it clear that were Rosemary to stay in Thurston "as things are" and "for a time", and "being so settled" the pleasure—Sarah pursed her lips grimly at Lawrence's lavish and not jointly accurate choice of that word—the pleasure would be all theirs.

Gifts from abroad followed the calendar—birthdays, saints' days, Christmas and Easter—and though they began with spectacular packaging and embarrassing richness, they soon fell away. The crested notepaper went. The niche in Forcalquier went—never to be regained. Addresses were in ever more exotic locations, ever changing—something which dismayed Lawrence and intrigued Sarah; but whereas his final opinion included admiration, hers was wholly disapproving. Just as he was moved to speculate about the baubles of Catholicism which arrived from the Mediterranean—crosses, pictures, beads—while Sarah was concerned only to burn them.

Towards the end, the presents arrived late, frequently spoiled through careless packaging. Often as not it was a box of sweets or something grabbed, you could tell, at a station or in the nearest cheap souvenir shop—a whistle in the shape of a watering can, a small bull in black velvet, a Georges Sand novel—objects most treasured by Rosemary.

Lawrence wrote informative and kindly meant letters twice a year and always said that Rosemary could return to France whenever she might be wanted, and never failed to add that her mother was welcome in Thurston whenever *she* wanted. One of the few of these letters to get through drew such an enthusiastic response about coming to "*cher Angleterre*" and "commencing life anew in your country" that the child was spun into a vortex of excitement for weeks. But nothing came of it, and Rosemary

6

pined into an illness which stayed with her throughout that winter.

Finally there was the strain of the last year when neither presents nor letters came: not even a postcard. Lawrence Armstrong went to France, to the last address, which he discovered to belong to a small, cheap hotel in Marseille near the docks. It was here she had died after her many flights. He brought back her ashes in a brown Provençal urn. The Roman Catholic church would not accept such remains. She was buried in Thurston cemetery, on a small hill which looked clear over to the fells, and the decencies were done by the Anglican vicar, a friend of Armstrong's and a fellow antiquarian. She had died, Lawrence told the curious, of "something like malaria".

Rosemary was just turned fifteen.

# Chapter Two

She had learned English rapidly and well: Sarah dressed her "like everybody else" ("everybody", that is, who thought "anything" of themselves): she went to the Church of England primary school behind Market Hill, then up to the National School and on to Thomlinson, a girls' school, where Lawrence paid a small fee for her to be gently taught lessons and strictly disciplined on manners.

Thurston was a typical northern market town with a couple of useful small factories which joined it to Industrial England. Its four thousand inhabitants were a fair microcosm of English life; its habits were provincial but no more so than that of every other place further than twenty miles from London. Between them, Lawrence and Sarah participated in a great deal which life in Thurston had to offer, and their commitment was founded in entire familiarity with people, place and country. All in all, Rosemary came to a town which was capable of absorbing her as completely as it had absorbed many others and to a household which was as sure in its local and emotional roots as in its unassailable right of freehold on the property which sheltered it.

Rosemary was a good mimic and although this talent disturbed Sarah and seemed to mock the holiness of certain acts, yet it served her very well in the beginning. At Sunday School, for example, she was as obedient (and this was the important fact) as humanly possible although the nature of the obedience—which Sarah saw when she and Lawrence took her to Matins and Evensong—somehow rankled with the middle-aged spinster. The Sunday-School prizes were always for attendance—which was Sarah's department; never for achievement—which was Rosemary's own. The girl could remember every single incident component to an event which had impressed her and be patient to tease and spell them all out: but she would never remember the books of the Old Testament in their correct order.

Only very hesitantly did Sarah admit this to herself because, of all the Christian texts, that of judging not lest ye be judged was closest to her severe conscience (as it needed to be with such a gossipy body), but in the end, when all was said and done, it had to be considered that Rosemary did not believe in any of it. God, Christ, the thieves, the miracles, the Church, the parables, obedience, Sunday School, none of it. Somehow, at bottom, it was no *more* than an act. Yet having concluded that, the troubled soul would discover, within the week, an altar in the girl's bedroom; cross, beads, candles and images. She would destroy such mummeries, to the most painful imprecations from the contradictory child.

"Proper little English girl," they would say as she stopped in the street on a shopping expedition with her "uncle" Lawrence: "You've made her into a real nice Thurston lass," friends would say, soothingly, to the difficult Miss Armstrong when they could see from the glitter in the pupil that all was not well between the grown and the growing women. The general opinion though was that Lawrence and Sarah had "got her beautiful".

There were times when the unquiet heart of middle-aged Sarah Jane Armstrong, spinster of the parish of St Mary's, Thurston, was stilled and consoled and even thrilled by the pleasure she found in what she had wrought in the starved-looking little stranger who had arrived out of the blue and howled like a dog, horribly and so unnervingly at the news of her father's death. She saw her fill out with stolid Cumbrian meals and long though troubled sleep. She loved her race to embrace the language and even the local accent was the more enjoyable in those early days because the little girl spoke it so charmingly. Later it was to be eradicated by Sarah—who always retained her own accent, however, and was not a bit ashamed of it. She was much tickled when Rosemary imitated some of Lawrence's ways and flattered when she caught reflections of herself in the small body. Moved, sometimes, too, by the unexpected nature of the concern and the uncommonness of the curiosity in the child. And thankful, when she saw the small head on the pillow, that she could be so useful to another creature, and that she had been called to do God's work in this way.

Yet despite the steady suck of the town, despite the kindly influence of Lawrence and the well-intentioned pressure of Sarah, despite her own instincts which recognized a course of self-protection and tried to adapt to it, Rosemary did not quite fit. It could be seen even in her clothes, which were always rigorously arranged in English order by Sarah before school and returned, not plain untidy like the clothes of a robust English girl, but somehow careless, coquettish, often with a flower in a buttonhole or even in her hair. In the talk, too, once the drive for grammar and vocabulary had yielded its treasure, Rosemary was content to bob on the surface of accent—never *settling*. In everything she did, you could always pick her out, not on account of excellence (though that, too, would have embarrassed Sarah, not as much, but to some extent) but because she was *different*. And this *difference* chafed at Sarah every day of their life together.

Her looks were never defined. She could look wonderfully attractive but it was so difficult to pin it down. Sarah would never call her "pretty"; "lovely" was wrong although it was nearer— "beautiful" was reserved for flowers or furniture—"distinguished" was out of reach—"*different*", alas, was the word which came to the rescue. "Different" spoken touchingly, admiringly, thoughtfully, with all the intonations of praise.

Her face was oval, not sweetly so, too broad about the cheekbones for that, but never faltering in the clean oval line. The nose, the index of the face, was strong, defiant, aggressive. Hair dark auburn, waving naturally and springing up from the head vigorously. A skin which was not quite white—not cream-white like the skin of some Thurston girls, nor white quick to respond to sun or hard weather—a pale skin which could seem tired and weak but then again could transmit a sense of herself which made the flesh soften and shine, almost translucently. Sometimes her mouth appeared thin, at other times it was full: in repose it was rather a delicate mouth, the lips long but not emphatically shaped. The eyes held you. Even people who did not much notice children were aware of that. They pinned you to yourself. Grey-blue with large pupils, bubbling with a sense of inner pleasure when she was on form, delighting in the world and irresistibly calling on you to share the pleasure which was both open to all and a delicious secret between herself and the person her glance had blessed. They seemed to absorb the spectator instantly, those eyes, and know him, appraising, flattering him with such complete attention but making him so conscious of himself that, in time, he might come to feel he was being almost "watched". Yet these same beautiful eyes could sink into bony sockets of desolate misery which changed her face completely and made you look away as if embarrassed to intrude on private grief so intense.

So you could never rely on the way she might look. Her state of mind was so volatile and had such an immediate effect on her state of body that you could fix her in your mind at mid-day and meet such a different character in the evening as might be a different person altogether. It was very unsettling.

There seemed a basic lack of consideration for the limits of others' tolerance in this as in her way with friends. At school it took her some time to uncurl from the tight and beleaguered position in which, at first, she set herself. Everyone seemed hateful and she ground their funny names around in her mind — Huntingdon, Parks, Lightfoot, Johnston, Middleton, Ritson, Corrigan, Connolly, Ismay, Hetherington, Robinson—syllable by syllable she whispered them to herself in her mind's voice and tried to chase out the fear by mockery. Tom, tom, tom; Hunt, Light, Middle, Stamp, Rob; Son, Rit, Parks, May, Hether; Tom, Tom, John-ston. The kindly disposed but strictly trained teachers—Miss Ivinson, Miss Steele, Miss Moffat—worried her by their concern or offended her by their apparent neglect. The school behind Market Hill was gloomy and damp in winter and on good summer days the treat of walking up to the vicarage to take lessons in the grounds was no treat for Rosemary who hated being stared at as she walked through the town in a crocodile line, hated, hated the fact of being so easy to identify. And besides, she was a little anxious, until quite old, about how to get back home if she started off from a place other than the usual place. Then she found friends.

Lawrence was impressed by the violence and changeability of her passions. Sarah was not. She saw the Thurston children— with whom she sided no matter how hard she tried to remember her responsibility to Rosemary—and knew that they were as baffled as she was by the contradictions in the strange child—now demanding leadership, now easy, placatory, tolerant, even servile, then indifferent and cutting: opening for the embrace at one moment, a stir on the surface of things and tight shut as a fist. There was a wariness in the local children which Sarah understood and with which she sympathized.

Yet, to make it difficult, as it always was with Rosemary, she managed to retain one friend throughout her schooldays, into

11

adolescence and, judging from the state of things, would keep her for the life-time. Nor was this friend a dependent, someone picked up and patronized by Rosemary: nor a slow country girl dazzled by the "half-breed" (which is what the children dubbed her at first): but none other than Jean Holmes, the prettiest, cleverest and nicest sort of person you could meet with in the entire county. Jean Holmes, short straight silky black hair, fine skin easily bronzed, lithe, co-ordinated in ways which escaped Rosemary and steady in a manner which totally eluded her: daughter of pleasant Thurston people, neither showy nor lacking but excellently respectable: Jean Holmes, who could play tennis very well and was good in the Guides; who was to be Head Girl of Thomlinson School and then become the girl everyone wanted to be served by in the local Post Office. To Sarah, and to a few others who took an interest in these things, the alliance was unfathomable. But there was no doubting its strength. Nor did it depend on daily nourishment or great two-way schemes; it was always there whenever the girls wanted to enjoy it. What puzzled Sarah most of all was that between the two of them it was Rosemary who took the lead. Jean revelled in her companionship and awareness of this greatly increased Sarah's respect for her charge.

Jean could become intoxicated by her friend, finding in her qualities and surprises which she discovered nowhere else. Rosemary was glorious. She would sniff at objects and facts as Lawrence did and then, if she found her store of information inadequate, she would imagine the rest, fantasize and lie, invent and corrupt the truth, adorning even the dullest matter with flourishes of fancy or bandaging it into an ageless mystery. Jean, who lived in a cheerful, accurate world, was very moved by these fictions, never calling them deceits even when they were revealed as untruths, as often they were by Sarah or by time. But Jean felt a part of her being nourished by these inventions of Rosemary's, something in her which could have died unawakened had been stirred by her friend and was kept alive only by her. There were times when Jean was irritated with confusion at Rosemary's behaviour and times when anyone just a little less secure of her position on the planet would have been frightened by the aimless excesses of the stranger—but a few moments back in her own house stilled this perturbation in a placid pond of family tranquillity. It was with Rosemary that Jean had her greatest adventures—though the word came from Rosemary to whom, on certain days, a short walk along a common field could be called and become an "unforgettable adventure". "Oh Rosemary," Jean used to chide her, lovingly, "there's no need to go *that* far": wanting her to go even further.

Her progress was erratic. At school she was gifted for literature and language but would become disenchanted with the set books for the former and the rules which pertained to the latter and come bottom of the class—to her form-mistress' irritation, Jean's consternation (Jean would always be in the first six) and her own self-amused gloom. Mathematics she found extremely tough, loved, and battled with ferociously adopting logic which infuriated the teacher and yet finally gained his admiration. Latin came easily but she was sloppy and the talent was no help. She was so nervous about French, so insistent on the rightness of *everything* she said or wrote in her mother's tongue and yet so prone to mistakes that each lesson was a painful forty minutes, best spent dreaming of something else entirely. A disproportionate amount of her time was spent in such dreaming—"dreamer"—a dreaded term of abuse—was often thrown at her and soon crept into her reports. "She continues to be too much of a dreamer," the headmistress of the girls' school would write, sorrowfully, "and she demands too much attention. Must try harder." She was not very good at games.

The decision to allow her to stay on at school was Lawrence's. Sarah thought she ought to leave and learn to earn a living; the headmistress could not press for the retention of a star pupil; and Rosemary did not address herself to the matter at all seriously. But Lawrence did not want her out in the world sooner than necessary. She needed time, he thought, and while he could afford it, she would have that.

Unfortunately, she decided that she must concentrate on French and Latin. She took English to make up the number of subjects necessary for sixth-form study, but the struggle really lay between the dead tongue and her first language. Lawrence, whose interest in the girl grew steadily and ever more strongly (within the limits he imposed on all external relations from within his bachelor keep) tried his best to dissuade her, seeing only distress in the French and failure in the Latin, with the English as erratic as ever. He was joined in this by the mathematics teacher who brandished her latest quite exceptional results before the headmistress and made an unexpected scene, saying that she was

13

the best mathematical brain the school had had in his time and it was disgraceful the way in which the brightest pupils in girls' schools *always* went for the Arts. The headmistress' reply that she was not one of the brightest pupils only made him more angry.

But Rosemary would not budge and soon everyone tired of trying to influence her.

Her career at school from then on was disastrous. "Sixth-Formers," the headmistress wrote, sadly but firmly in her royal blue ink, "are expected to work at the subjects they have freely chosen and in their behaviour to set an example to the rest of the school. I am afraid Rosemary fails on both counts." Distressed by her poor performance, Rosemary began to take it out on the rules and there was a limit to the amount of cover even Jean could give to her. Moreover there was the unpleasant and unmistakable fact that in any general argument—such as occurred on a small but significant number of occasions when the staff relaxed and treated the older girls as adults—Rosemary would not only insist on being contentious but never hesitate to show superiority wherever she had it. This was quite often, because the range of possibilities in her mind and the fearlessness which was part of her character both found great sport in conversation. It was her *métier*. The teachers, especially the head teacher, did not like it and would often respond brutally, by sarcasm and personal mockery which had Rosemary squirming helplessly. Academically, where she longed to succeed, she was trapped in the triangle of French, Latin and English literature which seemed designed to pull at her in the most profound and exhausting ways: the more she threw herself into it the tighter the bonds became. And when she shone—in debates—she could expect only criticism. After a year the girl was gaunt from the failure: at the beginning of the second year she went down with bronchitis which clung on and clung on until Lawrence came to the conclusion that the best medicine was to take her away from the school. She did not resist his suggestion, nor did those who had tried to educate her.

During these sick months, Lawrence anxiously noted an important change. She went into herself and feared to engage the world, kept her boldness private.

Harold Sowerby would visit her to cheer her up. He was a man of Lawrence's age—like Lawrence a steady bachelor, pleased "to be settled" in his way. But a bit of a snob. In Rosemary, he thought he detected signs of "a real lady" (the crested notepaper hurried along the first suspicion) and decided to call her "Milady". Rosemary was puzzled and indifferent. Harold was a simpler man than Lawrence and had only recently lost his mother —"whose hearth," he would say "I never left throughout her long and happy life." He was a great churchman, a church warden and also, odd for a man, they said, interested in flower arrangements. His own garden supplied bucketfuls in summer and in winter his inventions with evergreens were widely and rightly praised.

When she was fit to go out, in the spring, she went for lonely, musing walks about the edges of the town, yielding to the shy nervousness which her illness had nourished. She avoided the road past the cemetery, already overwhelmed with longing for contact with her mother. She went about with downcast eyes, afraid to be trapped into a recognition. She was ashamed of the failure of her mind, ashamed of the failure of her body, ashamed of its womanly pollution, ashamed of her utter uselessness in the world. The pressure of suffering she brought onto herself was intense and relieved at first only by nature, a sight, a sound, a smell: but even such a slight excitement would make her dizzy: she would feel she was falling, vanishing.

Jean left school at Easter, just a few months before she was supposed to take her final exams. She announced this to Rosemary rather triumphantly; they were walking around Brookfield, Jean having sought out her friend to break the news.

"You mustn't," said Rosemary. "Not when you've done so much work. You will have worked hard, I know that." Jean neglected to make the ritual denial. "What a strange thing to do."

"It is, isn't it?" Jean was tremendously pleased with herself. The decision had been reached after so much serious talking which concerned adults. It was such a relief to enjoy it. "Nobody knows why I did it."

"Do you?" Rosemary asked, playing the game.

"Oh yes."

"Well?"

"Let's sit here."

They had come to a bench placed in the lane by the ex-pupils of Brookfield School. Sitting on it, they could see straight across to the fells. Skiddaw centred their view, clearly cut out on this dull, placid day. The girls both wore coats and were glad of them. Jean snuggled up close beside her friend, delighted to be for once the mysterious one.

"Well?" Rosemary was finding it hard to keep irony out of her tone or her look: Jean was so sweet, she thought, bottled up with her news and itching to tell. She suddenly saw her friend, clearly, as a child, bursting into the house to tell her mother the great secrets of daily life.

"I think school's useless!" said Jean, recklessly. "After a certain point." She paused again. "For girls anyway." Another hesitation and then, rather lamely, "That is, for me."

"Did you tell your mother and father you thought it was useless?" Jean shook her head. "What about school—did you tell them?" Again her friend mutely confirmed Rosemary's suspicions. "You told them you wanted to earn a living, didn't you?"

Jean nodded: she was a little affronted at being so easily discovered. "There's a job coming up—the Post Office—next Monday in fact. Alice Press told me about it long ago—she's moving on to Carlisle. As soon as I thought it over I knew it was what I wanted to do."

"Did you?"

There was no irony in the voice but something quite different which made Jean look earnestly at her friend. She was afraid Rosemary was going to cry.

"How lovely to 'know'—how lovely that must be."

"Everybody knows sooner or later."

"Do they?"

"Of course they do." Then Jean, drawn by her friend's need, made a leap which proved to be the right one. "You should have stayed on at school."

"I was no good," said Rosemary, hopelessly.

"You would have been. There was just, there was just something up, that's all. It would have worked out."

"They were glad when I left. They hated me, anyway."

"Don't say that." Jean was hurt to think that anyone could hate a person she herself loved so much. But Rosemary had felt the hatred in the headmistress' final battles. She smiled.

"I'm sorry. It was my own fault. I wasn't clever enough."

"But you're *much* cleverer than *all* of them," Jean wailed. "That was what I could never understand."

Rosemary stood up and looked most affectionately at her friend. "And why the Post Office?" If envy could be sweet then that was her feeling for Jean at this moment. "Meeting people," Jean replied firmly. "And doing something that I can do without getting into a panic. I asked Alice Press all about it first. And of course," Jean smiled, rather slyly, "I'll be able to work my way up if I try."

Rosemary could have hugged her but simply held out her hand. As they dawdled back to the town she felt less tired than she had done for months. But how much older, how very much older she felt she was compared with her bright-eyed contemporary.

Lawrence had been re-telling her of the invaders who had come to this part of the world; the Romans, the Britons, the Norsemen, the Normans, the Scots, and Rosemary told it over to Jean who loved to be gently informed in easy conversation. Rosemary could make the past so vivid.

It was not only the past of the place, though in that she found refuge for her dreams. She could romance about the present in that mid-war period, protected, as she was, from the privations of working-class life and the excesses and ambitions of monied people. She could draw a picture which would seem ageless: the vicar and the choirboys, the spinster teachers and the cheerful shopkeepers; the "characters" and the old families of modest means and pretensions; the fields which came into the town, inlets of farming with the taste of real country: order and the solicitor who took walking trips to Scotland in the summer to pursue his ornithological passions and bring back rare birds' eggs (though only if there had been several in the nest): eccentricity and the newsagent who trained his five dogs to deliver the morning papers; security and the policeman who was bigger than all the bullies. Peace at night without traffic or rowdy behaviour: a train in the distance bringing coal from the west coast or the howls of a farm dog carried on the wind.

After Jean started at the Post Office, Rosemary made an effort and eventually she was found a place in the library at Carlisle. She caught the bus at twenty past eight in the mornings and got back from work at seven in the evenings, often extremely tired. Efforts to persuade her to take work in the town itself were fruitless: she liked the library, the museum in which it was housed, the Cathedral next to it, the Castle nearby; the strangers in the much bigger town—herself thereby one of many strangers, sharing a pleasant sensation of equality and comparative anonymity.

It was her own history which gave her real nourishment, the real food of her spirit which grew secretly and powerfully.

At school she had shown a talent for drawing and Lawrence still kept two of her works—both done at home as efforts for a prize—neither had been successful; in fact there was some evidence that their morbidity had caused offence and the head-mistress herself had judged them "far too worrying". Both the drawings showed a girl, sketched boldly, an angular, distressed girl, trapped behind bars while out of walls came malevolent heads of demons and in the walls themselves were outlines of skulls. The colours were dark, the subject matter powerful: and yet, in the execution and in the intention was something detached, amused, fantastical which forced a smile to the lips.

Lawrence had framed them, without telling anyone, and kept them on the highest shelf in his workshop, beside the faces of the grandfather clocks.

# Chapter Three

On the day of her twenty-first birthday, Rosemary went to London. She had saved up for more than a year. Having got a hint of her plan, Harold Sowerby had bought her an expensive case for her anniversary: too expensive, Sarah thought, and too personal. It was a fine case, dark brown leather, elegantly finished, with various pretty pouches inside in patterned green silk. Sarah bought her a new quilt for her bed: then, as the day approached, she felt increasingly mean and rushed out to Snaith's to buy a small bracelet as a supplementary gift; and was ever after irritated with herself for doing so. From Lawrence, with sweet inevitability, she received a watch, a tiny thing which, he said solemnly, "emphasized the slenderness of her wrist". Wanting to be extravagant, Jean sent her a bottle of French perfume, and gifts came too from others who knew her. There were more than a dozen cards.

Rosemary was very moved. Though she had been used to receiving presents from abroad and on her previous birthdays Lawrence and Sarah had never failed, yet the weight of gifts on this day which was so significant for her brought her close to tears. For on the day of her twenty-first birthday, as she understood it, she was a free woman. She could vote. She could certainly set up a home of her own. She owed obedience to no one. If the world beckoned, she was free to follow: if an instinct raged, she was free to yield to it. She could even return to France: she could do as she pleased.

In her bedroom she dressed as on an Easter morning. Some of the clothes were new—the shoes, the gloves, the stockings, the white blouse—and the other garments had been washed and heavily ironed. Her case was packed. All her other travelling things were well-wrapped. Neither tidy nor organized by habit or temperament, Rosemary was capable of making sudden efforts in that area, producing effects which were theatrical in their exceptional excellence. Everything about this trip had been worked out with loving efficiency. She was going to stay with Alistair, her uncle, and Wilfred, her cousin.

Even so, it was reluctantly that she went downstairs, full of portent. The sun was up and loose in shafts of warmth which had penetrated the chinks in the dour old house. Breakfast was laid as usual except for the cards piled high on the plate.

Sarah and Lawrence contained her awkward devotional trembling. Little was said. The ticks and tocks of the many clocks seemed a plumb-line of sound to an even greater silence: fathoms of warm silence. Fearfully she opened the cards and read the verses as if they had been poetry: without any hunger she ate her breakfast.

Lawrence walked her to the station and Harold met them half-way to relieve Lawrence of the weight of the case, hesitating to mention the object as it might have seemed like showing off but unable to restrain his pride in the thing as the three of them walked down New Street and past the old jam-works to the Railway Station. There wasn't, he would bet, another case in Thurston to match it: maybe the Duddings, of course, in their big house, or the Storeys, but even so, he would need see with his own eyes to be convinced.

And as for Rosemary! Words failed Harold Sowerby that morning. She was every inch the perfect lady, he said to himself; and to Lawrence he observed that the watch just "set her off—to a T". To which Lawrence replied that the case lent its class to her entire outfit. And so the two men feasted on her.

Rosemary's re-discovered daring and her will could be seen in the vigour with which she walked and the unselfconscious way in which she took the clothes, so recently laid out like a nun's habit or a bride's dress, completely for granted. While her apprehension refined the vigour, made more interesting the wildness of her step and the bold set of her head.

At Carlisle she changed trains without calamity and was lucky enough to find a window seat in her third-class compartment. Until the engine had pulled the coaches over Shap Fell she was able to do nothing but gaze out of the window, a rather mournful expression on her face, the slim lips turned down slightly, the eyes shaded sadly; a young man asked her if she minded his smoking (although it was not a non-smoker) and it was necessary for him to ask three times—his voice going from the caressing

20

interrogative to the embarrassed peremptory—before she acknowledged him.

When the train began to come away from Cumberland down the mountain, shaking with speed and set for the sprint three hundred miles south to the capital, she turned to her book.

Everything about this day and this event had to be special, including the book she read. Her reading had continued during the three years of her work at the library, although it was never planned or schematic. She would never tire of the Romantic poets, especially Shelley whom, from a frontispiece, she somewhat resembled: he would always be her favourite. She read the Brontës all and checked thoroughly to see if Branwell had left anything; Jane Austen made her shiver with pleasure but was somehow too compact to enjoy for long. Striving to maintain her Frenchness she tackled Victor Hugo and was rewarded. Dickens she liked but he did not stir her soul like Dostoevsky who made her feel turbulent, or Ibsen who drove her to dry tears. She dipped and pecked but she was always drawn to the French, in their own language, to the symbolist poets with whom she struggled—for their message seemed urgent—and with whom she failed—for her grasp of the language was not sufficient for her to endure the thought of what she was missing and her patience was not strong enough to plod through enough learning to make it whole. She loved the thought of the beginning of ideas and words: she had an unbounded awe for the Greeks—the names alone could thrill her—Homer, Thucydides, Socrates, Sophocles, Plato, Aristophanes—she did no more than glance at them, however, believing that she could not honestly read such until she had earned her way among the foothills. She thought that she did not deserve them yet.

But on the birthday, the 21st birthday of freedom and franchised womanhood, just as the clothes had drawn across the bathed skin with the frisson of novelty and the satisfaction of confirmation of a wished-for personality, so she could reveal herself in her choice of book. Finally, she had taken the Oresteian Trilogy by Aeschylus.

As the train jolted through Carnforth and Lancaster and Preston; Crewe, Rugby and Watford, she read of Agamemnon and Clytemnestra, Cassandra and Orestes, Aegisthus, Apollo and Athene, now reading a page or two, now looking eagerly out of the window, sucking in both landscapes with a feverish love for the newness of it all; yet keeping it private, containing herself. The names danced in her mind, but gradually the imagined world took over, especially the character of Iphigenia who was so innocent and so wronged.

She finished the Trilogy before the train arrived in London and then kept her eyes firmly on the passing landscape so that she would not have to look around and engage with anyone else: even a nod would be too great an interference with the private pleasure being distilled through her mind. She would have to read it again, have-to, have-to, the insistence copied the rhythm of the wheels, have-to-a-gain have-to-a-gain: they were all, all so magnificent. The murderers and adulterers, those taking revenge and those seeking another justice, she felt her own life somehow spoken for, already given words and shape, lacking only the events.

Rosemary had come to these plays as a poor Muslim goes to Mecca and everything was even more splendid than she had anticipated: if also more disturbing. For how could lives be glorious other than such lives lived with such intensity? Her own existence, which had often appeared full, now seemed unadventurous, even cowardly in its Chinese boxes of comforts, its cosy cocoon. She too wanted to challenge fate, ride with fortune, tempt the Furies. Now, on this day, which ought to be full of signs and significance.

# Chapter Four

Wilfred was waiting for her at the station but at first they did not recognize each other. He had come expecting the schoolgirl on the photograph which Lawrence had sent them some years before, and Rosemary was so confused about this magnificent cousin of hers that no one on earth could have fulfilled her vision. That she had a *cousin*, the word, the kinship, the poignancy of it! When Lawrence had first told her this she had pestered him about it so much—more than on anything else in her life—that he was reduced to complaints. For there was not a great deal of information he could give her. Rosemary's father, himself and Alistair had been step-brothers, each the only child of a marriage which had proceeded like a zig-zag. John Armstrong had married, Lawrence and Sarah were the issue: John Armstrong's death had been followed by his widow's marriage to Arnold Lewis, the father of Rosemary's parent: the mother had then died and Arnold had married once more, producing Alistair, her uncle, whose son was Wilfred, her cousin, three or four years older than her. The three step-brothers who were of insufficiently close ages to make them friends in youth, had followed such diverse patterns in manhood that their contact was pared down to an odd, inconclusive letter. Rosemary was now linking them together again.

It was surprising that Wilfred did not recognize her nor she him on that first afternoon at Euston, because they looked so alike. Despite the multitude of genetical permutations open to such a family history as theirs, Rosemary and Wilfred could almost have come out of the same gene. Thus as they stood, the one half-hidden by a pillar with a sunken heart miserably staring at her shoes and resenting the burnish of the elegant case and the other hovering about the barrier with many gestures and one rather unfortunate guess; they could have been playing the first scene in a comedy of errors. It was the unfortunate guess which revealed them. "Are you, I'm sorry, but are you Rosemary Lewis from Thurston?' he asked a young girl who, Rosemary slyly observed, amusedly, was extremely plain.

Rosemary made no move. She watched him. So this was Wilfred!

He was slim, she saw, approvingly, even though his saggy sports jacket and baggy flannels intimated a substantial filling. There was a silk handkerchief, rainbow-coloured, flopping from the breast pocket of his jacket and she liked that: she wanted to go and take it out, run it between her fingers, disarrange it in her own way and re-fill the pocket with it. He kept sweeping both hands through his hair as if there were an unruly mess of it although in fact it was nothing but a little tousle, a few days overdue for trimming. It was some moments before she saw or admitted to herself the likeness between them and when she did there rippled through her a yearning so keen she could have cried. Instead she intensified her concentration: the nose yes, yes—her father's nose, and the lips, somehow amused at the whole thing despite the act of agitation which was being performed by his hands. He would not be *really* disappointed if she had not arrived at all, Rosemary decided, grimly: but then she admired him for his self-sufficiency.

The last of the passengers came through the barriers and the bar came down as the cleaners moved into the empty coaches. Wilfred spun around yet again and yet again thrust his long fingers into his short hair. "You! You've been hiding!" he said accusingly. "Of course! How stupid!" He came up to her. "Didn't you know?"

"Yes." Rosemary answered carefully, rather unsettled with the shock of seeing her near-reflection face to face. She felt she could see his thoughts and already she longed for them to concern her.

"Well why didn't you sing out? Eh?" Cheerful and confident, he did not wait for a reply but picked up the case with an exaggerated "whew" of admiration which made Rosemary detest the ostentation of the thing. "Let's go. Dad's lent me his banger. If we tootle off now we'll miss the worst of the crush hour. Come on."

He strode away and she had to step out to keep in touch with him. As they walked, her apprehensions turned into physical anxieties and she felt a clutch of sickness in her stomach, the warning tightness in her head. An engine started up and the steam hissed out like fear from her heart. She felt weightless and wanted to sit down. He hurried on, dodging between cars, nipping across a street, bouncing Harold Sowerby's case against his thigh. Orpheus, she thought, as her sudden confusion deepened, don't look, don't look: but *if* you don't look I will be gone. She stopped still and discovered she was trembling. After an instant the noise of the London street split the will of her self-communion and she felt the sweat rise in her to repel this invasion. It was not until he had to turn a corner that Wilfred paused and looked back. He waved. "Magnificent, isn't it?" he shouted. "I love the city, don't you?"

Rosemary did not acknowledge him but forced herself to walk towards him, using him as a capstan and imagining an invisible rope between them which she pulled and pulled herself along. Wilfred watched her for a moment and then disappeared. She pretended he was still there and walked on. If only she could be back in Thurston, walking around Brookfield, quietly taking her way back home. That word—one she rarely used in connection with the Armstrongs' house—rose like a lump in the throat. "Home," "Home," "Home." She stopped once more and took a deep breath and plunged deep into herself to find courage. She *had* to stay. She *had* to be well, she had not to let loose once again the symptoms of that adolescent illness. She had to learn to overcome these sudden panics: Wilfred was waiting. She wanted to be with him so much.

She arrived at the car, breathless.

"Wave me out," Wilfred shouted above the noise of the engine and the ancient bodywork. "Make sure I don't run over a stray Cockney." He reversed expertly and Rosemary gazed up and down the small street only vaguely aware of her function.

"O.K. Hop in." He pushed open the door from the inside. It was not the first time she had been in a car but she had travelled in them rarely enough to be impressed. "Now, let's see if internal combustion's still a working principle."

"Is it far?"

"Kew? It'll take about half an hour if we get a good run at the Marylebone Road and don't find jams down at Hammersmith. Why? O God! Perhaps you're tired—would you like some tea here—or—I am sorry." At once, as if a cloak had been removed, the bluff manner of the University graduate which it entertained him to assume slid off and he looked at her, for the first time, directly and with affectionate sympathy.

"O no!" His look set off Rosemary's cure. "O no!" She could *feel* his interest like ointment on her nerves. "Please, I'm fine. I'd love to drive through London—right away!"

Wilfred laughed at the gust of enthusiasm and set off, chattering all the way in the manner which she now knew for what it was. Her confidence swooped up and was fully re-established by the time they crossed the Thames and went past Kew Green, so like a picture-book it looked with the elegant Queen Anne houses and the church of the same period, later, Victorian houses stretching up to the great gates of the Royal Botanical Gardens and in the middle of the Green a few young men in white shirts and white flannels loosening up for a game of cricket. Rosemary's first glance at once swallowed it and loved it—the pubs, the little white fences, the river beyond, sweet Thames, that line came to her mind just as she needed it, Sweet Thames run softly till I end my song! The fear and the anxiety, those harsh witherings of the root were finally spirited away by the magical gentleness of this gracious suburban village, full of leisure and civilization, a lush pasture fed by manna from industry, colony and stock-market: a man-made Eden fertilized by unseen sacrifices.

A place of such ease and intelligence, Rosemary was to think, as could fill out a life with ceaseless interest.

Those next few days' holiday were so crammed with events and impressions that Rosemary could later find days of recollection grown out of moments of incident. It was as if she had not only come of age but come into her estate. There were books in Lawrence's house in Thurston; of course, books to do with local history, with archaeology, with dialect, and also some sets of classics, Dickens, Quiller-Couch, Thackeray: but in Kew, in the rambling, detached house in Lichfield Road beside the Victoria gate, books were part of the general life. On the walls were not photographs but fine print copies of famous paintings. The house itself was large, the garden ample: there was a maid and a woman who came three times a week to help with the cleaning. Life was to be savoured.

Thurston was not eclipsed by the comparison, nor did it diminish. Indeed it was with a great welling of tenderness that she thought of the place which had succoured her so well and given her so much: a sentimental feeling came over her when, at night, awake with silent excitement, she would switch to thoughts of Cumberland to calm herself and, perhaps, to assuage some guilt that she was enjoying herself so very much away from it. A feeling of leaving.

For there was so much she could be alive to in this new place. On a morning stroll with her aunt in the Botanical Gardens, she recognized in the greetings and in the flux of conversation opportunities for the exercise of her talent which came only rarely in the North. Her uncle and aunt were very favourably impressed: her aunt by the girl's poise which surprised her and by her attention to her daily practices which flattered her: her uncle by her wit and curiosity. They went out of their way to ensure her happiness. It was the first time she had been on holiday and the first time she had been a guest for more than an afternoon: the tradition, in those roomy Edwardian suburban houses, was still, at that time, based on the customs of an English country house— insofar as the pocket allowed—and with such treatment, with such respect both for her privacy and for her entertainment, Rosemary bloomed.

They had anticipated a "case"—after the reports of failure and illness—and girded themselves to their familial duties. Her charm and talents bowled them over and, both in recognition and in compensation for the surly nature of their expectations, they delighted in her. Wilfred had most reluctantly agreed to take a couple of days off from his holiday work at the British Museum on his thesis, but the two days were spent without his noticing the cost and others went by carelessly.

They walked along the tow-path to Richmond, counting the barges which made for Brentford Dock, and at Richmond Bridge themselves took a rowing-boat which he pulled up to Kingston. Drifting back, close to the bank to get the shade from the willows, he told her of his life at Durham University and how he had always meant to come over to Cumberland but never had—dash it!—to tell the absolute truth he had been over to Cumberland, several times, to climb in the Langdales and sniff around Eskdale on a particular scholastic whim which he had conceived about the Norse settlements but somehow he had never got to Thurston. Would she forgive him? Never, she said gravely: never.

Wilfred had studied Romance Languages—Rosemary startled to hear the phrases what finer, more exquisite combination of words for study could there be than Romance Languages?—the

27

two great worlds were there, she thought, all that life was and all it could be. While he talked on describing the course and his progress along it, she found herself drifting on those two words as the boat drifted on the current and then she was sorry for her self-indulgence because she saw that he expected a response and she had no idea of the question.

"Well?"

"I'm sorry," she said. "This is so lovely. I've never been anywhere so beautiful before."

As increasingly often, Wilfred was both moved and taken aback by a directness which applied not to the top layer of exchange at all but was more vulnerable than anything which was open between them. Nevertheless there was a certain irritation in him that his account could be so very lightly received.

"I was asking you if you had been able to retain your French and if so what were the chief differences you noticed between the grammars." He paused. "Damn stupid question, I grant you."

"No," she replied seriously, "not at all." She hesitated. "I lost my French," she said, "all of it. I tried to keep it up but I failed."

"Tricky to do this sort of thing on your own."

"When I had help—at school—I did not take much advantage of it. I was lazy."

"Well . . . School." He shrugged.

"And afterwards I had not the guts."

"That's a bit hard on yourself."

"It's the truth." She dabbled her hand in the water which fondled her skin coldly.

"You can always start again," he said.

As he took up the oars to pull them round the final bend back to the boating station at Richmond Promenade, Rosemary looked up and saw the splendid line of houses on top of the bluff that was Richmond Hill; there, she decided, was where she would like to live with Wilfred: they would look out up the Thames and onto that gentle plain so long peaceful and protected; they would be on a cliff up there and welcome the force of a storm because they would be safe. She snuggled down to the dream in her mind and Wilfred was anxious about her preoccupation when he led her off the boat and along to the garden of a pub. She often slipped away where he could not follow.

28

She drank lemonade and looked around curiously, but with some disappointment.

"It's not a *real* pub," she declared, remembering Thurston and the terrible tales of drunkenness, the legends of weekend violence, the dour men in caps and waistcoats.

"Of course it is," said Wilfred just a little annoyed. He looked round. "It's outside, that's all. They have drinking outside everywhere else. In France they always do it."

"But in France they *know* how to do it," she exclaimed, ignoring her own ignorance: which again annoyed Wilfred who had been there.

"There's nothing to *know*," he was dismayed to hear some testiness in his tone and strove to eradicate it. "You simply sit outside instead of in and look at the river instead of gazing out of a window."

"O no!" Rosemary's eyes lit up with mischief, understanding his incipient irritation and finding it a spur. "People here sit as if they were *really* inside. They're exactly as they would be inside except that someone has taken away the walls and the roof. It's like one of those dolls' houses where you can take them to pieces and see all the furniture there. And look! These yellow and green tables and the red and green chairs—it's dolls' house furniture!"

"There are primary colours in France, too, you know."

"Ah, but I don't *know*. I haven't been there, like you, not for too long to remember such things. But I can guess it. This isn't a real pub anyway, inside or outside."

"You've never been inside!"

"I can tell." She seemed to hug herself, waiting for him to retaliate but he gave up.

Then she was dismayed that she had made so much of such a little thing: what she yearned for was that they would speak on the Great Subjects of Life and Art and Thought. Sometimes they were near it, nearer than she had ever been or thought possible. But too often she would take up this habit of teasing away at unimportant matters. Now as she looked at him who looked away and saw herself and her father, too, she was certain, in the profile, she longed to make a sacrifice and appease him. "Well. Well," she said tentatively. "So I have found my cousin at last."

"Yes." He turned, puzzled for a moment, and then smiled. "Do you know, Mother says we look rather like each other."

"We do." Rosemary nodded solemnly. "Of course you are so

much more full of life that it is difficult to see what you *are* like."

"You're talking about yourself, not about me," Wilfred replied with uncommon insight.

"No, no," she insisted. "I am timid. *You* are the adventurous one. You are like Zeus who could take on a thousand shapes, he could be a storm of golden rain, or a satyr or a warrior or a swan to make love to Leda. Great men have to have many shapes because they live so many lives." Imagine, she was thinking in some secret part of herself, a *swan*!

"Who said that?" Wilfred almost rapped out the question. Rosemary looked at him inquiringly. "That last sentence about Great Men—who said it?'

"*I* did." She allowed the pause for pride: and then to see through her decision to appease, she added, "But I am sure I read it somewhere. Anyway it is obvious."

"Who would you say are great men, then?" he asked.

"Those who become gods," she replied: and his laugh was so loud and startled that she laughed with him.

There were aeroplanes bobbing about in the sky, the soft putter of their engines a gentle peal to the pleasures of the afternoon. They walked back to Kew along the tow-path—Rosemary had insisted on this because she knew that Wilfred wanted to even though he could see that she was very tired from the day's exertions: she asked him the names of the machines and was delighted that he knew. She adored all his knowledge and he felt appreciated in a way quite foreign to his experience.

"I would like to be a glider pilot," she said as they sat on the seat outside the gardens, a rest he had suggested before the last lap back to his house. "Just to be near the sky with those wings and so much silence." She paused to savour it. The afternoon was almost over and before them the river and the sky showed the first tints of what would be a glorious sunset. Never had Rosemary been so full of so many fine sensations and she wanted to show her gratitude.

"You would be beautiful as a pilot," she said, not noticing the effect such caressing words had on this young man so long disciplined to reticence. "You would race with the clouds and wait for the winds to—no, what is it you said?—the air bubbles." She loved the word and blew it out, "Bubbles, bubbles, air bubbles to

30

lift you up and throw you into the sky. You would be like Icarus."

And again, he thought, she spoke of herself. "Icarus," he said, feeling rather stuffy but impelled to blunt his embarrassment, "Icarus is scarcely an inspiring example for anyone, is he? I mean, he did fly too near the sun and he did crash and he did kill himself."

"That's not the point."

They sat on for a moment or two and then the bell rang to announce that the Botanical Gardens would be closing in ten minutes.

"We can just make it if we step out," he said.

She nodded but had to wrench herself away from the sunset which, she thought, was casting a spell over her, ever ready to believe that nature itself emanated sensations which could be read and understood by those who chose.

"Otherwise we'd have to go the long way round, by the Green."

She jumped up and squeezed his arm. "How kind you are to me! I *am* tired, yes. And I love these Gardens so much. Quickly. Quickly!"

She kept his arm the few yards to the turnstile, way ahead of the present day in her reckoning of their relationship, and Wilfred enjoyed the closeness of her body too much to resist or comment: but there was something guarded about him, and once they were inside the Gardens—the gatekeeper letting them in free as it was so late and so her feeling of privilege topped up yet again—she made no attempt to link with him once more and he regretted his tremor of resistance although he paid his respects to the fineness of her sensibility in discovering it and reacting to it. Rosemary did not allow herself to investigate it: she did not want it to interfere with her pleasure in the moment.

They walked to the first lake and she scanned it for the two black swans she had seen on her very first tour of the Gardens, with Wilfred's mother. Wilfred's mother thought they were "rather obvious" when Rosemary had declared her admiration for them, and the older woman had pointed out her own preference, a rare family of exquisitely marked Cantonese ducks. Rosemary firmly stuck to her choice and said that she preferred grace to perfection. (Although even as she spoke it, she knew that, truthfully, she wanted both.)

31

"There they are!" She stood melodramatically still and watched the two slender swans, red beaks like broad-bladed daggers stained from conquest, black feathers glittering in the sunset.

"Oh, those two," Wilfred smiled. "They rule this place. There was the most terrible battle here the other week when they decided to have it out with the white swans."

"What happened?"

"These two chased the white swans clean off the lake. Vicious. It's a little unwise to have them around, in my opinion. A lot of children think you can feed swans just like ducks."

"We can't organize our lives for children."

"O God, Rosemary, I wasn't suggesting we could or should. I just think your favourites are rather savage."

"That's why I like them. Who wants pets?"

They were impressive, the two swans, he had to admit, two as one, gliding on the surface of water now taking its colours from the dying sun.

"That is how to go through the world," Rosemary murmured to herself; and on this evening she could see it, the possibility, the wonder, the glory of a life, linked to another in just such a free conjunction, as the swans swept over the golden pond.

# Chapter Five

Even among such days there were two which were immensely
more charged than the others; in a different constellation of
importance and significance. What they had in common was that
each was tight, crammed with incident and open to endless revi-
sion and reinterpretation. Yet neither day was one she con-
sciously enjoyed bringing to mind: for almost completely
opposite sets of reasons. They were too hard to bear. The one too
pleasurable, the other too painful: and yet so powerful were they,
so much gathered to them as life went on, they came to represent
the polarities of so many states of feeling and possibility, that they
were like a sun and a moon permanently circling her thoughts,
always to be seen, round and round.

Before lunch there had been whispering, at tea there were
significant nods and throughout the early dinner (they were to go
out to the local theatre—itself a rare treat for Rosemary) there
was badly concealed excitement. Mr and Mrs Lewis—Rosemary
liked to use their surname, her own surname, in her mind;
"uncle" and "aunt", though warm through the statement of the
link, were not as resonant—Mr and Mrs Lewis left the dining-
room and Wilfred took out a cigarette. She realized the importance of what he was going to say and wished that he had not
chosen to be quite so melodramatic about it. And so at first she
did not catch his mumbled "Would you like to go to France?" He
paused; there was no reaction from his cousin, none at all. "We
thought—a family birthday present. They do day-trips from
Folkestone to Boulogne—they're rather, well, I *imagine* they'd
be fun. And you'd get to France."

Rosemary nodded, almost brusquely, got up, carefully pushed
her chair under the table and left the room. Wilfred was worried
at the thought of the possible consequences: her extravagance
confused him.

Mrs Lewis found her in her bedroom, thrown on the bed, her
head almost hanging over the side of it, silent. The older woman

checked herself at the door, perturbed at the stricken pose and even as she was prepared to sympathize, simultaneously disapproving the spectacle. Before she had time to adopt a course of action, Rosemary rolled over the bed, jumped up and rushed towards her, arms outstretched, like a child, her eyes sparkling with tears. "You're so kind," she said. "You're all so kind to me."

The older woman hugged her gently, afraid that she too might cry. Rosemary had seemed so firm and independent throughout the week, in fact she had occasionally been a little apprehensive before this surprising niece: but in her arms she felt someone vulnerable and waiting for guidance. As if realizing the change she had brought about in her aunt's opinion of her, Rosemary stopped herself and a quiver of tension passed from her body into the body of the woman who held her.

"You're a tender thing," she said; and Rosemary relaxed, with such gratitude that Mrs Lewis was overwhelmed: yet with such abandonment of propriety that she felt, unfairly, exasperated. "Now, now, come along. Alistair and Wilfred will be having all sorts of guilts and glooms. Did Wilfred tell you about the trip?"

Rosemary pulled back from her, held her hands and nodded. She was incapable of speech at that moment and now Mrs Lewis, clear as to cause and effect and seeing the root of sentiment, allowed the excess: then, feeling she had been too stern, herself yielded to Rosemary's mood. She took the young woman back in her arms. "Well. We thought you might like to go back to the country of your birth."

"Thank you."

When they came downstairs, the two men looked extremely uncomfortable.

"She is a tender little thing," Mrs Lewis repeated, thoughtfully, after Wilfred had taken her off to the theatre. She shivered. "I don't know. She rather frightened me."

"Rosemary? Nonsense. We *all* get overworked. I think it's brewing up with Wilfred myself. That's the nub."

"That, too." Mrs Lewis shook her head. "She collapsed in my arms, you know, upstairs. Literally collapsed."

What Rosemary could always most easily bring to mind were the details of the day. They went so fast from place to place and yet the newness of things made time pass so slowly: though, again, the day was over in a moment: when it ended she could return to its beginning in an instant and join the day in a circle of memory, looping endlessly in her thoughts.

She seemed to notice everything: the spray from the bow of the boat, the cloud which looked like a fish, the tang of *thé citron*, the sound of French, rubbing against her mind, a velvet jungle. The *French*ness of everything touched and amused her and despite Wilfred's undeniable (but rather self-conscious) competence in the language and habits of the people, she felt herself to be much more part of it than he ever could be. He took exception to that, but with an effort let it pass.

It was getting more and more difficult for him to keep any distance from this demanding cousin. She read his thoughts and though he would deny them, both knew she had the gist.

That day, she was radiant. As she stepped on French soil she could have been its liberator and for a moment he was afraid she might kiss it. That anxious moment passed only to be replaced by another as he felt her thrill to the sight of the ordinary square in front of the church, the cafés, the bicycles, the *ouvriers* and bourgeoisie, the game of *boules* already begun. She might shout out or dance, he thought, worriedly, and steeled himself for a "scene". But all she did was ask for a *thé citron*. She was irresistible. Her pleasure, her just-containable pleasure at being Rosemary Lewis, twenty-one, with Wilfred Lewis in France on a sunny day in summer, sitting outside a café and watching the world go by, this glowed in her and sped from her, seeming to reach out across the length and breadth of the square so that everyone who came and went was made luminous by it. It was even as if they came and went on cue in some wonderful naturalistic drama in which they, too, though spectators, had parts. Life played the game of being itself.

Rosemary noticed his resistance as she had done, increasingly, throughout the week, but as it was accompanied by unparalleled consideration, she made a guess at its cause and was even more hard pressed to contain herself. It seemed to her that all things were possible, greater than that, all things were inevitable and her path had suddenly been revealed.

She was shy about going into the church and only because she was willing to please Wilfred did she agree to accompany him. Once inside she experienced claustrophobia. Wilfred thought that her subdued and abstracted air was a more intense version of his own feelings and he was glad to have it so: the candles, the gloom, the kneeling women in black, the echoing religiosity of the place appealed to all those mystical longings so scrupulously pruned by the low Anglicanism of his youth. Here, he thought, you could feel the power of the Church Militant, the Crusades, the great civilizing ventures, the paintings, the music, the scholars – what men! He remembered but ignored the Inquisition, the wars of Religion, the twisting of truth and of minds, or rather he thought that in some way they too fertilized this rich obscurity; carrying the summer's day and England into the ancient sanctuary, he thought it a place of strength for values and aspirations and mysteries all necessary to the fullness of life. Rosemary's influence was opening up his hitherto subdued and ignored taste for complexity and disorder.

Outside, Rosemary walked into the sun, looked up at it, and shook her head, like a puppy shaking itself dry.

"Impressive, isn't it?" said Wilfred, in rather a solemn voice, as he joined her. He felt at one with her.

"It's a tomb," she said. "Horrible." She shivered. "Even the sun can't break the spell." She shook her whole body for a moment and Wilfred looked around to see if anyone was watching. He had been mistaken about her and felt offended.

"I want a cognac," she said. "A coffee and a cognac. That's what they have here. That's what I need right now. Horrible, horrible place. It is a place for corpses."

She walked ahead of him, over to the café where she had recently so decorously relished her *thé citron*. Hurt and confounded, he translated his feelings into annoyance with her—for leaving him standing and for demanding this drink which *he* had thought to offer her at the end of the day—he considered letting her go off alone. That unworthy thought cancelled out her irritating ways. He caught her up; had she felt nothing of his solemn mystic yearning?

The cognac came and she sipped at it cautiously. "It's *lovely*," she said. "They never tell you that." She sipped a little more. "Delicious!"

"One's quite enough," said Wilfred and then he groaned at his primness.

He was losing himself in her. Wilfred Lewis, aged twenty-five, a capable scholar and well-adjusted young man; brought up with care and attention, pleasantly mannered, generally liked, able to be a "sport", perfectly at ease in his University blazer and flannels on this charitable little trip, was becoming bothered. She did not treat him as others did and he was beginning to wonder, just a little, if he *was* quite as others saw him. He was undoubtedly a person of greater consequence to her than to anyone he had ever known including his own mother: and yet by a glance or a gesture she could prompt him either to a flare of unimagined possibility or to the thought that what he held to was worthless. Hence, the moment he had warned her against the cognac, he almost winced to see her mocking glance.

Yet these reservations were small flecks on a surface otherwise rich and even. He picked them out because he needed to. Were he to admit that he was truly as entranced by the girl as his actions suggested, then he would be in real difficulties. Because Wilfred was secretly engaged to be married.

At Durham he had made a girl pregnant. The panic had been kept private as the two of them had met in horror day after day. The outcome was clearly signposted and Wilfred was just beginning to organize himself for marriage when she had a miscarriage. In the hands of a sympathetic doctor this, too, was kept quiet and after her recovery the two of them could have taken many different courses. Both, however, felt bound. Attempts to separate proved desultory: they were linked as accomplices. They became engaged. Their decision to keep it secret was mutual. She was still in Durham where she was launched on her course to be a nurse.

On this day, the realization that he would have to tell Rosemary about his engagement became insistent. He knew it would ruin her day: and his own. And the more he saw her fill out with such innocent pleasure, the more he felt trapped: both by the potential of his new pleasure and by the obligation of his old commitment. It would take a very great deal for him to duck out of his commitment: he would need help. His first course, class and custom dictated, was to hold firm to what he had.

Yes, if he searched he could find flaws and reservations in Rosemary: yes, he could see areas of irritation and anxiety—but what a feeling of life and joy came from her! They moved as if in a charm and he wanted to explore that, to ride in it and weevil its secrets.

He would leave the day unspoiled, he decided, for both of them.

It was on the boat that he felt most compelled by the idea of two of them. They had gone again to the upper deck and were leaning over the safety rail, looking down at the still sea being sawn open by the bow. It was cold. Everyone else had sought one of the bars or saloons except for an Englishman, middle-aged, white-moustached, plump, who paced the deck as if acting out a former part and was no interference to anyone, being entirely self-consumed. The wind hit their cheeks hard and she huddled close to him. He ought to have put his arm around her but thought better of it. She was disappointed and he sensed that: and more than that he felt an undeserved tribute coming from her, in glance and tone, showing how she appreciated the carefulness of his feelings. That undeserved acknowledgment almost cost him his secret.

He had to decide on something. They could stand there no longer as friendly cousins at the end of a jaunt.

Wilfred always carried a book around with him as a filling for those interstices which partition the day, and now he produced it. The pacing Englishman was out of earshot. He showed the title to Rosemary. "Have you read it?" Knowing she could scarcely have done so. She shook her head.

"Will you read it now?" she helped him implement his decision. "In the wind," she added, "on the sea—maybe it was a sky like this which Shelley saw last."

Feeling he wanted to live up to her request, though shy and anxious for fear of being pretentious, he read and, gathering confidences from the attentive attitude, so relaxed, read louder, and as he read he wanted to forget the link forged in the North and declare his love for this woman who had opened before his eyes over these days like a camellia. He wanted to and longed to: but he did not.

The last lines of the poem he chanted rather than read.

> I sat upon the shore
> Fishing, with the arid plain behind me
> Shall I at least set my lands in order?
> London Bridge is falling down falling down
> falling down
> *Poi s'ascose nel foco che gli affina*
> *Quando fiam uti chelidon*—O swallow swallow
> *Le Prince d'Aquitaine à la tour abolie*

These fragments I have shored against my ruins
Why then Ile fit you. Hieronymo's mad againe.
Datta. Dayadhvam. Damyata.

                    Shantih shantih shantih

When his voice ceased, they heard the wind again, and the engine, and the Englishman pacing the deck. Rosemary sighed in utter contentment and rested her head on his shoulder. "You are Le Prince d'Aquitaine," she murmured: and Wilfred was overcome by a feeling of hopelessness.

# Chapter Six

The day before she had originally been expected to leave (though the Lewis parents waited for a word to extend the invitation and Rosemary, too, could not believe that she would ever leave) Wilfred asked her what she wanted to do on her last evening. She said she wanted to go to the opera. Impressed by her choice, he promised to take her.

Two days had passed since the voyage to Boulogne, and Wilfred had gone back to his routine. On one of the evenings he had stayed out with some friends, on the other, Rosemary had gone with her aunt on an evening visit to Hampton Court.

Far from being made anxious by those two days' separation, Rosemary was relieved to have them. They allowed her to cull over what had happened and interpret her feelings to herself.

The strangeness of it all now impressed her less. She found the house not big but comfortable, the way of life not uniquely privileged and gracious but agreeable and possible, her own part in it not the workings of a fairy tale but a reasonable probability. She felt certain that this was her place, half-way between the far north and the Mediterranean, between the comfortable limitations of her adoptive Cumberland and the undeniable dreams of her native Provence.

If she was occasionally apprehensive about whether it could last or whether it was not too good to be true, then she merely looked around her and was reassured. Her aunt and uncle had accepted her with such affection that she could not doubt her welcome: while their discernment proved to her that her own assumption about the rightness of her situation was well founded. But it was Wilfred's behaviour which convinced her beyond all question. This retreat of his confirmed her intuitions; his failure to speak to her at any length about anything serious since their day-trip underlined the position: it was clear that he was (she could scarcely admit it even to herself but believing that lucidity was essential for a true conclusion, she forced herself) organizing himself for a statement. She watched every move he made.

Coming in late and tired—perhaps a little worse for drink—after his evening with friends, he was brusque to her and escaped the opportunity of being alone with her. Though disappointed, she was not hurt. She saw his tiredness the natural consequence of intense emotional perturbation; the wish not to be alone with her was clear proof that he had not yet come to a resolution. There was no hurry—she could wait for ever: in some essential way, she thought, they were bound and could never be parted. In every possible way Wilfred answered her wishes, her aspirations. She could be sworn that all his feelings and deeper thoughts were involved in the relationship between them and that was enough. When, the next night, it was she who was late and it was the parents who blindly insisted on staying up when it was obvious that Wilfred wanted to speak to her, she *knew* what he wanted to say and was rather relieved to have it wait another day: another night brimful of expectation was no punishment.

He had given her the book of poems and she read them over, finding romance in the mysteries of the erudite lines. She continued to walk and appraise the flowers with Wilfred's mother and with his father enjoy his enjoyment of her punctuations to his monologues. On the river the rowing-boat drifted down with the tide and overhead the few aeroplanes buzzed pleasantly to the airfield. Stillness gathered around her and as the day of the visit to the opera came and began to climb through its remorseless hours, they left her alone. Mrs Lewis, who lent her an evening dress, and then a bag and some costume jewellery, had expected to stay and chat with her niece but she felt that would be a violation and she left her alone. Her husband was looking forward to seeing "the young people" before they went to the opera—he always liked to see Wilfred in a dinner jacket; he had bought it for his son as "the one thing you *must* have" at Durham University and though the young man had very rarely worn it, the spectacle had pleased his father's mind's eye many a time—but when he saw Rosemary, startling in his wife's youngest dress, one she had long kept only because it was too perfect to give away, the dark wine velvet and the Flemish lace, and around the girl's neck a necklace his wife had last worn, he clearly remembered, on the anniversary of his survival of the Marne slaughter, then he abandoned his joviality; or rather the taste for it slid off him. The older couple watched them leave, looking through the window, almost mournfully.

"Twin Souls!" That was the phrase which had been in her mind since she had seen her cousin almost a week ago. Only because of that could the seven days have moved so marvellously well for them, she thought. She could not remember whether she had read the words but they had lodged in her mind all the week and now as they drove into the centre of London, knowing each other, changed, tense, she heard the words chanted by that silent voice which can be heard by the inner ear alone: strangely, the words were chanted in Wilfred's voice (though she had never heard him say them) and the stress and rhythm was the same as he had given to "Shantih, shantih, shantih" in the poem.

Wilfred was thankful to be anxious about the arrangements. He had never before been to the opera and while he would not have been ashamed to admit that, he was determined it should not be obvious. He became aloof, acted a little haughtily, appeared just slightly bored: and Rosemary, who had sensed his nervousness and guessed its cause, secretly delighted in his adolescent method of coping. She especially loved him when he was so boyish and not only his manner emphasized that but even the dinner jacket which ought to have confirmed his place among the Men only drew attention to the slenderness of his frame, the freshness of his skin (*there* was the one great difference between them) the insufficiently disciplined hair. She was pleased with this, seeing it as proof of his glorious innocence.

The opera was *Aïda*, and in the religious devotion of the audience, Rosemary felt deeply stirred. The music soared into her mind, completing everything. Wilfred, also, seemed absorbed and she felt that he too appreciated the work to its last drop—but more profoundly, she thought humbly, much more profoundly than she did.

Wilfred was using the distraction which the opera provided to work up his courage. The entire opera was a welcome *divertissement*. He was not especially fond of music and though it engaged him to hear and translate the Italian he could not get into it. He felt a little out of place, as well. From the faces and the attitudes he had noticed, he saw a higher class at play and while he did not resent the fact that his own class had not the other's advantages, nevertheless he was aware of a certain gaucheness about himself, coming simply from the fact that this was, in truth, a treat for him while to most of the others it was a habit or a well-fed passion. Wilfred had no other social ambition than an unasserted determination not to lose ground, but even so, the atmosphere was not one in which he felt he could forget himself.

Time was his chief enemy. She was due to leave the next day, at mid-day, and one or two tentative references had been made to that. But he guessed she had not packed. And his mother had said most pointedly "I think we should ask her to stay on for a while, don't you? I'm sure she could take another few days from that library—what do you think, Wilfred?" He had ducked the question.

But what did he think? He was caught between two imperatives but the difficulty was that everything in his training insisted on the denial of a private passion which would cause disloyalty. To do what Rosemary wanted would need revolutionary determination. Somehow Rosemary herself both incited and mocked that and he trusted neither mood. Above them on the stage Aïda stood outside the tomb which held her lover and decided to join him in his death: to be sealed up alive with him. The approaching end of the opera brought his first involvement in it, perhaps because he wanted to prolong it, to stave off the time when he would have to confront his cousin: or possibly in some unfathomable way, his own destiny and that of Aïda matched each other. Or was Rosemary like Aïda? She would certainly have acted like that. Her way of thinking was infecting him, he decided.

He drove down to Westminster and parked the car opposite Big Ben. It was ten to eleven: he adjusted his watch, feeling a coward and a fool. That would soon end.

They walked along the Embankment and he knew he must say it soon for he could feel Rosemary's anticipation coming at him unmistakably as the wind off the river. And she was fully justified —the opera, the stroll beside the Thames under the romantic gas lamps, the other couples using the darkness and the benches, the glamour of a great sleeping city around them and he, upright, honourable, why else there if not to make a declaration? She was silent.

And all the time his mind was taut, held by this old chain which he could neither loosen nor cast off: but which he resented, bitterly. "Have you read *Jude the Obscure*?" he asked, too loudly and looked around at the furtive dark.

"No."

"That would make a good opera. If only we had a composer who could do it justice." He paused. "I know nothing about it of course—music—not really."

They were near the wall and he saw her fingers trailing evenly on its surface.

"It's very bitter," he said. "Hardy, Thomas Hardy who wrote —of course you know—sorry—he hated marriage. Unbelievable." He saw the fingers break their path and waited until they resumed it. "Odd because just before *Jude* I'd been reading G.B.S. and been struck by his arguments against marriage in *The Philanderer*. Do you know it? Not as heavy as the Hardy of course and different altogether, but still—they were rather impressive arguments."

"People have always said harsh things about marriage," Rosemary spoke carefully; Wilfred stopped looking at her hand, thinking it somehow cheap to use it so as a gauge. "But they have still married. Most of them. Most of the strong ones."

"But times *do* change. Both these writers wonder how such a peculiar institution can survive modern times."

"Do you?" She looked at him squarely, stopping her walk: and he looked away, walked on.

"I have an ambiguous attitude," he said. "In theory there is nothing to be said for marriage *per se*: in practice it seems to be a practicable resolution." Yes. He *would* propose: all he needed was her help: she had him; she was certain.

"Wilfred?" her tone was only mildly chiding but it struck him with apprehension. "What are you *really* saying?"

"Nothing."

They walked on as people already much different. She knew he was lying but the fact had nowhere near penetrated her weave of dream and anticipation. He realized she had given him his chance and he was bracing himself to take it.

"Rosemary. I'm, I—am—I am engaged."

She walked on a little way though he had stopped and when she turned it was with no discernible anger. "You can't be." Still her tone was mild. "You can't be, Wilfred." Gentle, sing-song even, that first and lowest intimation of great pain. She came up to him and put her hand on his shoulder. In the half-light she trembled as she held onto him. He loved her but he could not move towards her. "O Wilfred," now she cried. "Please tell me you're joking. Please. O Wilfred. We have such a life to live, you and I. Please. Don't . . . well of course . . . I must realize . . . Yes . . . Of course. . . ."

She stopped and stumbled a little, but recovered herself and he let her stand alone. They drove back and, making a great effort, though still in that tone of lilting pain, she chatted about this and that and she left, as originally planned, the next day on the noon train.

Some months later, his engagement now openly declared and the marriage imminent, Wilfred went to see *Hamlet*. His bride-to-be did not come: she was feverish, she said, but both of them knew that Shakespeare bored her.

When Ophelia said: "There's Rosemary, that's for remembrance; pray, love, remember," it was as if he heard his cousin's voice and the force of it made him lose all thought. Then all at once, she invaded his mind so vividly that he wanted to shout out for her. Rosemary! She was gone. O God! Gone.

# II.   THE BOND

The pain was unbearable. Rigidly awake, she strained to discover a sound which could divert her. But there were only the clocks, muffled, syncopated, announcing their absurd measurements, she thought, to the immeasurable darkness.

Quietly she got up and lit a candle. There was a large packet of aspirin in the kitchen, hidden at the back of the cutlery drawer, for emergencies. She took three and looked at herself in the small kitchen mirror. Usually she avoided looking at herself because, as happened now, her image disturbed her.

In the candlelight she saw how much she looked like Wilfred: it could be him staring back at her. Drawn by an instinct which she knew to be dangerous, she let herself pretend, shifting the candle a little to make more shadows on the face and strengthen the resemblance even further. It could be him, yes, it could.

She stared at the glass as the pain circled her head, so fine, this pain, like a very high note, almost out of knowing but there, there, forever winging about the mind.

And then it was as if a layer of herself had been peeled away and transferred onto the mirror: it was not so much an image as a part of her. She raised up the candle and in the yellow light saw that it was herself. For some moments she stood, transfixed. And then she leaned forward and kissed the stone-cold glass.

# Chapter Seven

Nine years went by and the acuteness of the shock was not blunted or healed by other pleasures, nor did her memory allow it to rust. Other men did not compare with the vision of Wilfred and the two brief affairs she did have appeared squalid: acquaint-anceship was enough and safest.

Wilfred had married and later there was a son. She had bought a wedding present but the act of sending it was beyond her. The kind invitations from the Lewises to come again to London for a holiday were painfully refused. Nor did she go back to France: she was too afraid once more: who would be there to meet her?

On her return, Sarah had seen how strained she was and diagnosed "love" at once. Over the next few weeks, during which Rosemary was tired and upset, Sarah pieced together a story and concluded that Rosemary had fallen hopelessly in love with her cousin who had simply not noticed her. It was near enough the truth to enable her to understand the outline of the picture but the moment she began to make assumptions in detail she grated on the younger woman's sense of privacy and pride. The irritable reaction she provoked only confirmed Sarah in her diagnosis and while it would be totally unfair to say that she gloated over the young woman's distress, nevertheless, with the best will in the world she could not help feeling that just as the solution was entirely in Rosemary's own hands so the distress was not only of her own making but through her own fault. There were omissions which Sarah found it hard to forgive. For example, Rosemary had not brought back from London a present for either Lawrence or herself.

Relations between the two women did not improve as time went by. Sarah still had the talent and the urge to hurt this stranger who drifted so far from her. For she was convinced, many times in a single day, that what she said was unimportant; Rosemary seemed so above it, she paid so little real attention to it: Sarah felt as if she was bothering her and this inferior position was much resented. Even now she could strike back and in so doing damage something very dear to the woman: she burned the black velvet bull one day, for example, because she "found it just lying about and looking so worn out. . . ."

They learned a little: they learned to keep away from each other. Even that, even over the years, they did not learn very well. But like many constrained to live with those who do not fit, they contrived to meet each other rarely: even in the small house this was possible.

It was Lawrence who watched over her: but even he could not be what she needed. He mothered her but was not her mother, loved her but could be no lover. And the boundary of his concern was not a very great distance from his own preoccupations: to benefit fully even from the rather tepid, understated, wary bachelor devotion he could muster, she had to come close to him and take on his interests. This she did.

They were the like of her own interests—but much more pedantic and prosaic. Whereas she would enjoy the stories of the Dark Ages and amuse herself inventing great deeds and atrocities on slender knowledge, Lawrence would puzzle away with ordnance survey map and local histories as to what size the river must have been to give passage to the Long Boats. In Carlisle Cathedral when she was lucky enough to hear the organist practise at lunch-time, she would sit entranced by the magnificent fourteenth-century East Window and the music—far from the suffocating portentousness of that church in Boulogne (though she never failed to remember it whenever she entered the Cathedral) nearer the opera (which, again, she would always recall): but when Lawrence came down (as occasionally he contrived to do) he could not be still for longer than a few minutes and then he would be up and wandering about, guide book to hand, collecting more facts, making new discoveries.

Similarly, at Old Carlisle, he instigated a project to start a preliminary dig. Rosemary was content to leave it buried and imagine what might have passed there. She loved the place with its small amphitheatre so clearly discernible once you knew it was there, its potent hummocks and interesting contours all traced over by sandy paths which made it such a fascinating playground for children: and the River Wiza which twisted along through the covered camp. As it was it was enough: all revealed would have been better but the labour and the time involved in changing it from the secret to the opened did not interest her. Yet she made herself accompany Lawrence and go to a small roped-off square of field where a pit was slowly deepening. Slowly because Lawrence was far from certain in this particular enthusiasm.

In the first few years of her twenties, Lawrence was worried about her and badgered her. Like many who were in fact parents, he wanted her to like and do all that he had done and all that he had not done. He soon accepted that she was not like him, disappointed and anxious though he was made by her lack of that sense of application which really makes the difference, he would say, between a fad and an interest. What he never understood was why she did not go away from him; not in a geographical sense, though that too would not have been surprising: but why did she not join things, become part of a gang, get out and about more?

She stuck to her old friend Jean, to her books and occasional piano-playing, and to him. As her school-friends married, Jean first of all, she was left increasingly dependent on herself and on Lawrence's long formulated preoccupations. There was a pleasant enough though rather self-conscious group in Carlisle who formed a Literary Club and talked about poetry: she joined that but more and more it became a group of friends who preferred to meet in each other's houses and arrange outings: Rosemary was an outsider and to complete her alienation, it was with a man in this club that she had the first of her drearily unsatisfactory affairs. She remembered him by the touch of his hands on her skin and, at the memory, her flesh would cringe in distaste.

There were tennis clubs in the town and so on, and there was always the church of course: but she never had managed to set herself into the enclosed groups within the town: that was too intense; the town itself was enough for her without the further sense of community demanded by a self-selected section of it.

Perhaps in a larger town she would have found a "set", but in Thurston, she was detached from the centre of anything; particularly after Jean's marriage and her own undramatic but decisive break from the church. Even the house they lived in, up Longthwaite Road, a seventeenth-century alms cottage, one of three that stood at the bottom of a sloping garden which made them appear even smaller and more quaint than they were, was on the edge of the town.

She knew that she was lonely but tried to admit it to herself as infrequently as possible. No one could ever replace Wilfred: it was as if she had taken a vow so important to her that she could not question it.

At the library, she did the job well but she was diligent neither to be promoted nor to be a general favourite. Some were a little afraid of her and when she smiled it served only to emphasize the general sternness of her outlook. She dressed to please no one, not even herself.

People came to accept that she would end up single like Sarah and Lawrence and did not wonder at it, she *gave* very little of herself, they said. With Lawrence, on summer days, she would be seen walking slowly through the fields to Old Carlisle, carrying a spade, peering around her as if she were short-sighted: on the way to being an old maid.

# Chapter Eight

Rosemary liked to think it was the "day of the cattle" which had started it all—it amused her to have such a point of comedy to refer to for a beginning—but Edgar had noticed her over the years and in the months before that day had watched her shrewdly more than once, when she'd been with her uncle digging in the field. She was unlike anyone else he saw or knew; and that in itself intrigued Edgar.

It was a market day, a Tuesday, summer 1938. Edgar was with Scrunt. Most of his days since the spring had been spent with Scrunt and in a way they had lived like kings. They fished and went shooting and walking about the country; they got up whenever they wanted and thanks to their talents they rarely lacked a few shillings for a drink. Scrunt bred birds—crossing linnets and canaries—and an occasional sale would top up their account. And always they had somewhere to sleep—Scrunt's minute two-roomed house in Union Street—and always they could find a meal—at Edgar's mother's.

Edgar was almost twenty-five, Scrunt no more than twelve or fifteen years older but in appearance they were of different generations. To deal first with the nickname: in Thurston nicknames were universal in certain classes. It was as if the christened name was merely a formal disguise for official purposes: real life existed in the appropriate local appellation. These names formed a secret society, even, to a stranger, a conspiracy. At school, he had specialized in gobbling the cores of apples, colloquially called "scrunts": pips, stalk and all had vanished and the talent had earned him his name. His real name was Tom Calthwaite.

Born in a poor part of the town at the end of the previous century, one of nine, often shoeless, often—in that golden Edwardian Age—hungry and numb with cold; sent to work on a farm when he was twelve after which the War had seemed a treat. Scrunt had gone through without wanting a leave and come back to Thurston with an insatiable appetite for leisure. There were those who couldn't find employment and those who did not look: Tom Calthwaite belonged to the second category and in that group he soon became recognized as a master. He was cheerful; he did not cadge from his friends; he shared a good win; he sucked up to neither farmers nor the gentry; and he had undoubted skills, hard to cultivate, his peers appreciated that, as a breeder of birds, a fisherman, a handyman and someone who survived with style.

He had found himself a house, for which, permanently in arrears but never quite badly enough to be in danger, he paid rent of one and ninepence a week. It had a small back yard and garden which was covered over with cages for his birds and hutches for his rabbits and ferrets. Clothes were, always, other men's cast-offs; after the war, of course, his old uniform still served for about ten years. Food and drink in cash and kind could always be managed and fuel could be picked up. The entire system depended on the absence of women, but he bore that lack without noticeable strain.

He had achieved independence and a social equilibrium which was, in many ways, enviable. He was by no means the parasite so roundly condemned in the kitchens of the employed, nor did he bear any resemblance to the evil leech shivered over in the drawing-rooms of the comfortable. To a discerning eye, he was an interesting and original man; and Edgar was just the person to see that.

Edgar was the youngest of four brothers. His father, now dead, had farmed in a small way on the southern edge of Thurston, near the Roman Camp which had been Edgar's playground. He had played a lot. Two of his older brothers had stayed on the farm and by the time Edgar was old enough to need a job there was little for him to do on the place. And he would not go anywhere else to be hired. The second oldest brother went into the army and somehow it was expected that Edgar might follow him but he never for a moment considered it seriously. He saw that his brother went in as a private and stayed a private: he cross-questioned him on the chances of promotion for a man like himself and the answers, optimistic though they were from a loyal professional, quashed any ambition Edgar might ever have had. Not to be a general was one thing: not to be able to be a general was another.

55

Most of his notions about himself were highly pitched: general, first man to climb Everest (after a few days looking after sheep on the Caldbeck fells) Riviera Playboy, World-Wide Film Star, Great Inventor—for there was a curious respect and talent for learning in his character which had been cultivated by a Methodist lay preacher, a friend of his mother's. She herself was fondest of him of all her children because of this intermittent passion for books and beautiful objects, proof that her own unrealized aspirations to gentility had found root somewhere. For her husband was a rough old farmer and her other two home-bound sons, though they tried to be careful, were still gruff, inarticulate, slow-limbed men, drunk on labour. Edgar was light, attractive, restless; he too could be fierce, and after he had reached his full strength his brothers were careful not to bait him, but he could be tender, too, and for that his mother worshipped him. His father had taken note of this and beaten the boy far more than any of the others: his wife, he felt, had despised him since their wedding night, and Edgar was his first real chance to get even.

None of Edgar's schemes to advance himself in the world were successful, but each time he failed he would overcome the self-disgust by using his despair as a dynamo. He went to the factory to make himself some quick cash but lost it, such as it was, on the purchase of a hound which was supposed to fly and could scarcely run. He went down South but soon came back, too fond of his home place to stand the isolation, too impatient to bear the trial and having little to offer as urban man without a course of training and re-education he would not submit to. A friend of his father's took him on in a butching business but the steaming entrails overpowered the thought of eventual triumph as a merchant prince. Between times, he laboured, sometimes for his brothers who admired his ability to do a job rapidly and easily but soon fell out with him over his insistence on doing a job and then quitting: their code demanded length of service, work was never finished and to leave the farm at three because you had finished ploughing by three was totally unacceptable, an insult to all they stood for. The nearest he came to achieving a goal was when he decided that the future lay in motor cars—the thing was to invent a new one and sell it world-wide—and he managed to attach himself to Claud Porter's garage.

He had charm, Edgar; in that time of great difficulty he would always get a start somewhere—of course the fact that he would always have farm-work to fall back on gave him confidence and a certain independence. But it didn't work out. The smell of oil and petrol sickened him. He had been a good mechanic, though, and Claud told him there would always be a place if he wanted one.

He had gone back to the farm as the prodigal son but the older brothers had been less compliant and understanding than their biblical exemplars. His ideas for modernization, for borrowing from the bank, spending on dairy cattle, building up a pedigree herd, all this was met at first by amused wonder and finally by anger. The argument was violent and it was only the mother's will which kept it from coming to blows. But Edgar would not be thrown off without a portion. To get rid of him and his claims forever they gave him a seven-acre field and the barn which stood on it. All signed the forms in Charlie Ritson's office—an unprecedented occasion and shameful, the older brothers thought, dressed in their suits as for a wedding or a funeral. Edgar knew he had been sold short but was happy to settle for something solid, well aware of the pain that the loss of land was inflicting on his elders and, in some small way, finding comfort in that. They deserved no better. His ideas could have made them into rich men all, real farmers, even landowners, why not?

He still kept his bedroom and the right to live in the house: at one stage he had wanted that down on paper, too, but seeing that his teasing was upsetting his mother too much, he had left off. The signing away of a field was enough of a scandal.

After this, Edgar came upon Scrunt. He had always known of him, of course, though he had made no previous contact with him: Scrunt was never one of the drunks you could bait on a Saturday night, nor did he persuade small boys to help him driving cattle or leading horses. Scrunt kept his distance and they might never have got together at all but for one evening in late spring when Edgar was sitting against his barn, looking at his field and wondering what to do with it. The older man was out with his nets and his calling birds, looking for linnets. Unobserved, Edgar watched him working along the opposite hedge; watched him set up his own half-tamed linnets which sang out to their fellows; saw the man nuzzle in the gap between dyke and bank, the net in his left hand soon to rise like a monstrous butterfly and drape itself gracefully over the guileless linnet. He caught two and as he made to leave, Edgar came around the corner of the barn which had partly screened him and the older man stopped dead in his tracks. He had been trespassing and farmers were unreliable. Edgar walked up to him very determinedly and Scrunt relaxed, ready to ride rather than retaliate.

"How do you train them?" Edgar demanded. "How do you get them to call when you want?"

Scrunt was a great relief to Edgar whose own contemporaries were either progressing steadily, in which case he envied them and they irritated him: or they were doing badly in which case he felt exasperated through his inability to help them. He had made close friendships but none long-lasting and as he went through his twenties his friends fell to marriage one after the other until there were very few free and those, often, half-ashamed that they were unchained. Scrunt did not remind him of his place in the world. Everybody else did. Moreover, the older man had managed, out of apparently very little, to construct a rich way of life, or so it seemed to Edgar who regarded himself as a connoisseur. The fact that his brothers thought of Scrunt as a sly old bugger added to his enjoyment.

He was never short of something to say, the older man, and could make a story out of his passage from bed to the mid-day drink. Some time each day was spent loafing: either at the fountain or against the front of the Victoria Arms. The town was seen on its way: assembled and re-arranged. Like a sailor watching the sky, slight fluctuations were noted as portents of great events. The story of one day following another was good meat for imaginative speculation. In the pub he would compare notes. Through him, Edgar came to see the town as great readers see the world of their authors.

And Scrunt was clever. Everything he did he did well and when he and Edgar turned their attention to this field, then for the first time Edgar appreciated a mind as uncluttered by past obligations as his own.

They had sat against the barn all one hot afternoon with a can of cold tea provided by Edgar's mother and some flat cakes which Scrunt had traded for his morning's small excursion for mushrooms.

Both men were shrewd enough to enjoy the play of their roles. Scrunt would never be without a look of affectionate mockery, a look which would always lighten Edgar's feelings. The younger man enjoyed the gypsy-like living off the land and the elaborations of life which could be cultivated in the extensive periods of leisure they allowed themselves.

The cold tea went from hand to hand: the flat cakes were digested ruminatively, the afternoon turned into evening and the light held; by about nine o'clock a solution had been discovered and there was still time left to stroll down to Thurston for a nightcap, stopping on the way to collect a little kindling wood from a recently felled tree.

One of the stumbling blocks had been the question of Capital. Edgar owed 22 pounds to his mother, and 35 shillings to a brother but he was not going to pass over the considerations which a man with Capital might have brought to bear on a seven-acre field and a rather neglected barn. Scrunt, too, enjoyed the thought of Capital and the first two hours went by in pleasant speculations to do with dealing, trading, building, general investment prospects and so on. When they turned away from it it was without regret, pleased with the exercise, honour maintained, deciding ultimately that, times being what they were, Capital was best kept In The Hand.

Then Edgar suggested he might borrow. Scrunt gave short shrift to usury: he could never see how paying interest was ever any benefit to anyone but the lender. He opposed.

Edgar, he suggested (this was his pet hope) could keep pigs. He, Scrunt, would secure food—one way or another—and a few pigs—Christmas—butching ... but at this word Edgar recalled his nauseating experience in the slaughter-house and argued against pigs, superficially on the business level but really out of a revulsion for the butching: because to make a real profit they would have to butch themselves and that thought would have ruined his appetite for the trade; however fat they had grown, the end would always have been distressingly in sight: indeed the fatter the worse.

Tentatively Edgar suggested that he might sell his "collection": the horse-troughs, small millstones, pottery, brass, one or two yards of leather-bound books, broken statuary, oddments and junk items which he had accumulated with a good eye over the years. Scrunt, who considered the "collection" to be totally valueless, his young friend's one aberration, sadly pointed out that the objects could well be priceless one day and anyway a man must have his hobbies.

The tea went down and the moon came up; a white, wafer crescent; the northern light held clear.

Hens were too fussy and building too messy: re-selling too unpleasant and letting out of the question.

The final decision was this. They would find out the rate charged by the auction company for keeping beasts in company fields and undercut them. Farmers who bought and could not transport that day or farmers who bought and wanted to keep the beasts for a few weeks only before re-selling could take advantage of the competitive terms. Moreover it would fit in with the pattern of Scrunt's week—picking up jobs on auction days was the nearest he came to regular employment—and so the operation would not introduce new and unwelcome strains into his system.

So, a week or two later, Scrunt and Edgar opened the gate of the field in which Lawrence and Rosemary were digging, because it was a short cut to their own field, and the sucklings had been a nuisance on the road.

# Chapter Nine

The sucklings were young and frisky and they galloped across to the roped-off area wih clumsy curiosity. Lawrence, who had been taking a breather and glancing through a book of place-names, heard Edgar's shouts and turned to see a stampede. They had often been known to charge people down and trample on them, these playful sucklings; besides, Lawrence was too much a countryman: all animals were guilty. He stepped over the rope very briskly, backed on to the edge of the pit and decided to climb down into it. Oblivious of the excitement, Rosemary dug on, enjoying, as she always did, the hardness of the spade in her grip, the tension from her calf to her shoulders when she pushed it into the earth: she liked the dank smell and the heaviness of the wet soil. They had found nothing but a few stone chippings.

"Give me that spade," said Lawrence, nervously. "Please. There are some cattle. Up there." He was fussed.

"I'll go," she said and with only a token demur he let her pass. She climbed the ladder and looked over the top of the pit.

Cattle were all around, their solid mask-like heads pushing against each other for a better position. The rope was already going down and the pressure was building up to push the cattle forward. At first not quite taking in the danger—for the beasts would soon be at the edge and there was nothing to prevent their own panic tumbling them into the pit and crushing the two of them—Rosemary just looked at them. Particularly at the nostrils streaming and the eyes, bloodshot. And then, as when a nightmare suddenly grips the conscious mind, she understood the danger and a rush of panic swept over her skin.

The rope on one side went down and the cattle began to move forward. Those at the front, seeing Rosemary and sensing the pit, turned to retreat. Encouraged, she waved her arms and shouted; panic was now all her character. Catching her fear, Lawrence scrambled up the ladder behind her, holding the spade in one hand and waving it even before he reached the top. "Go away.

Go away. Go away," he kept repeating, and though he too was full of fright, the words were mildly uttered.

The check was temporary. More of the cattle were curious than cautious: more pressed than stayed. Despite the loud and louder warning noises of those beasts at the front, the later arrivals pushed forward to see. Now the leaders were sideways on to the mass, leading into them, holding them back for a few moments and then forced to yield two or three paces. The noise swept up louder and amid the noise there was a sound which Rosemary never forgot: in the terror of the animals and of her own mind it lodged like a solid particle in a seething mass. It was Edgar's laugh, clear, merry, full-throated. Even at that dreadful moment, it touched her heart. "Clout the buggers!" he shouted. "Belt them, Mr Armstrong! Go on—they're nobbut beasts—belt them on their bloody noses."

Further confused by the arrival of the two men in their rear, the cattle now began to push and jostle dangerously. The leaders could not hold them. They slithered towards the edge. Tentatively, Lawrence tapped one of the sucklings on the brow.

Urgent now, Edgar appeared, wading through the middle of the beasts, knees and elbows working violently to clear a path, swearing and shouting at the angry herd. "*Hit*—the buggers. You! Miss! Get that spade and hit the buggers! *Hard!*"

She never remembered taking the spade: nor did she remember swinging it: but she never forgot the shudder of contact when it landed square on the face of a beast no more than three feet away.

"*And* again, miss. And *again*. Come *on!*"

Rosemary flailed about her and Edgar roared her on as he came through and turned the cattle, physically pushed and kicked them away from the pit. Scrunt had worked around the other side, his stick prodding and slashing like a sword, and he had succeeded in forcing some of them to lead away. The rest began to follow and Edgar's urgency changed to triumph. "Away! Away! Away home, you stupid sods! That'll do, miss. You'll spoil their looks! *Away!* Get out! Git! Git! Away!"

Scrunt took them through the field and Edgar helped Rosemary out of the pit. She was trembling very badly. Lawrence stood where he was on the ladder, unwilling to move at all until he had recovered himself. Where the cattle had been, all around the pit top was churned up, torn, fouled, disturbed. The sight of it seemed to match the mood of Rosemary and she covered her brow and her eyes with her left hand.

Edgar offered her a cigarette but she refused. Lawrence too rejected his offer and he hung about uncertainly and then, rather lamely, began to set up the posts and push them into the ground once more. Scrunt saw the sucklings through the bottom gate and began a thoughtful trudge back towards them.

"That was near," Lawrence said, eventually. "Thank you, Edgar. That was very near. Yes, it was. Thank you."

"He shouldn't have brought them into this field in the first place." Rosemary was still shaking and this vehemence added to her perturbation. Edgar was embarrassed.

"We didn't see anybody," he said. "We often use it as a short cut."

"Well you shouldn't! Bloody cows!" She looked at him and he grinned that she swore. "Yes, bloody cows! And bloody men who chase cows, too. How would *you* like the thought of tons of cow meat jumping on top of you?"

He banged in a post with his open hand, still grinning, enjoying her anger, hoping for more, feeding, as he did, on confrontations. But she had stopped, captivated by his casual strength: the thick pad under her own thumb tingled as his hand pumped up and down on the top of the wooden post. Aware that he was being observed, Edgar set himself up to be admired: he was not unused to it. Rosemary noticed the change in him and censured him for it, but fleetingly, and while Lawrence hoisted himself up the ladder wearily and slowly, she examined this man.

He was well built, rather burly, his skin tanned by the weather, his battered clothes given grace by the coloured scarf knotted at his neck, the way the cap was pushed back from his forehead, the incongruous cuff links bright against the dull grey jacket sleeves. Satisfied that the post was firm, he picked up the rope, ran it between thumb and forefinger to clean off the worst of the mud, and twisted it back into place. Then he went to the next corner, lifted the pole as if it were a walking stick, and jammed it deep into the ground, so deeply that there was no need to hammer it in further. He looped the rope around the top of it and moved on but not before he had glanced directly at Rosemary, returning her interest, asserting his awareness and commanding her to take note. She did. His look was very bold—far, far too bold, some

63

ancient voice of circumspection warned, but the boldness awakened her.

The fear had shaken her, reached into the roots of her self-concern and, in those few moments, refreshed her belief in the value of her existence: and now, immediately following, this bold stare which strummed her senses.

Yet he was not handsome. His eyes were ordinary brown, his features regular—nothing magnificent or distinguished—his hair dark but not black, his bearing strong but not marvellous. It was the health of his face which caught you, the health of someone who dares and is reckless. Where she should have been most wary, she was least resistant; recklessness was a characteristic which Rosemary considered to be a great quality. She turned away from him but as she turned he began to whistle, loudly, tunefully, and she smiled at the boyishness.

"I think we'll call it a day," said Lawrence who was far from recovered from the shock.

"I think we might have to finish altogether if this young man insists on making this property his short cut!"

"No, no, dear. Edgar would mean no harm." Lawrence knew as much about Edgar and his family as he did about everyone else in Thurston. "He would just be wanting to save himself some bother."

"And give it to us!" Rosemary was reluctant to let the matter drop: it would be sweet to turn it into an argument, a connection. But neither of the men would let her.

"Here's your coat, Mr Armstrong. I am sorry."

"Yes Edgar. Of course. Oh—hello Scrunt. *You* might have known better." Lawrence eased himself by being a little reproachful. "There are often children playing around here, you know; often. And those sucklings can run."

"So can kids," said Scrunt, and reiterated in the local slang "Chavvas can nash, Lawrence, thou knows that. *We* did."

"Yes, well. It's the principle—but there we are."

Lawrence had been very frightened and he had expected a little sympathy, not least from Rosemary. But she seemed fully recovered, and there was only token sympathy. He was further hurt by this, deserving better, he thought. "We'll call it a day, Rosemary," he said.

He brushed himself down with his hands and began to walk over to the gate: inside, he was still shaking but by now he was angry with himself for his show of fear and so an equilibrium was being established. Reluctantly, it seemed to him, Rosemary trailed at his shoulder: Edgar followed a pace behind. Sensing the probable consequences, Scrunt rapidly assessed his own position, turned and went down towards the town another way, to the station to collect some of the coals which so often seemed scattered about, unheeded and unattended on busy market days. Winter was not far off.

"Have you come across anything?" Edgar asked. The broadness of the dialect was there in his tone and accent but he took care to avoid local or slang words, treading nimbly between them as between exposed land mines; fully capable of it; he had never in his life felt outsmarted or put down despite his limited formal education.

"Well," Lawrence welcomed the chance to assert himself at this moment, "we've found a few bits and pieces which may add up to something. W. G. Carrick at Carlisle is going to look them over. We haven't the tools, though, really: and then, if this was nothing *but* a military camp—cavalry quarters really—then there would be little of a town about it. Graves and palaces are what you want."

"That's lovely!" Rosemary clapped her hands and took her uncle's arm, kissed him on the cheek, exciting Edgar both by ignoring him completely and by showing affection which he knew had been inspired or at least set off by him. "Graves and palaces! If ever I write a book, that's what I'll call it. Everything's there— *Palaces and Graves!*"

Much appeased, her undivided affection was something he loved, Lawrence felt able to re-assume a little dignity. "And what brings you down to driving cattle on market days, Edgar Crowther?"

"Oh, business, Mr Armstrong." Lengthening his step, Edgar came alongside, Rosemary now between the two men, one so solid and so known, the other so fluid and mysterious. "I have plans, you know, for one thing and the other."

"You should be helping your mother and your brothers," the older man said. "Not taking land from them. Demanding your portion! You're a rascal, Edgar, always have been, always will be. Your uncle Frank was the self-same man and so was your grandfather. *He* used to go out shooting on a Sunday and maybe never get back until the Wednesday—with all that lot to feed. You're the same make, my lad, so don't give me this 'business'. When times are hard, poor men have no business." Lawrence delivered his admonishment in a recovered humour; he liked Edgar and he liked many of Edgar's relatives, particularly those with whom he had been comparing Edgar. They were wild, in his opinion, but there was no bad in them, he thought, and they had always shaken down in the end.

"Now then, Mr Armstrong, we're not all like our fathers even though it might seem like it on top. There's things can be done with that field: there's money in it and I intend getting it out."

"And how do you propose to do that?"

"Well ..." Edgar rapidly rejected the idea of revealing the truth of his present position or the more likely of the speculations: a mixture of caution and superstition forbade that. On the other hand he did not want to be in the position of someone who talked emptily. To meet this small crisis, a new notion occurred to him.

"Well," he repeated, "I could start off a little riding school. That barn would convert and take a few fell ponies: they're cheap enough to buy. I could get a few as foals and bring them up myself. Tackle shouldn't be too hard to come by—Jo Willie Stewart always has plenty that he picks up at these farm sales. Feed would be no problem. And there's plenty of little lasses would love to get up on a pony once or twice a week." It was not such a bad idea. In fact he promoted it into the top three on his mental list. "Only at weekends, of course," he added. "Through the week there would be other uses."

"Who could *afford* to go pony-riding?" Lawrence asked.

"There's plenty with money: don't you worry." Edgar was firm and certain. "There's plenty not at all badly off. They'll come if their daughters tell them. And pony-riding can catch on soon enough."

"But in Thurston there are some little girls who don't even have the money for a handkerchief," Rosemary broke in. "I see them. They use flour bags—beautifully hemmed and nicer than handkerchiefs. You would be pandering to the rich!"

"I don't know about that," Edgar would not have been able to give a respectable paraphrase of the meaning of the word "pander", but from her tone he perceived its intention and from that he deduced enough of its meaning in that context to keep him in the hunt. "Pandering's a strong word." The use of it was,

66

in its small way, another example of his boldness: he was placing the noose around his neck and offering her the rope-end. "But there's no other method for a man to get money excepting by taking from those who have it."

"Most people get rich by taking from those who don't have it," she retorted. "They don't take money, they take labour and use ignorance and helplessness. Surely you realize *that!*"

Edgar resented her tone and he did not reply.

They walked down the hill and then up towards Thurston. Edgar's house stood on a corner of this winding road, a four-square Cumbrian farmhouse and farmyard, once separated from the town by a few score acres of fields, now slowly drawn into it as first the private houses along High Moor were built and then the council earmarked Brindlefield (no more than two hundred yards away) as a site for development. Still, it was surrounded by its own land and on most parts of the compass faced green fields unlimited.

"I have a collection of stuff you might like to see," Edgar murmured, after some thought. "I've fixed it up in one of the stables. Would you like a look at it?"

Lawrence phrased his reply carefully; he had no wish to offend the young man but he was tired. He wanted to be in his own house. Moreover, he had taken out Edgar's mother once or twice before she had been married or even met Edgar's father: nothing serious, just an amiable friendship which had turned to courting because that was the way of the world. When Lawrence had realized his firm addiction to his single status, the parting had been amicable enough, but he never forgot those long walks around Kirkland with the slim, eager young woman so keen on "bettering herself". So full of interest not so much in local history for itself, but in local eminences, local splendours, local glories. If he went in with Edgar he would have to call on her and that would take the best part of an hour: he was not in the mood.

"Edgar, I'm not as young as I was. Laugh if you want to, but those blooming sucklings of yours worried me. I want to get home and have a quiet sit down. There it is—broadcast it if you have to, a few fresh young beasts upset the old fellow—but that's the truth of it. Another time, gladly."

"What about *you?*" Edgar turned to face Rosemary. She wanted to go: all three of them knew that.

"I'll go back with Uncle Lawrence; that would be better."

Edgar turned his interrogative gaze to the old man. "No, no, of course not. Stay if you want to." He repressed the spurt of jealousy which rose within him. "We'll expect you in half an hour or so. Bye, Edgar—and take care where you drive in future."

They watched him go, the pair of them standing together looking after him as if he were setting out on a long voyage. In the silence, Edgar searched furiously for a remark which would give the right tone to their time together. Lawrence turned, sensing them, and waved his stick before stepping out, into the town, a sturdy, self-reliant figure, brisk and firm.

"You really hit those poor animals," Edgar said at last. "You really did."

"Didn't I?" Rosemary smiled at him, delightedly, her eyes brimming with fun at the memory. "It was *awful*."

"It was bloody necessary, I can tell you. They were all but going to jump on you."

"Yes." She paused and half-closed her eyes, seeing the scene once more and seeing Edgar appear, high above her, above the beasts, not like a centaur, she had been looking for an analogy, not a centaur. "A Minotaur!" She laughed, not realizing her mistake.

"Pardon?"

"You—like a Minotaur."

He smiled politely and waited for an explanation but she had gone too far beyond the present stage of their relationship. She turned and went into the farm, breathing in deeply. "I love the smell of a farm," she said.

Edgar followed her, closing the gate behind him. He could see his mother looking at them through the kitchen window but he pretended he had not noticed her.

# Chapter Ten

The stable was dark and he lit a paraffin lamp whose yellow light revealed the deep brown of the beams and the stall; the walls were whitewashed, and recently, she noted, but he had left straw on the ground and the overall colouring was of ripe yellow and oak brown, potent colours which warmed her. He closed the door behind him and the outside world was shut off. The pungency of the straw slaked her nose and throat: the sweetness seemed to be tasted in her blood.

"There you are," he said.

This collection moved her deeply. She said nothing for a few minutes, just looking at the millstones and miners' lamps, the fragments of pottery and the troughs, the half sets of china and the elaborate horse-brasses, the leather-bound books and, as an altarpiece, a half-size statue of a naked woman, an eighteenth-century copy of a Roman figure, but still, distinguishing the pile of odds and ends into something which could be called a collection. She would have laughed for pleasure in his temerity, his affection, his determination to seek out and preserve what was beautiful, but she knew that the laugh would be misinterpreted; she could feel his eyes on her waiting for the merest hint of mockery.

Rosemary felt no sense of privilege and yet even his mother was not welcome in Edgar's retreat. He had offered her, instantly, the best. For the place was not only a retreat, permanently to be defended against the curiosity and taunts of his brothers, it was also the spot where he had experienced the most unnerving conscious strain in his life. When his father had died, the very moment he had heard of it, he had come to this stable, his mother had thought to be with his grief. But there had been only joy. He was perturbed by this—no excuses from the past of oppression from that bullying, disappointed man could preserve him from the disgust which his conscience expressed. Yet it could not be doubted. He felt not only relief and a sense of triumph but real joy at his father's death. He wanted to laugh, to dance on the grave.

And the knowledge of that pressed on his mind now: Rosemary seemed so very indifferent to him that he grew agitated. She looked through the collection calmly, but he was sure he sensed contempt: and in that apprehensive state the shadow of guilt at his strange joy swept across his mind.

"Where did you find this?" She held up a stone head.

"Same place I found her," he pointed to the statue of the woman. "Out at Whitehall. . . ."

"Where George Moore used to live?" she interrupted, and instantly regretted it.

"Yes," continued Edgar, calmly. "Him. A millionaire wasn't he?"

"It's beautiful," said Rosemary, looking at the head, rubbed by the weather, given more distinction by the weather than by the artist. "Beautiful," she repeated.

"And you never know," he came over to her and took it out of her hands to examine it, as if for the first time, "it could be worth a bob or two one fine day."

"But that isn't the point, is it?"

Edgar sensed his next move unerringly. "No. I don't suppose it is. It answers for itself."

She was satisfied.

"What was that Minotaur?"

"O, nothing." But he waited for her explanation. Still unaware of her mistake, she continued. "He was a man with the body of a bull. He used to demand twenty virgins from Athens every year as a sacrifice. Theseus killed him with Ariadne's help. The Minotaur lived in a labyrinth and she gave Theseus a thread so that he could find his way out after he had killed the beast." She paused. "It was just that—you came through the herd and they were packed so tightly you seemed to grow out of them." She hesitated. "It was a myth, of course."

"There's usually something behind them, isn't there?" His interest, his grim insistence on eliminating his ignorance thrilled her as much as that first appreciation of his recklessness.

"O yes," she agreed. "And they *found* a labyrinth when they excavated there. This is lovely," she picked up a piece of china, a Spode display plate, badly cracked.

"Did they find a Minotaur?"

"Of course not." Now she did laugh, but gently, and he joined in.

"It was a daft question," he admitted. "I mean, we might come from monkeys, but bulls is pushing it a bit."

"I think maybe we're like all the animals in some way," Rosemary exclaimed, delighted that he had the talent to keep the talk open and not close it through glumness or banality. "I think some of us *are* like bulls."

"And some are like sheep," he replied.

"Yes! And foxes. Thurston's full of foxes."

"Old Scrunt's a bit of a fox. What about Mr Armstrong?"

"He's . . . you would think he was a nice old cuddly Russian bear but he isn't—I know—he's a polar bear, perfectly suited to its surroundings but very dangerous when attacked."

"So we all are."

"I *did* hit that cow, didn't I? Do you think I hurt it badly?"

"It'll probably be concussed for a week," said Edgar, straight-faced. "In fact it might lose its memory for names."

"No . . . but—will it?" Then she realized that she had been wrong about the Minotaur and blushed. As Edgar stood there, a dark figure in the dark stable yet touched by the tawny glow from the straw, she felt apprehensive and yet her guilt at having been rather pleased at his original ignorance forced her towards the truth.

"Your turn to ask a daft question," he said. "Like when I asked if they'd found a Minotaur," he reminded her, severely. "One daft question apiece. Quits." He could have been talking to the wall.

Perhaps, he thought, she suddenly saw him as a mucky farmer, not even a farmer, a labourer, he would appear to her—a curiosity, someone to take an interest in and smile at later over tea and cakes. He turned away, picked up a hammer and a couple of nails and banged them into a beam as if he intended to split the oak in half.

Behind him he heard her lift the sneck of the door and the outside light and air gushed into the place, extinguishing his fragile hope as the lamp was extinguished.

Still she pondered. Why did it *matter* so much to tell this man the truth? Why would she risk the inevitable intimacy, as she saw it, which would follow such an admission which revealed such concern? The strength of her attraction to the man less than one hour in her life before had been exhilarating: this new desire pointed out consequences which she needed to consider. Yet the pressure to set right a simple mistake was growing: to hesitate would be to enter into further complications because the lapse of time would undoubtedly breed them and nothing but the truth would do.

"Have you a cigarette?" she asked.

He had only one. This had been saved throughout the afternoon. The money he had received for driving the sucklings, after being halved with Scrunt, was put in his inside pocket, designated for his recently begun savings. Like everything else, Edgar had entered on this as if nothing else on earth mattered and no miser gloated more over his hoard. He gave her the cigarette and handed her a box of matches. He knew he ought to light it for her but it would have gone against his present mood which was a little resentful: he could not see why she had suddenly slipped out of his knowing. His mother would see her smoking at the open door.

"The Minotaur," she said, and as she began to say it, a smile seemed to start inside her and race to her lips; how stupid she had been to hesitate? What could possibly be simpler? "The Minotaur—I was wrong—it has the body of a *man* and the head of a *bull*. I said it the wrong way round. So when I saw you on top of the cows it could not have been a Minotaur."

Catching her smile he returned it, the mood being far more important than her words which only set off in him the instantly repressed thought that bulls were more likely to be on top of cows than men or minotaurs or any other beast.

"I'm sorry," she concluded, as if expecting admonishment: and her bowed head filled him with exaltation.

"I'll set you home," he said, "I'm going that road, anyway."

Though they only edged around the town, Rosemary was very alive to the fact of their walking together, a young couple, as might be a courting couple. She scrutinized him every step of the way but he was well aware of this and he enjoyed it, in a way, this strange experience of being put on his mettle by a young woman, made to work, to think, not allowed to slip into the somnolent ways he had taken with the other women he had known.

"Tomorrow," he announced, as they came near her home, "I'll take you up into the fells. There's some old stones there that a

72

man told me were from before the Romans. You would know. Are you off again tomorrow?"

"Yes, I'm on holiday all week." She was taken aback and unnerved by his confident assumptions.

"I thought you might be. Would you rather walk or bike."

"Neither, thank you. I don't intend to be so energetic on this holiday." She regretted her rather haughty tone but he had to be checked in some way.

"We'll go to Abbeytown then," he said. "There's a bus just after dinner. 1.35 it goes, the Silloth bus. We can look around the Abbey."

"I have already. . . ."

"I knew you would have. I'd like you to tell me what you know about it. And I'll show you where all the stones went after it got knocked down, when was it . . . ?"

"At the Reformation."

"There you are, you see—we could help each other. The farmers nicked the stones. And there's a bit of a bird sanctuary round about, on the Wampool—you'd like that."

"I'm not sure."

"I'll see you at the bus-stop."

"Perhaps."

"That's good enough for me!" He left her abruptly, for an effect which came off, for she was forced to watch him stride out the first few yards, his jacket flying behind him, his boots fairly kicking the ground, whistling like a ploughboy, she thought, comforted by the cosiness of the comparison. A ploughboy.

Edgar strode away up Longthwaite and into the Show Fields, where he had no business at all but to stay long enough to exonerate himself from the lie of having said he was coming her way: he spent the time lying on a bank of grass, watched rather nervously by the heavy-breasted shorthorns munching interminably.

That night he took her round the head as a present, wrapped in thick brown paper and tied up with coarse twine. Handed to Lawrence who opened the door and accepted the gift with great surprise. Edgar thrust the parcel into his hand and left without a word; untypically unnerved. Through the open door he had seen Rosemary, looking lazily across to the intruder, those eyes which he had seen so vivid and penetrating, now clouded, preoccupied, unlit by life around, almost unseeing: and yet she saw him, unseeing, and after his hopes of her since that afternoon, the indifferent glance wounded him. The gift was shameful evidence of mistaken presumption. He got rid of it into the old man's hands as furtively as if he were passing over stolen goods.

# Chapter Eleven

And yet she was at the bus-stop. It was he who was embarrassed and felt the eyes of King Street riveting their gaze on the base of his skull. Few did look. Scarcely anyone put one and one together. Edgar and Rosemary—a pair of odd birds anyway—happened to be going on the same bus. Nothing in their greeting or their behaviour suggested much more than the constrained politeness of acquaintances thrown on each other's resources through circumstances alone. There was nothing of the sense of meeting when Rosemary came down the street. In fact, for a few moments, Edgar was fully convinced that her appearance there was merely coincidental: for she stopped outside Johnston's shoe shop and examined the display in those large windows as if nothing in the world interested her as much as boots. But when she did come up to him, her gentle smile beat out all doubt.

The Abbey had been razed but the chapel remained and in the chilly interior, their feet echoing as if in a canyon, where a whisper was a declaration and a comment a solemn statement, both of them felt uneasy. Edgar had no pace for such an occasion: more than once he had looked in churches but always to have a glance at something in particular, something someone had told him about, and then he would enter, rapidly, almost lurching forward, his head drooping with fear of being seen by the vicar and challenged on his mission or, worst of all, on his faith; a quick scan and he would be out again. His interest in the past was a magpie's and found enough to feed it out of doors.

Outside, that very characteristic thrilled her. He had more physical energy than anyone she had ever known, the darting curiosity of someone much younger, and a certainty in himself which took her breath away. She could not see how anyone, anyone at all, could appear so self-assured. To Rosemary, her existence and that of anyone she knew was at this time coloured by absurdity, by mortality and by the final foolishness of all effort. Melancholy was a perfume she had come to trust. Life had to prove itself. And here was the man lording it over all, living in his glory!

He led her over the fields to Abbey Farm where Ned Bland was farming; fortunately unaware that his property was being pointed out as a classic example of ancient thieving. Edgar walked under the lovely arched entrance to which he pointed as if he owned it and calmed the barking dogs. Rosemary followed him tentatively, not to be out-dared by him, impressed by the proprietorial way in which he led on, though simultaneously amused that he should want to.

Edgar walked around the farmyard as if it were for sale, prodding walls, picking things up and banging them to test their strength. Mrs Bland came out to see if a horse had broken loose, with the noise but Edgar waved his hand at her and shouted he was just looking around; once she had established that he *was* Edgar Crowther, Jane Crowther (Miller that was), her boy, then she went back to her baking. He would be up to no harm and the oven was too hot to waste.

He led her through it as a young Russian landowner (someone out of Tolstoy, she thought, giving him every advantage she could) might have shown her through his estate. And yet the place was nothing whatsoever to do with him: when they finally came across Ned Bland and that tolerant young farmer let himself be interrupted and drawn on the connections between the Abbey and the farm, it was quite plain to see that the two men did not know each other especially well.

So it was all for her benefit. She remembered the silence in the house the night before when she had unwrapped the clumsy parcel. Sarah had looked at the head as if it were some terrible omen; Rosemary herself had laughed at the sight though the heavy stone seemed to sink into her flesh and even now she could feel the imprint on her hands, and the coldness. Lawrence had accepted it as an endearing attempt of Edgar's to make up for his mistake over the sucklings. Once he had cleared that up, his mind was at rest. But Sarah accepted his explanation no more than Rosemary herself did and she burned both paper and string at once: a rare example of waste. Rosemary had left the head to Lawrence but just before bed he had insisted on her taking it— she, after all, had hit the animal! What an adventure it had been! She had struck out "like a trooper", he told Sarah (and, later, many many others) "like a trooper" and "bang on the nose!"

76

Now it was in her bedroom, on the window-sill, the deep sill which was broad enough for a seat, a spot she had often used as a retreat when younger, a place to lock herself silent and hold hard. There the grey head sat, propped upright by books, and in the gaslight it took on a focal quality. How it seemed to have suffered; the eyes, she decided, were those of the blinded Oedipus. She looked and looked on it as intensely as Oedipus himself had looked at the Sphinx, and slept with the curtains open to let the moonlight keep the stone illuminated. What had Edgar to do with such a thing as that?

Still less could she see a connection in the daytime. From the farm he took her along the Wampool, where he spotted some of the birds which hovered about the coast only four miles away over the moss or marshland. The black-headed gull, the herring gull, the eider, godwits, greenshanks, spotted redshanks—he claimed to identify them all—just as boys at that time claimed to see all makes of aircraft in the few planes which went over this part of Cumberland. She could not contradict him, for her detailed knowledge of nature was minimal—she adored the broad sweeps, the great effects, the symbolic concatenations; local detail was outside her real interest and beyond her grasp. But she admired it, greatly, as she admired Lawrence's mental map of Thurston's past and present.

Yet doubts remained. He was a chameleon, she decided, and would alway be. Because his interest in the past was not earthed in knowledge through books she did not believe in it.

Yet it was there, and as real to him as her literary fancies were to her.

What she did not fathom was that Edgar was fundamentally nervous. He had never met anyone like Rosemary before. It was this which caused his nervousness because he sensed he had to act quickly, and yet he knew so little about her; and if she caught him at it she would push him off—he knew that much!

He had to bowl her over.

# Chapter Twelve

That day and the few days following he played the part until he was the part. He showed off his paces as a horse might be asked to do to a suspicious dealer. He was aware of the element of buffoonery but risked that, believing that laughter never hurt a good cause and knowing that flaunting is always comical and the peacock's tail is soon plucked for ladies' hats. But he persisted because he had no other way; and in some peculiar part of him took pride in the assault, for what he was doing was to smother her with himself, trap her with all he had and not only did that call for skill, it called for the faith that yourself once fully shown was still worth knowing. All or nothing, he concluded, jackpot or bust.

Rosemary, too, soon ceased to count his comedy as foolishness. She was alert to his intentions and while dealing with him was not too difficult, it drew her into an involvement with him which he wanted; she was not at first aware of the full extent of his ambitions. For this nervousness of Edgar's gave his cause its sincerity and that was a quality which Rosemary could perceive and respect. She was definitely intrigued by him. He was like no one she had known—no one, that is, she had spent thought on. His local reputation, his lowly circumstances and his ridiculously speculative prospects were not only no bar, they gave him additional interest—the *gall* of the man!—and that drew from her both a sympathy for those ill-spoken of which a long suspicion of Thurston's judgment had bred in her and a pleasure in the fact that there was *far* more to him than anyone ever said: she was pleased with her unique perspicacity. And she could see that he loved her.

There was no question of that now. He had to see her every day. He would station himself to watch her get off the bus on her way from work. He grew shy, he told himself he was not good enough, he let her walk up the street and then he whipped through the warren of back-alleys, through Reed's Lane and the

Warren and Water Street, up to the top of Church Street to meet her at the church square as casually as if he had just strolled down from the auction. It was then that the network of alleyways and yards which made up the centre of Thurston struck him as being so friendly. They kept his secret. They sped his passage. They nurtured his desire.

He would walk her from the church up to her house every night. When he did not appear at the church, she missed him and to his delight she told him so. She was now the sum of all his ambitions and to court her in style he procured a car. The deal was complicated. It entailed two weeks free and hard labour at Claud Porter's, the realization of all his funds, speculation on a hound dog and a promise to work two free weeks for the previous owner, who was Mr Banks, the licensee of the Crown, over the busy Christmas period. Even so, it was a knock-down price and it needed immense devotion just to make the wheels go round. Edgar was fortunate that the farm was halfway down a hill, so he could be sure of some sort of start by letting it roll: pushing it back up again always seemed to discover a few willing boys who would heave for the sake of a sit at the controls, or labourers, friends who knew when weight was needed.

She began to draw once again. She would ask, still ask, as she had done since her arrival, if she could go into the parlour when she came back from work and there, amid the domestic treasures of many years, she would spread her sketch pad on the green baize and concentrate, utterly. When she was in that parlour, Lawrence was restless. It was as if he heard her calling to him but he was not allowed to answer; and yet the call was of one in danger. He felt about her as he had felt twice before: during her illness and then after her return from London. Then her need had been plain to him and he had tried all he could to help her, conscious of confused and unusually excited emotions, a turbulence uncommon to his normal days, as much tired as tantalized by this, but managing to hold on to his task, which was to be ever-available.

On both occasions she had leaned on him, he knew that, he had had the certainty of that loving dependence: now, the wall between them was real in every sense. For though he longed to be wanted and knew he was needed, she did not ask, she did not depend. Lawrence looked at some of the objects Edgar had brought and they seemed crude things, a tinker's taste, poor

79

bribes. Yet when he went up into her room one afternoon with the shameful intention of looking to see if her drawings were scattered about, he saw the head, in the window, wedged with books, and a small jar of wild flowers to one side of it. She, then, saw things differently. This was cared for as nothing else, he saw, looking about the room sadly, as nothing else. He left without searching for the drawings and, to punish himself for his bad behaviour, he did not take his usual evening tot of rum.

She had carefully put them away in the bottom drawer, the dowry drawer, of the old mahogany chest which Sarah had long ago provided for her.

Rosemary was a little ashamed because the drawings seemed so childish. In all of them there was, centred, a castle. She was in the castle, sometimes outlined, sometimes drawn just as a face, sometimes indicated only by a single brush stroke. Trees bent under the stress, rocks cracked, winds blew their fullest force—and riding the wind was a raven. Edgar had taken her to see a raven, among some crags, way past Ullaby in the fells; and she half-remembered echoes of its importance in legends and myths. She did not look it up as normally she would have done, for that would somehow have broken the spell. But Merlin she remembered, and that led her to Arthur: to knights, to great deeds, to Edgar recklessly climbing the crags to look for the nest while the ravens swooped above him in the bare hills and the wet rock slid under his fingers. The raven in her paintings and drawings was black, of course, but its shadow on the earth beneath the storm was white: the shadow could have been a reflection or even another bird, or merely an acknowledgment of the force of symmetry. But there they were, one in the storm, the other on the earth, poised, both, between the edge of the page and the centre; and there was no doubt what they wanted. They wanted her to leave her fortress and come into the world.

Did she have to, oh, did she have to? It was dull like this, walled around by library, routine, Lawrence, tidiness, Sarah, a few acquaintances, walks: but it was safe. She knew how safe by the feeling of danger Edgar gave her. And there were the books she read, they took her where Edgar would never take her, never could he fulfil her spirit as Shelley had done, not all the promises of physical love, she thought, could equal one verse from that beautiful genius. No, she would stay in this castle of self and let the world mock her spinsterhood as it thought fit. There was a good memory to feed on and she was never bored. The depression had sweetened to melancholy and in those twisting glades she had found a sort of ease. But he was flapping at the gate, this raven, beating his wings against her cage, thrusting the passion for liberty into her mind.

Weariness was what she felt, a weariness of the flesh. It would be hopeless. Edgar was a boy, with all his strutting to throw her off the track by making a mockery of what he knew she feared, he was still, as she did fear, a boy. If only he would let her be. She would survive him. He had not touched her as Wilfred had done. There had never been any question with Wilfred; Edgar had not leaned in and plucked her soul to his own, he could not do that: he had stormed through her, wind and rain, noise and show, he would pass away.

But what was it then, this life, with nothing ventured? The ancient line dropped down onto her poor reason. Nothing gained. She wanted no gains. At night, often sleepless now as their relationship approached a climax, she looked long at the head, now like a skull, now a stern patrician, now an obscure shape scarcely defined, once more Oedipus; an absurd gift.

She had to leave the castle, yes. No coward soul was she. She would leave. She would go. She would go out into the world once again. This time with no certainties, no great expectations, with some fear and the sole hope that the years since her virtual breakdown after the London love, the years of retreat and a certain quiet would have given her the strength to endure.

# Chapter Thirteen

His hand on her back seemed to melt into the flesh. She ached for him once more to sweep his palm over her skin. How wrong, how stupid, how like a child she had been to think that there was anything more wonderful than two bodies lovingly entwined! She could not instruct him, she dared not interfere with her pleasure, it was a new world which had swum into her mind; her skin and her blood were drenched in a sweet exhaustion which drugged all her senses.

A new form of herself seemed to grow out of his contact, to encircle her and protect her, to give her primitive warmth and unwilled security, to give her the chance to grow. She could be new as this feeling was new. The squalor of those other rushed and embarrassed times now seemed furtive and a mockery; but she did not altogether destroy them in her memory; without them she would not have had the irresponsible nerve to give Edgar what he had wanted: and without that she would have missed this new life. Out of squalor came beauty.

His hands moved over her as the hands of a mother bathing an infant, she thought, and as he stroked her back she thought of the Hindu's snake which is supposed to sleep at the base of the spine and, at times of ecstasy, rise up through the spinal cord to kiss the brain. Her body seemed to be alive in many ways, some so deeply, sweetly pleasurable that the skin was loath to impart the message to the mind, others so silly that her eyes stirred with laughter at the idea—snake up the spine, indeed! It was Edgar's hand, gently rubbing a skin which was as thirsty for contact as a desert for rain.

The suddenness of her capitulation (for so the action must always seem to Edgar) had surprised him. Until then, despite the car, there had not been so much as a kiss. This was not policy on his part but, curiously, a sort of politeness. They always talked, on their trips and outings, and the talk would both bind him to her and emphasize the distance between them. Her accent was more refined than his, her vocabulary wider, her attitudes lined with easier habits, her assumptions more secure: she reminded him, in some ways, of a young woman teacher they had had at school, hugely "fancied" by the older boys, a woman whose slightest condescensions were interpreted as the wiles of whoredom, who walked the no-man's land of pubescent lust, a living testimony to the saving grace of repression. Edgar listened to Rosemary as he had listened to that teacher: both excited and impressed, not unwilling to declare his own position, indeed insisting on claiming equality, but fundamentally the recipient, the taker. Yet he talked. He had never talked so much about personal feelngs and personal reactions with anyone. Silence, to Rosemary, was either a sign of failure or it was a mark of respect for unutterable feelings, usually before nature but occasionally, he came to think, before the fact of the two of them together. For in her talk he sensed her growing love.

They had driven to Dash Beck and walked up the fells and along the ferny path to Half-Way House behind Skiddaw. The season was over, the colours at their best, tints of yellow, brown, orange and gold flecking the bare hills and ornamenting them when the sun shone. That strange settlement with its small allotment of conifers, a civilized blemish on the rudeness of the fells, an awkward reminder; a failure, just the one short row of cottages so significantly placed in hills, full of resonance, like a post on a pilgrimage: but here no holy place save perhaps the mountain top. Edgar had grown to enjoy these walks—altogether a new experience for him her type of walking; with no particular aim, no nest to see or trap to set, no business to do or friend to visit, no deal or notch of adventure, just the free air and the hills, the silence and the impulses which landscape worked. It had taken him some time to get used to it and though he would claim that he now shared in the pleasure of such aimless wandering he could never rid himself of the need for a purpose and a goal: and here he had one. Conquest.

But by Christ he was not going to make a mistake! He was not going to rush it, he was not going to be crude; he had gained admittance by brashness, that was over now. She might intimate that she enjoyed the effectiveness of his crude assaults on the world but he was too canny to follow that trail. It would lead him straight to the kingdom of the clown. He had other ideas. And so, although he could not help but impress her, although the vivacity of his glances and movements were themselves bold declaration, although his courtship was active and magnificent, he did not touch her.

But after these hours of solitude, where even footsteps on mossy ground seemed too heavy, and, on the return, speaking seemed too loud, the bowl of hills became a cathedral for whispering, then his body had declared itself. He had put his hands on her shoulders and looked at her without disguise. Her eyes were mischievous, she was ready to evade him and fully capable of it and yet at the same time she was daring him; and, such was the clarity of his perception at that moment, he saw fear behind the play, saw her saying "Are you *sure*? Be *sure*. That's all I want, be certain, be sure, if you take me you will have me, be sure, be sure because otherwise I will break. Yes. Truly, I am in your hands." Perhaps love is just such a total perception for at that moment she, too, saw into him and perceived the love beneath the need. He loved her. There was bravado and uncertainty, there were furies and even misgivings, but he loved her. With that knowledge she anointed herself and her head rested against his chest. Both of them were shivering slightly and they clung to each other as if for safety.

It was as if a glacial change, emphatic and enormous, took place there on that spot: she nodded slightly and yielded utterly to him. She summoned all the images of love and wanted to lay them before him. And yet, even as she indicated they could make love, even as she felt his skin on hers, at the very moment of penetration, hard in the middle of the effulgence was the scar of Wilfred's memory and the disappointment of knowing that there was desperation in this choice, the stigma of the Last Chance. But maybe the physical pleasure would wash all that away, that and more, even down to the split root of her inner life; healing, healing flesh in flesh. On the mountain side like satyr and nymph, she thought, again fleeing to the past for protection. Greek men were contemptuous of Women. Edgar. She loved them. They left weak children to die. This body on hers was so warm and solid, so nervous and strong, violent but without hurt: she would not have complained of any hurt; no death there.

Edgar was able to understand her. He did not think that she was cheapening herself by giving him all at once, by giving him everything without the insurance of rings and promises. On the contrary, her action made other girls' politic gradations seem cheap, he decided. She was fearless, that's what he concluded, she was neither a hypocrite nor a schemer. This much he knew and, rightly knowing, made love to her with great care and tenderness. More than that, though, he thought that she was independent of him, he did not want her to be, still less need her to be, but he thought that the independence she had in words carried over not only into actions but into the consequences of actions. One of his causes for satisfaction when they rolled from each other and pulled the heap of clothes over themselves was that she would not use this occasion for future pressure. If necessary, and this seemed to make her golden in his imagination, he could see her going on alone whatever happened, regardless. There would be no need of course because he had been careful: but the thought excited him to even greater love for her. The love-making itself while giving him so much did not quite match one of the less open, less full, less splendid couplings he had managed along the way. He needed his admiration for her to stir the affection to love.

Yet the qualifications were murmurs in a benign storm, heard only in the most private part of the mind and heard as much in the confidence that they could be overcome as in the fear that they might damage what was there. There, together, was a new union. They knew each other, now they could look clearly.

All the way back to Thurston, he whistled the latest tunes, loud and clear.

# Chapter Fourteen

He watched her through the glass partition. The way she "carried" her head, Edgar had not noticed it before. She worked inside a circular desk, like a pen, he thought, and was at the beck and whisper of all those using the library. He admired her efficiency as she pulled out indexed files and dealt with the old man who would not go, but spoke and then stood aside while she attended to others, preferring the exchange to any solution. And she did not flirt, he observed, a little complacently. Inside the library they seemed to move as if under the sea, the reading people, trudging slowly, unspeaking, looking up every now and then as if breaking the surface of the water for air. Rosemary's "place" was on a raised dais and she appeared to sail above it all, head and shoulders above the rest: perhaps it was her embarrassment at this distinction which made her carry her head in that way. Edgar was pleased with this analysis. A swan! That was it—she reminded him of a swan, her neck rather elegant, her head dipping to the murmuring claimants who fed her their requests. He rubbed his hands with pleasure. He would tell her that. It would please her.

She had seen him of course although she did not let him know it. She preferred to catch a glimpse of him out of the corner of her eye, afraid that recognition would embarrass him and cause him to shy off. She wanted to dwell on him when he thought himself unseen: and half glances were better than nothing. How deliciously awkward he looked! Scrubbed, suited (his brother's, she was soon to be told) hair recently barbered and head still smarting from the ruthlessness of that masculine shearing, he stood there, well, like a boy, really, she had to admit with a frown in her mind, but surely like something else as well, such innocent strength, such naïf unironic bluntness—a warrior? He looked too cramped there in the hall of the library, too crushed in that space and that suit. She could not find a suitable analogy.

But he had come for her. On Saturdays she finished work at

twelve-thirty and he had called for her: as promised (or rather, she remembered, as threatened!) and one thing was certain; he made everyone else in that place look anaemic. There was some satisfaction in raising him up by putting others down: she could hate this tepid place and all the feeble exercise of turning leaves of printed paper. Edgar took his stand outside all of that! He was what was written about, she thought, the hero of books, not their myopic reader. She glanced at the clock. Five minutes before Miss Bennett should come and relieve her: Miss Bennett would not be early.

Caught in her own conspiracy, Rosemary grew restless: she wanted Edgar to be gone, to be out of this place which fitted him so badly. She resented the library that it should make him appear so very awkward: she blushed, not for him, she thought, but in vexation at the place's limited capacity for accommodation. Yet she could not let him know she had seen him for now that her pleasure had been mysteriously transmuted into resentment, she did not trust herself to be kind. She concentrated on her work, manufacturing activity, encouraging the thick pointers on the monumental clock to move all the faster without her attention.

When Miss Bennett did arrive it was almost twenty-five to one and Edgar was gone. She hurried out.

He waved at her from the other side of the road, and in clumsy dumb show, indicated that he would get the car from a side street and bring it round. He acted as if Castle Street Carlisle were a tunnel of roaring traffic: two bicycles, one motor bike and side car and a baker's van passed by while he did his act.

While she waited she glanced down at the castle which crowned the end of the street. It was a picture-book building, neatly raised on its mound newly mown; drawbridge, moat and crenellation and on the other side the sheer drop to the River Eden and views to Scotland, the old enemy, beyond. She had often taken her sandwiches there and dreamed of the sieges and battles, the Romans and the Norsemen, but most of all the Scots, Wallace, Duncan, Robert the Bruce and Bonnie Prince Charlie, pipes and drums, fifes and guns. It was a secure daydream, sitting there behind the neatly reconstituted walls. Henry II had given it its present outline almost eight hundred years before: and the cathedral just beside her built up about the same time: strength and spirit, she thought, with scholarship, the library, in between. Soldiers, scholars and saints, three archetypes, three masculine graces; Edgar was the soldier; he would have marched with Bonnie Prince Charlie, she thought, would have seen the romance and righteousness in the Stuarts' cause and swung in behind the young pretender on his southward triumph. Yes: it could vibrate, the castle. In her happiness, she felt the attraction of it as keenly as she had ever done.

"W'll go to Watendleath," said Edgar, "you'll like that."

He had never been there. He knew the Lake District very poorly. It was there. It was beautiful. It was the best part of England. You could not find better views the world over. People came from all over to see it and live in it. Edgar accepted all that and in any debate would emerge as a lover and staunch champion but in fact he knew only a segment of the northern rim of fells at all well: and Lake Bassenthwaite—the nearest large lake to Thurston—was the source of all his rhapsody on lakeland. Rosemary knew the Lakes fairly thoroughly. Lawrence had made it his business to show them to her, one by one, and many holidays had been spent on meandering bus trips in and out of that romantic shrine. Watendleath had been the goal of one of her very first trips—it was one of the most popular places to visit; but she said nothing.

They drove on the high road, by-passing Thurston and looking down onto it. Little was said; they could always use the excuse that the car made so much noise, but that was not the problem. Nor would it have been difficult for them to have uncovered a conversation. What had happened, though, since that easy coupling, was a definite shift in their relationship. As if to counterbalance the easiness of that first physical communion, an unmistakable formality had entered into their subsequent meetings. They had made love again once since that time and it had brought out a tentative awkwardness entirely missing from that first occasion. Rosemary had already worked out what was happening: they had done things the wrong way round, that was all—the union had come before the overtures: there had to be a time for courting. She loved that word—"courting", at once gracious, aristocratic, redolent of chivalry and, as used in Thurston, homely, solid, rather bawdy and planted in certainty. Yes, she wanted to be courted—even to Watendleath.

At Ireby he stopped, at the edge of the village, just beside the church, and asked her if she would like to go in the Black Lion for a sandwich. He was not sure of her attitude towards pubs and although hikers did it, and some holiday makers, he did not want to "put her out". She could have battened on his face with kisses as he earnestly explained all this to her, but once again she restrained herself—used to that reflex—and gravely assured him that the saloon bar at the Black Lion would not compromise her position in society.

When she asked for "the same as him" which meant a glass of bitter beer, Edgar was over the moon. What a woman! And yet she drank it like a lady and sat in such a way as to let no one assume familiarities with her. They ate beef sandwiches and just in time Edgar refrained from the pickles which were left, three of them, damply neglected on the willow-patterned plate.

In Keswick she would have loved to have stayed to look at the market which packed the quaint main street with bustle and cheerful barter—but she saw his face set against this request and realized that though persuadable he was pursuing a well-prepared plan which deserved her respect. They drove on, once more in the gracious wilderness which could impassion her and seemed to Edgar the proper place for courting; for he had caught her affection for that word and that play and he built on it. There was enjoyment there. To play the plain man reassured him, for if she would accept *that*, then his real self, he felt, must be far more acceptable. He needed cover still.

On Ashness bridge they stood and looked down Derwent-water. The picturesque elided into the magnificent. The lake and its islands, fells riding each side and curling around the small town which stood between the two waters. Rosemary let herself go even further, let herself open to it all, felt the chill freshness of the world rustle into the nooks of her mind. Edgar waited until she had finished looking and then walked on up through the woods: he had parked the car at the foot of the hill.

Rosemary was soon confirmed in the suspicion that he had never been this way before. The walk to Watendleath was a fair trudge in Edgar's terms, with the car available; he must have thought it just around the corner over the bridge. She could hear that assurance being given him by the acquaintance he had probably asked—"no distance, no distance at all"—and guessed that Edgar had thus chosen what he would consider her preferred and the romantic approach, on foot, through woods, silently. She was understanding him well, now, she thought.

He would have missed Surprise View. She went over to the

edge of the path and looked out at this spectacular vista of Borrowdale, Catbells and the valley floor, waterfall and sheer rock face, presented with a suddenness which checked your breath. Edgar came up behind her, passed her by, and went to the edge.

"Do you like it?" he asked proprietorially; turning to smile he seemed perilously balanced. The drop was sheer behind him.

"It makes you want to fly," she said and then she remembered Wilfred and Icarus who would always be a guide. But Edgar was not to do with that. He was the Minotaur. Her mind sorted itself slowly through the simple distinction—so much had been buried in her self-sought retreat (for she herself, was she not Narcissus?). Edgar was not from the myths—he was an Englishman, she thought, or rather a Celt, changeable and potent, unwilling to commit himself utterly but always at grips with what he did. She had seen him in the English novels and in the border ballads, in the lives of English heroes and in those Tudor portraits, faces dark, quick, full of temper. No—she must see him more clearly—*not* Elizabethan, not English, not Celtic, not anything other than himself—Edgar Crowther—a rough, rather remarkable farmer's son of unusual tastes and aptitudes who was trying most painstakingly to impress her. It was his body she must think of, the white skin under the heap of clothes, the weathered hands and wrists, the man as he was. And sex—that reality: truth could be found there. It was hard for her; idealized images had made their own laws in her mind. Only the evidence of her senses could overthrow that rule. But did she want such a revolution?

"The view doesn't greatly matter," Edgar said, turning to look again. "It's what you give to it!" He paused. "Isn't it? Anyway no view for me is as good as the sight of you."

"Edgar!" Her tone was almost chiding, just caught in time and left with the colour of pleasure.

"It's true. You're lovely, Rosemary. *I* think so, anyway."

Rock beneath her feet for ten thousand yards the books said and before her a man whose ancestors had been in this region long long back, working the land, marrying, making a living. What a hopeful phrase. "Making a living." If only one could—and the living one wanted. He would weld her to him and his. She held out her hand and stepped towards him. He opened his arms and she came into them—and there he held her, on the very edge of that sheer drop, both of them conscious of the emptiness below, both accepting it.

"You're very young," she said. Edgar was prepared for that.

"I feel a hundred years old," he replied, "and anyway, what does it matter?"

To that last phrase she rarely had a convincing answer. He knew that.

"You don't know anything about me."

"I know all I need to know. And you'll tell me the rest, won't you?"

Rosemary pulled away from him and put her hands on his shoulders—gazing at him fixedly. "I can manage as I am," she said. "I am happy enough to remain alone."

"That's not the point."

She went back into his arms. No—it was not the point. Contentment was all very well for those who were fulfilled by it: she could never be. To her it would be the fortification of cowardice. He was right. She closed her eyes and saw more clearly—the strong, bold man able to hawk his way through the world and herself, ivy on oak, follower to leader, wanting to travel, to dare, to see.

The strain of holding her and himself on the edge made him tremble; both of them were aware of the dangerous drop and accepted the dare. He was hard against her; but there had to be more time now. It was serious now. It was not a day nor a few months but a life which was in question now.

"Let's walk on."

Edgar wanted to make love but yielded to her initiative, accepting it as part of the price.

When, finally and much later, they reached Thurston, he slowed down at the fork in the road: his place lay up Southend, hers up Longthwaite. "Which way shall I go?" he asked.

"You choose."

"No." He tried to be playful but was too self-conscious. He had made the offer.

"*You* choose," she repeated, looking at him. Even in the dim light which came from the single gas lamp marking the fork, her eyes sparkled, full of vivacity, mischief, mockery.

"You must be tired," he said.

"O Edgar!" Her laugh confused him further. What should he say?

"Well—you've had a busy day—I mean—you were up for work this morning, weren't you, early?"

"What are you trying to say?" And yet her tone was so gay, so loving, so fresh to his mind—how could he capture it—*she* was the wild finch; *she*.

"You're the wild bird—what you were saying before—about Scrunt's finch—"

"Yes, yes. I remember." She paused. "You must call me, then."

"That's what I've been trying to do."

"O Edgar, you're so sweet," again she laughed and he felt foolish.

"I'll take you home," he said, preferring to lose, at this stage, rather than to force anything. She kissed him on the cheek. "Thank you," her tone was grave. He had done the right thing. His relief carried him through the final indecision of parting.

He put the car in the open barn and smoked yet another cigarette. The car was already sold to his two brothers but he had made it a condition that he could use it one day a week. His brother's suit was badly creased and the man would be raging, he knew, missing it for his Saturday night. Best to climb in through the back, change, and give it to his mother to clean up. At least return it "smart". And maybe there would be no fight. "Courting" got you off a lot. They were as curious as anyone about his strange adventure.

He did as he had planned but was too restless to sleep. Besides, his brothers would only come in and wake him however he tried to jam the door. He wrapped himself up well and went out for a walk. There was no moon; he kept on the road and went towards the fells, going through the day in his mind, trying to work out what she meant here, what he had done there.

She was all he thought about. Meeting her had extended him and excited him as never before: there was not the sensual thread of physical certainty but that did not matter, he thought, where there was so much else. She rasped against him and he wanted the fleshy indolence of his small-town self to be shaped. If he had in his pride been able to admit it he would have said that she was hard on him also in ways he did not like, in ways he could not but resent and against which he must eventually strike back. But all

that was so little as he walked the dark road and turned back at
the foot of Brocklebank. There was no reason to it. He wanted
her. She was all he wanted. He was after her and he would not
give up.

From Thurston he heard the few cars leaving the Saturday
dance, boasting their existence by the sounding of their horns.

# Chapter Fifteen

As the autumn passed and the trees were finally stripped, as winter settled, harmlessly at first, around the remote northern town, so Rosemary began to understand that something real and total, something definitive and vital might indeed happen. The bandages protecting her from misery were loosed by the pleasure of the days; the veils which had helped her hide from the world and live in the muslin folds of her mind were drawn aside by curiosity and then by a secure feeling of confidence. Edgar was being very careful, she realized that, but perhaps she ought not to be suspicious of it. He was learning from her; he knew now how to impress her and because she would not change her creed though she might take risks with her life, she *was*, duly, impressed. He had felt out her need to be complemented and she could feel him manoeuvering into just the right position. She was being pursued, no doubt of that, and the defences of inheritance and experience were being mined and breached one by one. As Christmas approached she dreaded it. He had already proposed several times and would accept neither her refusal nor her prevarications. At Christmas, she knew, there at the winter festival, clamped between the two halves of that bitter season which so feelingly reminded her of her foreign birthright, the sun, then he would attack and she had no defences. Like the trees themselves, she was uncovered.

It seemed that year the people had just a little more money for the festival. The shop windows were bright, the children decorated the sitting-rooms more lavishly and in early evening festive frames shone onto the streets, Harry Moore's toy-room was crammed, Aladdin's Cave was the notion that year and by a coincidence it was the name of the pantomime to be seen in the parish rooms. There was just a slight feeling of having pulled through the worst of the depression; the Rayophane mill was employing almost a hundred men, Redmayne's took in about two hundred women, farmers were at the beginning of their long road to mid-century riches; the radio was cheerful; the popular songs were good. Rosemary took more of an interest than ever before, smiled at the urchin carol-singers who scattered through the streets when she walked home from the bus and chanted her up Longthwaite Road with long-known verses firmly delivered; she thought of presents and felt that special gifts were due to Lawrence and Sarah and even to Harold Sowerby who believed she was letting herself (and him) down badly by associating with Edgar, she admired the decorations and went to look at the dressing of the Christmas Tree outside Carlisle Cathedral. She felt part of the mood for the first time. On the wireless one Sunday was an adaptation of Charles Dickens' *Christmas Carol* and that throbbing spirit which once would have made her sceptical now seemed full of love and healing insights. Jean's second child had been born that summer with a bad leg and Rosemary thought of the baby as Tiny Tim and wished that she had agreed to be godmother to it; her principles seemed a poor excuse now; she took time and care to find a large present. Edgar had found work at Hetherington's sawmill driving the delivery lorry while the regular man was ill. It was cold every day and the coldness of the clear air made her eyes smart. She longed for the snow.

The school term ended, the streets filled with children, night came in mid-afternoon and the lights in the library were on all day. Even that dour place regained its early savour and she began once more to be open to the gentle chafings of the gentle readers. She had never been a "favourite" and her attitude did not change that much, but she smiled much more often at those she knew—which was a difference generally remarked.

She had started on Sir Walter Scott, finding much in the bold romantic adventures of the heroes to fill out her impression of Edgar, discovering in the fiction great territories of fact about "her man"—as she had once heard Edgar referred to. *Redgauntlet* was her reading matter that day and she got on the red bus—bright as a stage show on those faintly lit streets—and ignored all the sensible warnings so often given her about ruining her eyes. The bus swept through the dark countryside, waited for by children in the farms and cottages back in the fields which swallowed up their narrow lane, as much a treat to them as Scott's pages were to Rosemary.

Edgar was doing special deliveries of logs that evening and her plan was to make some Christmas cards. She had not done this for years. It would give her the opportunity to get out her paints again. The thought of being snugly tucked in the front parlour, deeply secured and ensconced in brown furniture, brown curtains, brown wallpaper, brass, some photographs, no mirror, that place with the fire which was now always lit there in the afternoons (it kept Sarah's bedroom warm as well which mitigated the extravagance of the fire in parlour *and* kitchen) drew her through the town almost tangibly. She hurried, that evening, nodding back to the many greetings, filled with the comforting pleasure of being known by so many people, smiling at Scrunt on guard at his usual post at the fountain, leaning against the railings, as regular in his surveillance as a sentry outside a Royal Palace. Up past the church where she regretted Edgar's work and missed his company, past the school which she had never once re-entered since her time there, the vicarage, over the tiny Floshbeck and past Flosh House, the fork in the road and up the final slope, the cold air slapping ceaselessly on her face so clean and sharp it could only have left the fell tops moments before, busy in her mind with *Redgauntlet* and painting, Edgar's hands on her breast, fondling so wonderfully gently, questing, certain, the thought of the fire pulling her to the very depths of solitary pleasure, there the dour, the pretty, English cottage, picture-book, protected, and through a chink in the curtain the light from the paraffin lamps. Perhaps she had never felt so finely relaxed, the will unwound, the feelings unstrained and yet the flesh and the mind firm with excitement and hope.

She saw the boy first, crouched on a low stool before the fire, his fair face red from the flames, a heavy book in his hands; Lawrence next, near the boy, sitting with unusual rigidity in his favourite chair, and taking a glass of sherry which was even more unusual. Wilfred stood up. Rosemary heard her mouth clutch at the breath and her hands fled there as if to pacify the threatened features. Before either of them spoke she noticed so much about him and herself. He was no longer like herself, had grown thinner; it made him appear taller and his face was drawn in fatigue and sorrow. Yet despite the superficial proofs of some physical decline he still stood gracefully, dressed with untroubled elegance, had about him a manner which needed no interpretation from her, being her own. The years between their parting and this their reunion were snuffed out. And that was what most of all, to her surprise and confusion, she noticed in herself: despite all, despite the recent upheaval of Edgar, those years between were no time. She could forget them. There was a rightness about herself and Wilfred which cancelled out both debt and credit. She was shaken and physically shaken, too, feeling a shiver threaten her. She nodded at him, pressing her lips together to stop any words, making her face look severe so. He, too, he too, as she—oh how instantly they were as one, she thought!—he too did not trade a word but looked and acknowledged by an inclination alone.

"This must be Stephen," she said.

The boy looked at her and blushed. He could no longer pretend to read the book. It was as if he had been caught doing wrong, the guilty way he responded to the sound of his name.

"You'll be eight?"

"Nearly nine." The words threatened to choke him.

Rosemary looked at him and he felt himself rock under the scrutiny. Her look seemed to fix his flickering consciousness of himself, to freeze the flame. He smiled.

"You have a lovely smile," said Rosemary and he felt he had been acquitted.

Sarah came in, best pinny billowing before her. "I've put your tea in the parlour," she said. "I thought you and Wilfred would like to eat together. Lawrence and myself had ours with Stephen." She looked affectionately at the boy: he was a good-looking child, well dressed, finely tempered, well mannered—Sarah's ideal.

"I'll play a game of cards with Stephen for company," she added.

"You never did that with me," Rosemary cried out: and then she checked herself.

"You weren't a nice little boy," Sarah replied, though not playfully.

"What are you reading?" Wilfred asked her.

"Your first words!" She laughed and the sound sent a peal of joy through her. "Your very first words!"

He took the book and looked a little quizzical. It was the Scott.

"Verbose," was his verdict, "and fundamentally dull. Nothing but action." Her own thoughts *exactly* on Scott until she had begun to read Edgar into him. Yet she was reminded, by this similarity, of the reasons behind her change.

"I like him," she countered, a little too stoutly. "Books about thought are too often dull."

"You don't mean that," he replied.

"Oh yes I do. I've changed, you know." Sharply she remembered the pain. "I'm not a lost little girl in London any more."

"Your tea'll be getting cold," said Sarah. "Go through, go through."

Rosemary took off her coat as Wilfred went ahead. Sarah pulled back the table cover and took out a pack of cards. They looked incongruous in her careful hands. Rosemary noticed the brown spots on the back of the hand. She went over and kissed them.

"Get away with you!" Sarah was more flustered than pleased. It was Lawrence who was warmed by it: this was the impulse he loved.

"He resembles you," said Lawrence, tentatively. "Surprising isn't it? By blood you're not all *that* close. But the resemblance is quite striking."

"That's why cousins can't marry," said Sarah, in her blindness finding the most tender spot of all.

"I thought that was all disproved," said Rosemary. How stupid to be so shocked by Sarah's words.

"So did I," Lawrence helped her as best he could. "I was sure I read something somewhere."

"It's in the Bible," said Sarah without needing emphasis. "Come on, Stephen, sit up at the table."

At the door Rosemary turned back hesitantly. Lawrence was still looking at her, willing to be of service: why was she afraid?

"Edgar says he can help you to get some more books in dialect. He says his mother knows a woman who has an attic-full."

She was as much reassured by the disapproving flinch of Sarah's shoulders as by Lawrence's understanding nod. She went through to the other room.

# Chapter Sixteen

Wilfred told her about his life since they had parted. It was as if he had deliberately sought her out to deliver it all to her. She had no time to object and no defence against the intimacy of the confessional. He told her much on that first night while she felt the uneasiness of danger; on the second and third nights he repeated and embellished and concluded. On the third night she cancelled a meeting with Edgar in order to hear Wilfred out. She excused herself on the grounds of her cousin's "need" for her.

And indeed he was not well. He had been up in the North-East, near Durham, and came over to Cumberland "almost in a dream", he said, intending to give Stephen some fresh air and exercise in the Lakes, often best at Christmas time and anyway it would be a treat for the boy, get him away from their London flat which would be depressing. Again, as he talked, as before, almost a decade before, Rosemary felt each word to be her own. She tried very hard to resist the consequences of this: she did not want to abandon herself in this way. Apparently cool, she fought violently to hold onto the new love for Edgar: but memory, family, nostalgia, first love, kinship, intellectual affinity, the whole loyal longing for Wilfred so painfully and silently suppressed over those years, was now released with irresistible force. She had lived so long in the past; she was a prey to its potency.

He had called at Thurston almost by accident, he said, seeing the name on a bus when he and Stephen had got off the train at Carlisle. His Uncle Lawrence and Aunt Sarah had welcomed him and he was to stay "as long as he liked". He shared the spare bedroom with his son.

He had no inhibitions in the telling—it was too urgent and too necessary for that—and Rosemary fortified herself against shock. I had to tell someone, he would say, at the beginning, but by the second night both of them knew that it was her he had to tell, her alone. This area of his life when he had been as dead to her, had to be pictured, revived and seen to have passed. And as he talked, Rosemary thought how *could* you know I had been waiting?

She was insatiably curious about him—wondering all the time if his life during the absence had somehow matched her own. All the facts were fuel to her long-subdued passion. He liked giving lectures; he enjoyed talking to the students and had established a routine whereby they could drop into his flat at any time on Saturday or Sunday evening—for coffee or beer and perhaps some music would be played or they would play games—Chinese portraits, word games and charades were especially popular. But most of all there would be the talk and this Rosemary ached to know of—what did they say, these blessedly fortunate students? What books did they read? What did they discuss on the last occasion?

Her peculiar nature, a compound of gossamer fragility where she was like the Princess and the Pea, and direst courage where she was in a masculine and almost an heroic mould, found the bond with Wilfred unfractured. He was so sympathetic to the nervous side of her character: even in those few days she felt her mind bathed by his care; and he appreciated her boldness, she could see that. He would not have made the confession had he not trusted the confessor.

But he had no energy left from his own consuming obsession to spare her the thoughts which his appreciation demanded. Wilfred was at his wits' end: he was afraid for himself and for his son; though able to maintain a well-mannered relationship with the external world, he was only just caging the chaos in his mind. For inside that well-bred, well-educated skull was a sick rage, a self-tormenting devil which screamed to be loosed or killed: or it would itself kill. Rosemary answered his need—he could see that: and see little else.

Each night, Sarah cleared away dishes despite Rosemary's protests—enforcing her benevolence with a knowing smile at Wilfred. His misfortune had brought out the best in her. A man whose wife was dead, a young widower, was, to Sarah, more romantic than anyone else at all.

# Chapter Seventeen

"Everybody feels guilt at the death of someone close to them," he said, "it must be part of the sense of loss. But what makes it difficult in *my* case is that we had quarrelled, we had separated and Stephen had become a rope in a tug of war. It's not as if her death can be set apart from what happened between us; the illness she had was quick and sudden, it ate her up like grief or despair. The point is that I was not there, and not only that, I was in the process of following through a terrible argument, a vendetta it would be better to call it. We had disappointed each other so much that revenge was the only consolation."

The confession came out like a prepared statement. It was the third night. Stephen was in bed, above them, and could hear his father's urgent murmur; the sound of it like the suck of the back-reaching wave drawing across the pebbles. He could not sleep, the boy, in this felted silence, in the small room with the empty bed beside him, the thought of his dead mother enlarging by the minute in his head and him too old to shout out, too proud to cry. In the living-room Lawrence sat at the table as he did every weekday evening and worked away at his book, enjoying the peaceful certainties of reorganizing his indexing system and repatterning his quotations. In profile to him was Sarah preparing a parcel of clothes for the "patched and darned" stall at the Christmas fête. Both also heard the steady insistence of Wilfred's voice and each watched the other surreptitiously to make sure there was no eavesdropping. The manner of Wilfred's attentions to Rosemary had raised the younger woman in Sarah's estimation. If only she could be stopped from having anything to do with that rough-neck Edgar Crowther! And if, not only *that*, but she could be assisted into marriage with the poor lonely young widower. . . .

Sarah enlisted all her energies to further that end: before going to bed at night she prayed and before leaving her bed in the morning, she schemed. There was excitement and real pleasure in it for her—it was the first time she had been able to enter into the adult life of her disappointing charge and the attempt at alliance could compensate for many previous disunities.

Wilfred had delivered his news as might a messenger who has run far to find its recipient and found himself with the energy to do no more than utter the barest information before collapsing. After stating his terrible guilt he had run both his hands through his hair, looked ahead, abstractedly, dully, not wildly, and then his upper body had collapsed onto the rest of his arms on the small table. Rosemary swayed backwards as he sobbed as if in danger and then stood up, walked around behind him, nervously stroked the back of his hair, desisted, took out a cigarette; and waited.

He felt no relief inside the skull. The release had not brought ease. Nothing had left him except those sounds breathed into pellets of meaning. How stupid to expect it! The stretch of darkness around the shocked nerves would not be illuminated so simply: would not, he thought, be illuminated again.

What Rosemary now knew beyond doubt was that Wilfred needed her. Edgar's need was not to be compared with this. Any balance which had been held between the two men fell to Wlfred's side as she absorbed his news. She had never before been needed.

"I'm sorry," she heard him say hoarsely. "I shouldn't have told you that."

"Poor woman," Rosemary replied, speaking without self-conscious thought. "Poor woman."

'Yes."

Once more a pause, but not so long this time. Wilfred lit up his pipe and visibly "pulled himself together". Rosemary felt a twinge of failure that she could not help him avoid this face-saving.

If only, she thought, there was something glorious she could say. Some second statement which would echo his first at once and in kind, some healing response which would forever bind them together. Life should at least let you do something poetic and exact and grand at a time like this; or was this the delusion only of her reading and of her dreams? "I didn't know her, but I know you," said Rosemary, boldly. "You would have stayed if you could. You would have stuck with her if you'd been at all able to. I know that." Convinced by her desire to be convincing she went on, looking above his head, seeing him as he had been almost a decade ago. "You loved her as much as you could. I'm sure of that. If people fall out of love then they have to discover other things. And perhaps no one can stay in love forever," she hesitated. "Do you know anyone who has?"

"No," Wilfred sat back and considered the matter as if it had been just any other question. He felt that he had exposed himself over-naïvely and searched to recover his poise. "No—although my tutor at Durham—my Moral Tutor funnily enough—he and his wife were always loving to each other."

"That's not the same," cried Rosemary. "In fact I *hate* it when people are 'lovey-dovey' as they say around here. Love is too private and too marvellous for that. People who let it leak out all over the place are like burst old pipes."

"Icarus," he said suddenly, "I'm right, aren't I? You admired Icarus, who flew too near the sun and saw his wings melt and fell back to earth. Do you remember?"

"Yes," she paused. How well she remembered—how *much* she remembered! It shamed her to acknowledge it as Wilfred sat so proud of his feat. "Yes," she said sadly. "You have to fly," and she thought of Edgar.

"When you came to London," he said, "I thought of flying away." (Rosemary did not allow herself to react to this declaration but its sweetness slid under her skin and she saved it there, to feed on later). "I could see you and I could see her: you were clear and yet mysterious—you were tantalizing; she was obscure and blatant, but she caught me by the tail. It is a sort of madness to admit that a form of social habit prevented me from flying from her. Letting her down and letting myself down and letting the side down was worse than seeking happiness. Fear drives out love."

To Rosemary there came the corrected phrase "perfect love driveth out fear" but for once she managed to leave the words unsaid. She felt very nervous: she sat on the edge of her seat, her back straight as if a schoolteacher had told her to "sit up properly"; tense and attendant, her mind galloping over the future as Wilfred stumbled clumsily and painfully through his past.

In the end they had decided to sacrifice themselves for Stephen. But nothing was worth a sacrifice.

The word was spoken in a new tone; real pain and fury went

into it and Rosemary instantly saw the Druidical knife, the palpitating heart of the Aztec's chosen noble victim, Abraham and his only son.

Nothing was worth a sacrifice, Wilfred repeated. If he had to try to set up a structure of right behaviour then the cornerstone would be that nothing was worth a sacrifice. It would not serve, but then nothing else would serve better. The drive to bad would always find a way as water comes down the mountainside. Yet in private relationships at heart it would hold: between adults and their sensible children, nothing was worth a sacrifice. Where suffering could be avoided it should be avoided: after a while, to hold on without expectation that things would get better was a denial of the possibilities in life. It was following the rules to their roots and in the end those roots had been planted by man and could be torn out and replanted by man. Your own nature in revolt against the nature of society could often be right: the majority were only right when they did right.

So eventually he had left his wife. He had taken a flat of his own and another woman lived with him there for a while. Without her he could not have survived the separation. His wife had not taken a lover. Because of Stephen he had tried to rejoin her: in his mind many times the resolution had been clear and firm but when he saw her again on those Saturdays and Sundays when he went to visit his son, then he would be plunged once more into an uncontrollable passion of irritation.

The other woman . . . Rosemary tried to be cool about that but his confession was too much all at once. The poor wife, she kept repeating to herself, but she did not know how she meant it, for after all there was undoubted rejoicing in Wilfred's presence here with her: in his freedom, in his confession. But the other woman . . . how did that fit in . . . ? Surely that lowered the whole thing, she thought, made him less of a man.

How she would have liked to have kissed him, though. As he sat there she could "see" them together endlessly, evening stretching into the future, talking, reading, thinking together, being one mind, one spirit, one body. That hopeful thought drove off all doubts.

"And I did not realize how weak she had become," he said. "What I did not understand was how much she loved me. Not me as a man—though that, too, sometimes—but me as a husband and as a father, as a provider, as a companion, as all those people she needed in order to live. There are letters she wrote but did not post. I read them. And those she *did* post, if I had only read them with understanding. There is no doubt in my mind that I killed her: by default."

Wilfred spoke that last solemn sentence with such unhappiness that Rosemary's only response should have been to kiss him and hold him. But she could do neither. The self-accusation was so terrible. If it were true it was horrible; if it were merely a pose, it was also horrible. It had to be false: and yet he had convinced her. A sense of wrong informed her.

But there he was: in need, as once his wife had been.

"You cannot force yourself to love someone," she conceded.

Wilfred nodded, gratefully.

"It must have been unbearable for her. And for you ... perhaps she saw her death as a gift of love."

He looked up, sharply, as if she had said the remark most likely to stab his feelings. But saw that she, too, searched, as he did, for meaning in words to cover the act decently.

"I shouldn't have told you," he said. "It's selfish to give anyone else the burden."

"No," Rosemary wanted to help and forced herself to move to where she knew he needed her. "No, you needed to talk. Now I just—I just keep thinking of that poor woman."

He turned to her as her hands lightly settled on his shoulders. His eyes looked hopelessly into hers and the chill of his despair was sent to her. She knew what to say: and wanted to; for her own sake, she would admit that.

"You can always live," she said. "There is no alternative. None. None at all. You must live because that is what we are for."

# Chapter Eighteen

She lay silently awake on the narrow bed. "None," "None at all,"—the call of her sympathy rang loudly in her mind. Had Wilfred been slightly embarrassed by the vehemence of her support? She could not believe that—his need was so enormous, surely, no help could be subject to such trivial laws as those governing embarrassment. And yet he had reddened a little; his shoulders had stiffened under the tender consolation of her hands —she was confused by his sudden switch from the confessional to the unapproachable. Her indulgence was all for him, however, and she could soon explain away his inconsistencies. He had not meant to go so far, she guessed: the description of his marriage sounded like an account tabled in the mind for the sake of clarity, for sanity even, certainly for reference in times of unbearable remembrance. He had not meant to tell her. Despite his avowal to the contrary, she was certain that the words had simply slipped out. The closeness of their natures, the strength of retrospective alliance, perhaps the security of finding her still single and his aunt and uncle still welcoming (for she could see that he regarded himself as a moral outcast) all had combined to release the wounded story.

No doubt he was merely rehearsing it in his own mind, treating *her* mind, she soon concluded, merely as an extension of his own—Echo to Narcissus. This pleased her.

But what he had said could not. "That poor woman" was what dominated her mind. That poor, poor woman—to have gained so much and then to have lost so much. Rosemary could feel a print of the other woman's pain and even that small intimation distressed her. She considered that Wilfred had been weak to have married the wrong woman in the first place and, despite her best intention, the corollary was undoubtedly that he ought to have married herself. She allowed herself to take no pleasure in this.

Yet she still loved him. If love meant an instantaneous empathy which followed and wanted to follow every flicker of another's mind and temperament, she still loved him. If love meant being proud of a man, acknowledging the way he stood for himself and in the world, she still loved him. Yet this terrible fact was between them. She could not fit it into her idea of the man she loved and yet there was no seeing him without it.

She got up and sat on her window-ledge, not minding the cold, looking out towards the white frosted fields around the little school they were building for the juniors. In bright red bricks. Like a toy, it looked, an age away from the ancient building in the town centre which had heard the obedient chants of so many before. "The town's starting to creep away from itself"—the observation was Edgar's. He'd been talking about a scheme to buy up fields on the edge of the town in the certainty, he maintained, that the old town, the knotted puzzle of Thurston which he liked so much, would have to be unravelled. She remembered the phrase for its sense and nonsense: how could anything "creep away from itself", she had thought; and yet the meaning was perfectly clear.

Yes, it was time to get to Edgar. Her cold feet rested on the colder stone of the head he had given her. However hard she looked at it, the face remained the same: no longer would it transform itself into a thousand shapes—it was a badly chipped head, probably a piece of inferior eighteenth-century garden furniture given an air of significance only by accident and dirt and age.

It was time to get to Edgar. From what seemed the far, far part of her mind Rosemary hauled up the awful realization that on the next day, Christmas Eve, she had promised to go to a dance with Edgar where, she realized with painful certainty, he was going to present her with an engagement ring: willy nilly. It did not bear thinking about and yet she had to do *some*thing.

How completely he had vanished from her thoughts! A few days before, she had been schooling herself to accept what she feared, having already embraced what she loved. She had been prepared to organize herself around this odd man, convinced that there were talents and possibilities in him which she could encourage. Confident of her ability to mould him even as he appeared to dominate her. He had given her a great deal, she acknowledged that, though aware that her easy manner of yielding her body to him had been more than a just return. Now she wondered, rather, at the very ease of it. Would she give as freely to Wilfred? Were he to walk into her bedroom now—and part of her, she had to admit, hoped that he would—would she let him make love to her?

The frost was white on the half-built school, on the fields, on the few roof-tops she could see. She herself felt as if the night had painted its stiff whiteness on her. Her flesh was block cold. Yet she could not yet leave the self-imposed exile on the window-sill, locked into herself, only the mind warm.

She must see Edgar and ward off the evening. It would be difficult and it would be decisive, she felt, and she could not act in any other way.

Eventually in bed, as she shivered off the wilfully encouraged coldness on her flesh, she used the painfulness of it to re-enter into her perturbation over Wilfred: the body providing both a distraction and a parallel.

She knew him so well and yet this dreadful fact of his life made him a stranger to her. How could he have done it? How could he have married her? And then, compounding that mistake, fathered her child? Then, a mistress? There was so much to absorb and disentangle—but how could he have done that? Then the leaving and the uncomprehending her plight. Who was this man who could abuse first his instinct and then his position and finally his responsibility? Compared with him, the flat openness and untapped mystery of Edgar seemed much more true.

Yet there was never a fight, never a struggle. Wilfred had reminded her that she was his. The obligations she had to Edgar could be severed if she took her courage in both hands: and if Wilfred took up his courage he could identify his enemies of the past and lay them low.

Then they could meet once again. As warmth seeped into her and the dour dawn rose reluctantly to illuminate the hoar-frost, she fell asleep, and woke late,· her head clustered with urgent dreams, indecipherable.

# Chapter Nineteen

She caught up with Edgar finally at the sawmill. Although she had only looked for an hour, the smallness of the town and her apprehension had made the quest seem long and arduous. Nor was the mood of those she asked any help: they assumed her to be chasing her sweetheart and the friendly smiles, the affectionate conspiracy depressed and irritated her.

Wilfred had decided to go down to Carlisle to do some Christmas shopping. Sarah was delighted to have been able to persuade him to stay over the holiday; the pastry was slapped on the board and smacked like a new baby's bottom, the pudding-spoon flew, tins lined up to be greased, and all the festival recipes were employed to stock the larder shelves deep. Lawrence had found, in Wilfred's son, a bright, apt and willing pupil, the best listener, he solemnly declared, that he had ever met. With Stephen he had struck up a true friendship; the boy enjoyed watching him work with the clocks and was soon able to help him in a useful way; he liked the older man's local stories and above all he was blessed with true curiosity.

Rosemary had been aware of this settled state of affairs throughout her afternoon and it had comforted her. Everything seemed so very much in place. She had never felt as close to Sarah, as much *part* of that household; never before felt that she was really contributing. Wilfred, in a few days, had made her more part of that home than ever before. Now she was giving instead of taking, an asset, even a benefactress.

And in that mood, the town which Edgar had made so vivid and full to her seemed a dreary little place, still the harbour it had always been, but only until the wind dropped and she could sail out to sea again.

It was Wilfred who had taken the initiative on the morning of Christmas Eve and Sarah had welcomed his request with a warmth which Rosemary had scarcely ever seen before. But she was certain that a great part of his reason for staying on must be herself. His parents would be disappointed not to see Stephen —Rosemary could so easily flick her mind to see them in that house in Kew; would she know them again? Would they welcome her again? They had continued to invite her to go for holidays— perhaps they really did like her—how much he must want to stay to be prepared to deprive his parents of a certain chance to feel useful and be happy.

Rosemary felt, on further consideration, that Wilfred's confession had been the greatest compliment ever paid her. He had come, he had talked, he would stay—those were the tributes to cherish.

She stood, just inside the gate of the sawmill, behind her the new paper factory; another mill and the railway bridge to her left and to her right yet another factory—Redmayne's where the women of the town found employment—the whole small area bleak with walled industry, she thought, so soon forgetting the warmth of Edgar's vision of the place. Edgar, utterly confident beside a perilous stack of planks, was sawing logs for the last Christmas sales. He saw her and waved and in dumb show indicated that he would not be long. She watched him, grimly: he was putting on a display.

How well he did it! The whine of the machine soared into the darkening sky as he walked between the yellow planks, heaving large branches of stripped timber onto the plate, pushing them towards the sawing wheel and back again as the log was executed. The process hypnotized Rosemary. Edgar was so capable. He could attend to so many things at once—kicking the belt of the saw, stopping to pick up the log with one hand while sliding the branch back with the other, stacking the log as he turned. The sound of that machine could be heard all over the town. Its wail could be very painful; oddly, on this evening she, who hated noise, found it enjoyable, even a little exciting.

He took his time.

It was only when he joined her that she saw his anger. His face smiled—but the smile was menacing: his gestures were energetic, apparently cheerful but, to Rosemary, threatening. He did not look her directly in the eyes—such a look, she thought, would ignite a rage she already feared in prospect.

"Well," he demanded, the tone of his voice incapable of disguise. "I thought we were meeting later on." His attempt by glances and implication to pretend that his brusque manner was due to the urgency of his work touched Rosemary unexpectedly. He had looked forward to it then, had he? So much?

"That's what I came to talk about," she said, and shivered; standing there had made her cold. And it seemed unnecessary, such drama: better to have written.

"What's that?"

Now he did look at her and was still. She remembered, vividly, the first time he had made love to her. The trace of his hands on her back turned to print in her memory as she remembered his confident flesh. He *had* given her much.

"I can't come tonight." That was not good enough. She collected herself. "I'm sorry, Edgar, but it'll have to be all over between us. My cousin from London—it doesn't matter where—anyway; he's staying with us. I can't—do you understand."

"You're in love with him," said Edgar, sternly, so sternly that Rosemary's head jolted back. She could not reply.

"If that's the case then there's no more to be said." Edgar nodded, *briskly*, she thought, wonderingly. "You must choose who you will. All I can do is press my case. You know my feelings for you, Rosemary; they won't change."

"I'm sorry, Edgar." Her throat was full, a weakening about the eyes let in the tears she had never expected.

"Ay well," he replied, still unyielding. "That makes two of us. I'm sorry as well."

She turned so that he would not see the effort to hold back the tears. She admired his strength which gave her such liberty.

"Don't cry," he said, softly this: and her tears came.

"I'm sorry," she murmured; still he did not touch her, he, whose impulses were always expressed by his body. She felt the omission as neglect and could understand it only in terms of his massive strength, the resources she had so relied on in their imagined future together.

"I hope you're very happy whatever you do."

By the time she had turned to meet this most generous release, he was gone and over the dark yard she saw him swinging the bags of newly cut logs onto a lorry, in a fury of effort.

She walked away from the town, up towards the cemetery, to calm herself. There she went to look at her mother's grave and stood over it as night fastened on this cold northern town, regretting that she had no flowers for the mound which looked so forlorn under the winter grass. She resolved to come again, on New Year's Day, and bedeck the place.

So, it was done: and through the natural tears, good tears of clear sorrow, she felt the pleasure of freedom rise up. Down into Thurston she returned, unburdened, unattached. Before her the prize of a life which could be so fine, she knew, so compact with interest and quiet thoughtful pleasures—she could forget the raw appeal of Edgar, that could be lived without, that was not so important, she was certain. Though the flesh needed much it could make do with less: but the spirit, once touched to life, as hers had been with Wilfred, once joined in a union which made matrimony appear the very coarsest analogy, she thought, the spirit could never "make do": once aroused, it could only reach out again, go further, take on the whole of life.

# Chapter Twenty

Christmas Day and Boxing Day were the best ever known in that house, Sarah declared. There was such a "family" feeling about it: the older woman's hints and innuendoes were now as plain as banner headlines. They went to church, the five of them, and took a pew to themselves, which Sarah thought particularly fine. And the treasure she had laid up in the mysterious and distinguished appearance of Wilfred!—well, from the appreciative glances of her good friends on the Townswomen's Guild she knew there was gossip there to crochet out the winter.

At last Rosemary had redeemed herself in the older woman's eyes. She treated her like a superior. Rosemary was even more discomfited by this than she had been while living under her aunt's reproach but the strangeness and the privileges underscored the richness of this time.

Perhaps it was because they stood in a peculiar relation to each other in terms of manners and intimacy and idealizations that the redolence of those days was so very strong. Wilfred was as much if not more Sarah's ideal than Rosemary's: Lawrence provided Stephen with all the solidity and certainty in the world, while the child's cultivated intelligence charmed the self-taught clockmaker. Rosemary was clever enough not to impose on Stephen and he could see her as a friend and not resent her as a substitute for his mother. More profoundly than that, all of them ached for lack of family: the older ones had no children, the boy no mother, Wilfred no wife, Rosemary no one at all—and in the sentiment of each one the notion of domestic felicity was cherished most sincerely especially at this festival time. They were well met at this season when all over the town as all over England families retreated into themselves, for richer or for poorer, for better or for worse, to remember and even sing the carols which were as comforting as cradle songs and acknowledge a birth which had informed their history. Christmas trees and tinsel, paper chains and mince pies, the heavy pudding and the child's stocking, the charm of commonplace things made twopence-coloured for the short festival and the unabashed declarations from church doctrine and traditional rites, all settled around those two days and bound them in as effectively as a fall of snow.

Wilfred took two walks a day: Stephen was allowed to miss one of them. Rosemary also skipped the evening walk, somehow more enjoying the thought of Wilfred alone doing something he so liked. And she was taking care not to arouse Stephen's jealousy: the boy was very alert. He watched her as she watched him: once or twice they caught each other out and smiled a little wryly.

The day after Boxing Day, Lawrence arranged to take Stephen to Carlisle. There was an exhibition in Tullie House about the Roman Wall and then they would look at the Castle and the Cathedral. Wilfred announced his desire to climb Skiddaw as it promised to be such a clear day. Sarah enlisted Harold Sowerby's help to borrow a car from one of his neighbours and she waved off Rosemary and Wilfred as if they had been setting out on their honeymoon. The presumption was not lost on either of the two young people, but a sympathetic smile was all their comment.

It was amazing, she thought, how fluently they could reach each other. Words were only the tip of the iceberg. Compared with their communion, the short letter from Edgar was like an indigestible lump: yet she carried it round with her unwilling to destroy it, unwilling to leave it behind in her bedroom. Now it was in the breast pocket of her jacket. She could not get rid of it.

Dear Rosemary, it read,
    This is to wish you all you wish yourself. You know how I feel about you and I can't see that changing. But we are all free as you have said many times and I agree. It would be wrong of me to wish you good luck because your good luck would be my bad. But I do wish you happiness, Rosemary, and hope you will remember the happiness you have had with
                                        Yours,
                                        Edgar.

There was nothing she could absorb in that, she thought, without being swallowed whole. It was not a communication but the statement of a position. Yet she could not dislodge from her mind an obstinate fascination with such a weighty plainness.

But by the time they had reached Applethwaite and driven a

114

little way further to park the car, to reach the lower slopes of "stupendous Skiddaw", the old man of the lakeland fells, Edgar was far from her thoughts and the wad of his letter on her breast forgotten.

Having conquered the first, steep ascent, they sat down to eat some of the sensible sandwiches which Sarah had insisted on making, not allowing Rosemary to "waste her day" with such work. Before them lay as splendid a view as could be seen in the world, Rosemary thought. The winter sun was strong: the sky blue with cirrus clouds scattered high and stretches of shapely cumulus resting on the fell tops. The balance of hill and valley, lake and cloud, town below, and above the top of Skiddaw, slate reflecting slate, the grandeur and the workaday gave a sense of harmony which Rosemary wished into herself as sun-worshippers offer themselves for infusion.

"It's remarkable how recently this was appreciated," said Wilfred, reading her thoughts, she observed with a flush of gratitude. "Only about two hundred and fifty years ago. Before then it was the land of the barbarians—the place the Welshmen fled to when the Romans came, where the Celts gathered to resist the British—and the last battle against the Normans was fought around these hills. When people spoke of the mountains they spoke as if these hills were the Himalyas—'immense' 'dark' 'dreadful'—Coleridge is the man who changed that. Wordsworth, of course. But at first Coleridge was the more ardent propagandist. He was the first fell-walker—his descriptions of the walks he took are some of the best prose he ever wrote. I'll send them to you."

She enjoyed his tendency to lecture, understanding, too, that it used up nervousness, but she could have wished for more courage on her own part. She had read much of Wordsworth and still knew pages of Coleridge by heart and yet Wilfred's fluency overawed her. Temporarily, she was prepared to endure it, even to encourage it as it further increased Wilfred's stature.

As they walked up the rest of the fell, he talked more and more about Wordsworth for whom he obviously felt a fascination on that day. Rosemary relished the tie and saw Wilfred's attraction to this very northern poet to be yet more evidence of their destined unity. She would be Dorothy to his William, would help and make notes and unobtrusively feed the man; and then, later perhaps, she would be Mary, his wife. For he wrote "only articles", he had said, so far; but he was a "writer", and a blaze of pleasure swept through her whenever she brought it to mind.

They were walking on the back side of the hill now. Beyond, towards Blencathra and the Caldbeck Fells, the sun was in full flood. The edge of the shadow was a ruled line above them. Below, to the right, was Skiddaw House where she had taken Edgar. She fingered the note in her pocket: it was a dignified letter, she thought, manly; Edgar was indeed a remarkable man. She stopped and faced the sun, closing her eyes, letting its mild wintry warmth be full on her face.

"You look like someone praying," Wilfred observed.

"I suppose I *was* praying," she said quietly.

Wilfred jabbed his finger towards the summit of the fell, now no more than fifteen minutes away. "Up there we'll find a cairn and a trig point." He smiled—"Our barbarian ancestors would have prayed to those phallic symbols." He hesitated. "Do you know the story of the worship of the first phallus?"

Yet again the coincidence was too perfect to be accidental. Rosemary long ago had come across a book on Tutenkhamen at the public library. The young king's beautiful eyes, even on the death mask, were so intelligent, sensual and tragic, she thought; and she had developed a secret passion for Egyptology. She had read the book and discovered the hieroglyphics and learned that it was a Frenchman who had cracked the code and translated them. Since then she had kept up a loving interest in Egyptology. But she preferred not to admit it and encouraged Wilfred to go on. She could see him as a grave Arabic scholar.

"Isis," Wilfred said, "the wife of Osiris, went around collecting each of the twenty-four fragments of her husband's dismembered body, and everywhere she found a part she would raise a monument. However, the principal part—the *membrum virilis,* had vanished. So Isis built a simulacrum of the Phallus, high and mighty in stone—the biggest monument of them all and immediately the most popular. It makes sense. After all, that is what starts off the whole damned business."

His glance was boldly returned. Seeing her tentative yet intoxicated expression he saw how beautiful she was. Painfully he now remembered her words to him beside the Thames—yes, they *could* have been so wonderful together. There was still time— but as soon as that thought came to him he dropped into hopelessness. He was unclean. He could never promise anything to anyone again. He had found the word for himself while reading *Antony and Cleopatra*. When Antony calls himself "unqualitied". "Unqualitied" was he, too, with all virtue drained away and no foundation within him on which to build that private moral world so essential to the sort of life he believed in.

In the distance, but still clear, was the spot where Edgar had taken his body into her own. That was unnerving, but she could suppress it, if only she could rid her mind of an image which had quite suddenly seized it. It was so vivid.

It was of the stone phallus which Wilfred had referred to. First she had seen it alone in a desert, a monumental length of stone pointing to the sun, challenging it or at least returning the challenge. Then she thought of the centre of the planet, surrounded by fire and molten minerals, it was a ball of iron. She imagined the ball of iron had begun to grow a skin and push its way through the fire—she could see it, undestroyed by the flames, the gorgeous yellows and scarlets licking the black iron but only hardening it. It had driven through the minerals, unstoppable, growing steadily towards the surface where finally it met this, Skiddaw mountain, the "oldest rock in the world", and up the centre of Skiddaw it was driving now even as they walked, to burst out before them, she thought, the instant they would touch the cairn at the top. Simultaneously, something in her head was matching the pole of iron, for inside her brain she felt a definite growth, reaching through the layers of blood and nerves and tissue, driving down to her throat where it would break through. The double image was full of a great pleasurable pain: she wanted to hug it and hold onto it and yet it had to come through or she would die. Silly as she told herself she was, when they *did* reach the top and Wilfred conscientiously tossed a slate stone onto the cairn, Rosemary watched it, hypnotized by the certainty that it would suddenly lift into the air and be replaced by the rod of iron from the centre of the earth. The force inside her brain, too, became urgent, and she parted her lips, aware of the lunacy of it all yet caught up in it. "Wilfred!" The word made her feel dizzy.

"Yes."

"I must be . . . I'm feeling tired."

"You've done too much."

She nodded: the words had relieved the pressure.

They sat in one of the stone shelters against the wind, looking over to the far side of Lake Bassenthwaite, and ate more Christmas sandwiches. Wilfred's thoughts turned gloomy: again and again he thought of the death of his wife. Time would not heal it—he knew that. The wound would forever be open. If only he had behaved well. How he envied those with a clear conscience who "did all they could". The world seemed full of loyal people. Why did he not scream his pain onto this landscape which had seen so much unjust blood and loss? Munch like the sheep went the jaw of the lecturer. Sang with sick rage the guilt and pain in the skull. It was truly human to shriek at death, he thought, to be let howl and tear your hair. This stoicism battened down too much, made less than true the reality, robbed the feelings of expression, stunted that growth of pain which must have its way as evil itself must have its way. For in his neglect there was evil, he was convinced of that: it was something he could not understand but he could see it. What else was it to turn away from the cry of need from one you have loved? To turn your back.

Rosemary sensed that he had gone from her and, sadly, made no attempt to follow, glad to sit out her own strange pain, agitated that such an intrusion should have come to interfere with this seeding time. As if to exorcise the devil of it, she slipped Edgar's over-folded letter from her pocket and unobtrusively placed it under a stone. But the second her fingers withdrew their grip she imagined a stranger discovering it, reading the lines, knowing this fact of her life. She retrieved it and held it in her hand.

"You look very tired," said Wilfred, dragging her mind back to the present. "I don't suppose you're used to so much walking." The flatness of his tone depressed her. She did not stir herself to deny or affirm.

Side by side, there on the top of the fell, each sucked by an inner world more powerful even than the spectacle of nature round about them, they sat mourning the waste, closed to external impulses, shut off even from each other; between them the abyss of self.

"It's probably as well to go back the way we came," Wilfred suggested. "Any other route down means a long trudge back to the car unless we go *straight* down and I don't really think we're equipped for that."

She acquiesced and they stood up together. The sandwiches

and wrappings were put away. Driven to lick his wound, Wilfred wanted once more to talk to this woman who was so marvellously sympathetic. And yet he could not be direct. He must find a way which did not deal with his own realities—once had been enough to ask of her.

As they walked down, the jolt of feet on the slope warmed her up and she felt sure again. Casually she let Edgar's letter slip and fall from her hand. She needed such a gesture.

Again they stood looking down the length of Derwentwater: the light was more mellow now, some of the clouds pink and mauve, extraordinary tints, Venetian in their sumptuous lustre, and the lake so still, no boat, no wind in the valley.

"People believed that Wordsworth's poetry could heal them," said Wilfred, suddenly finding himself again able to link his pre-occupation with an act of public communication. "In fact, when John Stuart Mill, the philosopher, had his breakdown, it was Wordsworth's poetry which cured him, so he wrote: nothing else could. I can understand that."

"Yes," Rosemary was over-eager to join in, "he's so calm and certain about everything."

"Yes and no," Wilfred paused, then, still looking straight ahead at the view, he went on "I think he appeals to those who have witnessed a personal breakdown because he himself had such a breakdown—or even two such breakdowns. Once when he was an early adolescent, when he describes having to hold *onto* rocks and stones and trees to feel their solidity and reassure him as to his sanity, and later in his twenties after the affair with Annette Vallon." He hesitated. "Have you heard of Annette Vallon?" he asked. Rosemary shook her head, hoping that this admission of ignorance would not break the spell which she wanted to grow and bind them together in the old way. "She was his mistress when he went to France just after Cambridge and he made her pregnant." Wilfred used the word deliberately, to shock. It sounded bitter. "Then he came back to England, pre-sumably to fix things up, but there was the war between England and France and he never got back there. But there are always ways. He abandoned her. And he was lucky that she proved so independent: she did not die on him, she made no claims, she let him let her go without a cry, it seems. His break-down may be seen as a redemption but what if he had had to redeem a death?" Rosemary almost held her breath: once more, she saw, he was calling her. She must answer; she must help.

"But how could he go on as he did after that?"

He paused and then continued vehemently, "He concealed the fact of Annette to his friends, to the world and even to his poetry. And yet if Wordsworth stands for anything, he represents the truthful, questing spirit, finding proof for instinctive good feelings in the 'goodness' of the natural world. Yet he lived with a gross deceit: he had fathered a bastard and abandoned a woman he'd sworn to love forever—how could he be so convincing about right and wrong?—you should read not only his poems but his letters, especially to young admirers when—and he was only in his early thirties himself—he urges them to be ascetic, to be moderate in all things, not to drink and above all to be chaste—how could he do it?"

"Perhaps only those who have done wrong *can* know what is right and what is wrong. Feeling the unhappiness and enduring the consequences, they are maybe the only ones who can be certain."

Wilfred was silent. "Yes. That could be. But where does he get the faith? How can he be such a hypocrite?"

"That could be his sacrifice."

He looked at her most keenly. "I'd never thought of that," he said and she blushed. "Do you think it is possible not to hurt others?"

"Yes," she laughed. "Of course it is. You have to work at it, that's all." She paused and then asserted herself. "We can make ourselves into what we want."

"Only if we kill those parts we don't want."

"That has to be done anyway."

"I'm against all killing," he said, "even of the bad."

How much she wanted to speak plainly to Wilfred and say— "Look, forget the past, forgive her, let her go—and see, see what we have together, what a life we could make." But a whole culture of manners and practices forbade her to say that. Metaphors were all she had.

As they set off down the last stretch, he returned to his theme. "What *would* he have done if Annette had not been so strong?"

Rosemary hesitated and then made her decision. There was no way to ease the pain but to pretend to certainties. "No one is finally responsible for anyone else," she said.

He looked at her sharply, his face instantly altered, as if a tight-wound spring behind the eyes had suddenly been released. This was the heart of it! His eyes held her own, shining as if in exultation—"But they *are*!" he cried, "they must be!"

Rosemary shook her head, dismissing his desperate need to be disapproved. "Not if they are adults," she insisted. "Children, very old people, very sick people," she stumbled over that last category—how ill had he *known* his wife to be? Even in this warmth of contact there was the uncontrollable tremor of suspicion. "But adults are firstly responsible for themselves. Otherwise they take away too much from another's freedom." Liberty, that was her faith. "To be too dependent on someone is to appoint him your executor in life and that is to give him too much. Some people can accept it. Some look for it and need it. Lucky people find those whose strengths complement their weaknesses. But there are those who don't. And when the realization arrives, then you have to say that one person is *not* responsible for another."

"But they *are*! We *must* be responsible for those to whom we give our loyalty—whether we give it voluntarily or whether we give it because we have no choice, as in a family. Once it is given, then a contract of dependence is entered into and to break that is wrong. It can even be evil." He was vehement.

"No. No!"

The more he pressed her the more she knew he needed her to stick to her argument. "If that were true, no son would leave his mother, daughters would stay as companions to their fathers, everyone would be presumed to make the utterly right choice of partner, friendships would never wither: people change, Wilfred," how boldly she used his name, now, which had so often been murmured in sleep, "they change every day and often the change makes them unable to bear what once they had accepted without a word. You must acknowledge that."

He was silent. They were walking slowly now, across the level last field which joined the lane where the car had been parked. She could see that he was attentive. She concentrated even harder and tried to keep her argument as lucid as possible, nerving herself against the odd feeling—almost as odd as that feeling of growth inside the mountain and inside her mind—that her voice might be turned into a substance in the air, that this sound of herself, so determined to be lucid and intellectual and so altered in tone from the normal colour of her voice, might turn into a thin tube of glass, unformed glass, writhing its way about both of them like a snake. "In these country places, there is so little variety of change that the assumptions of knowledge you make in a courtship and a marriage must stand a good chance of holding true for the rest of your time. Particularly as your pace of life will go on the same for both. But in the city, I think, two people can live at entirely different speeds." She wavered: she knew nothing about the city; she feared she had lost his interest: she made another bid. "Morality reflects society: the only absolutes are ideals, which are much more important."

"I would completely reverse that sentence," Wilfred exclaimed. "Ideals are simply the sparks which fly off a busy society to be shaped into patterns by ingenious artists: morals stay the same forever."

"Every act has been justified by some society—and by societies we admire," she asserted.

"Murder."

"War."

"Theft."

"Property."

"Promiscuity."

She paused. "Sanity," she replied firmly. He nodded.

By now they had reached the car. The climb had been a stiff one, the strain of finding communion with Wilfred had been severe and though their argument had exhilarated her it had also exhausted her. She was not used to it. Moreover such a swift process of dispute concerned her. So much was said just for the sake of making the next point. There seemed to come a time when the argument simply had to roll on like a snowball suddenly feeling its weight and rolling down a hill to be stopped only by a solid object or the termination of the incline. The car was her solid object.

Wilfred opened the car door and looked up at where they had walked. Yet another layer seemed to slip off him, she noticed in her consuming passion for knowledge of his nature—he had something of the gaiety which had been so vivaciously present on those first few magical days in London. "In one way you're absolutely right, of course," he said, "Wordsworth's lines will be read long after his ideas have died. There's something which escapes reason and morality and all prosaic expressions of life."

"Poetry," she affirmed, a little uneasily dutiful.

It was the retort he had aimed for. They smiled in mutual recognition, and yet still Rosemary felt uneasy. It could not, perhaps it must not, be so simple.

# Chapter Twenty-One

When they reached Thurston she excused herself immediately on the grounds of having a headache. Sarah was amazed and appalled to discover how Big their walk had been and cast a reproachful look at Wilfred for such masculine foolishness. Rosemary was ushered to bed with all the status of one ennobled by a great feat of exploration. Stephen, too, pleaded a headache—his day with Lawrence had gone on long enough; the man's zeal for his pupil's good was remorseless and the boy needed a rest. Wilfred could not face the prospect of sitting in front of the fire alone with his aunt and uncle. This clear realization rather troubled him for he had taken some comfort from the feeling of "family" during the previous days. He saw now how much it depended on Rosemary's presence. He announced that he would take his evening walk, to be rewarded, most unworthily, by a song of praise from Sarah on his constancy, his iron will, his physical endurance ... the wind blew hot and hotter from that quarter.

He walked around the Syke road, his stick occasionally tapping the iron railings which ringed what once had been a magnificent estate with deer parks and grand avenues, private golf-course and imitation Venetian tower, representing Thurston's brief fling of squierarchic elegance. Lawrence had told Wilfred all its glorious history. It was seductive, Wilfred thought, this dense knowledge of a small patch of land. Colleagues did the same in their research. For himself, though, he preferred the most idle speculation on the grand scale to any detailed burrowing, through perforce he did his fair share of that. What he most wanted from knowledge, however, was not an ever more refined version of an ever more constricted area of fact but a map of the world of the mind where he could tramp at will. Something comprehensive and gorgeous like those coloured maps of the world in his early school books. If he had been more courageous, the unwritten books which lay unborn in his mind would have been directed by huge flights of fancy: but instead he produced the regulation articles on "his" subject and kept his nose clean.

This night, elevated by the memory of the magnificence of that view from Skiddaw and the exhilaration of the release of his mind so stirringly in him, he regretted his lack of courage. It would be so fine to see these notions in print, even if they were no more than a jumble of little significance: it was what excited *him*. Duty called him to specialization and textual research. The appetite for wide reading which had, in his adolescence, first enticed him to take books and learning seriously had originally inspired him with a Romantic passion for the French poets from Villon to Rimbaud. Soon he had begun to construct patterns to find grand themes, to discover a taste for what his tutor, a predictable old pedant, had called "lamentably pretentious and woolly thinking". Boyish dreams but never entirely flushed away. He had wanted to relate the medieval poetry of Italy and France to the philosophy of Aquinas using the aphoristic techniques of the ingrown Danish intellectual dandy. He wanted to take Nietzsche's sentence "a man must pitch his tent on the side of Vesuvius" and under that title compare the religious development of the German philologist and Cardinal Newman. Croce was his ideal, and he wanted to write an essay on Croce and English thought as seen in R. G. Collingwood. No note of these essays existed on paper, but now and then, on his sober process through the academic hoops, he slipped aside and thought over his ideal and vain hopes: without them the rest would have been unendurable: his nature would not allow him unrelievedly to serve the sort of scholarship his times dictated.

Stars, clear and bright, and the milky way a milky gauze. No moon. He stopped twice to attempt to look for constellations. In such silence, so warm in his skin and mind he remembered the conscientious visits to the planetarium. His mother and father had been very good to him. He was fully aware that Stephen's life did not interest him as much as his own had appeared to interest them. Part of his pleasure over the past few days had been in having Stephen off his hands. Besides, the boy would turn against him some day, bound to, and the slow burn of his son's accumulating accusations was another fear. This household contained him, though, Lawrence and Sarah and Rosemary.

She was a remarkable woman, Rosemary.

It would no longer be contained; he had to allow his interest in her to be admitted. She had broken down the self-consuming unhappiness which had been around him like a blockade for months now. If only he *had* married her. Fool, fool, fool, fool and fool a thousand times not to have followed pure instinct where only that can be true. Let it be admitted to those glimmering constellations at least, he had done a stupid thing, done himself harm by his stupidity, preferred duty to nature and been dealt a terrible return. Yes, Rosemary, yes! To myself I can say it and you, too—who is there to be afraid of here?—you, too, feel as I feel which is why, perhaps, you have been constant. His mind now tuned higher than it had been for a very long time, he began to see Rosemary as the Lady of Shalott, idealizing her.

Careful, careful.

It was not the same, she could not be the same as before, while he, under the skin, was a totally different man, he thought. How could you honestly make people believe that you were so very different, though, when in looks, gestures, attitudes and a hundred visible and sensorial ways you seemed exactly who you had been. While away from that pageant of self, on the real battlefield of character, all which had once shone through those same eyes and been enlivened through that same flesh was vanquished.

As sentimentally romantic in his way as Rosemary, he feasted on the stars and thought of ancient mariners, of ships in the desert and lonely cenobites, of St Jerome, who was part of another unpenned masterpiece, that holy man most insistently portrayed by late Middle Age and Renaissance. Someone who denied the flesh so violently that he had castrated himself (what *agony* as the knife slit the skin!) as high-Christian poetry—like Donne or St John of the Cross—castrated sex and relegated the organs of erection and ecstasy to the zone of deadly silence. Poetry and pain. His inheritance. Circle in circle of stillness, even the copses quiet, corpses, Speetgill and Forester Falls, only the occasional car spluttering officiously through the night; bodies good and bad alike, in bed in farms and in the villages. A cigarette, the railings hard against his back; there was the North Star, follow those three along and it led you straight to Venus.

Yes. She loved him. He had to consider that and act on it; quickly, or it would be unfair.

Yet the suck of his guilt was so strong. She would have to

heave him from the swamp. He had no strength to move out of his past without help.

Earlier that same evening, Edgar had seen them return. He had watched them whenever he could, trying to resolve the mingled anger, pride and disruption of his feelings into a plan.

Stage one of the plan had been carried out. For when Rosemary had come to the woodyard she had not broken the news but confirmed the reports he had already received. The town was like the gallery in the dome of St Paul's: one whisper against the wall sped around the whole circumference in a moment. Sarah had been very pleased to be cross-questioned on this distinguished personage whose dress and manner so clearly marked him out as a gentleman, and a catch. It would be untrue to say that she had pointed the trumpet at Edgar but when a close friend of his mother's had made the usual polite enquiry about the "visitor", Sarah had had no compunction in giving her an embellishment of the facts: they had once been almost engaged, she said, but then they were too young, alas, yet out of tragedy might come ... his young wife dead ... tragic ... new beginnings ... loves the Lake District ... nephew ... lec-tur-er ... writer, too ... so well-mannered and the way he *spoke*—Education and a good bringing up always showed through ... Rosemary, of course, in her element ... books ... all that ... nothing for her *here* ... must hurry, lamb to buy, he likes lamb.

Edgar had gone to Scrunt who had seen them, and appreciating that his young friend's seriousness wanted no equivocations, yes, he said, she seemed very happy. "Women," Scrunt had concluded comprehensively, hopelessly. So Edgar had been prepared. He had decided to act with the greatest dignity and make no fuss, be strong and hard: and this he had done.

After she had left him he had driven the lorry-load of logs way into the country, found a village down on the coast where he was hardly known, and got seriously drunk, ending the night in shivering sleep in the cabin of his vehicle, having unsuccessfully attempted to return to the home of a young woman who had come into the bar.

Fearing his brothers' taunts and afraid of his own violence he had spent Christmas on the hoof, pounding about the area, looking out for them, soon discovering the paths and times of Wilfred's regular airings around the Syke. Inside his trouser pocket, in a small, hard box, blue with tiny gold clips, white silk lined, was the ring: emeralds. An old-fashioned design he had sought out in an antique jewellers in Carlisle; potent, it had seemed to him when he bought it, with all his feelings for Rosemary, her grace, her independence of mind, the older ways she had caught and held to, her uniqueness.

Much of his energy was spent keeping a check on the jealous and turbulent feelings which his sense of loss had stimulated. Sometimes his thoughts were so vicious that he feared for himself. Since the survival of a ferocious childhood fight with his father, he had coped with the force of such pressure by refusing to acknowledge it.

What was he to do? No one had fondled him as Rosemary had. No one had taken his sex in her hands and made the lightning shoot to his brain. No one had so richly made love to him and afterwards so gently laughed at their passion. No one else would serve. The prospect of returning to that tentative small-town marriage-market made him frigid; he would not be able to stand it and yet he would have to find a woman—in their short time together, Rosemary had broken forever the possibility of solitary existence. He knew now that a woman was essential for pleasure, for company, for what he could give as well as for what he could receive, for any life worth the word—he could not go back to being a bachelor however available short liaisons might be: he wanted a steady complement. He wanted Rosemary.

He walked so as not to burst with frustration and rage, wanting the cold Christmas air to douse his brain and let him think through to his next move. It was so difficult to be calm for long enough to work something out, think it over and then act on it. Rose-Mary. Mary. Rose. The words pounded in his head like a ship's pump clearing a flood. All that day he had forced himself to reduce his inchoate lusts to a clear decision: in great measure he had succeeded; but the mere sight of Wilfred and her getting out of the car that evening had exploded all his tranquillity. Yet he had to act or it would be too late.

He did not want drink; there was no man in the town he could talk to; Scrunt had served his purpose. Like most ambitious people, Edgar had always found the development of close friendships a drain and an encumbrance. For common intimacies he had his brothers; but what he needed now was either a confessor or a catalyst.

He went home, knowing that his mother would be there.

In the old-fashioned kitchen, she was spending the evening on shirts, turning the collars and cuffs, a task which seemed scarcely even to occupy her, so easily did she do it so that the hands flew before her, apparently unattended. There was neither electricity nor gas at that farm—much to Edgar's disgust—but this night the shadows were welcome. Two shapely lamps stood on the table; the fire was banked up. It was hardly fair and certainly lacking in filial piety to compare this idyllic hearth with the spiky evenings in his father's time, but a brutal eye—which Edgar could employ—would be forced to observe the improvement in both the scene and the woman. Mrs Crowther had been made younger by the death of her husband.

She offered him tea and he declined. She turned off the radio, a good play she told him, but she was sure she had heard it before and it bothered her so much wondering where and how that she had lost all concentration. Nothing else was worth listening to. She elaborated her excuse in a leisurely fashion, having waited long enough for her son to come back to her and sensing the strain at once. Mrs Crowther had long since ceased to chase him about his work or ask any question on that sore subject: a strong act of will had repressed her anxiety and curiosity both: her reward came in amusing fragments and in his transferring to her the general certainty of his faith in himself. She had adopted a similar policy towards his affair with Rosemary but had been unable to stick to it quite as staunchly. The woman in her son's life was, after all, much more important than the job. The rebuffs had not discouraged her.

Now she could sense that she might be taken into his confidence. He sat uneasily on the old horse-hair chaise-longue. She said nothing though her mind raced for tittle-tattle to set off an exchange: but all that her mind delivered dissolved on the tongue. She had rather hug the silence between them.

He could make so much of himself, Edgar, even now, she thought. For the other three men she had bred she did not stint in admiration or affection: but she loved Edgar. His talents had been her greatest pleasure; watching the graceful, quick child, so like herself in his lightness of manoeuvre in mind and able, also, to translate this into physical analogies. Like all true love it contained much self-love. Insofar as her self respect would allow her, she had doted on him. And known the bitterness not of a thankless child but of an outcome which indicted her care—for the quickness had grown wild, the individuality lodged on obstinacy. In the eyes of the world of Thurston and thereabouts, he who was her glory had brought white hairs to her head with his irresponsible ways. The hope she had nourished, the secret strength she had felt herself giving him, the potentiality she knew was forever in him had to remain a private matter. She realized that she had been foolish enough to care for the good opinion of the majority: that she had wanted such second-hand fame was sufficient reason for the punishment of her son's notoriety.

She expected nothing from him now. Or rather, this is how she schooled herself, for her thoughts still lapped about him as she went through the daily grind of cleaning and cooking and mending and baking and generally slaving for men who thought she wanted no more than such bondage. Edgar knew she could have made more of herself—no, away with self-pity, her life had been not half bad, and away with fond hopes and conceits, this was certain: she could have made a more graceful, more contemplative, altogether more feminine way through the world. Edgar knew this sexless drudge was a consenting shell. He loved her, too: perhaps the only love from any man which had reached her.

He was bruised, that was plain enough; perhaps even wounded, but he'd slink away with that, not let her see. She had heard all about Rosemary's betrayal (as she instantly called it) and was impressed by the effect on her son. Oh, the torment of that regular ticking clock and the solid brown oak, the hams bagged in muslin hooked to the ceiling, white pendulous limbs and the flagged floor clean as a table-top—could the flare of her feelings ever melt down such a weight of world-ordered sobriety? She wanted to burst through the tranquillity and nurse this boy who had laughed like a magical child and opened her feelings to a world which they had only dreamed of—she wanted to tell him that he had made her live, just for a while, in a way in which she could find nourishment. She wanted to thank him for that. Rough now, his boisterous tenderness had then led her to laughter and adventure: her recollection made more of it than had ever been there and the laughter may have been short, the adventures the merest trifles—but to her this large man before her, unaccustomedly sunk into himself, glowering over his thoughts so fiercely she was made tense by the very feel of it, yes he and he alone had given her the reasons for visitations to a past which would have been unburnished without him.

"You must do something," she found herself saying and had to stay the tremble in her voice. The space between them was still calm: into that pond of air her gentle, unthinking advice dropped like the smallest pebble. She held her breath. The words pushed out to him over the thin surface of the silence which connected them and did not break it. After a short pause, Edgar murmured: "Yes," and in the monosyllable, though grudged, encouraged her to continue, cautiously.

"I've never met her of course, not to *talk* to," the woman went on, unerringly touching on the very centre of his concern and yet taking care not to interfere. "But I've *seen* her often enough. I like the look of her, I must say. She looks very intelligent and, I don't know, very *different* from anybody else around these parts." This simple declaration was far from describing the spiky complexity of her feelings towards Rosemary, but in that tangled web it was a clear thread: sometimes she *did* think that Edgar could do much worse than marry such an unusual person although, of course, he was in no way ready for marriage. "I thought you were well suited to each other. I was looking forward to getting to know her." This was truthfully said and brought from Edgar a burst of confidence.

"I wanted you to," he replied. "I was going to . . ." he touched the box in his pocket and the texture of the cold smooth surface on his rough fingers remembered the waiting body of Rosemary; the words lurched from his mind, "We were going to. . . ."

"I know." Mrs Crowther bent her head slightly. "Rather, I guessed that was why you were working so hard."

He nodded and though she did not look she knew he was near tears. Then she put aside all caution. "Why don't you go and talk to her and tell her how you feel about her?" She looked at him and he turned away. "You'll expect her to *know* what you feel without saying anything I suppose. But she won't. Maybe she'll think you never had much interest in her if you can give up so easily."

Edgar nodded. She had clarified his resolution. "But that man," he said: he hesitated, "It isn't as if, from what I've seen, it isn't as if he's even interested but he just turns up and I'm out. I'm just out—just like that."

His humiliation was bitter. Knowing that he had to control it if he were to achieve anything at all, he kept it strictly repressed, but even in the slight reference there was the force of his rejection. Revenge was due sometime.

"And so . . ." Edgar spoke carefully, each word, it appeared, having to quench the self-pity which threatened to flood through him. "And so what is she like? Just one look at him—and that's enough for her to leave me she's been with for months on end."

There was no answer.

"I know I'm just a mucky old farmer's son, an ignorant lump compared with him. I can see that." This time he spoke powerfully, the words fully expressing the resentment and his mother welcomed the discovered strength, seeing him capable of great things as his rage fed his will, only afraid, as he was, that the one might pervert the other. "He's from a university, he's in a different class altogether—who can blame her for wanting him, eh?" The voice flushed out as his pain found some relief: watching him, his mother wondered that any woman could stand against the full expression of his want of her. "I can understand that," he went on, standing up so that the light from the lamp on the table suddenly caught his face. "And why shouldn't anybody change their minds? She was decent about it—most women would have been frightened to do what she did but she came and told me—she didn't write a letter which would have been an easy way out. He's her *type*, that's the word, isn't it? I was all right until he came along. But beside him I'm a nobody. He's educated, I'm not. He'll have money, I'm broke. He *thinks* the way she does. To me, she thinks she has to explain things. He's finer clay, that's all—why shouldn't she want the best? I respect her for it."

He hated her for it. Mrs Crowther knew that and simultaneously knew how to keep the insight to herself. She had rarely seen him blaming himself for anything: once or twice in his childhood he had yielded to the insistent demands of guilt and shame but since becoming a man he had fortified himself against their erosion. What kind of woman would turn down her son for some stranger who arrived out of the blue with a handful of books and a mouthful of educated sentences?

"You do yourself harm," said his mother, firmly, rich in the depths of their communion, able now to twist and turn wherever she willed. "The last thing you are is a mucky old farmer. If you'd wanted you could have been a good scholar. Mr Scott was willing to give you every chance and so don't pretend you're an ignoramus, Edgar Crowther, because that won't do. If this young woman has to explain things to you it'll be because you're being canny and not because you're in need of the knowledge." Her jocosity was the very tender rub his rage longed for: it must not be fed, nor must it be thwarted—this mother's milk sweetened it towards resolution. "I don't know what the young woman sees in you but *I* see no lump. I see a man who will make something special of himself when the time comes for him to need it. Oh yes, you well know how much I've worried about your playing about with those men no better than gypsies down in Thurston but in the end if it was play he needed, I thought, then it's play he must have because he'll only go one road through life and that'll be his own. There's fine clay in you, Edgar Crowther, if not from me then from my mother and my father who were as fine as any your young lady could ever show. So don't you be sorry for yourself. If there's something to be done, do it. There's no one you have to bow the head to."

With a rush like the rush of the wind he was over beside her and lifting her slender body out of the chair and into an embrace of thanks and love. For a moment, she closed her eyes and let her mind liquefy to thoughts too deeply secreted within her to bring to word or even image; the stir of feeling must serve. It would do.

"She's a bit like you," he said, "that's why."

She wanted him gone now, herself left in peace to harvest the memories even while they were so fresh and store them lovingly for the empty evenings to come.

He set off for her house. It was not late. No matter the time. He had to see her.

The decision to act penetrated the confusions as clearly as those stars pierced the sky. He felt bull-certain of himself now, his body roaring to challenge. Rapidly he crossed through Brackenlands and came towards Lawrence's cottage.

Up the slight hill before him came Wilfred, not anxious to finish the walk which had left him somehow cleaner, cleansed by an exhilaration which he did not care to analyse for fear of acting rashly: the feeling had been the most positive he had felt for so long.

Edgar's impetus was strong and he passed the gate of Rosemary's cottage to meet Wilfred head-on. The warmth inside him was too well kindled to be quenched and besides he had not sought a confrontation (which he would instantly have done with a man of his own class) believing it would not "do": but if he let this chance slip he would not deserve to win her back.

Wilfred's path was blocked. He looked at the offender without seeing him, smiled slightly and politely and took a pace to his right. Like a mirror image the man moved with him and Wilfred's smile warmed a little in appreciation of the comic aspect of such tangles. "Excuse me."

He took a pace to the left and was again mirrored. Now he looked to see the face of his opponent and found in it nothing that he recognized. "I'll stand still and you walk around me."

Halfway through his sentence Wilfred realized that the obstruction was not accidental. In the pause which followed he tried unsuccessfully to remember if he had met this man anywhere before. He did not feel particularly nervous for, despite the obvious strength of the young man, his dark face and the menacing muffler around his neck, he struck no threatening attitude.

"I want to talk to you about Rosemary," Edgar said and Wilfred's overwhelming first thought was how redolent the name sounded spoken in that rich Cumbrian accent—a long-vowelled Rose and then Mary to rhyme with "wary". The pronunciation illuminated her in his mind vividly. He did not reply. Edgar went on, riding on the back of an anger which was controlled at great future cost. "I want to say this to you. . . . Before you came here, Rosemary and me were going out with each other regular. Regularly. We have been for some time. Now if she wants to drop me for thee that's her own business but I want to say this. I'm not givin' up. First off I thought that right thing to do would be to step aside. But it won't do. So I'm glad we've met like this. It puts everything above board. I was on my way to ask her out for a walk because I want to talk to her. Now then."

Edgar was prepared for anything, but not for Wilfred's long sympathetic look which was followed by an acquiescent nod. For a peculiar moment he thought that the man was going to shake his hand.

"I had no idea," said Wilfred. He glanced around as if seeking a more secluded place for them to talk: they were alone in the road. "Of course," he added, and then could get no further on.

Edgar still tense, still consumed with the effort to hold himself down, was overwhelmed by the resemblance between this stranger, now seen at close quarters for the first time, and Rosemary. Wilfred felt a burden of explanation on him which he could neither shake off nor carry. "I was planning to leave in a day or two," he said. It was all clear now.

"You're very alike," Edgar burst out, "You and her. *Very*."

"We're cousins. Other people have said we're alike." Wilfred paused. "Perhaps—is there a local nearby—we could have a drink."

Edgar shook his head, resenting the other man's attempt at seizing the initiative. Yet it was going to be very hard just to turn his back. Wilfred was equally unable to let the exchanges break off jaggedly. He was not prepared to act as if he had rights or even as if he had interests, afraid to commit himself to his cousin. Such a commitment needed certainty or boldness: the first was gone from him, perhaps for ever, the second was reluctant to act. Yet she loved him, or could come to love him, and he, without any doubt, had found refuge and balm with her.

"Right then." Edgar wrenched himself away from this man. He would have liked him as a friend. He felt pain at leaving him even after their handful of minutes. He hesitated. "It's very difficult for me to go and knock on her door with you coming in just after." Edgar bent his head a little as he said this: it was, after all, asking the man to go away and give him a clear run at the field. It was in every way asking too much.

"Yes." Wilfred considered for a moment. "Probably the best way, you know, is for me to go in and tell her you'd like to see her. If she can't make it I'll come out and tell you myself. Is that all right?"

The other did not trust himself to reply. How *could* he be given such favours by a rival? Perhaps Rosemary had been swept away by her own fantasies (always possible in Edgar's grimmer reckoning of her character) or simply been thrown in some way. For this man obviously had no wish to keep a tight grip on her. Or perhaps the man was a fool?

As they walked together to the cottage, however, Edgar realized that it was *he* who was being foolish. The man was so sure of her that he could allow her perfect freedom. She would respect that more than any display of jealousy. So he was being walked into a trap. The stranger would have all the credit for being the big free-hearted one and himself seem like a boy creeping about the streets at night abashed even before the tepid action of knocking on a door!

"Here we are," said Wilfred. "If she can't make it, I'll be right out again."

As the door opened, Edgar automatically pulled himself back and then once more castigated himself for being so timorous. What *was* this? He was out to win back the one woman who could raise up his head from the trough as he saw it of a rackety life in a town too small to nurture it yet too tenacious to let him go. Besides, he had made love to her and she to him. This was no boyish courting. And like a bloody fool he had put all his immediate future into the hands of the one man who must be his enemy. How could anybody be so stupid as to let himself be tricked like that? How did that cultivated accent so easily defeat his determination? Or was it that, really? Wasn't it rather the resemblance which had confused him? No lights appeared upstairs that he could see, no sound or stir to encourage or inform. Perhaps it *was* the likeness which had unsaddled him. And the man was so gracious and so hesitant: there was nothing to push against. That was the trick of it.

Rosemary opened the door and closed it sharply, her gesture and her manner a little flustered, her coat undone despite the night, her hands down in her pockets, head bent slightly. She walked firmly over to him, however, and smiled in a friendly way. Edgar needed all his courage then not to see in this casual attitude the very end of his hopes. "Wilfred told me you would be here," she said. He nodded, that lilt in her voice leavening the ache in his mind to real pain. "Let's walk along to the first gate."

He trudged along beside her and they arrived at the gate of a field a couple of hundred yards on without a word having been exchanged. She had hummed a little, now and then, and each time she stopped he thought it was to save him further pain and each time she started he felt the irresistible force of her happiness breaking through. Not for him, though. At the gate they stood side by side looking ahead into the winter darkness. A few beasts came up to them for food and nuzzled through the bars.

He reached out for her hand and held it firmly though she was clearly reluctant. With his free hand he flicked open the small box, nudged out the ring and dropped it onto her captured palm.

136

"No." She flinched and he almost let her go. Oh, Rosemary, Rosemary. That you could flinch. Am I a leper to you now? He held on and closed her hand into a fist, his own strong around it.

"This is your Christmas present," he said, speaking wearily now. "It was bought for you and you must have it. Throw it in the river if you like, but it's yours."

He let go, she opened her fist and then clutched at the ring as it rolled down her hand, seeing in that instant his love letter which she had so deliberately dropped on the mountain side that very afternoon. Why, *why* did she have to make this choice? More important, how could she salve this man's pain whose very intensity (she had to admit it to herself) also flattered her. "Thank you." She pushed it on a finger of her right hand. "I'll wear it with . . . I'll be glad to wear it."

He nodded in dark against dark, the strong shadow silhouette of his face turned from her. There was nothing more to be said: each had been firm and strong and the suffering came from clean wounds. But something of pity and something of the remembered wholeness he had so fiercely restored to her made it impossible for her to turn away.

"You must go." He said this decisively but with such sorrow she was drawn to lean against him, in some way seeking comfort also. "Go away." But she did not budge: her eyes closed, she paid her tribute to the life their flesh had brought her spirit. "Please." Still in reverie she saw Edgar pulling gently away from her, pulling part of her body with him, pulling her towards him now in the reality as he held her more and more tightly and kissed her hard, sweetly, passionately.

# Chapter Twenty-Two

Wilfred was waiting up for her. She came and sat down before the fire, neither unbuttoning her coat nor taking it off. She shivered and prodded the spent coal with the poker, gazing intently as if longing for flames in which to discover dream pictures.

"I could make you a cup of tea," Wilfred suggested and took the silence to be consent.

She did not move when he returned from the kitchen. He poured out her tea and placed it before her, glancing at her as he did so, shocked to see the strain on her face. "You ought to be in bed," he said. "You look too tired."

His sympathy seemed to strike her so that she shrank into herself, huddled around her cup of tea, her eyes socketed in scarcely bearable distress. Wilfred saw that were he to throw his arms around her she would be helped. But that commitment was too grave. What did she *think* of him? He waited with unobtrusive patience. The clock-maker's clocks ticked away the chances.

Eventually, Rosemary, unsummoned, turned to him with a gaze of such mournful intensity that he felt uncomfortable. She held his return glance fast and to look away would have been cowardly: but the discomfort grew rapidly more acute. He was expected to divine her look, he realized that, and at the same time assert a claim or assuage a terrible fear.

"I was with Edgar," she said at last—O why did she have to do it all alone? Why would he not help her? Yes, it was justice that she should tell, but one who loved her would surely not claim justice. Edgar had acted not on rights but on needs. And in doing so had displayed the passion she reverenced. What she had done had been in some way to do with honour, with kindness, with debts, but she had acted badly also. "We used to be together before you came. I just turned away from him—when you came. . . . He brought me this tonight."

"An engagement ring."

"Yes."

"It *was* serious then."

"Yes, it was."

Wilfred nodded, though why, he could never have answered. His chief concern was to be absolutely still, to let nothing interfere with his concentration. What courage she had, this woman who let nothing pass her by!

"He wanted . . . " she could hear her voice way out there, beyond a tunnel of fear which she had to drive through although in the attempt she would surely perish. Unless Wilfred pulled her to the light. Her head dropped onto her knees, suddenly, as if struck. Wilfred wanted to tell her it was all right, she need make no confession, not to him.

"How important do you think your body is?" No, she would not flinch. "How important," she went on very slowly, "is it, do you think, that somebody, that I, let, allow, he was so unhappy, Edgar, and I felt this obligation, to love him?"

Her eyes were full of tears but she forced them back. She had no right to cry, she thought, no right to play on his sympathy. But if only he *would* reach out to her.

"It is difficult," Wilfred began, coughing slightly to lubricate his dry throat. "It has, of course, been at the centre of the argument—the argument that is about love—for a long time. It depends on whether you think the flesh is as it were independent of the mind. It's a very ancient argument, a very respectable one."

How elegantly he began his evasion, she thought, lazily in a detached part of her consciousness, and a small smile coloured her expression. And how, at the same time as she admired it, she despised it.

"It *is* difficult," she agreed—but she could not pretend. "Do you forgive me?" Her caution was at an end.

"What is there to forgive?"

"O Wilfred, please." She reached out and took his hand. He noticed the ring. She pressed the knuckles of his hand against her cheek. "I want us to be honest and that does not mean just telling the facts. It means looking for the truth of things behind their appearance." As she imagined the greatness of this attempt, all her fear seemed cowardice. "We could find out so much about the world. That is all that matters. We could be daring together —don't you see? Don't you?"

So near alike to sentimentality and to inspiration were her words and so encircled by an inviolable innocence of life Wilfred thought, that he did not know where to begin.

She looked up at him, even mischievously. "I can't do *all* the talking," she said.

He smiled and knew then that no one would ever be as complete to him as she was, no one would ever complement him as she would. And yet there was a prohibitive tension within him which was definite. "Perhaps," he began, breaking straight into his own thoughts, "perhaps it *does* matter more than we think. Perhaps to give your body *is* to give yourself. I don't know. I would've thought that for a woman it might be the case."

"And a man?" Rosemary made the obvious retort only to gain time. She could not follow his tack. Why had he suddenly changed? If only it were jealousy.

"A man *is* different. He goes out to the world—while, to put it crudely, a woman lets the world come into her. A man's sex is part of the adventure he involves himself in when he tries to make his way in the world. To a woman, I think, her sex is the seal of her acceptance of the world. It is her proof of fidelity."

"Why should *you* mind? You've never said anything to encourage me to believe that the practice of fidelity was part of our friendship."

She had gone too far.

"I never said *I* minded," he replied, gently. "We were speaking generally, I thought: and as for our friendship—as you've said yourself, there are many things which do not need to be spoken."

"I *want* everything to be spoken," she said, recklessly, adding, "Silence is for slaves or saints: like suffering!"

"You believed in it until a few moments ago."

She hesitated, all at once overwhelmed once more by fearfulness. "What are you saying, Wilfred? What is it you want?"

"I don't know," he answered.

Energy left both of them and the room grew colder. He stirred and she glanced once more with hope, but his face was deliberately unresponsive.

"I looked in my diary," he said, "while you were out. Stephen is due to start school on Monday. It's only fair on him to give him a day or two to organize himself. I thought of taking him back tomorrow."

She nodded and turned from him to make it easier for him to leave her. She would not have him against the smallest ounce of his will.

"Are you sure?" she asked, finally, sensing his uncertain pause at the door.

"Yes. I'm sorry," he said, hesitated, and then went away.

Rosemary wept spasmodically without a sound until the last heat left the fire.

# Chapter Twenty-Three

But when first light came she could no longer deceive herself and did not sleep. Cold and upset as she was, she rose stiffly to go out and see in the new day.

She turned up the hill to walk first away from the town. Soon the cold grip relaxed and she shivered towards warmth.

Little stirred in that grey and gradual dawn. Now and then she stopped at a gate to see back to Thurston across the fields. How restfully it snuggled in its nest, the church tower solid in the centre of it all, dark sandstone and slate holding their ground, a sturdy compact place with the country running into it like rivulets only to be dammed by the two factories which bound the town to industry. She liked it well enough.

"Like"—what sadness was in that pleasant sound, she thought. To like was to lap, to accept, to believe that tepidity was a good alternative—yes, she had understood that when she had withdrawn into herself all those years, then she had been grateful for the soft wind and drizzle of everyday, an undemanding world respectful of fragility. Now, for better and for worse, she was in a bigger world and had outgrown her old cocoon. She could devote herself to spinning another or she could attempt to fly as she had bid herself do. But to fly needed more than a "liking" for it: to fly she needed faith and passion and force.

As she walked, circling the edge of the town, seeming to awaken the dogs on the farms, catching the occasional clatter of men's boots as they hurried across the farmyards to start the day, the rhythm of her body gave her a detached fatigue very near exhilaration. Edgar had taken his leave and asked only for a last coupling; she would not lie to herself—there had been great pleasure in it, both in itself and for the poignancy and finality of the act, and this had forced away the guilt. She had put away all thought of consequences as unworthy. She could not weigh the one man against the other in terms of their needs: all she could do was to satisfy needs insofar as was in her power. Edgar had

had great need of her, she was well aware of that: his pride, his dignity, his sense of wholeness, his sense of the power of his own love all had been impaired. She had no regrets about helping him to rediscover them, to help once and for all. And it would be a greater lie not to admit that she had loved him in some way and always would: love was not a skin you could shrug off after a season, she thought, it printed itself on the inmost cells of your mind and though it could fade and even be beaten down it could never be lost, only be turned to hate.

Perhaps she had been glad, she thought, to go to Wilfred with Edgar's love so fresh. For Wilfred had to be brave. She could not tease him into passion. He had to know of their love-making just as he had made her know his pain over his wife. Perhaps, for she let nothing pass on this bleak morning, there was some sympathy in her actions. There could be nothing between them to stain honesty or truth in any smallest way, rather risk all than expedite the smallest deceit. Risk, risk, risk!

In these desolate northern country lanes where the sun would not shine this day or ever as in the south of her closest dreams, she wanted to dare the world. If she were going to abandon that private fortress in which most of us eke out our survival then she wanted to meet this world face-on. What it was must be enough —that was why she was glad to have the gift of being able to love nature. It was without God or the Devil, she thought, it was without purpose or glory save in the individual who could work with others for great change—she was not one of those, was not and never would be a co-worker to alter ways of thought or work or habit. She could not stride on the highways of life. There was a narrow, steep path left though, she believed, for those such as herself and Wilfred, not cast in the mould of greatness to the world but capable of making some attempt to insult its terrible indifference, to soar above its miserable repetitions of tyranny and chaos, privilege and anarchy, destruction and impotence. And to do that you had to fear nothing and love truth.

As she walked down now into the town she grew more sure that she was right. Wilfred would come to her—of his own free will he had to come despite all impediments. He would see through the meaning of her offering herself once finally to Edgar. The birth-coupling-life burden had to be thrown off and a time out discovered. Two were needed: she could not do it alone.

Such expectation and ferment was in her mind, such excited

stirrings of hope and vision, that she scarcely noticed that she had arrived back in the town itself. It was still early morning. She had re-entered it under the railway bridge just beside the paper factory and towards her, coming down the hill making for the gates was a steady stream of about a hundred men, dark-coated, cloth-capped, huddled against the cold she had long shaken off, marching in to work. She stood beside the high sandstone wall which banked the stationmaster's garden and watched them stream through the little green hut which pinged to the sound of their clocking-on cards. Until the last one was gone she stayed there, afraid to move against such a solid, earthy, materialist intent.

When Station Road was clear, she set off, merely tired now, her private inspiration overwhelmed by that wave of men who represented, she saw it clearly, the engine which gave her the time and leisure to consider such alternatives as the morning had allowed her. Without remembering, she passed the woodyard in which she had seen Edgar to tell him he had been superseded. The men had made her expectations seem insubstantial.

Alone up Station Road, her feet rattled the pavements like sticks on a drum and she came hurriedly out onto the main street only to be met once more by a moving mass of purposeful bodies, this time the women coming towards Station Road to begin at the clothing factory which started up fifteen minutes later than the men's works. Rosemary felt as if she were being hunted and had been discovered in open country. Her tiredness and the oscillation of emotion over the past thirty-six hours had left her finely sensitive and horribly nervous. These women, heads covered in headscarves and bent as in mourning, dark-coated under the dour Cumbrian sky, wrenched from sleep, how irresistible the suck of the real world, the terrible wheel on which you had to stretch yourself in order to "make" a living. She stood back in the entrance of the Blue Bell Pub, a large Victorian doorway, baronial and excessive, and from this retreat watched the sweep of about seventy women, most of them young, most of them younger than herself and everywhere half-recognized faces half-remembered as mother or sister or cousin in the town.

When they were gone, the street once more was empty and Rosemary too felt herself to be empty. Though the shops were not yet open nor the milkman nor the paperboys to be seen, she dodged off the main street and proceeded to the church by one of the routes through the back alleys which Edgar was so fond of. She remembered that.

Tired at the church and unnerved by the way in which the sight of the men and women had thrown her feelings she suddenly wanted a rest and she went in. Early communion was being celebrated. She hesitated and then decided to stay.

" . . . who in the same night that he was betrayed took Bread; and when he had given thanks he brake it, and gave it to his disciples saying, Take, Eat, this is my body which is given for you: do this in remembrance of me. Likewise after supper he took the Cup; and when he had given thanks, he gave it to them, saying, Drink ye all of this: for this is my Blood of the New Testament, which is shed for you and for many for the remission of sins. Do this as oft as ye shall drink it, in remembrance of me. Amen."

After he had said the words, the priest received communion in both kinds himself and then turned to the congregation. There were eight communicants, among them Harold Sowerby whom Rosemary saw with affection, remembering kindly the afternoon when she had been convalescing as a schoolgirl and he had played hymns and psalms to her. He saw her, in return, as he came back from the altar to resume his pew and his smile was immediate and welcoming. She returned it. She did not herself go to the altar-rail having as an excuse that she had not made the general confession nor been absolved nor yet repeated the Credo.

She joined in the saying of the Lord's Prayer after which the priest's voice again rose in solo to incant "O Lord and heavenly Father, we Thy humble servants entirely desire Thy fatherly goodness mercifully to accept this our sacrifice of praise and thanksgiving; most humbly beseeching Thee . . ." but the word *"fatherly"* had unexpectedly struck deep into Rosemary's pain— *why* had he left her, that father she had so loved? She went out of the church.

Mother, too, born to bear me, why did you go when I needed you so much? Now you see me, both, from some part of my mind that is yours you see me and what I am, stumbling along an alien street on a grey morning, confused and afraid again, between the unlicensed love of one man and the undeclared feelings of another, till lately content with daily burial in a library as my only salvation—you should have stayed alive long enough for me to

145

know by what standard I had to fail. O God, if you exist, you are a killer: you who would kill even your own son.

Poor Judas, she thought, betrayed.

At that fork in the road which would take her to Edgar's or home to Wilfred, she paused to throw off the troubled thoughts which the town had laid upon her. She could not take on the burden of exploitation—the mechanical subjugation of those townspeople going to work in the factories was not her doing nor was it in any way in her power to relieve their lot. As long as she reckoned their lot to be unjust and stood for that in as much as she was able, then she had to consider that was all. It was her lack, being able to do no more, it was her incompleteness. But it must not impair her resolution to do what she could do just as the Church must not tempt her to believe there was no Faith but theirs, no struggle but Christ's, no solution but Eternal Life. She preferred the Cross. She would believe in Christ up to the cross, right up to the moment he cried out "My God, my God, why hast Thou forsaken me"—she believed him then most fervently of all. And no further.

Look! Look! At that dour grey sky! Smell the dead tang of mid-winter! Feel the blood in the dull limbs! Even that sense of being would have to be enough to build on.

Edgar was waiting across from her house in the archway he had often used for his lair. She was not surprised to see him but a little sad that she had no more to give. So tired now that her mind seemed to swoon away every other moment yet she stood for a few minutes and answered as he spoke. He took no liberties and forced himself to talk of this and that. His policy now was to maintain a contact with her; that was all.

Persisting in her duty she nodded, smiled a little, chatted a little and waited for a chance to leave which he soon gave her and she went straight to bed and to sleep.

Wilfred, who had slept most uneasily and finally woken with an impulse to redeem what he saw as his failure on the previous night, had observed the pair from his window. He assumed that Rosemary had sought out Edgar after his own quitting of her. So he had been right. She would find what she wanted without him. He was glad. The positive nature of Edgar's love for her had illuminated the poverty of his own gifts. All he could do was talk, talk, use the words to relieve the guilt, and use her, as he now fully realized, in contradiction of the first philosophical precept he had tried to live by—Kant's rule that you must never *use* another person.

He had used Rosemary. But she had not been hurt by it, he had seen that. So he would go back to his empty flat and face himself alone.

# Chapter Twenty-Four

Sarah thought it served her right but was determined to say nothing of the kind. The poor young woman looked so worn out; and Christian charity restrained her also.

"*When* did he go?" Rosemary asked again, unable to digest the sudden information.

"Just after eleven. Lawrence arranged for Mr Sowerby to drive him to the station. There's a connection at Carlisle for a very big train to London."

"The Mid-day Scot," said Lawrence, wanting to fill Rosemary's silence with neutral talk. "Or it *could* be the Flying Scot, although I believe that comes *up* from London like the Royal Scot. They're all fliers. They're all capable of over a hundred miles an hour and they all have fully equipped restaurant cars. It would be the Mid-day Scot. From Glasgow."

"Why didn't you wake me up?" Sarah turned away from the accusation which was in that question.

"He said you would need some sleep." This foolish young woman had ruined her chances, her reputation and her future in one night. Sarah bit her lip to keep it in—but she had seen Rosemary go out with Edgar, heard her return to Wilfred and then awoke to see her as it were coming back after return from a night with Edgar. It was unforgivable!

Rosemary looked wildly to Lawrence, frightened by the double blows of the man's disappearance and now this woman's anger.

"He left you a letter," Lawrence said and withstood Sarah's reaction. She had wanted to keep that back for a while. She went to the sideboard and scuffled a little while in one of the drawers. Rosemary took it from her and went back to the bedroom.

Just to leave like that: she had *known* him, hadn't she?

She sat on the edge of her bed but felt the lack of support for her back. The bed looked unattractive, unmade in the mid-day light. She put on a cardigan and went to her window seat. Her feet rested against the stone head. There was no way she could work things out. Reluctantly she opened the letter.

Dear Rosemary,
I thought it better not to disturb you.
We are to catch the noon train which will give us time to settle in this evening.
It has been a great pleasure meeting you again. I'm sorry if I bothered you unduly with my troubles. Your sympathy was very welcome.
I'd like to think we could come up again sometime in the not-too-distant future. Stephen seems to have enjoyed himself enormously.
Finally, please don't think me impertinent if I wish you every happiness.
Yours sincerely,
Wilfred.

She could not understand the last sentence at all but it was the overall tone of the letter which most upset her. So closed. A gulf seemed to appear in her mind and she felt herself drained of all feeling.

She had a vision of her future: starting the very next day, her holiday would be over, back to those glum early buses in the dark, the deadening routine of the library, fidgety affairs, fatigued weekends, cheering outings with Lawrence, a doleful and wounded figure. She would slouch through the days—O God! It was a settled, painful, protected, privileged, decent spinster's lifetime there before her and she could not bear the thought of it.

Why, why, why had he left her so?

This pain, she reflected, as the desolation began to percolate to the innermost layers of her feelings, could grow until it was all her world. Whose boundary would contain it? What could he mean by that final sentence?

She was too proud to show the letter to Sarah, who could have explained it: and Sarah too resolute in her charity to bring the matter up.

Rosemary dragged herself back to work the following morning and after that one day felt a lifetime's exhaustion. All her preoccupation was with divining the reason for Wilfred's disappearance. Obvious causes were all rejected out of hand. There was something much more profound, she was convinced, which had thrown him off: and that conviction tormented her because its roots must be deep in her expectations. What had she done?

Then it would appear most simple. She had told him that Edgar had made love to her, that was what she had done, and who was the man could be expected to absorb that? Yet ... effective as that explanation could seem, it would not serve; in her eyes, Wilfred was stronger and truer than that.

Down she burrowed as the New Year broke and the days drew through their brief and recalcitrant daylight hours: he could have decided that she would be too intense for him to engage himself with so soon after the shock he had endured. But it was for that very reason she had not pressed him, and had avoided the obvious course of telling him that she loved him. Perhaps she had been wrong. Perhaps what he most needed was such a straightforward and reassuring declaration.

It could not be as easy as that. She saw his guilt and his loss, she had caught something of the scale of his private ambitions. She understood how much retrospective pain would be further invoked by the recognition of their affinity.

She began to lose weight and a cold clung to her; but she went to work, needing the days to be filled.

Surely they were twin souls.

She ought to write a letter. Many times it was begun but what could she honourably say other than to give him a cheerful account of the gossip of the day? She would not hold his affection to ransom. Moreover, was it not he who ought to write a letter, a real letter, not this marginalia she had been left, not this wounding token of respect?

Edgar had no way to read her. Gloomily pursuing his plan to keep contact with her, he would wait for her return from Carlisle and often walk her up the street as in the old days, worried by the strained look on her face, the heavy cold, the lack-lustre eyes. She gave him common politeness and even that cost too much.

Just to go, leaving such a scrap behind.

She ought to write him a poem, really, expressing her feelings in the only possible way, describing their relationship in the only possible way. *Tristan and Isolde*—she would send him a copy of that: he would know, that was all he'd need to know. And Shelley —*Adonais*—yes, Adonais could represent the old love that they had had, he could be the spirit which had to die, it seemed, perhaps through destiny, so that a new love could be discovered. She thought of Dido, too, and her passion for Aeneas: of how she had sacrificed herself on the funeral pyre when Aeneas had sailed away. She got down the Fourth Book of the Aeneid which had been her text at school and chanted the stubborn Latin to herself as if it were a spell to cast out all doubts.

But it was Shelley he would understand. Frantically she searched through her collection to discover the poem which would perfectly and definitively express everything, everything she felt, everything he felt, all that was between them ... her search was unsuccessful: whatever she lit on said too much or not enough and that "soaring spirit" depressed her, which was bad. Always before, even in the depths of her distress she had come away from him with some pleasure but now he was like the Ozymandias of one of his own poems. . . .

> "My name is Ozymandias, king of kings:
> Look on my works, ye Mighty, and despair!"
> Nothing beside remains. Round the decay
> Of that colossal wreck, boundless and bare
> The lone and level sands stretch far away.

It was important to be sensible. She would simply write and say that she had made a mistake and that she loved him—no, *he* was not the "mistake", of course not, how silly! She loved him— could he not see that his foolish turning away was killing both of them? The letter would be sensible: she would type it. Perhaps that would be too formal? Better to write it in her own hand, he would appreciate that more. Or she might type *some* of it.

One Sunday she caught a bus to Keswick and struggled some of the way up Skiddaw. The day was very dull. She was afraid on her own in the February emptiness. The sound of her own breath panicked her. There was no hope of getting to the top or even of going high enough to retrieve Edgar's note. Somehow the crime of dropping that note needed to be expunged and then everything would be on its proper course.

Her cold grew much worse after that but she would not desist from work. The pain was welcome, the struggle was all she had in the world.

Lawrence wrote a letter to Wilfred at the beginning of February. It was a careful letter but firm, indicating Rosemary's condition and suggesting that even an uncommitted communication would be helpful as an act of kindness. There was no reply.

In contrast, Edgar's behaviour at this time recommended itself to both the old people. His escorting Rosemary from the bus in the late winter evenings had now become most necessary as she often arrived from the library in a terribly debilitated condition. Sarah would never approve of him but she saw that he had qualities: Lawrence was greatly impressed by the loyalty and tenacity of the young man and saw the cost. For Edgar, too, was under strain. He left other women alone, he existed in a state of blocked lust; he threw everything over for this pursuit, this was his will, and all the time his will was being fed by a pride which writhed at being so completely consumed and needed revenge which his ambition denied it.

The collapse came as no great surprise. She was found unconscious on the bus at a place called Maryport, about eighteen miles along the route from Thurston. She was taken on to the Whitehaven cottage hospital and, after about a week, sent home to convalesce.

While cleaning out her room, thoroughly, to receive the invalid, Sarah had discovered literally hundreds of crumpled sheets of paper, stuffed in drawers, in pockets, under the pillow, heaped on the window-seat, everywhere: and grotesque drawings which upset Sarah dreadfully as they *seemed* to be pictures of a man and a woman making love. How could anyone, let alone Rosemary, how could anyone in the world put their mind to sitting down and drawing such a thing? She burnt them all.

The papers proposed a difficulty. Sarah was sufficiently informed of her brother's practices to be aware that scraps of paper were often valuable reminders and even on occasion were inscribed with Ideas. She respected such notes. On the other hand, there were so *many* of them here—scores of letters to Wilfred half-finished, heavily corrected and revised: poetry; quotations from the Bible with comments which Sarah did not read in order to save herself pain. What was she to do with them all?

Rosemary's illness far away across the county in the miners' hospital spurred Sarah to the most delicate considerations. The young woman would unquestionably be upset if the notes were destroyed: Lawrence had been on the rare occasions his notes had been accidentally removed. On the other hand, this crumpled heap which was piled up like a paper pyramid, white on the young woman's bed could just as well be very disturbing: Sarah herself was disturbed just to look at it. In some way this terrible intense inbitten misery had to be ordered.

She had the sudden and strange idea of ironing out all the scraps of paper—every one and, thus made neat, placing them most tidily in a file, one of the kind she usually bought for her brother at McMechan's. The idea seemed peculiar but also it seemed completely right and she was relieved.

Beige was the colour she chose for the file and she did the ironing on the day Lawrence went through to Whitehaven to visit Rosemary.

As she worked she could not help glancing at the words on those twisted pages. Some were obscure, some made her blush, the overall effect was to move her to a feeling of pity for this unhappy lovelorn child. One passage above others fascinated her, however, and as it had been copied out several times she took the liberty of keeping one of the copies for herself. It read:

> What pangs the tender breast of Dido tore,
> When, from the tower, she saw the covered shore,
> And heard the shouts of sailors from afar
> Mixed with the murmurs of the watery war!
> All-powerful Love! What change canst thou cause
> In human hearts, subjected to thy laws!
> Once more her haughty soul the tyrant bends
> To prayers and mean submissions she descends
> No female arts or aids she left untried,
> No counsels unexplored, before she died.

She placed the beige file in Rosemary's deep dowry drawer, underneath her lavender-scented summer clothes.

The poem she read again and again in her own room, and then she picked up a similar piece of paper on which was written out another poem, this time in Wilfred's hand. She had found it in his room after he had gone. It read:

> No motion has she now, no force
> She neither hears nor sees,
> Rolled round in earth's diurnal course
> With rocks and stones and trees.

Between the two was a bond she could not understand but could not deny and from both the old woman caught an overpowering sense of loss, of severance and of waste. She pinned the two poems together most carefully and kept them in her prayerbook. If only love had touched on *her*, she thought, even to wound.

# Chapter Twenty-Five

Lawrence thought that the best thing he could do would be to try to engage her interest. She lay there day after day so tired and yet getting little sleep, despite Dr Dolan's prescriptions. His constant advice was that she needed an interest to take her mind off herself.

At first, Lawrence tried to catch her attention by bringing up the notes he had made following their digs at Old Carlisle. By now he had read Dr Bruce, Camden, Hutchinson, Maugham and Ferguson, the last of whom had given Lawrence immense satisfaction as he had not only stressed the size and importance of the site (others had done that) but had also proved that the Roman road system in Cumberland had its *centre* at Old Carlisle, near Thurston.

"I never thought of that," exclaimed a delighted Lawrence. "Imagine. The *centre*."

But the gobbets of information—was it originally called the Castro Exploratorum? Did Augusta Gordiana quarter there with an Ala or Wing? Was the River Wiza the Virosidum?—each of which was a gem to the old man—brought only a polite acknowledgment; after several attempts, he gave up and merely gave her town gossip.

Attempts at help came, too, from Harold Sowerby, who made it his business every evening to copy out a passage from a book which, he said, had often comforted both his mother and himself in times of stress. The book was *Reflections for Every day in the Year on the Works of God in Nature and Providence from the German of Christopher Christian Sturm*. Each morning a new reflection in immaculate copper-plate and black ink would be unobtrusively slipped through the letter box. This duty Harold laid on himself as an act of Christian duty, and it was something he would never omit, hail or snow.

The reflections were wide-ranging, one for each day, and Harold copied out the relevant passage whatever it might be even though they might not at first appear immediately relevant or even Christian. Rosemary's February sample included long *Reflections* on "A Temperature Always the same would not be Good for the Earth" (Feb. 3): "On Fogs" (Feb. 6); "The Sun does not always appear" (Feb. 8); "On Earthquakes" (Feb. 9); "On the bodily Advantages which the beasts have over us" (Feb. 15); "The Causes of Heat and Cold" (Feb. 23); "On the use of mountains" (Feb. 28). They brought her much pleasure.

Determined to obey Dr Dolan's injunction to help her take her mind off herself—and not to be outdone by his old friend—Lawrence next decided to make a "scientific" effort to teach her the Cumbrian dialect and proceeded with William Dickinson's glossary of words and phrases. To please him, Rosemary let him believe that she was an eager pupil and for about half an hour every afternoon—she was soon tired by any effort—the small upstairs bedroom sounded with the cracking of that strong old language. "Brig"—bridge, "Bummel"—blunder, "Cadger"—retailer of small wares. "Carl"—a coarse fellow, "Cat-wittin"—conceited, "Chunter"—to reply angrily, "Cockly"—unsteady, "Cofe"—calf—and on through the alphabet, learning by rote, the whole made more presentable (as Lawrence thought) by readings from Richardson's *Cummerlan' Talk*. Like the slapping of butter it sounded, she thought.

Sarah was a good nurse and gave Rosemary the cradle of care she needed. The older woman was as attentive as a penitent. She blamed herself a great deal for idle talk over Wilfred and Rosemary which might (who knows?) have got back to that refined young man and tipped the balance against this poor girl. Certainly she needed all the comfort she could get. It was she who encouraged Edgar to come up and would leave them alone, the young man feeling twice his size and unbearably clumsy in the feminine bedroom. But Sarah guessed that Edgar's nervousness would soon leave him and she guessed too that it was only his utterly determined faith in his own love for Rosemary which could give the woman any belief in a future. Sarah never grew to like him, though.

Edgar would talk to her about his childhood and his family. He could make her laugh with his caricatures of his grim brothers, stupidly angry or self-defeatingly mean and ignorant, a family always making decisive gestures in hopeless directions, his mother accommodating herself to these blundering males. He rarely mentioned his father—or only to dismiss him. The stories of his boyhood were better for her because she could "see" him so clearly—the troubles he had got into were so very like the troubles she herself would have adored to enact.

She needed to pull herself out of this whirlpool she had fallen into. Only occasionally was the world clear and then Edgar would be there, steady, smiling; flesh and blood.

Always, though never insistently, Edgar would end his visit on the same series of questions, tenderly begun. "Why don't you marry me?"

"I'm not sure I could love you."

"I'll do that for both of us."

"Oh Edgar," she laughed. "You're so *certain*. That's what frightens me."

"Yes I am certain. I always will be."

"No. You have a limited time just as I had." She paused. "I'm too old for you."

"I feel like a hundred."

"You're a boy, Edgar. You need a nice young Thurston lass to look after you. I'm too tired to do that."

"I'll look after *you*."

"Would you?" Rosemary looked at him directly, honestly and questioningly. At one and the same time he was prepared to go to the stake for his conviction and yet he felt unsure, even in some way scared of the awesome responsibility such a direct appeal entailed.

"Of course I would. I'm strong enough for us both. They say God makes up in marriage what he missed out at birth. We can both benefit."

"I couldn't manage you. You'd run away from me." Again, she was so clear and so sure it made him feel that he was in danger of perjuring himself.

"Never," he asserted, aware that the denial was uttered too stoutly.

She smiled, as if reassured. "How can you say that?"

"I can," he played on obstinacy. And then a happy retort occurred to him. "How can you *ask* that?"

"Good!" she laughed at him and took his hand. "A fine, big hand. Strong. Are you?"

"In some ways." Though he was embarrassed as she seemed to "test" his fingers, he did not draw his hand away.

"Which?"

"I'll be all right once I get you. I'm half a man till then. You make things clear. You always see through things. You'll keep me at it—and I can always keep going. So you see—we'll fit each other."

"Oh Edgar—you're so sweet!"

"Why do you say that? When you say things like that—it's worse than when you say anything else."

"I'm sorry. I don't want to insult you. You've been very good to me."

"That doesn't matter."

"It does. It *does*, Edgar. Kindness might be the most important thing in life—don't you see? We *have* to be kind to one another—what happens when we forget that is too horrible." She let go his hand, gently.

"Kindness." Edgar pronounced the word as if he had never articulated it before. He would have loved to contradict her, to argue with her, to point out that the very desperation with which she exclaimed the word undermined his faith in her commitment. But he could not organize his reaction into an argument. The most he could ever manage would seem to be a riposte and here he could not even rise to that.

"Yes," she continued, fervently, "and that is why you must be strong. To be kind is to be patient and comprehensive and loyal —that means being a man. To be kind means that you have looked at the chasm which is the opposite of kind and decided to turn away because what I mean by kind is not just being 'good-natured'. That is an accident of circumstance and birth. To be kind is something you fight for and sacrifice for—you earn it. It isn't just doing good turns like Boy Scouts either although it's also that. To be kind is to be a Christian without that depressing humility and that destructive addiction to suffering. To be kind is to be the best sort of man: lovers are kind and mothers to their favourite children and sometimes, in books, it seems that some men have been kind to each other—comrades or friends. You must consider the other person's feelings equally with yours— love your neighbour *as* yourself and that means loving yourself first and well. If you hate yourself then you will take revenge on others. If you are kind to yourself then you will be in a fit state to be loving to others. 'Loving' kindness—there you are, in your English language they come together often, don't they? Once we cease to strive to be kind then we accept chaos. That is all the progress any human being ever wanted—for society to be kinder. All the rest just doesn't matter. It doesn't matter that we have motor cars and aeroplanes and electricity—it is of no importance whatsoever, candles and horses and eagles are much more beautiful anyway."

"Oh no, Rosemary. We can't go back to horses! Ask my brothers about horses on a farm—bad enough there, more trouble than they're worth. They broke my bloody father's back, he said. No, no—you need progress if the ordinary man's going to lift his head out of the trough."

"Out of the *trough*! Really, Edgar, what *do* you think of your fellow men! Trough indeed!"

"You know what I mean. I mean, what you say is all very well—about kindness—*once you have the basic essentials*. Most people don't."

"That need make no difference."

"It does though and that's that."

"No. No! *That* isn't *that*; not at all. Poor people can be kind. They needn't be kind to the bosses but they can be kind to each other—they can be kind to those they love. Your philosophy denies them their rights as full human beings. Your philosophy says 'poor people are only half-people or quarter-people—they can't have the full range of life—that is reserved for rich people.' No, no." She hesitated, and then with a wicked smile concluded, "You're a snob, Edgar!"

He held his mouth tight shut but his facial reaction was enough expression. Yet he saw how pleased she was, how happy this release into words had made her: her face sparkled and the pallor was entirely thrown off; her eyes were once more full of mischief and nuance, bewildering him with their vivid animation. And the way she declaimed her convictions made his heart sing.

"You must marry me," he insisted. "You can't get out of it now."

# Chapter Twenty-Six

She went back to work after Easter and still no word from Wilfred. Edgar's incursions into her thoughts were brief indeed, mere sprinkled showers compared with the saturation of Wilfred. The work was more irksome than ever.

Edgar had secured himself a steady job at the sawmill as if his role as attendant or sentinel demanded regularity in all things. People noticed a change in him. He had begun to settle down, they said: his mother worried how long he could hold on for what he had decided he could not be without. She asked to meet Rosemary and invited her to tea one Sunday. Both of the women were agreeably surprised: and with the two of them there about him, Edgar felt like the King himself.

In this period Rosemary re-established a more constant friendship with Jean. She would often go to her friend's house and as the evenings became lighter would sometimes slip there straight from work and stay until late.

What sensible, ordered, unpretentious, undemanding contentment there appeared to be—there *was*, no doubt of it—in that house. Jean and her children, well-behaved but not at all constrained; Jean and her husband, loving but not over-attentive; Jean herself, still with her talents, her sporting skills, her place in the town and in her set, the uninterrupted progress of a clever, modest English girl through a society which took her as its standard and pride. Rosemary was very touched by the way Jean still gave her precedence and saw that it might be because while she could, in imagination, encompass her friend's life, Jean could not do that with regard to hers. Yet how silly that explanation seemed. Much more likely that Jean was carrying a schoolgirl fantasy into an adult habit of politeness.

They lived over on the other side of town, at a place called Standing Stone, in a corner house which was extremely pretty, a place rich in domestic felicity, and Rosemary's nature and her love for Jean were such that she could enjoy it undisturbed by envy or regret. For the contrast between their lives could be thought of as quite harsh.

As she wandered back through the warm summer town, where people walked up and down the two main streets to see and be seen—not only the peacock young, but old couples come out for the soft air and a quickening of acquaintanceship, families digesting their enjoyment the cheapest way, boys on old bicycles, strangers in from the villages, lovers—Rosemary would return to wondering what was to become of her. In some ways she was as secure as she had ever been: but she could not go back to rest in the nest of Lawrence and Sarah's hospitality, however much they said they wanted her to do so.

Apart from anything else, it appeared an imposition. They were getting older: goodness knows they had done their duty by her. They needed to be left to lead their brotherly-sisterly life. She was an intrusive body now. Besides, to be honest with herself, an alchemy had occurred within her, a taste of liberty, a blossoming of all her affections however cruelly nipped, a relish of herself being bold. She was not who she had once been: and there was shame, too, which made her unwilling to retreat.

But what was she to do? Wilfred she tried to shut out of her mind unsuccessfully of course but at least the attempt restrained the furthest lunges of pain. She could leave Thurston and seek employment elsewhere—but she was sadly alive to her limitations. New places would frighten her: no, for better or for worse she had been dumped in this spot by fate and she would manage no move easily out of it. Perhaps, if she were *really* bold, if she could reach the heroism she so longed to see in others, then she would have left Thurston, Cumberland, England, the entire island and gone across to France to find in that alluring mystery access to the source of life which was dammed up here. If only she had *that* courage! Nothing else could match such an ideal.

Like her shadow, Edgar.

Yes, he was devoted but she mistrusted his devotion, well aware of the obstinacy which was in him. Could she manage that? He would most certainly tire of her: she would be too hard on him—could she endure that, or could he?

On one evening he came to Jean's with her and stayed. He got on famously with the children, his vigour never bruising them. She watched him most carefully. If he could be tender to the children—could he not also be tender to her?

They walked back with little said, through the populous town, out again onto *her* side of Thurston and beyond her house a little. At that same gate where he had taken her body months ago as both thought for the last time, they stood once more in the dusk and looked over the fields to Skiddaw and the other fells. The cattle were far away in the bottom corner of the field, in the long sweet grass of summer.

"That's what I would like," said Edgar, softly, "a place like Jean's. And a family like that. Two or three children, a garden to occupy me, a nice house for you, somewhere to rely on and be happy in. What more can you want out of life?"

"Oh Edgar! You'd be restless in six months!"

"No . . . no . . . " he turned to her, utterly sincere in his self-conviction. "You think you know me so well but I'm not too sure, Rosemary. Anyway, I've changed a lot these last few months, and thought a lot as well. I know what I want now—oh, as regards work, I can't guarantee I won't take a few risks here and there, that's how I see work; that's my nature, that's nothing fresh. Not that. But it isn't what I want from life. How I see life. If we could be together and have a decent family—that would satisfy me, that would be the real part of it all. The rest's a racket anyway. I used to think all of it was until I met you. Now I don't. There's part of it that could be oh, decent, you know, something you could be proud of. . . ."

How restful that vision was and yet it *was* a vision. As if he had read her innermost doubts of him Edgar had given the lie to her belief that he was a man barren of ideals, a man utterly without a non-materialistic vision, without a soul. It was not the greatest ideal, this evocation of domestic plenitude, it fell far below the great pictures of life she had breathed with such exhilaration from books and her own thoughts, but it was some sort of aspiration. And in Jean's life, of course, it had made an undeniable beauty.

Perhaps to trust or not to trust was finally a question of need.

"If we marry, Edgar," she said, and instantly his breath was held, her tone commanded his concentrated hopes, "then you'll have to take care of me." She spoke very quietly looking not at him but out, over the plain, towards Skiddaw Fell. "I'm not strong like you, I'm sorry to say, and I'm not your ideal Thurston lass. If you marry me, then it will be difficult for you."

He nodded; too happy to dare spoil it, too exalted to listen properly to what she was saying. The sound was enough for him, the sound alone told him she would come to him, they would marry. He had won! When she had finished talking he kissed her gently and tentatively and they walked back in silence.

"We'll tell them now," she said when they came to the door of her house, "we'll tell them right away and then we'll go and tell *your* mother. Let's marry soon."

On the eve of their wedding, Lawrence took out the two unhappy paintings he had kept secret to himself since Rosemary's adolescence and he tore them up into dozens of minute fragments of which he made a pile to burn.

They rented a small cottage at the top of Station Hill: equidistant between Jean's house and the cemetery with a view clear across Thurston to the hills. Each of them could easily make out their childhood houses. It was much too far for Sarah to walk but she could walk into town and catch a bus and so make something of an outing of it. Besides, young people like to be left alone at first.

War was declared less than two months after their wedding. Edgar chafed to go into the army but was kept hanging about until the following spring.

Soon after he left her, Rosemary gave birth to a daughter. Sarah invited her to move back in with them and Lawrence would have loved it, but the young woman declined. She had come to love her tiny old-fashioned cottage and feared that to leave it would be to abandon the surprising happiness she had discovered there.

There was the question of the name. For a time she was much tempted by Isidore or Isadora—"gift of Isis"; its perfection could not be approached. But eventually, and for complex reasons, she chose Eleanor—"bright". Isadora was too personal to her: Eleanor lent itself to the diminutive Ellen (which she would resist, but still it was there) the name of Edgar's mother. More important, Eleanor of Aquitaine had married an English King, Henry II, thus uniting the two countries; and later Eleanor of Provence (who was much more important for the connection with her own mother) had also been the female half of an attempt an Franco-English wholeness. While the connection with France now, when France was over-run by the Germans, seemed as important as it had ever done.

Most important of all, however, was something she kept entirely to herself. Eleanor was from the same name as Helen, daughter of Jupiter and Leda, sister of Castor and Pollux, carried off by Theseus later married by Menelaus and loved by Paris. This magnificent myth gave Rosemary great pleasure and it pleased her endlessly that her daughter, her child, should represent such a force here, at the northern edge of a beleaguered England which settled down grimly to find in itself the strength to endure the terrible assault from the Nordic will to power through fire.

# III. EDGAR

# Chapter Twenty-Seven

It was raining, but such a light, fresh summer drizzle as could have been manna, she thought, or drops of honey. Everything was transformed on this day of Edgar's final return from the war.

The news was out and all her neighbours managed to see her during the day and happily refer to the fact. Rosemary had slowly become rather a favourite up in this isolated part of the town, placed as it was almost as a posting-station on the very outskirts. There were two or three farms there, a number of cottages, half a dozen bungalows farther along the road housing the well-off or the retired, and in the middle of the huddle stood Highfield House, the Workhouse, a beautiful sandstone mansion now turned over to the old and to the destitute. Tramps would climb up Station Hill and wait for the legal hour of admission, filling in the time by cadging work or more usually just sitting under the hedge with their sacks and coats, objects of terror to the children. So the outside world was always intruding and always in the guise of poverty and despair: there *were* jolly tramps, you heard, but Rosemary never saw any.

She had kept herself very much to herself at first, totally absorbed in the child, afraid that she might not be up to it, this motherhood of which she had heard so much. As the child prospered, her confidence grew, her pleasure increased, her love for herself became more constant and she sank deeply into the life of herself and the child and the dream of her warrior husband south in the desert at war. She read a great deal and listened to classical music on the radio: on the days she received one of Edgar's letters she was happier, probably, than she could have dreamed. Certainly she would keep telling herself that she did not deserve to be so happy.

As she did not presume, the neighbours took to her. This one saw to it that her wood was chopped, another offered to keep her garden "down"—do the heavy work for her—another would bake something tasty for herself and the baby every baking day. At Mr Pearson's small grocery store she met them all and, with milk and eggs from a farm whose fields backed onto her garden, she was well stocked. "Things" that were needed in the town could always be got by a boy only too eager to use his bicycle for such an outing—one of the Pearson boys or one of the Lowthers —and do a good turn for the young lady whose husband was in the war. For most of the people about her were country people owning more of an interest in the land than in the town, and the cottages housed labourers exempt from military service: she had an unexpected eminence there, through Edgar.

Slow peaceful days though the occasional aeroplane going to Silloth or Kirkbride were reminders and the BBC news a constant pulse—she spun the reality and the dream about her, cows peacefully looking into her garden, the occasional chatter of cyclists on their way to the seaside, before and below her the earnest town about its business, the farmers' slow walk and cheery smile, the politeness in the shop, the helpfulness, Eleanor's miraculous existence which day to day was more of a wonder than rainbows or shooting stars. Deeply she sank into her contentment: Edgar was such a man! Never the smallest murmur of complaint. She missed him greatly, she asserted to herself, although it was strange the completeness she could feel without him. And without the job, also: she had anticipated certain lone-liness on leaving the library but there was very little loss. She preferred her own company and that of her daughter.

Besides, she was so occupied! Eleanor took a lot of time and Jean came over twice a week; those visits must be returned: Sarah struggled up now and then and Lawrence arrived every Sunday as Scrunt arrived every Saturday. The two men were especially difficult: each bursting to help her—but what was there for them to do? As Eleanor grew older Lawrence could occupy himself in teaching her but poor old Scrunt who was meticulous in his loyalty was often left to invent work out of nothing at all, to search out an unsteady slate on the roof or a wall that needed attention or whatever: very trying for both of them.

She received some insurance money after her work at the library and with the money Edgar sent her and the allowance which Lawrence insisted on making (easing the exchange by saying that it represented a quarter only of what she had paid them weekly since her work had begun) together with her own savings she felt comfortably secured. The local library gave her material to fill her leisure together with the radio.

Once again, then, she plunged into herself as to the bottom of a great ocean with the outside world somehow distanced, out of real knowing, safely removed. Inside this silent world she could watch the darting of dreams, follow the sensuous and fantastical shapes which beckoned, satiate herself on the tranquil density of such a life.

Now the day had arrived which would see Edgar once more with her. She had cleaned the house daily for a week. Jean had brought flowers, Scrunt had brought two large bottles of stout and some mushrooms, Lawrence had brought a small carved wooden figure he thought might be of interest, probably a piece of ornamentation from a ship's cabin circa 1600, Sarah had brought some of her famous scones, Mrs Pearson from the shop had brought round a quarter of butter, a clutch of eggs had been left on her doorstep, Harold Sowerby had brought a lovely prayer-book with a white vellum cover—all had left hurriedly, not wanting to impose. His mother had sent him a new white shirt.

Rosemary could scarcely contain herself. She changed her clothes three times, finally deciding on what she had worn first of all, a simple black skirt, a white blouse, a black ribbon in her hair, her best shoes and thank goodness the one article she had bought herself during the last winter had been a decent stylish raincoat. Eleanor was dressed with the usual elegant carelessness which distinguished her from most of the other children.

The hardest thing of all was to wait until four o'clock. He had written that he would arrive in Carlisle at three and catch the train to Thurston at 3.55. It would take her no more than ten minutes at the very most to walk down the hill to the station. She was ready at dawn and from then on the clock seemed stuck in itself. The rain, too, seemed to drag out time.

She had not seen him for more than two years: three short leaves at the beginning of his service had been followed by a move to North Africa and there he had stayed until his injury. He made light of it as the custom was, but Rosemary thought his attitude rare and distinctive. A bullet had nicked his kneecap, painful but far from serious and comical really, as he'd been a tank-driver most of the time! Enough though to guarantee his discharge.

At last it came, the hour, and the few strokes sounded sweetly

on the grandfather clock which Lawrence had given as one of his
wedding presents.

Would he still find her attractive?

Eleanor was put into her pushchair. She could easily have
walked down but Rosemary had worked it all out carefully: walking back could be tiring and Edgar would certainly have luggage
—"kit", they called it, she remembered—it would be too difficult. Edgar's brothers had offered to come and help her but been
quite happy to withdraw the offer when they sensed she would
rather receive him alone: they stood in awe of her. Now she
temporarily resented her possessiveness: Edgar would almost certainly need help and she would have both hands occupied with
the pushchair. How stupid of her not to think of that before!

Would he love her as much as before?

Be calm. It would sort itself. That was one of Lawrence's most
soothing sayings—"it'll sort itself". "*Sortes*" were the fates; that
was something to rest on.

Please let him still want her.

Down the hill they went at a steady pace, past the grander
houses further along until they came to the high sandstone wall
which barricaded the railway from the road. It was cold alongside
that wall. Little sun ever got there because of the height of it and
on the other side of the road was another wall and paths leading
up to two large houses, the Oaks and the Beeches. Before she
turned under the railway bridge she was forced to stop and look
at two horses drinking in the fountain at the junction there:
Eleanor was obstinate in her love for horses.

As she turned into the station, through the first gate, up the
driveway, a handsome little station with stationmaster's house to
one side, her body melted and then tensed together, seemed to
swoon and then leap to recovery. It was hard not to cry. The
ticket collector waved her in and she wheeled Eleanor onto the
small platform. The drizzle had stopped and the sun was pushing
through, catching the newly fallen rain with glittering reflections.
O God why did she feel so weak? Please let him still love her.

Three others were waiting for the train, none of whom she
knew though all knew her and she was politely greeted and
returned the greeting. Faces were unclear. Would she remember
what Edgar looked like? How ridiculous! But would she? Which
side did he part his hair on? The sun was now too hot on her face
and her skin seemed to burn coarsely.

Eleanor was content: on the side line an intricate piece of shunting was in progress and she could occupy herself with the clatter and steam from the engine.

There was the train, charging towards them along those iron ruled lines. Where was she? Her throat was dry—had she time for a drink? She might do something idiotic. She pushed Eleanor back from the edge of the platform though they were safe enough already.

The engine shook the station and hissed and shuddered to a halt beside her. The driver grinned down at Eleanor who looked lovely in a white rain-hat: he saluted. Rosemary smiled nervously and began to push the child down the platform: two people got off in front of her and blocked her view. They moved away. The porter shouted out. The guard blew his whistle. The wheels turned once more.

She was crying. She could feel the tears down her cheeks sweetly stinging her lips; the porter turned aside and Edgar stood before her in an island of baggage, thinner, awkward, almost at attention. As the train pulled out the sun flooded over him and its warmth seemed to be the help he needed. He opened his arms and she rushed to fall against him, sobbing with relief and exultation and overflowing happiness as he gently patted her hair.

# Chapter Twenty-Eight

Edgar felt certain he was at a turning-point in his life and that this decision would be crucially important to him. And then again out of nowhere he would be swept by the conviction that nothing he could will could much change the way his life was to be. But he had to do something.

During those first few weeks he spent a good deal of time in his field, sitting in the sun as he had used to do leaning against the ruined barn, sucking on hand-rolled cigarettes. He would walk the long way round by Cuddy Lonnins and Longthwaite to avoid passing through the town. It unnerved him to see it so very much the same.

Mostly he thought about his time in North Africa. He would never admit it to anyone in Thurston (they would have been shocked and upset had he done so) but he had enjoyed the war. He had discovered that though he had an alert natural fear he had no depressions or continuous and melancholy anxieties about combat. He had found friends and would undoubtedly have been made a sergeant if his regular drinking had not led him into unfortunate entanglements; and one man in particular had palled up with him—Tom James he was called, from Wiltshire, a man who'd been to university and so on but preferred to "serve in the ranks". Edgar had been as suspicious of him as the others but then his better nature had moved him to pity this self-made exile who was so often also excluded from those he had sought to join.

They had teamed up. Tom's quick, fair leanness was in complete contrast to Edgar's dark secretive vivacity and they became known (a striking example of army wit) as "The Differents", addressed, each, as "Dif", or "Dif 1" and "Dif 2". Tom first of all exercised his socialistic theories on this new companion who in no way was a pupil: but Edgar had no time for that nor for any other overt attempts to "improve" him. What he appreciated was the chat of a man whose gossip was so elegantly phrased and so well-informed. Tom could relate the most commonplace event to a cluster of circumstances or see perspectives behind obdurate facts: it was, quite simply, a pleasure to be in his company and a peculiar pleasure in that they were in this strange land which might have been the moon, so foreign was it from Cumberland or from Wiltshire. Tom enjoyed meandering about the place made philosophical by the bleakness of the desert and Edgar rediscovered his own enthusiasm for rooting about: they even started a "dig" at one camp where there had been a Roman town, pretending they were making holes for the latrines.

Now, back in Thurston, he would catch at those days as easily as that very morning and hold them clearly, brightly in his mind. They drank. Tom introduced him to gin, praising the "spiteful spirit" as he called it. Sometimes Edgar went on a blinder: got drunk, played pontoon all night, ended up in the glasshouse for a couple of days after a rather rowdy incident.

And then Tom had been killed. Edgar had seen his friend's tank broken and burning as the rest of the corps had turned back. Tom would be sealed into the machine. He had stopped and despite the danger run across to the stricken vehicle. But it was no use. The tank was his friend's tomb.

On morning after morning after that he had woken up sweating, panicking with the sensation that there was no reason whatsoever, none, none, for him to enter into the world. The army routine had kept him sane. His own wound came almost as a compensation, soon afterwards.

There was a little money would last a few months. He let it.

Everything had a new smell. Everyone seemed a different size or shape, alterations slight but disconcerting: and yet there had been no change.

Sex was very important to him. He would not leave Rosemary alone. For the time being she welcomed him but he feared that her compliancy would pass. Sometimes now she made mocking references to Messalina and the Golden Ass and often questioned his intention—as if there could be any doubt! He would have liked to have been able to tell her of his need for pleasure, in from the wilderness, pleasure, the flesh-stung lick of pleasure. She would have taken issue with that: to her, pleasure was an inferior aspiration: harmony, love of course, even happiness—these had meaning and resonance for her—pleasure was coarser stuff. While Edgar wanted to rut until his sweat blinded him.

He could talk to his mother now, without strain or irritation. His brothers, married, had stayed on the farm and treated him with great caution.

If he'd had capital he would have bought the first farm that came onto the market and bid for every neighbouring acre from then on. There was no doubt, he thought, that all governments for some time would feel obliged to subsidize farming heavily. You could not lose. His brothers, of course, curdled lumps that they were, would probably kick all gift horses in the teeth. They had not even claimed their quota of prisoners of war from the nearby camp though this represented the cheapest possible labour—often by good men who liked the chance of a real job: but they didn't want foreigners on their land, they had declared, virtuously. Edgar gave them up. They would never make a success but even they could not fail on such prime land.

Yet when all was taken into account, he was sometimes glad not to be able to be a farmer. He had no misconceptions that he would be any better off anywhere else in the world, but a farm was too solid a claim: there would be no room for the elusive play of alternatives.

Night and morning. In the morning, Rosemary would often pretend that she was afraid Eleanor might come in. He knew, sometimes, she really was afraid of him. And his temper could be erratic—though both would excuse the violence on the consequence of war. But those outbursts—common to his early life on the farm—punched her hard.

Scrunt came up to the field a few times—but the old spell had broken and each liked the other too much to push it.

He could not understand the shift inside himself, the blind irritations, above all the weariness. Except for the drive into Rosemary's body it was all weariness.

He would always keep this field. Tom used to speak of a retreat he had somewhere on Exmoor. This would be *his* retreat, this decaying wall for his back, the unkempt hedges his screen, a place to trap memory.

A pub came up to let, The Mitre; it stood next to the market hall in the middle of the town. Thirty pounds would see him through the fixtures and fittings and the Brewery would loan him for his first two weeks' stock and allow him a month's arrears of rent. It would do.

# Chapter Twenty-Nine

"No. Please, *Please*, Edgar, let's stay here—let's be happy where we are, we are happy, aren't we? Let's stay—*please*. We ask you."

Eleanor had long since been in bed. Edgar resented the calm appropriation of her vote. But he kept his peace. Rosemary had taken his news badly. She sat in the small kitchen, not gracing it as she had previously done, effortlessly accommodating herself to it, but with the look of someone trapped, confined and panicking for liberty. "Please, I like it so much here—you'll see how nice it is. It's just that you're restless after the war, you're bound to be, it's quite normal. But what would *I* do in a pub, Edgar?"

"I'd thought you might help."

"I know nothing about pubs. Neither do you."

"I haven't got it yet, Rosemary, I haven't even sent off the application."

"I'll burn it if I find it. I will." She looked wildly about her, longing to pounce on it.

"We'll talk about it again tomorrow."

"We'll talk about it *now*, Edgar Crowther, and look me in the eye. Why must you have this pub?"

"O Rosemary—don't go on. I've thought round things and it seems the best bet. It'll give us a steady income and a place to live and I'll have free time through the day to get on with other things."

"What other things? And we already *have* a place to live— *here*, this beautiful cottage you brought me to. What is this about a steady income? That's not you."

"Well it is now. I've yourself and Eleanor to consider and I'm older. I want to feel secure about you both."

"Edgar. Don't use us as your excuse, thank you very much."

"What are you talking about?"

"You know. You know exactly."

"But I don't!"

"Of course you do. What other things?"

"I don't know. It depends on what turns up." He smiled. "I'd like to breed basset hounds."

"Nobody needs a pub for that, Edgar. I'll *hate* that pub. Your wife will hate it—does that mean anything at all to you?"

"Yes." He paused, somehow enjoying her rage, rising to the fight: her look flickered so rapidly between shades of scorn and temper. "I've thought about what to do and this seems the best bet so far," he repeated, stubbornly.

"What's wrong with your old job? What's wrong with our life as it was? We had a home and we managed on the money. I could work again if you want. Eleanor will soon be at school, I can see if Mr Anderson will take me back in the library for two or three days a week. I'm sure Jean would give Eleanor her tea."

"Eleanor should be given her tea by you. And I'm not having you going back to work just to top up my pay packet. I married you and I'll support you. When I can't, I'll let you know."

"I *love* this place, Edgar! I love our life here." She smiled, wildly: it made him feel uncomfortable.

"It's very nice, granted." He looked around with approval. A few old fashioned knick-knacks, one or two solid pieces of furniture from Lawrence, touches of elegance here and there—a watercolour, a beautiful blue vase: it was a very pleasant place. "But there's no work here for me."

"*Work!* You'll find work! Men like you can always work. That isn't important."

"It is to me."

"Nonsense." She looked at him with such a challenging mischievousness that he felt a clay-footed dullard to be so dour about work. "The question is not work but life," she said. "Work is the means to an end. If you take that blessed pub, what you are saying is that the means are very important? That is not work, a pub, it is a way of making money. Not man's work. A man does what he has to do in the spirit of one who seeks something greater. Only the weak respect the rich."

"Money is important."

"Of course! It is a remarkable invention. Civilization would be very backward without it. But in the end it is the lubricant and not the engine itself. And the engine is man. A real man needs money only to take him somewhere."

"What if he wants to go somewhere expensive?" Edgar could

not but admire her tenacity—even finding something splendid in her scolding—and yet the accretion of his guilt and her dissent was beginning to strain his tolerance.

"Money is never a bar to real achievement."

"Rubbish. Poor people, people I saw in Africa, people with nothing—they can achieve nothing at all without some money first."

"We were talking about you," Rosemary replied promptly, "not about anybody else."

"It still applies."

"No one's remarks can encompass the world."

"I have to have work I want to do." Feeling that Rosemary was slightly off balance, Edgar pressed his advantage. "I got sick of pointless routines in the army."

"Yes." Any reference to the army halted her: Edgar could always exploit that.

"The pub would take a lot of energy—I need that—and it would give me time, I know, for other things."

"These 'other things'—" She was quieter but no less persistent. "What are these 'other things'?" There was more than curiosity in her tone now: she was jealous.

She was onto it. How could he explain that the only stirring of anticipation he had felt in considering his move against the opaque and placid world of opportunity awaiting a soldier's return in Thurston and the seductive lethargy had been in the contemplation of the wheeling and dealing she found inscrutably degrading? It was an aspect of his character she would not accept and he did not want to thrust it down her throat. What he could see for himself was maybe a little cattle-buying, one or two bargains from the farmers who used The Mitre, a building-up of trade there, perhaps a petrol pump at the back, use the big upstairs room there for receptions, weddings and funerals; he would be someone who could call a tune. What else was there to keep him going forward? What other things?

"Politics," he lied. "I would like to have something to do with how this town changes—because it *will* change. Nothing can be the same after a war like that. Once the shock's over, it'll change."

"You don't need money to be a politician," she said, stubbornly, although without much conviction.

"Which of the men on Thurston Council today are broke?"

177

Edgar demanded. "They're either shopkeepers or they're farmers —they haven't *much*, but they have enough for Thurston. That's what I want." And as he spoke, this vision which had taken him by surprise appeared to be as substantial as any long brooded plan: he grew enthusiastic. "I want to have some sort of say in the place Thurston becomes. But I'll be no good unless I can have a bit of a show, Rosemary, not show, no, no—something where I can be my own boss and have some time to myself. Those two things are very important. Anyway I've been ordered around for long enough. A landlord is independent. If I can be free—those two ways—then I can *do* something—don't you see."

Rosemary hesitated and then nodded. His appeal had almost convinced her. She was fair; and his declaration had made her doubt—for what had she to offer against it? "I hope I'll be some help," she said sadly, and it was here that Edgar almost threw up the scheme on the spot. How *could* he imagine Rosemary pulling pints behind a public bar! Some pictures simply did not fit together and this was one of them. Saturday night crowds, whisky-sipping farmers on market days, inscrutable boyos playing darts throughout the afternoon—Rosemary would think that she had been transported to another planet. And yet . . . he was so confident in his own capacity to cope that he felt sure he would have the energy to spare to look after her. He would make it—he would keep her away from the harder jobs—perhaps she needn't even come into the pub at all except at busy times; there would be ways.

"Please can't we keep living here, then?" she asked gloomily. "In my lovely little cottage."

"There's a flat above the pub. It's supposed to be very nice."

"A *flat*! What about my garden? And Eleanor—where will *she* play?"

"People manage. Anyway, cheer up, I'll probably not get it."

"Oh, you'll get it," she replied carelessly. "You're always lucky, you know that; you count on it."

# Chapter Thirty

For Edgar the pub confirmed his best hopes; for Rosemary it far exceeded her worst fears. She hated it with unalloyed detestation. Edgar thrived on it. Within two years he had made The Mitre into a noted and profitable house.

Yet by any strict standards he was not a good landlord. He spent too much on help, for a start: he had two women in to clean in the morning—so that Rosemary could attend to the flat; he employed a barman every lunchtime; he was generous with measures and with his own rounds. He was not at all meticulous in the finer points of being a publican—the bottles were not wiped before they were put on the shelves, the pipes for the beer were cleaned but not often enough to give the beer the exceptional clarity which obtained at one or two other pubs. Nor was he a hearty "mine host"—often rather preoccupied: often absent; never bothering to jolly people along.

The profit came from his popularity, and that followed his farming and sporting interests. The Mitre had always been a farming pub but to have someone in who knew a deal about the business (though he'd never made anything of it himself they said) was a great relief for those tillers of the soil who found their own company good and more of their own company even better. Edgar applied for an all-day licence for the two chief market days; it was granted and, as the pub was so central, it thrived.

There were so many auctions in Thurston in those days—horses, cattle, sheep, pigs, poultry, all centring on the open-air market around and about the church which was only a few yards from The Mitre. And the thing about Edgar was that he encouraged the old lads to come in; Scrunt, Kettler, Noney, Patchy—the group which cannily got itself known as the "real old Thurston characters" and who clustered around the auction shrewdly, ever ready to drive your purchases down to the station or walk them back to your farm. But most of all they were full of good daft talk and mad tricks, forever gambling and cadging and arguing and holding forth—better than a theatre. Then there was the sporting side. Edgar had fallen in with Dick Waters, a rather cavalier motor-mechanic who was the best shot and dog breeder in the district. Edgar had given up his idea of bassets—that corner was secured, anyway, in the town, by George Johnston up at Flosh House—and turned his mind to hound dogs. With Dick he had invested in two pups. With Dick he had plans to erect that petrol pump and part-time repair station in his large backyard. And Dick brought in the sportsmen.

On Market Days, the pub was like a cauldron. Pies came in from Glaisters, teacake sandwiches from Johnstons across the road where the farmers would take their mid-day meal and soon after send for more. Always ham—home-cured, thick, well-fatted, well-salted. Whisky was the farmers' drink and a waterfall of scotch went from shelf to stomach on a market day. Dogs would curl about the corridors—loud hillside greetings—exchange of prices—barter—disappointment—a new story about Scrunt—a pair of horses for sale—a man with a pony he had to get rid of—children rushing in for pennies for sweets or with news from their mothers who were pecking thriftily about the bargains on the trestle-tabled stalls and, to cap it all, in the one quiet area of the pub, a small room which Edgar had turned into a saloon bar, uncovering beams in the ceiling and getting an old-fashioned grate for a log fire, there would be Rosemary, unsure, always unsure of herself and the prices and which bottles contained which drink, but trying her best, and being rewarded by the sight of Edgar in full cry for fulfilment and the courteous appreciation of the customers who were glad to see her joining them, understood her wanting to be away from the main brawl but all the same liked to feel that she still joined them. For she was so very out of place that her presence added a definite distinction and perhaps there was a cruel feeling of triumph in having toppled someone who was so obviously out of her own world but more likely there was the warmer comprehension of the love she must bear for Edgar to entertain such employment. She was popular, though she would never believe it. And Edgar was proud of her—that mattered a great deal.

Each time she went down into the pub she made a great effort, a major sacrifice of her instinct which cried to be away from this too worldly, world-stuffed, worldly wise, world-consumed place, away to graze in solitude; abandon hope all ye who enter, she thought and in her imagination this was indeed Hades. The boyos whom Edgar encouraged were like gargoyle-faced and malignant imps full of slyness and malice, utterly foreign to her, utterly repugnant however much she might appreciate their idiosyncracies in the abstract. The genteel she disliked even more; the regulars appeared to be like scarcely animated mummies—she had no feel for the complexities which might be concealed under a pose of silence, no entry—how could she be expected to have?—into the ways of a largely rural working class which thatched its culture close and so tightly you never saw the binding. Conversation was her test and by this standard all failed dismally except the boyos whose teasing and deceitful monologues baffled her. Yet she tried: she kept at it. And though she grew angry she did not grow bitter.

The flat, too, was dreadful, she thought. Though the rooms were bigger and more numerous than they had been in her cottage, the outlook was so bleak. Across the street she could look into the front room of the Tomlinsons and Fenwicks who also lived above their businesses: and this meant that they could look into her room across the narrow street, a thought that made her shiver. Nor was the back any better, looking out over a courtyard and the blank side wall of the Market Hall. She felt trapped.

How could anyone who really loved her have brought her here?

She observed Edgar's bloom angrily. He seemed to run rings round her and confuse her completely by the rapidity of his organization; though he provided help for her whenever she might seem to need it, it was always Rosemary who was left bound to the place while he was away with his dogs or to do a deal. He found the work easy and congenial, the quick switching of his mind from task to task was a pleasure, an entertaining exercise. Rosemary's type of mind could neither grasp external matters anything like as fast nor, once she had them, let them go without a second thought. Edgar was like a mirror, beams bounced off him and sped away in the correct direction as he angled himself shrewdly; Rosemary was more a pool which rippled uneasily at any intrusion but then let it sink and become part of the whole. She was jealous of his talents: beside him, she felt herself terribly slow and half-witted—not a sensation she found it easy to tolerate. She could endure it, but it was extremely wearing.

Her man had gone away. Baffling as it seemed, Edgar was at one and the same time more about her daily life than ever before and yet she had none of the richness of contact she had felt during those first few months before the war when he had been out of the house at work all day. All the fallow silences were charged with busyness: he became very irritable, short-tempered, sulky, tired despite his pleasure in it all and excusing everything on the grounds of future benefit. When finally pulled to a halt by the insistence of her demand he would sketch out a justification for his intense activity in terms of future security and present unrivalled opportunity—"I have cash in hand. I can save for those fields I want to buy. Of course you wouldn't understand that—that's just to do with dirty old money." She was shocked by the viciousness in his tone, but held on. "We could work up a nice little business here if we didn't spend our time thinking we were too good for it." He paused, suddenly wild to gouge what he most admired. "Nobody's lived on ideas *yet*, Rosemary—us ordinary people need money and prospects and hobbies to keep us going."

"Why do you need all those things? You never mentioned them before." She spoke calmly, ignoring the fear his tone raised.

"When before? Eh? Before the war?—I wasn't concerned with anything at all then except getting into it. When before?"

She flinched before his aggression, saw the truth in his remark and felt that he did have a grievance; yet she persisted. "You said that you wanted a quiet family life—like Jean's. That statement was very important to me—it stayed in my mind more than anything else you've ever said."

"Said what?"

"You wanted to be a man out in the world for all financial purposes and for your adventures but what you really saw life to be was in a quiet home with a wife and children. I must admit I was surprised but you were very serious and sincere and I believed you."

"Then I must have changed."

"I don't believe you've changed. I don't believe you'll ever change. The man who spoke to me then was the true Edgar Crowther. All this—chaos—is just a whim."

He was intensely uncomfortable when she addressed him by his full name and also rather afraid to be told he was other than he himself thought. He respected her intelligence and her insights too much to be able to dismiss the charge out of hand. It always seemed to Edgar to be very likely that she was right.

On the other hand, he could not go back to that quiet little idyll in the months just after war had been declared. They were gone. They had been his convalescence, the war had been his university, his grand tour and his time of reckoning. Now he had to get a move on. "I can't get as much out of my own company as you can," he said. "You have inner resources—my mother said that."

Rosemary laughed: Edgar, taking this as a slight on his mother, concentrated on holding his peace. "Your mother never said that," she contradicted. "It's simply your way of trying to keep me quiet."

"She did say that."

"You want me to be the contented slave trotting up and down your stairs in and out of your pub while you tear over the countryside with your new friends."

"I've known Dick Waters for years."

"Don't be so childish, Edgar—you know what I mean."

She would often go too far and insult him, hoping that the sting would cure. But he was set on his course: he wanted to fill the abyss he had seen after Tom's death, to be cramful of doings, to slake the desert which would always gasp for more.

"I am not childish," he said—yet these words themselves, he knew, were childish: and he writhed in the noose. "Don't help if you don't like it."

He knew she would: yet just as some horrible perversity caused him nowadays to attack what he most admired—so a similar pain drove him to taunt the very constancy which needed his support.

The more she grew wearied in this prison, as she saw it, the more exuberant Edgar became until she began to think that his access of life and the ebb of her own were connected. That he was feeding off her to stride fully charged through what she saw as his masterful days—organizing the pub in the morning, working there, setting up outings, solving people's financial problems, dealing in dogs and furniture (he became an habitué of the sales which were forever taking place in the market hall next door) serving behind the big bar, involved in the auction on market days, trying to get the garage going in face of opposition from the chairman of the parish council (himself the proprietor of two garages), racing his dogs, dealing in horses, playing cards for money—his life began to appear monstrous to her, so attached and beset by the world which stuck onto him in lumps until he was barnacled against the flow of the subtle private intimacies she lived for. He could not do enough: even though his day thronged with activity his whole urge was to look for more.

In his shadow, Rosemary found herself diminishing. The greater his force became, the greater the number of his roles, the more he grew into a man for all occasions and all situations, the less there was for her, the less she saw to love, the less she understood, admired or, she believed, desired him. Though his sexual demands continued ceaseless and urgent she found a score of excuses to deny him and found in his bitter denunciation of her attitude yet more proof of his waywardness.

Neither of them liked to talk about sex, about the act between them, both were shy, believing perhaps that it gained potency and charm from being unworded. Also, of course, their education had taught them to refer to sex only in sniggers and the snigger tainted speech on the subject forever after. Yet it had to be brought up and Edgar attempted it most fully, after false starts over a number of weeks, one Sunday afternoon when Eleanor was up at Sarah's for the day and the hours between business allowed for sufficient time. It was a bleak winter's day and they had been in the pub for about a year. Outside, the sky was a mass of heavy dark grey clouds moving portentously in from the Solway to meet the challenge of the fells. No one was on the street: the Sabbath in a small northern town was sepulchral: the spirit of Christ, it seemed, required there to be a blight on all positive or playful or amusing or congenial activities. God wanted the place to look as if it were shut up against imminent plague and the people had responded. On such a day as this, Rosemary felt soul-sick; for sun, for gaiety, even for Catholicism which was at least rich, for anything but this door-within-door retreat which made her feel so alien she could merely long for night.

Edgar's first caresses were dismissed impatiently. She was pretending to read. He went back to his chair and picked up the newspaper but he could not pretend. The moment to him seemed constructed solely for the pleasure he should take in the body of his wife and the satisfaction she should find in him; the second half of that supposition was tagged on, in his mind, to salve the swelling of selfishness, for the truth was that he wanted her. Nor did this initial resistance either deter or dismay him. He had still enough good memories not to be too upset by her rejection: he could understand her plea of fatigue.

He tried once more, reaching out to touch her shoulder, taking it gently and as she felt the pressure she knew that the encrusted complaints were only a small scab: she still loved him. But revenge, finding a way even in such pettiness, shrugged off the tender grip.

"Come on," he coaxed, and her mind was still thrilled by that voice which had called her to so much pleasure, pleasure which must not go down fathomless in unremembered chasms of the past, pleasure which she needed for present confidence. But the burden of anger pressed out the light. "We have all the afternoon," he said, "let's not waste it."

What had begun almost as a casual whim was becoming a fuller desire. So many times had Rosemary's body been under his own, socketed as one, the buck and swoon of sex. She rolled her head from side to side, her eyes tight shut between pain and ecstasy and whether or not he satisfied her she would look at him with tender delight. She knew about love.

He put down his newspaper and leaned forward in his chair. Aware of the approaching attack, Rosemary smiled, but to herself only. She would not avert it. "Look. Through the week we're often tired, me from work, you from Eleanor. I understand that —Sunday is a good time; you know."

"You can't have certain days as 'good times'," she said, without looking up. "That's turning the whole thing into a performance that you can turn on or turn off any time you want."

"Nobody said that," he replied, sullenly.

"O yes you did. If you want a fuck at the drop of a hat, get a mistress."

Edgar was speechless. The careless use of the word shocked him: and its association with such an odd and old-fashioned phrase—"at the drop of a hat"!—made it slightly unreal; while the bald suggestion that he should take on a mistress was overwhelming. At one and the same time, it seemed to him, he was both disconcerted and intoxicated by the woman: no one but Rosemary would come out with a sentence like that. He would never forget it.

"Don't be ridiculous. Why should I want anybody else?"

"Because I'm not giving you what you think of as your 'conjugal rights' and you're in no mood to be denied for long," she said, evenly, emphasizing her conclusion by closing the book and looking up at him. "You're going around building empires at the moment and there's no reason to think you'll stop at sex. Conquerors get the habit."

Edgar was intrigued and excited. Noticing this, Rosemary realized she had gone too far too soon, presenting him, as she often did, with the conclusion of a long line of thought instead of arriving at it by stages; and dressing it up in sensationalist language because she loved to shock him.

"What would you do if I ever *did* have—a, a mis-tress?"

"O I don't know. Scratch her eyes out, I suppose."

"I don't like all this. I don't like the way this is going."

"O come on, Edgar; you're quite worked up at the thought of it."

He was.

"I'm not," he said, bruised by the obviousness of the lie.

"Sex is important," she said. "Sensuality is another matter. To be sensual you must be in harmony—your mind and your body. For sex you are asking to penetrate me and I have to make myself vulnerable. I don't feel able to at the moment."

Edgar was silent, angry with himself because he was still unsure of her distinction between sex and sensuality and he was angry at the way she seemed to degrade his desire. "It isn't like that. You'd think I was going to harm you."

"Of course. A woman is assaulted in a sexual encounter. In a sensual encounter she is equal and each absorbs the other. But when your big cock comes charging into my poor little body I sometimes think I'll need to buy some shock-absorbers." He smiled: her imagery could always sweeten him. "It doesn't hurt. Come on! It doesn't hurt—I make sure of that."

"What if I asked you to drop your trousers every time the thought of your naked body crossed my mind?"

"I'd love it."

"Yes. You *would*!" She frowned and then smiled at him, so that he felt unworthily honoured. "All right. I can never be angry with you for long. I *mean* to be." He drew her towards him and she snuggled beside him in the chair. "I *want* to be, I really want to tell you what an awful man you are running about involving yourself in trivialities." Her loving scolding was great flattery: he began to kiss her brow and, carefully—remembering his protestation that he did not "hurt"—to undress her. "You're better than that. You're better than pubs and garages and dogs and all the company of fools who believe in such things. Stand up for what is inside your head. That is what makes you a man. That's what is different about you. Not those terrible pirate's hands of yours, or that cheeky smile or even the bustle you make about the place as if you were Dick Whittington."

"Sssh," he said, "ssshhh."

Though, as always, she was generous to his failure to satisfy her, appreciating that the root of her need might be too deep for him to tap, yet she could not stem the flow of misery which filled her like a vacuum when finally he rolled away. He would doze now, for a few minutes, and then be up like a pup, she thought, able to shake her off with one shudder of his mind while she would smoke and brood and compare and remember. Storing past and present, analysing the event, the act, the reasons for it all. A car going past, the first she had noticed throughout the afternoon, made her cringe. Why could not she, too, forget?

"What you are is a strong man," she said, eventually.

"You usually say I'm a child."

"Those who manage to remain children in adult life *are* the strong ones. It's we who lose our childhood who are weak."

Edgar had noticed her turning away. Love-making always brought him back into a sensitive mood. He felt as if she quickly cleared away part of him by that simple act. Resentment thudded into his mind but as yet it was still secure in good memories of love. Besides, he thought that the external world could give him just as much intensity. That was what he had always looked for and was rich in the belief that it was to be found wherever he sought: the pain he had felt when Rosemary had kept him waiting all those months and made clear his position—second in line —that long and refined endurance together with the memory of the agony he had gone through seeing Tom's death—these, the most powerful feelings he had ever passed through were transformed through his physical health and the spring of his self-esteem into a drive for pleasures and satisfactions wherever they could be found.

He dressed quickly and went out to Dick Waters' allotment to look at the dogs.

Rosemary appreciated his leaving her alone. She needed solitude to breathe over her thoughts. There were times, she thought, when his manners were so much better—so much more direct and sensible than her own. At other times she was appalled. He had no respect for her privacy anywhere in the house at any time of day or night. He claimed right of entry to her person whenever the spirit moved him. The thought which she gave about interrupting him or disturbing him or bothering him was, it seemed, totally absent from his make-up. When rejected he sulked, kept away from her altogether for a short time (he could never last out a full day—she could have endured weeks, she thought) and then came back. Like the Bourbons, she told him, having forgotten nothing and learned nothing. He was no respecter of words. To lash out with his tongue—though as yet he did this rarely with her—was done without any realization of effect or consequence although when *he* was accused of this or that failing he would be both astonished and hurt that such a wounding remark could be uttered by one supposed to love him: in short, her role in many ways was the role of a servant.

She never forgot a small incident which had occurred on one of their visits to his mother. Edgar had been sitting in the big armchair and nearby, just out of arm's reach, was the table on which were tea-cups and so on. His mother had handed him his tea and then returned to the kitchen for some cakes. He had tasted it, grimaced, and then hollered the old woman back into the living-room because there was not quite enough milk in his brew! And without a murmur, his mother had come over to him, taken his cup while he sat there, borne it to the nearby table, poured in a little more milk, brought back the cup, stood over him until he had tasted it and then, without any irritation in her expression or in her voice, resumed her chores. On their way home, Rosemary had said that she only imagined such service being given to a Pharaoh or to Louis XIV. Edgar was well pleased at the comparisons. His world was made for men to work in she said and women were their midwives from the cradle to the grave.

All right. Rosemary would accept that, as she also accepted his carelessness about personal hygiene, his obsessiveness about tidiness inside the house, his distrust of open windows, his gambling and his gin. In many ways she could fake delight in it; sometimes it really did amuse her and she was nimble enough, she thought, to avoid the worst consequences.

But how remorselessly Edgar now chivvied her! To dress more

smartly, to be tidier, to be more cheerful, to be more welcoming, to do this, to do that—he wanted to create a Thurston lass out of her after all, she would think, sadly, and be helpless.

Yet a day would come when they would go for a walk, say, and the views of those ordinary hills, the feel of the wind and the sun, scud of cloud and pressure of his arm around her waist (he always walked as if they were lovers, his arm around her waist: for that alone, at times, she would have followed him to the end of the earth) all these simplest things would fill her with such a pressure of pleasure that she would feel herself a child again, a lover, a sweetheart—the word he always used for her when he felt most tenderly; sweetheart. Against such fulfilment nothing could weigh in the scales.

Almost invariably she would end such musings by re-discovering what she considered to be her great good fortune. In the Sunday silence she fell asleep.

When he came back, she scurried, guiltily, into the routine of making him a light meal and dressing herself up—what a mockery that was, she thought: every day of the week she paid all this attention to her looks—and for whom?

Half-way through the evening she felt a surge of repugnance for the whole doleful ritual of masculine drinking. She went upstairs, put on her dressing-gown, found a play on the wireless and smoked, heavily, defiantly doing something decent with her time. She expected him to come up to her in a grimly suppressed sulphurous mood and all but giggled when he appeared exactly so. He had stayed downstairs after the pub had closed for longer than he need have done.

"I'll make my own tea," he announced before she had time to move, "don't bother." And before she could respond, he barged into the kitchenette and clattered his way through the simple process. If she left him alone he would laugh himself out of it, she knew that, but wished she had made the tea ready beforehand all the same.

This attempt to sustain his sense of grievance was lamentable. He could not look at her; he was too self-conscious to pretend to do something else.

"I don't mind you coming up," he said, "really." He looked up; she smiled and suddenly he was full of rage, his voice bitter. "It can't matter to you whether we have any customers or not.

189

You don't believe in money. You've found it too bloody easy to get it."

"You always think that your work is the *only* sort of work," she chided him.

"Oh yes. There'd be something wrong with *me*. *You* walk out: *you* make it plain that you despise the bloody place and it ends up with *me* being in the wrong—Oh yes! I've known that trick!"

"Edgar!"

His look was full of pain. He recognized the stupidity and injustice of his words but some ineradicable daemon goaded him on. "Of course I know I *dragged* you here," he went on, his restraint utterly gone, "We all know how I *forced* you to come and lower yourself—*demean* yourself—that would be your word, wouldn't it?"

Poor Edgar, she wanted to say, from where do you feel such distress? What was it? Tell me, she wanted to say; tell me. But the shock of his unjust and brutal accusations still stung the surface of her mind and froze the superficial response as cold chills the skin while the blood still runs hot.

"What did you say?" he rapped out, though she had said nothing at all. Now he was sunk into the surliness she most feared, became alien to her entirely, drawing on that unhappy source of character which his normal temperament could keep secret and controlled.

He held the cup, small, between his hands, and concentrated his gaze on it.

"You see," she said, gently as she thought. "Pleasure doesn't lead to happiness."

It was as if his mind suddenly twisted itself: he snapped off the handle of the cup, looked at the break and then hurled the article across the room against the wall.

Rosemary felt sick, but, seeing his mortification, she had compassion: but he had to be challenged.

Edgar waited to be condemned, and was amazed by her silence, eventually and rather despairingly attributing it yet again to her superior comprehension.

"You don't know what you want," she said, "except that you want *more*. When I met you you used to amass all sorts of things; you made an accumulation and called it a collection"—she could not resist that jab—"and it's the same with the whole of your life now. This pub, the dogs, Eleanor, friends, deals, whisky, gin, myself, you're like a common-or-garden Midas, just piling more in more on more—and *that's* why I hate you touching me so often—don't you see? Because I don't want to be part of your nosebag—everything cannot be experienced in the *same* way or we become nothing but a set of jaws connected with yards of bloated intestines."

Edgar laughed at the image. It was the mark of his compunction.

"Well. What *do* you want of life? A man must want something. Come on, Edgar, don't just sit there like a log." She was in good humour once more, he looked so comical, mouth-open, shocked. Her mischievous, loving tone and glance pierced him utterly. He was not worthy—he thought—of such devoted and intelligent attention. And he felt numbed by it: as if a central nerve had been paralysed: like someone transfixed by a snake, he had once thought when Rosemary had read him a poem about a snake. "Well? Well? What-do-you-want-of-life?"

"Everything!" he was desperate and struck out wildly. "I want to have everything I can get! Yes—that makes me a greedy man or an unthinking man or whatever you want—but I would like everything! Food and drink and sport and—in bed with you—and more of a family, more business, dogs, more friends, more knowledge, more of all there is. I would like to stuff myself—right—yes—so I would—to pile as much life into my life as I can! I want to be packed full of it! *Full!*"

He had spoken coarsely and his vision had chilled her spirits. Yet she was fair and it *was* a vision, it was an ideal which the most refined or the most distinguished minds had never acknowledged but to despise, but it was *some*thing.

"Harry Hotspur!" she suddenly burst out—and clapped her hands so delightedly that Edgar felt as if he had been decorated. Rosemary smiled with relief: she would read the plays again to be certain—but he was, surely, something like that reckless, voracious, life-rich English lord, wasn't he? Even the fact that he baffled her best attempts to penetrate his real self added to that richness which fed on darkness, she thought. "As long as you never *really* change," she said, coming close to him and holding his look very steadily. "Then what you do to that old carcase of yours or mine doesn't matter at all."

"Doesn't it?"

"No." She put her arms around his neck and he was distressed that he should feel such an impulse to look away from her intensity: he held on. "No . . . our flesh is only the sacrifice."

She pressed against him and he had a curious feeling of her having surrendered everything to him, of her being unable even to stand without his body there to grow on: he did not even clearly admit this to himself and as for burrowing through to the consequences, he was too far from that kind of concentration or courage; it would have meant such a superimposition of will on his normal character as only the greatest danger or the greatest desire could prompt.

She would not let him sweep up the broken crockery: his offer was victory enough for one day. One battle was not the war.

She took some pleasure in the thought that she was plotting against Edgar, like Penelope deceiving her suitors. And then again like Penelope when Edgar seemed so loving and promised her that this was temporary—he *had* to fight his way through the real world, a woman did not understand the brutality of it, the ruthlessness, the strain and so the effort needed if you were to stand alone and kow-tow to no one in no way—then he was Odysseus and she would wait a lifetime for him. She fell out of love with him again and again during these few years: but something he said, or the sound of his laughter, a caress, an unaccustomed expression—and she was once again entranced by him.

Sometimes, too, the very Protean nature of his life made her feel that she was being unjust to him—she should be pleased to be with a man who, in her eyes and by her standards, did so very much, should be proud of him; his was the race of doers, of makers and workers. She would always be a spectator, she thought.

The further afield he went to unearth activity the deeper she enclosed herself in the dark flat, sucking on her pain. She could bear that. She could nurse it and up to a point control it, she could live quietly with it if she was not too disturbed. Like Echo, she thought, she was in a cave waiting for Narcissus out there, striding through the lush lands with all the world to trample over.

She could wait, she could wait. Life would surely change. She would do her best and she did. By Edgar, by his business, by Eleanor and by herself. And after that, what was left drowned its sorrows in fiction. She read *Tender is the Night* several times. André Gide beguiled her in a different way: he spoke directly as it were to her inner ear, as if she shared a secret language with him which was neither native French nor native English but this translation. She read as much as she could of Colette, ravished by her; and she struggled with James Joyce and John Cowper Powys. It was lonely though, reading books like that which inserted themselves so insistently in the surface of your mind and having no one to talk to about them, having no one to earth some of the electricity and relate it to life around. It was even dangerous. At times the fiction was too moving easily to bear alone. But she had to get used to bearing things alone.

From within the dug-out she watched her husband's progress with amusement, with anger, with disappointment, with affection, with irritation but always with an intensity of concentration which beamed on him without fail. Edgar absorbed that, staved off the hurt, digested the positive part, and made his life. If only he did not have to feel the flick of her contempt. But he could live with it.

In the town people were surprised how well the two of them took to The Mitre. They'd said that Edgar would never settle down but he had confounded his critics. *She* was even more unlikely, really, if ever anyone was *not* cut out for pub life! Yet they said she coped very well, looked well, kept that daughter of hers beautifully turned out. They were a very striking couple, really, it was thought: surprising altogether.

# Chapter Thirty-One

One day she discovered again a letter from her mother. It had been written, as she learned from a postscript, by "an English gentleman Friend" because "I have not a sufficiently clear grasp of your beautiful language. And so I have sat with him and dictated, like Madame de Récamier, from my sofa, and he has translated and inscribed it all like the village clerk in olden times."

It was a sweet letter, full of gossip and womanly chat. Far and away the longest message she had ever received and kept so dearly for that reason, wrapped in brown paper with a few others (scrawled notes, generally) and tied with a red ribbon which had come from a large box of chocolates sent her one Christmas. When Rosemary read it she found herself at first very moved at the thought of this lonely, dispossessed woman obviously (she now deduced) passing down the ladder of fashionable Mediterranean resorts from lover to lover, self-propelled onto a path of independence which had led only to greater subjugation. Yet that first impression soon passed away. In the asides and the reflections freely scattered, thanks to the unaccustomed luxury of an intelligent translator and amanuensis, Rosemary detected a spirit of gaiety which, though almost desperate, she loved. "How I wish I were a few years younger and you, my darling, a few years older," her mother had dictated. "Then what fun we could have on this wicked ancient sea! We would take tea—English style!—in the morning, but in my bed. You would come from your room to tell me of your adventures and I would tell you mine. A full heart needs a true friend and alas one of my many faults is that I am incapable of making a true friend from my own sex. Men can only be friends if they cease to be men—that is too much for the best of them—and who cares about the others? Grow up quickly, quickly, my pet, and perhaps I can keep away the wrinkles a little while longer. Eat oranges at mid-day."

She often read the Georges Sand novel: having forced herself to read it through in French soon after she had gone to grammar school she now knew it almost by heart.

Rosemary grew used to letting her mind slip its moorings from the present and drift into a dream world of France and her mother, creatures from literature and those from her imagination. She had been long used to slipping into the past: it was there she had spent many of her happiest hours, reassembling the sensations and expressions of previous days and years, fondling long in memory what she had often scarcely even caressed in life, making in those catacombs of thought secret contacts, meanings, patterns for survival, and in that reconstructed past nourishing the faith in her own ongoing.

She found comfort in the memory of her mother and the days passed by vaguely; only Edgar brought her into sharp contact with the world and though she needed that, it was generally painful. They would argue. She would try to appease his swelling temper. He would accuse her of not wanting him as he was, of not liking him as he was, of thinking he was someone he was not: then he would demand more children. She saw the rise of his guilt as the enthusiasm for life became involved with a kind of gluttony and she tried to salve that sore.

It was as if he wanted to test the last ounce of her love. His way of life was an affront to her, he thought, and because he did not modify it, there was reason to suspect he flaunted it. She despised superficial acquaintances: across the bar he made, literally, hundreds. She was careless of money: he had to grow shrewd in all cash transactions; she deplored materialist grossness—he had plans which if successful would bring him large chunks of the town's commercial life. Above all, perhaps, Rosemary loved conversation: she believed that all actions should be turned into thoughts and all thoughts must be expressed and challenged. In this she found her zest. Edgar's tradition, however, was to move largely by silent recognition, by gossip and sudden wrenches of direction. Her insistence on talk at first merely irritated him from time to time and then grew to offend him. To be forever explaining himself, to Edgar, meant to be forever excusing himself which brought on guilt and exposed his limitation in this area. Very often he could not explain why he had acted as he had done: it had seemed all right, to unearth the reasons for it was to tear up part of his mind.

He wanted more children. He could not defend this desire and he knew that he was asking her to undertake another burden—although her use of that word dismayed him—in his heart of hearts he believed that a child added as much lightness as weight to the life of a woman as well materially secured in the world as Rosemary. She was not adamant but she was argumentative. And so he thought he was imposing on her and that worried him.

He was aware, too, that her demand to examine his day was resulting in his ceding a great deal of essential responsibility to her. He was trained for that. Most of his contemporaries in the town put their moral safe-keeping in the hands of their wives as readily as they gave them their wage packets. The Right-and-Wrong Mother was Jehovah, and Wife took over the load. Edgar's behaviour had been subject to the circumference of his mother's toleration: he had surrendered sovereignty over those boundaries to the woman early in his life when he had little choice. When he had gone his own way he had dispossessed her. Only the bad boys broke out of the settlement. Edgar wanted to give Rosemary his conscience but was afraid because she mistook it for his whole self. She sensed the strength of his need to give this to her and she dimly understood the contract which he clearly saw and lived by—that he would support her in the world and take care of her passage through it in return for that security in internal distinctions which he was used to rely on in the woman. But she mistook him and thought he wanted her to take care of him, to be his voice and his body and his character. Unable not to give, Edgar was pushed into a trap: he had no alternative but to yield to her and yet she took too much. While she saw no alternative but to take him on, as that was what she understood him to desire, blaming his mother for castrating him. And despising his lack of self-containment.

His external enterprises were not very successful. The dogs did not prove to be fliers, one scheme to open a bookie's shop, another to develop an early market for new potatoes, went the way of the petrol pump or the housing 'consortium'. He was a great one for getting into things, it was noticed, and getting them started—but then something else would crop up and he would be away: his lack of capital exaggerated his natural business restlessness.

He had started on the road of desire, she had said that and he accepted her word and he saw solutions only in terms of more.

Often, when the pub had closed in the afternoon and he went upstairs to find Rosemary richly involved in a book, he would make some tea and take the cup to the window to look down on the street of the town which was winding its way so encoilingly into his life; and he would look out, bleakly, waiting for a sign.

# Chapter Thirty-Two

Stephen came while Edgar was away doing some dealing in the cattle he still kept in his field from time to time.

Rosemary recognized him instantly. She had been called from downstairs by Annie Waters, Dick's wife, who helped out every morning now, and came reluctantly to the head of the stairs. He stood at the bottom, his back against the wall, one foot casually on the bottom step, elegant, self-contained, amused. She stopped and let the swirl of memory and desire rush through her. As she came down to him she found that she was shaking. Yes, he did so much resemble his father.

"Stephen?"

He turned and smiled; shyly, gently, a youth of eighteen or nineteen, a little taken aback by the effect he saw he had had on the woman before him: then he smiled more broadly as he remembered something.

"Father said that people used to maintain that you and he could be twins."

"Did he?" Her whisper was painful to her own ears. Without a pause, her feelings were back where they had been ten and then twenty years before.

"Yes. Often. But that must have been long ago. He's going bald now: you would be his youngest sister now."

"Thank you." She spoke gravely, for his compliment did not flatter her. "You should have written," she said, "I would have been ready then. Never mind."

"I just drifted up here to do some walking," he said. "The long vac is terribly long and I've not the money to go abroad. Besides, father always spoke about the Lake District with such enthusiasm."

"Did he?"

"I thought I'd better give it a go for myself. I've been up to see Uncle Lawrence and Aunt Sarah. They've given me the bedroom

I shared with the old man last time. Do you remember that? It was Christmas."

"Yes."

"Oddly enough, it's one of the things I remember most clearly from my childhood. Uncle Lawrence hasn't changed, has he?"

"No. Perhaps mending clocks keeps Time in its proper place." She smiled and indicated that he was to go upstairs. He stopped, half-way up.

"I say, do you mind if I get myself a half of bitter? It isn't often I'm in a pub but being in one and not having a drink doesn't seem right, somehow."

"Of course. How forgetful of me. You're a young man now."

They went into the small saloon bar which was empty on this weekday lunchtime. The sun came through the window and picked out the fairness of his hair. Rosemary drew inexpertly on the pump and the beer frothed over the top of the glass, running down her hand. A little more was spilt as she handed it over to him. He drank a third of it at his first pull. "Excellent," he said. "There are pubs in Oxford, you know, where one can still get beer from the wood. But," he added with hasty loyalty, "it's no better than this." He raised himself onto his toes and looked around appraisingly. She watched him, appreciating this cool independence. "What a nice place this is, isn't it? It's either there or it isn't, atmosphere, don't you agree?"

"O Stephen! You don't have to be so polite. It's just a pub."

"But I like it. I like pubs!"

She changed the subject: the unexpectedness of it all gave her confidence. "What do you study?"

"French," he said. "If I'd managed my affairs better I'd be in France now—you have to do the speaking part on your own initiative."

She took a quick breath; he would not ridicule her. "Do you like Gide's books?" she asked.

"Well!" He put down his glass with a hearty emphasis which was contradicted by the expression of delighted but puzzled interest which came to his face. "I've just read *The Immoralist* on the train coming up. His language is so clear!"

"I'm ashamed to say I read him in English."

"Rosemary!" How her name rang about her ears! "Disgraceful! That won't do at all."

They began to talk about Gide's philosophy. The young man's unspoilt undergraduate bumptiousness was infectious. In the small brown-beamed room, with a single span of sun coming onto the carpet, dust floating in the light, occasional chatter from outside, Rosemary sensed freedom: her mind was released from its troubled dealings within the skull and the thoughts soared out. She did not care what they were worth: at last they could be uttered and understood and they were her own. Later, she was to think that she was finally being "read".

They swopped authors as greedily as gamblers exchange tips.

When Edgar came back, he found them still in the saloon bar though the pub had been closed for an hour.

Stephen, by this time loosed from all the qualifications he had felt at first about her request that he should read her some poetry in French (and also a little drunk) merely nodded to the stranger and concluded, sonorously—

> "Les cris aigus des filles chatouillées
> Les yeux, les dents, les paupières mouillées
> Le sein charmant qui joue avec le feu,
> Le sang qui brille aux levres qui se rendent,
> Les derniers dous, les doigts qui les defendent,
> Tout va sous terre et rentre dans ce jeu!"

"Oh—that was wonderful!"

Rosemary clapped her hands together there, in the sunlight and Edgar felt a sweat of jealousy break out in him. Never had she offered herself to him as she was to this youth, he thought! Stephen turned, nodded to him once more and raised his glass to accentuate the greeting.

Edgar slammed the door and walked away.

Rosemary smiled at Stephen in almost a triumphant way: knowing that he, too, would be amused, in the last instance, by such a display. Yet it made her think very tenderly of Edgar. In one respect it was thrilling to be so forcefully wanted; in another way it was shameful.

In the back yard Edgar stopped and considered that he had acted like a fool. He was irritated with himself and savagely aware of the inadequacy of his behaviour. A petulant rage would not be cooled, though, however grimly he stood in the open air and tried to force himself to be calm. He had guessed who the young man was and seen the resemblance to Wilfred whose power, so unworked for and yet so very strong, had once made him feel so unarmed. Had Wilfred wanted Rosemary at that time, he only had to ask. Edgar had lived with that and endured it. But to find her plucked away by a boy!

It was impossible for him to pull himself together and despite his best wishes, he was forced to do what he knew to be most stupid: to get up and walk off, walk away out of the town towards Oulton, a direction he rarely took, in a common sulk, full of unspeakable notions of revenge. How she would laugh at him!

He nodded calmly to those he passed, but he was totally unable to subdue his feelings: the best he could do was to keep away from the two of them. Walking around Thurston was his only hope of exorcising the devils which spat so malevolently inside him.

Rosemary was too excited by the newcomer, too afraid to lose a drop of his presence, to give full consideration to Edgar's feelings. It was pique, she decided, no more.

Eleanor's arrival from school brought a fresh impetus to it all. Stephen was delighted to see her and became so boyish they could have been brother and sister, although she was only ten. They played dominoes, the three of them, and though Edgar did not come back for opening time, Rosemary was not anxious. He had asked John Connolly to come in and open up for him as he often did on days when he went dealing. At five-thirty as the bolts came out of the front door, the three of them went out by the back to take a walk down to the park.

He walked unhurriedly, Stephen, without letting the activity interfere with his attention to the conversation. She found his pace exactly suited her own: Edgar walked much more rapidly.

"It must be fun, keeping a pub," he was saying, airily, a little drunk, but she dismissed all critical reflections, "being in the middle of things. One gets so cut off at Oxford. Even though chaps come up from, literally, all over the place, it isn't the same as being, you know, in the real England. That's why I'm rather sorry they wouldn't accept me for National Service. Flat feet. Shaming."

"You're not ashamed at all. It rather nourishes your sense of what is ridiculous."

"Quite right! I say, you can see right over to the fells from here, too. That must be . . . no, I'm lost."

"Skiddaw," she said and steadied her mind against the wave of longing love which the single word swept up.

"Dad's favourite. That's it. I'll climb it before I go."

"When are you going?"

"Oh—a couple of days. It depends on what happens."

She let them go over to the amusements in the park and found a bench to rest on. Eleanor was on the roundabout, beaming with delight as Stephen spun it round faster and faster. Two small boys watched the speed of it enviously and Rosemary nodded when Stephen abruptly tugged the roundabout to a standstill, let the two boys mount onto it, and started once more, this time spinning around the three of them. Suddenly she saw herself between Wilfred and Edgar as Eleanor sat there between the two boys—each in a segment of the roundabout, each holding fast onto the iron bars on either side which marked their boundary. Round and round and round. The thought made her dizzy.

A great weariness engulfed her. She had offended Edgar deeply—there was no denying that and it would have to be remedied.

"She's just like you," said Stephen, having raced Eleanor back to the bench.

"Is she?"

Stephen nodded, happily, and flopped down beside her, tired from his games.

# Chapter Thirty-Three

They lay silently in bed. She had not been able to penetrate the shell of his resentment. Both were wide awake. They could hear Eleanor's deep sighing breaths in the next room.

She was frightened of him when he cut himself off from her, when he sank into himself. His sullen face frightened her: it seemed cruel. After all, no crime had been committed, no breach of trust—over-enthusiasm, yes, bringing back painful memories for Edgar, but she had never disguised her love for Wilfred. Edgar had never mentioned Wilfred but she knew that he wanted her to cut the former lover out of her life and leave no trace.

And indisputably she had flirted with Stephen; disgracefully. But she could not *really* regret it.

The intensity of Edgar's anger provoked her own. Surely her affections were free provided they did not contravene her primary loyalty to him! If only he would grow up! How *could* anyone expect another to be so shackled? If love was not accompanied by trust and tolerance then it was unworthy, wasn't it? Her thoughts flittered around her mind disturbing all chance of sleep and she got out of bed, found her slippers and dressing-gown and went out to make herself a cup of coffee. Edgar considered coffee to be an affectation.

She could not but smile at his provincial responses sometimes.

Smoking, sipping, curled in the corner of the sofa with a novel, Rosemary soon slipped away into a world circumscribed only by her own imagination. The night and silence of the town seemed to give her energy in a way in which the daytime bustle never could. She was safe, charged by the sleep of others, able to let her mind prowl in peace. All the more potent, such quietude, in the middle of so many buildings and machines and sleeping bodies.

"You wouldn't think of making *me* a cup of that stuff."

She smiled at him, lovingly, glad to be interrupted by him,

however gruffly he did it, relieved at any contact. "Of course I would," she said and lightly got up and went past him, humming. He smiled: the request for coffee had been a shrewd concession.

"You can hum," he said. "You can *hum* all right."

"And why shouldn't I? My husband comes to look for me in the middle of the night. That's very nice, I feel like humming my head off."

He stood at one door, talking down the short and empty corridor of their flat. Rosemary was inside the kitchenette.

"Why do I feel like that, Rosemary? Why do I *do* things like that? Why could I not just say hello and welcome him?"

He had come through! What a magnificent man he was, she thought. He had considered his feelings and weighed them and come through. It was a real victory!

"Because you're a man," she shouted, gaily, and then dropped her voice. "Because you're a marvellous man."

He laughed and the effect of that was to make her shiver with pleasure. How warm he could be! How isolated in frigidity she would be without him, she thought.

They sat down opposite each other, sipping from the steaming cups.

"I know it's stupid," he said, "and unfounded. I *know* that. But when I came through the door and saw him reading to you —the way you looked and *he* looked—I thought I was going to throttle myself."

"That shows what a *good* man you are," she replied, promptly. "A bad man would have felt like throttling Stephen or me or both of us! You blamed yourself from the beginning and you could work it out in the end. Good men aren't those who do the best thing out of habit or fear but despite habit and overcoming fear. They love to be bold."

"You want people to be good though, don't you?"

"I don't care how people are as long as they live to the uttermost in their minds or their bodies."

"That could lead to terrible consequences if what you wanted to do was bad."

"You mustn't harm anyone else—That's the Law. That's what makes civilization. If only the Greeks had not kept slaves."

"Some people might like to be slaves."

"Well they must be made to dislike it," said Rosemary, grimly, "it is a condition which debases us all. We must be free to find out how confined we are: and the next stage is always to break the bonds."

"What if it does us no good?"

"I'm not talking about progress. I don't think you can get better. I think you can be more comfortable and people should be as comfortable as they want to be. But that is not the point, not really. Really you must—there's a poem by D. H. Lawrence—it starts 'Not I, Not I, but the wind that blows through me'—that's what we must make ourselves—free to listen for the wind and let it take us over the world. Death can never be defeated but life can. Life can't be cheated, either."

There was nothing he could say when she took off like that, no way he could follow her. It was as if he stood on the earth, sunk in it unalterably while she beat the wings of her mind and lifted and raised and soared above him. Her hair was swept by her nervous fingers, her eyes fixed on the ideal.

"We must go under—like Orpheus into Hades—we must be re-born—we must endure if we seek the crown. And the crown can be different for different men but it is invisible to the greedy and the vain and out of reach of the feeble and the complacent and alas to those poor people whose daily lives are too oppressed."

Her confidence awed him. "And Stephen, I suppose," he replied, humbly, "he is another, is he?"

"Stephen? Oh no. Oh no! *You*, you donkey, *you* are the adventurer it was my luck to meet."

"No."

"But yes—yes, yes and yes! Don't you see that?"

"No!" Edgar's tone was firm and even admonitory. "Nothing you have said includes me. I am an ordinary man. I want property and money and I want more children and I don't know what the other thing you are talking about, what it *is*. I recognize it. Some people have it. *You* do. But *I* don't have it, Rosemary, you mustn't say I do. You must not."

"I *know* you do."

He wanted to believe it. But he was too compromised, he was too earthly, he was not strong enough. His mind could not concentrate itself on such an unworldly objective for long enough to achieve anything.

"Let's go to Allonby tomorrow," he suggested, briskly. "You,

Eleanor, me; give us a bit of sea air to brace us up." He paused. "And Stephen of course."

Rosemary came across and flung her arms around him, kissing him until he protested he would suffocate.

# Chapter Thirty-Four

Allonby was a village on the Solway Firth. At one stage, in an excess of late Victorian enthusiasm, it had been thought a shrewd location for a genteel resort. Three hotels had been planted on the flat coast, and a charming front assembled of large houses and a few shops—offspring of the big department stores in Carlisle. There was a pleasant turf green dividing the village from the shore and ponies were gathered there for the children; a stream ran down the middle of the green and small white wooden bridges were prettily placed for those eager to race from the hotels to the sea. Before the expected bather was a far range of Scottish hills, behind him the fells, and above him nothing worse than the usual boisterous climate of the north-west coast.

But fashion never made its bow. The front remained one-deep in houses. The offspring of the department stores dwindled from malnutrition and two of them were long deceased. The school which had been carefully placed to be in the centre of the boom town stood at the very edge of the village and two of the three hotels became pubs. Yet Allonby had a melancholy grace about it which, Edgar knew, charmed Rosemary. And Eleanor loved the ponies.

That day, being a weekday, it was sparsely patronized.

Edgar parked the car beside one of the pubs. The tide was out, so far out that it seemed you could walk across the flat firth to Scotland. A desultory game of beach cricket was going on, and three old ladies were combing the shore for stones: every so often one of them would dip like a toucan and rise clutching a white pebble. It was not particularly warm: Rosemary and Eleanor kept their coats on. "You see what I mean," said Rosemary to Stephen and instantly Edgar grappled with the jealousy which had started to ferment in the car when Stephen had found such clever things to say to Eleanor, such clever games to play with her. He could not address the girl in such a humorous-serious manner and she was his daughter.

"Yes," Stephen looked round, carefully. "It's rather like a ghost town. A fastidious, late Victorian ghost who refuses to come out of the bathing machine. I love all the greys. That's the colour around here, isn't it? The hills, the sky, the sea, the houses, the road, the gates—so many tones of grey. It's pathetic that all I can say is 'dark grey' or 'light grey'. One simply isn't educated enough: there ought to be a score of tones—"

"There probably are." Rosemary's interpolation came as a rebuke. She had noticed Edgar's struggle and was attempting to help him. At the same time, though, his inability to cope with this youth did give her a feeling of amusement which was most difficult to conceal.

"Yes," he admitted. "I generally blame something else for my own ignorance. But what grey is *that*, for example, over there, where it says TEA SHOP. Lead?"

"Lighter than lead."

"What do *you* think?" Stephen turned to Edgar.

"It's like a pigeon," said Edgar, "it's that grey."

"Pigeon grey—of course. There probably *is* a colour called that. If not, we'll invent one—here in Allonby, a tone of grey was first named."

Eleanor had wandered off towards the pony-riding school and the three adults went over to her. She had opted for a donkey because of its brick-red saddle.

"I wouldn't mind a ride myself," Edgar proposed. "How about you, Stephen?" His question was half-hearted, but Stephen jumped at the chance to accompany this man already so singular in his experience.

Stephen's mount was a little fresh but he refused to change it even though he did not look quite comfortable in the saddle. Edgar had chosen the biggest horse and he sat it firmly and strongly. They looked so well together, she thought, Edgar in his mid-thirties, burly but not stout, highly-coloured, dark-haired, dressed in dark tweed jacket and trousers, his face never still, his whole attitude looking for greetings and challenges: Stephen, beside him, fair, slim, nervous in an entirely different mode, *his* face alive too but revealing the tumble of thoughts within rather than reflecting the many claims before it. Eighteen was a lovely age. And she, how was she, she wondered, as the two men rode away down the hard sand and Eleanor plodded up the green on her donkey, how did she look?

She rarely thought of her age: linear developments of any sort were not particularly important to her real life. Her attitude towards the time of day was uncertain. She was always taken by surprise and yet never much moved by it. Similarly she did not regard herself as a woman approaching forty. She was lucky in that her appearance was one which age refined and did not rub away. She looked as well, even better now than she had looked ten years before: the skin was less elastic, of course, some tension gone, but her attraction had always lain as much in her aspect as in her features and on the whole the world had done well enough by her. But in her mind she was still seven, still and forever landed shivering in this northern island, clinging to a father she could sense she would lose if she once let him go; she was still 8–9–10–11, waiting for her mother's letters and then, eternally, gazing at the urn which contained her ashes: she was always, always in London with Wilfred beside the Thames, twenty-one, wanting to re-align that one moment of private history, she was alone in her bedroom with cigarettes and books, soaking up the pages to blot out the pain—it was impossible for her to be her stated age. When it was brought to her attention, the number of her years seemed impressively long and yet no more than a prologue to a real life ever-attendant.

Edgar and Stephen went further down the coast than they had intended and had time to make up when they turned. Edgar had enjoyed it—the strangeness of it tickled his sense of propriety. It was such a peculiar thing to be doing, this trotting along the sands on a large chestnut stallion in mid-afternoon for all the world as if the world were merely the stamping-ground for his pleasure. He never had the same feeling of leisure at a hound trail or even at a day at the races. Stephen looked a little anxious and had been mostly silent, giving Edgar time to glance at him, to understand the boyishness in him, to look his enemy in the face and conquer his bad feeling. To the older man, though, he was closed: there was no way he could enter the younger man's world without crawling or breaking something, he thought, and yet he would have enjoyed it there. Like Rosemary, there was in him the humour of someone whose inner life was interesting, self-nourished, always alive however damped down by the world. Edgar envied that and considered it the mark of someone quite unarguably superior to himself.

The horses began to pull as they approached the seaside village and Edgar was keen to let his mount have its head. It needed to stretch itself fully from time to time, such a powerful animal. He knew, however, and retrospectively it was this clear memory which most distressed him, he clearly knew that Stephen was uneasy on his horse, that he was a little tired and the slightest bit apprehensive of the horse's temper.

"Race you back," he said. "Go on! I'll give you a start!"

He leaned across and slapped Stephen's horse hard, twice, on the flanks and whooped loudly as it dashed away. He waited a moment and then spurted after them.

What a marvellous sensation, the air from the sea so bitingly rich and fresh, the power of the animal yet sensitive to a touch, the feeling of speed as the wind swept by! Stephen kept his lead. Edgar rode faster.

Within sight now were the people on the beach and among them he distinguished Rosemary, standing apart, looking over to Eleanor who was playing with the running waves. He came up alongside Stephen and saw the tense nervous face, so like hers. "Oh! Away! Away!" He shouted and slapped the rump of the young man's horse after each word. The response was immediate and Stephen seemed to sway in the saddle as the horse bolted.

Excited by the race which she had just noticed, Eleanor ran across to her mother, across Stephen's path. Stephen struggled to avoid her. "Let it go! Let it go! Stephen!" Edgar's voice flustered the young man even more. "*Let-her-go!*"

Stephen was pulling hard, trying to stop the horse which was now frantic from the desire to have its head and the nervous brutal tugging against its will. However he kicked, Edgar could not reach them and near Eleanor Stephen pulled so savagely that his mount reared high, hooves flailing, and landed on stiff fore-legs, bucked and again reared high, squealing frighteningly. Once more it bucked and this time took off with every ounce of its speed and determination and Stephen was thrown. He landed awkwardly, stunning himself, breaking a collar-bone and fractur-ing two ribs.

When Edgar reached him he was convinced that the young man was dead and that he had murdered him. He lay so splayed out on the shore, his head nestled against the rock which had wounded it, his arm grotesquely twisted, his face horribly pale, and dark red blood coming from his nostrils.

"Don't touch him!" Rosemary commanded. "Don't touch him!"

Even then, in that emergency, Edgar was hurt by her sensible words and the tone, and yet aware enough of himself to condemn such selfishness.

"You stay with him, I'll get a doctor."

He went across to the riding school. There was no doctor in the village. Edgar phoned for an ambulance, got some brandy and blankets and rode back. A small crowd were gathered about the body. Far in the distance Stephen's horse was trotting home along the edge of the sea.

# Chapter Thirty-Five

They kept him in hospital for three weeks. Rosemary visited him every day. The visit was the fixed point around which her day revolved. Edgar went twice. Both times he felt ashamed and intrusive.

It was Lawrence who informed Wilfred. Rosemary could not do it and she kept to herself the mingled feelings with which she responded to the news that he would *not* bother to come up "as Stephen is in such capable hands".

Both Edgar and Rosemary knew that the accident was a decisive fact and waited for the consequences. That incident had given her the chance she needed to take the initiative for which she was always contending. His guilt sapped his will and the primitive system of retribution which seems to operate between married equals demanded that her voice be listened to.

She bided her time, nursed Stephen, and was especially thoughtful to Eleanor. Edgar too sought refuge in Eleanor but the child was able to be independent of both of them through the ever-ready affections of Sarah and Lawrence whose house was her second home. She could still physically shrink away before her father's rage and he bitterly regretted the few times he had cuffed her.

He was apprehensive and grew morose and self-pitying.

When Stephen was released from hospital, it was decided to have him stay with Sarah for a week to ensure his complete fitness. Rosemary went up there every day. Her action was impossible to criticize and she knew it. Eleanor saw Stephen as the hero who had sacrificed himself in order that she should be safe; she, too, practically lived at Sarah's.

Edgar's restlessness became wilder. Adequate help was available for the pub. He organized it and drove to Carlisle to look for relief in the city.

The pub he found was a sombre, rather stern establishment

with a style of decor more suited to a country house in the Gothic manner.

The woman came in at ten to ten. He had been watching the clock and considering whether to have another drink before closing-time. She walked to the bar uncertainly, not having seen him as he had settled behind a draught screen. Edgar went up to get himself another drink and the woman started when she realized she was not alone, bent her head to sip at the sherry she had ordered, and sat at the nearest table. She drank quickly and ordered another. When the barman told her that it was time for last orders, she asked for a third glass and drank off the second while he was bringing it. Again she sat down and, after some fumbling, found a cigarette.

Edgar was sitting sideways to her and could examine her without staring. She was about forty or a year or two older, he guessed. Her face was striking in that it reminded him of the current film-stars; the heaped and waving hair down to the shoulders, bow-lips, slim cheeks, forceful eyebrows; the gestures, too, were familiar, the way she held the cigarette, lit it while shading the flame with her free hand, the very act of inhaling—all intrigued him by their approximation to a manner he had seen several times at the cinema but never so confidently in real life. She was smartly dressed, though not at all showily; on sitting down she had opened her coat and he could see the outline and excellent figure. She drank far too quickly.

Time was called and she looked around, frightened, he thought.

"Excuse me," his voice almost boomed, in the large room, "I don't want to butt in or anything, but if I can give you a lift anywhere, I mean, if you've missed a bus or a train or something." She was looking at him steadily but without the sense of fun which Rosemary would have had; he was conscious of that; had he been making such a pass at Rosemary she would almost certainly have made him feel a blundering donkey by this time. The woman nodded, almost gravely. "Thank you," she said. "But I'll be all right."

Her expression gave that assurance the lie. She looked stricken and Edgar felt a chord of sympathy. Her plight, he was sure, was as bad as his own. She finished her drink and got up, rather unsteadily. For a moment she looked around as if wondering where she was and then she went once more to the bar and asked for a bottle of sherry. The barman wrapped it up in brown paper.

Edgar opened the door for her. She paused again and peered out at the dark street, rather short-sightedly and fearfully: she looked at him.

"I live along the Brampton Road," she said. "Do you know it?"

He nodded, not daring to speak as a surge of dangerous expectation lifted through him as it were thickening his impulses: even his throat felt thicker. She nursed the bottle of sherry in the crook of her arm.

They drove in silence, both staring straight ahead. Edgar had not gone for more than a few yards before his policy was absolutely clear. He would take her home, open the door for her, wish her good night and then return to Thurston without a backward glance or further thought. His strength and clarity of mind made him feel cheerful and he hummed to himself, quietly.

They crossed the River Eden and quickly mounted the easy hill. Noticing his hesitation before the roads which forked to the north she pointed out her route and he followed her directions.

Yes, he would probably be back home just about the same time as Rosemary on whom he had undoubtedly been over-harsh in his thoughts. After all she was temperamentally under strain the whole time in that pub and Stephen's action, while foolish, yet deserved all the gratitude of a mother: the youth had undoubtedly (though unnecessarily) tried to save Eleanor from harm. It was understandable she should nurse him.

"This one."

He braked hard and both of them were jerked forward in their seats.

"Come in for a drink."

Edgar got out feeling winded. She was already out and walking towards a small green gate. The nearest street light was some distance away and she was not easily discernible.

He followed her. It was a very large house, early Victorian, which had been turned into flats. Still without a word from him, he was led in, side lights were turned on, curtains drawn, her coat taken through to her bedroom, the wireless switched on. "Coffee?" she asked and he nodded. "And a scotch?" He nodded once more. He could not help thinking he was in a film: and the room overwhelmed him.

Edgar was very raw. His knockabout experience of women

before Rosemary had taken him little distance beyond the physical contact: with Rosemary he lived an austere life. Here he was in a woman's place; soft materials, shaded lighting, gentle colours, a feminine smell, pretty objects, paintings on the walls, everything warm and lulling. It was not only sin and luxury which were represented but a world which he had thought he knew well, a woman's world which yet was far away from his mother's plain traditions and his wife's severe ideals. He breathed softly so as not to disturb it.

She brought him coffee and beside it she set down a bottle of whisky, half-full, and a jug of water. "I'll stick to sherry," she said. "It's a stupid drink but I started off on it about four hours ago and if I change now I'll just fall down flat on my face."

She sat across from him at one end of a large couch and he in his wide easy chair found himself transfixed by every move she made. She crossed her legs and the rustle of nylon was like a tickle up his spine. She flicked back a fall of hair which had loomed onto her forehead and the sharp upward tilt of her breasts stirred him.

Then he saw she was crying and any next resolutions or last defences simply slid away in pity and curiosity. Yet he did not move, using the moments to gather some strength into himself, to settle his mind.

"I'm sorry," she said, "you shouldn't have to see this."

"Please," he protested, moved by the strength of his own feeling of tenderness, "please."

She poured another drink, rather sloppily, he noticed, and he was even more aware of her vulnerability. As his awareness sharpened so his strength increased until he felt as he had done when first he had seen her, sure in himself and intrigued.

"Can I do anything?"

She drained the glass, again tossing back the lock which strayed down onto her forehead. "You can fill this up for me. My hand's not steady enough."

He got up and went across to pour out the sherry. The sound of the liquid falling into the glass seemed unnaturally loud in the room, and significant. She took the glass from him with a nod of thanks. Edgar hesitated, and then he sat down beside her. She was perfectly still for a moment and he held his breath. Then she took another cigarette.

Still now his mind dwelt on exits. He would stay for a few

minutes longer until she pulled herself together, that was only decent. She was in a bad way; Rosemary would most likely be leaving Sarah's now—he had left no message. It would take no more than twenty minutes to get back home—at the most—the road would be empty, no one was out at this time of night.

"You'd better go," she said.

This relief was met by a swift rise of disappointment and once again curiosity picked at him. "Are you sure I can't help?"

She looked at his hands for a moment and then turned to him, intently. "You're married, aren't you?"

"I . . . yes. Yes." The affirmation made him feel free.

"Go back to your wife. Go on. Go away!"

She spoke violently. Her weeping had not ceased. He reached out to comfort her and she came into his arms softly and fully, pressing against him, murmuring onto his shoulder. His patronizing intention was unbalanced and thrown by the excitement her body brought to his.

"No, no." She pushed him away and looked at him, hopelessly bedraggled and, now there was no mistake, drunk. The realization reassured him completely.

"You'd better lay off that bottle," he said. "Tomorrow morning'll be terrible if you don't."

"Tomorrow morning will always be terrible."

"Don't say that."

"Why not?"

He shook his head. "A good sleep," he said, "and you'll be—"

"*Go away!*"

The pain in the words touched him more closely than anything she had said or done. He stood up and felt himself too large and obtrusive, hovering over her grief. "I'm sorry," he said. "Of course I'll go."

Edgar hoped she would ask him to stay for now he was caught by the net of sympathy and curiosity and budding affection: she had been so yielding in his arms; he had not felt himself so potent for a long time.

But she said nothing more and he left.

In the hall he saw a telephone and scribbled down the number on a page from the notepad neatly placed beside it.

The adventure had taken him much longer than he had guessed and the church clock was nearing midnight when he came to the pub. He had driven back slowly, carefully, quite unable to disentangle his thoughts, preferring to wallow in their confusion.

Rosemary looked up from her book the instant he opened the door and in that instant he thought that she saw right through him, saw his potential infidelity, waited on an explanation. Nothing could be hidden from her, he thought, and his soul shuddered.

"And how was Stephen today!"

"Edgar! Really. You ask as if you hated him."

"Don't be daft. I just want to know how he is."

"Don't be daft," she repeated, lovingly imitating his accent, and stretched out her hands for him to take. He went forward feeling like a traitor. He took her hands and she drew him to her for a kiss. Though he had not kissed the other woman he felt that he wanted to wipe his lips in some way. Bending forward stiffly he administered an emotionless kiss.

"You can do better," she said and circled his neck with her hands, locking them. He tugged against them. "I won't release you until you kiss me like a lover," she said, "that was a husband's kiss."

He grimaced and was bewildered by the rebellion he felt so strongly inside himself. Why should he not comply with such a sweet request? Yet to do it seemed to demand some sort of betrayal. He blotted out his thoughts in an energetic embrace. After all, he had done nothing wrong, he told himself, and yet he knew at the very moment of release from Rosemary that soon he would telephone this other woman; and at the same time the part of his mind which loved truth and loyalty and his wife was summoning resources to fight against this danger.

"Hm! *That* wasn't right either," said Rosemary, mockingly cross. "But I'll let you go."

"How *was* Stephen then?"

"Oh—much better. He'll be leaving on Saturday."

"You'll be sorry."

"Don't sound bitter, Edgar—yes you did," again her eyes smiled at him amusedly—but so lovingly, too, could he not accept that? "I have been neglecting you, I appreciate that and you've been very good about it."

"I had little choice."

"That's not true. You could have been sulky or even downright obstructive."

"As a matter of fact I think I *was* a bit, you know; what do I mean?"

"Jealous?"

"Why did you say that?"

"It must be like that. If your wife pays attention to another man, whoever he is, you *must* be jealous."

Edgar clearly saw that she could be right but he resented what he considered the imputation. After all he had taken a lot of trouble not to express his jealousy and to be told, as it were, that all his work was for nothing was a bit much. Besides which, in the very centre of himself he thought that he was not at all jealous. There was something in their relationship which precluded his jealousy, he thought, something early nipped in the bud by that icy age during which he had taken on the burden of the knowledge of her love for Wilfred.

"Who could be jealous of a boy?" he demanded and almost bucked with anger when yet again she smiled.

"You were like a boy yourself when you said that."

"O for Christ's sake!"

She jumped to her feet lithely. "I'll get some tea," she paused, "or would you like something else?"

Her docility when she brought in the tea worried him as much as her mockery. She did not really feel docile towards him, he thought, not a bit! He watched her settle down opposite him and seem to appraise him.

"I want to persuade you to leave this place, Edgar." She spoke quietly, taking great care to keep all colour out of her voice. This, he thought, is the price.

"Since when did you want anything else?"

"I've tried to be a good landlord's wife. If I could stick it out, I would. But I think it has worn me down. Eleanor doesn't benefit either."

"No need to drag her in."

"I don't have to drag her in. She's here already."

"You know what I mean. It does Eleanor good. She sees all sorts." He too was worried about Eleanor, but she would never consider that he thought about his daughter's welfare.

"Can we talk about moving? We never have talked it through."

"We never stop talking."

"How else do you expect us to communicate?" She regretted

even such a light sally and then dismissed her regret. Why should she treat this man as if he were an angry bull?

"There are other ways."

"How?"

"You know what I mean."

"Perhaps you can move out of a pub on an instinct," she said, "but I doubt it. Otherwise we would have been out two years ago. My instinct simply hasn't counted for anything. I've repressed it. But that can't work forever if the situation stays the same. And I couldn't face another attack of asthma." She wanted to stop: these were complaints, not the calm reasons she had rehearsed so carefully. And the grudge which had come into her voice would be no good for this argument which she had to win. Yet everything in her panicked at the thought of staying in the place any longer.

"Yes, you weren't well," he said.

"I didn't mean that."

"And you think it was caused by having to live here, do you?" Edgar persisted. Her asthma worried him: the desperate breathing common to those who suffer that illness had sounded like the last gasps of one only just hanging on to life. He had been upset, unused to illness and unsure of the melodramatic effects despite the incontrovertible evidence.

"I don't know. That isn't what I mean. No. It isn't that." She struggled to regain her balance. She would not *use* her illness. "I'm asking you to face up to the fact that your wife has tried to do something because of her love for you and she has failed. She is sorry. I *am* sorry, Edgar. But now you must try something for me. You must try to see my point of view. Marriage *must* be between equals. Don't you see?"

"You *were* ill, weren't you?" His decision had been reached. It was over. He ached to compensate her for all the past difficulties and the present deceit he was practising on her.

"No. No. Please. Listen. When two people decide that they will love each other fully—then they must take on all challenges together. Don't you see? I want you to live by what you enjoy, by dealing; you could go back to those antiques you collected, why not? You had a feeling for them—I loved it when you took me into your stable the first time, do you remember? and showed me your treasure-chests. You were like a pirate. I think I fell in love with you then—it was so sweet seeing you there so proud."

Rosemary spoke quickly, conscious that her tenderness was becoming the flattery which nowadays made him so incomprehensibly annoyed but scarcely able to apply the brake to herself so excited was she by the clouded but certain feeling that she had won, they *would* leave the pub. Yet this did not give her the exhilaration she might have expected because of something about him this evening which she could not fathom or decipher, however finely she swept the scanner of her understanding. "Don't you see?" she urged him. "Two people come together as we did by such a human accident that it cancels out the accident of birth. I mean, how I came to Thurston was so much to do with luck. So in a sense we start clean, owing nothing to fortune as we would have done if I'd been your Thurston 'lass', don't you see? We have the chance, then, to build our own lives, you and I, and we have the luck to be strong in different ways so that we can help each other. But we must be bold, Edgar, don't you see?"

Yes, he was thinking, tenderly, she had been painfully ill. He could not let her go through that again: he would not. "Dealing" —did she say?—he liked dealing, he liked pulling off a bargain, travelling, he liked the gypsy in it all. She talked so fluently, Rosemary, and when she was serious as she now was he would always agree with her: she was always, it seemed to him, so exactly right. Enfolded in a burrow in his brain, however, like the enemy within the gates, his keenest thoughts occupied themselves with the other woman, velvet curtains—red they had been, wine-red: he would deceive his wife, he was saying to himself— no, no; would he? Rosemary was so true. He was not worthy of her.

Thus by diminishing himself he prepared himself for an act which needed him to be less than he could be. He listened.

"I believe we are born base and we die base and all that matters is what we do in between." Now quite carried away. "I can understand why the Chinese love philosophy and fireworks. And for no reason. Except to *live*, just for the *fun* of it, to see yourself in life—do you understand, Edgar? I'm being so useless tonight, I feel I love you so much—you'll never be able to—oh, that's silly—I love you because I know you are a good man and a brave man and a true and honest man."

Her praises thudded into him like darts.

"We'll leave," he said. "We'll go. You're right. We'll do it."

He had been happy and fulfilled in the pub. He was taking a big loss—she would never understand that.

As she kissed him he shivered at the treacherous thoughts which would not shift from his mind and wondered what would happen to them.

# Chapter Thirty-Six

She was called Margaret. Her husband had been killed at the beginning of the war after a marriage of a few weeks—the marriage itself, she explained, hurried forward because of the war. She had sustained herself since by working as a secretary and, at first, by joining as many evening classes as she had the energy for. She lived alone. It was her husband who had been the local man, she had come from the Midlands and knew very few people in the small city of Carlisle. His parents, who had never much approved of her, saw her only occasionally and grudgingly: her own father and mother were in New Zealand, living with her immensely successful brother who had become a farmer. She had stayed in Carlisle during the war for want of somewhere better and for the memories of those weeks with her husband. Since then she had felt less and less able to make the sort of choices which allow someone to influence their own life vitally.

There had been a long affair with a man who had separated from his wife. He had promised to divorce and to marry her, but in the meantime they met as surreptitiously as schoolchildren. This had dragged on for four years and Edgar had witnessed the aftermath of one of the "last meetings" which had begun to occur increasingly regularly. The affair was exhausted but a kind of honour towards its former potential kept it just alive despite the pains of fatigue and failure.

Edgar learned this over three long afternoons during the next month—two Saturdays and a Sunday when he sat in that seductive flat and let the complications of someone else's life pour into him. For some reason which he could never understand, her unhappy story acted as a salve to his own feelings.

It was so easy to find excuses for the times he saw her. He would say he had been "out dealing" and Rosemary would nod happily, understandingly, confidently.

They had left the pub. She was full of this yet concerned not to let it appear that she had won a victory. Her triumph, though, was very hard to disguise. The lovely cottage they had once rented was now taken but there was no trouble finding a place. They soon came on one up at Highmoor, near the old mansion. Edgar had found a small, detached place, standing where there had once been a lime tree on the mile-long avenue leading to the big house. The rent was reasonable.

The mansion amused Rosemary. Sarah and Lawrence had taken her there a couple of times on Sundays when she was a little girl. At that time the grounds with the golf course, the miniature zoo and the ornamental lake, were being run down, but the house itself was still inhabited by a lady who did good works in the town and continued the tradition of opening the place to the local people on special Sundays. The furnishings had strongly reminded Rosemary of places she had been hurried to in France by her mother. She had mentioned this to Sarah and the old woman's immense solemnity in front of these unimaginably splendid rooms was given savour by this direct contact with the great world. Rosemary had soon sadly realized how she could win over her guardian; and done everything to avoid using that method.

Now the zoo was gone, the pond was neglected, the golf course was farmland, the mansion was eleven flats, the avenue of limes was an avenue of two- and three-bedroomed houses on one side and neat garden-allotments on the other. Yet the place remained; the lovely Georgian house and on top of it, the imitation Venetian tower, planted there by a nineteenth-century owner who had loved Venice; now a landmark. Once there had been a bell in the tower whose strike could be heard for ten miles around; but it had been too heavy or badly slung and threatened to destroy the entire building. It had been removed. Rosemary saw a parable in that, the tongue being taken out for fear it would destroy the body. She amused herself drawing simple parallels between her own situation and this odd structure, this extravagant foreign stalactite on the calm and reasoned Georgian proportions.

But in the end it only amused her: she thought it rather ugly. Edgar admired it.

From her front room Rosemary looked down over farmland to the small sandstone grammar school and beyond it to the auction, the church, the town and on the facing hill, to the cottage in which she had spent such a timeless age of insulated contentment.

It was only when she was settled in the new home that she realized how tired she had become during the couple of years in the pub. The strain on her resources had been considerable. She had tried, there was no doubt, she *had* made the effort to remember people's names and what they drank, to keep up a conversation with mere acquaintances, to get the prices right, to be clean and bright as Edgar wanted. She had worked out exactly what he wanted, she believed, and tried to model herself on this ideal. The difficulty was that it contained so much which she held in contempt. Yet she had wanted to be helpful, she had been determined to be useful and not an albatross as she had once called herself, and her considerable energy had been harnessed to this task.

Now, however, in the peace of the afternoons, snug in the small, elegant little rooms, with quiet neighbours, far from any crowd, a fine open view, free, she saw the distortion she had forced on herself and she gave daily thanks that she was rid of it all. Despite her efforts and in complete contradiction to her wishes, however, she was extremely irritable and edgy with Eleanor and Edgar: she was adamant on trivial points and infuriatingly playful and ambiguous on matters which needed decisive action. Though she was sure she had done the right thing, for the moment she felt exposed and unprotected.

This helped Edgar.

He had not made love to Margaret on his return visit nor on the subsequent three or four visits. Reassured by his shyness (for this was how she interpreted it) Margaret let herself relax in Edgar's company, found him a good listener, ready with full-blooded common sense when his advice was demanded; just the strong friend she needed. But she, too, from that first night, had felt the hum between them; and each movement was a significant gesture. She talked.

Whereas Rosemary's experience was derived from the mind, it seemed to him that Margaret's came from the world. The discovery of this distinction pleased him. He was shamefully easily pleased with himself over these three weeks. He was giving Rosemary what she wanted, he was giving Margaret what she wanted, he was boldly cutting himself off from a lucrative trade and setting up alone in a tough world and giving himself what he knew he ought to want. He was Jack-the-lad all right.

"Please, Edgar, no, I'm sorry," Rosemary turned from him in bed and he let her go, his anger lightened by the thought of the other woman. And she *knew*; he was sure. Her love was lucid.

He noticed an aversion in himself towards his wife. It had come on him several times before and stayed or passed quickly as his mood spread or shifted. Now he tagged it onto his everyday observance and matched it against the alternative.

Aware of the danger, Rosemary dug into herself for explanations which were only to be found outside her own state.

As Edgar prepared himself for infidelity by degrading that part of himself which loved Rosemary and undermining the Rosemary who loved him, so Margaret too found herself set on a course. She waited for him as an experienced woman waits for a hungry man.

If their physical tie was so repugnant to Rosemary, he reasoned, what would it matter if he found physical satisfactions elsewhere?

What the hell, others did it. No one he admired, and when he thought of it now he felt that he did not belong with any of those people, not with the man who left his house at ten o'clock every night to take his Alsatian for a walk and briskly brought it back at six the following morning—not with the lodger who had the woman while her husband was on night shift—not with the professional man who whisked away his secretary to lakeland pubs and excused himself with talk of "conferences". Edgar cringed to think he would join that gossiped band and refused to face that fact.

He was quite safe, he thought, as long as he did not make love to Margaret. The company was enough. A woman he could talk to, who agreed with him—what a relief!—who obviously thought him quite straightforwardly attractive and not "good and brave and courageous" and so on which made him feel such a shallow hypocrite. And there was also this fetid turbulence within him, which could not be denied, as if something dark and bad and irresistibly powerful was thrusting for attention.

Sometimes, oddest of all, it seemed a matter of little consequence, a meeting, a mating, a skirmish on the surface of life, a friendly fornication, why not?

Why someone voluntarily seeks out complication or danger, his own worst interests and even pain, is inexplicable: to look, as Edgar did, for a kind of damnation needed maps of his mind beyond his knowing. He was certain that this would be the day, this grey Saturday, and as his car jogged over the cobbled streets of Carlisle he deliberately refused to slow down, letting the impact shake him.

He pressed the bell but had no sense of announcing an arrival for the sound was only heard, and quietly, in the lounge. It still disconcerted him a little. She opened the door, paused for just a moment, and then led him in.

She was dressed to kill. Though it was day, the sidelights were on in her lounge, which faced north.

"Scotch?"

"Please. Yes."

She went out: the minimal exchange keyed him up. There was no doubt this was the time. Too nervous to sit down, he looked at the paintings on the wall. One, in an impressive gilt frame, showed a galleon in a storm, the centre of the canvas almost white with spray. There was a strange intensity within him, almost, he thought for an instant, a smell of cordite in his nostrils.

"Here it is."

Her voice was very soft. He turned as she placed the rose-patterned tray on the small inlaid table beside what had become his usual seat.

Where was his instinct now? Where was that clear message which had once long ago propelled him towards Rosemary and impelled him to hang on when he was bleeding from her wounding rejection?

In the middle of the bewilderment was a kind of love come perhaps from trivial rebuffs, and disappointments from Rosemary, but founded on that groan of longing which is beyond words and beyond reason and so widely held to be base and dirty and worthless, but despite or because of all that, Margaret attracted him most powerfully and he moved forward to her, slowly and nervously through the hurricane of his conflicting feelings; he reached her and was unable to stop himself trembling.

She stroked and soothed him.

They made love most unsatisfactorily for both of them. She had tried to defend Rosemary's claim on him; he had agreed but it made no matter now. It was done.

Yet though it had been no pleasure for either of them, though the act which both had enjoyed with others had passed in dismal and unbalanced frustrations, the bodies had been conjoined as one flesh. There was no joy.

He was cold as he drove back to Thurston and he felt sick. Along the road just past Thursby he drew into the side where there were some woods and climbed over the fence to see if he could retch up his sickness. The stench of the winter woods broke from his trailing feet and the two smells, the one inside, the other outside, matched each other for unpleasantness. There was cold sweat on his forehead and his thighs were weak, felt clammy: his own breath stank to his nostrils. But he could not vomit. He leaned against a beech tree and rubbed his forehead against the bark.

A few cars went past on the road, their lights on, night falling.

And in bed it was all he could do not to scream. Rosemary was very tired; Eleanor had fallen and hurt her arm which had become so painful that she had taken her to the doctor's. The wait had been endless. "Internal bruising," the doctor had declared and advised a couple of days in bed. Oh—and Lawrence had come around with news of an old friend who was selling off his farm and might well have some bargains for Edgar in the outbuildings—things which he could have for the price of removing them; and in the novel she was reading . . .

His back to her, he felt curled into himself tighter and tighter and ever tighter with no relief. He had broken their trust and God alone knew the consequences.

Yet at the heart of the despair and the self-contempt, he found a certain inexplicable triumph.

# IV.  THE DUEL

# Chapter Thirty-Seven

Rosemary was now just over forty and Edgar had been out of the war for three years. Like many self-absorbed women, her attractiveness had been retained without any effort: as if it appreciated the lack of exploitation and found nourishment in the lack of vanity. Eleanor was nine now. Her mother, she realised, was *not* like other mothers and in the end, she resented this. She was ashamed of this realization on her strong days, but generally it vexed her, this distinctiveness, and she wished it away. Rosemary saw the young girl's dilemma and tried, sometimes, to do as other mothers did, with little conviction or consistency. Rosemary would inevitably forget to buy her daughter the *absolutely essential* white plimsolls and a fortnight later spend two days putting together a fantastical dress for her as Harlequin in a school production of Pinocchio. She would forget, so many times that it became a bore, that on Mondays her daughter needed dinner money and then, even worse, come to the school itself sometimes, mid-morning, *with* the money, and, worse still, *stay* to have lunch with the headmistress and set off the staff table in chuckles. Or she would decide that Eleanor would have, for once, a party and choose a day: on that day, there would be such a wealth of invention in the house, from the kitchen and the garden and from scraps and tokens she had "made up", that all the other children would be doe-eyed at the resources of this lovely woman who gave them such an original but rather wild afternoon—and after it Eleanor, bursting with a mixture, again, of pride and shame, would find herself crying and Rosemary laughing. Then all would be clear as a simple walk along the Syke road where her mother would pick a few flowers and bask passionately in the richness of the present. But soon the cross-patternings would again enmesh her. So, slowly the daughter learned to keep a distance. The learning of this lesson brought her a good deal of unhappiness.

In the house, such a refuge after the highway of the pub, Rosemary made a reckoning.

Her expectations from life were as small as her aspirations were large. She had, in a sense, constructed a life for herself. She paid little attention to the fate of her body and similarly, in the small town's society she was utterly careless of the accepted distinctions. Her attitude confused people and made some who would have looked up to her think less of her and those who expected to be able to look down on her feel snubbed. She made her own way.

Deprived of the mother and father from whom she could learn by the surest method, imitation, and of the country and like friends who could have been substitutes, she had, in exile, been forced to cunning.

This private self which was where she felt most "real" (everything else being like a graft of new skin) was founded on the golden age of her childhood, idealized by time and distance and death. In that age she spoke a different language, the sky was a different colour, the smells and sight were different, materials were different and there was this wonderful flickering memory of her mother and father which troubled her mind like certain slang phrases in French which she would half-remember in dreams and wake to find tormenting her. Round and round this golden orb she had wrapped herself and mummified that inchoate past. Adolescence had stirred her, Wilfred had awakened her and his neglect had almost killed her: Edgar's bullish strength had forced her out once more against her better judgment but according to her will and now, with a child and a home, she was secured or trapped in the substantial, the real world, and could no more return a second time to her oblivious Hades than Orpheus.

Her private secret self which in times of crisis emerged as her only strength was nurtured by books, by paintings, by solitudes and above all by the idealized dreams of love and glory which works of the imagination and worldly gossip together combined to describe in such primal colours. Nothing was more important than the discovery of a like soul, she thought and passionately believed. Without that you were a savage.

By this time Rosemary had sifted Edgar to the last grain of his character, she thought. Though she would tell him that he was "bewildering" that was often flattery or really a stratagem to lead him away from his own bewilderment at her. She knew that a large measure of his love for her had been driven by that obstinacy which both dismayed her as being unthinking and impressed her for its will to make life. She disliked his easy charm though she found him, at times, so simple and innocent that she was disarmed as never by anyone else.

What she loved was the power in him. This, though roundly appreciated, though fingered lovingly in the hands of her mind, was still a mystery, its source and its possibilities alike unfathomed. It was this which she wanted him to ride on, this gift he ought to pluck out of the collection of his talents, she thought. It was rare, and what it bred was a contact with the whole of life which took her breath away. When all his power was about him, in a gesture, in a walk, in making love, simply in the look on his face, then Rosemary believed that something grand and marvellous was in the world and she loved this man for revealing it.

Now there was the chance to do more than wonder. Now was the time. She had to create the opportunity. He had to find the core of himself and she too had to come into her own.

In a couple of months she was organized. The house was adequately furnished—rather sparsely but she preferred that; the spaceless clutter of Edgar's mother's house, and Sarah's similar taste, oppressed her. Edgar had sorted out the small gardens front and back and given both over to lawn and flowers, doing away with the vegetable patch which she regretted but did not object to, knowing he thought she would prefer the flowers. As far as she could tell, he was beginning to establish himself as a cattle dealer and all-purpose middleman: true, he would look tired and complain of obstacles but she never took his anxieties so very seriously: she was confident of his talent to survive.

What she set about doing, by stealth and in all good faith, was so to engineer their lives that they might live gloriously.

# Chapter Thirty-Eight

Edgar never conquered his nervousness and Margaret never truly abandoned herself to him. Though this made their sexual contact disappointing for both of them, it did leave free ground for friendship and companionship. Margaret used Edgar as a confidant. He seemed to enjoy listening to her: she would stop every now and then and ask yet again if he was bored or sure that he wanted to hear all about this—but he would encourage her, genuinely. The guilt became bearable.

Underneath all Margaret's words was a confession of vulnerability and a fury against failure which is the last redoubt against despair. Edgar was being asked for comfort.

He could offer this: he enjoyed offering comfort. He could give advice which was not only asked for but acted on. She made plain her needs and yet the demands were never made with that insistence which aborts sympathy. Edgar discovered that his judgment was valued and he was truly flattered. Margaret would present him with ever new combinations in her puzzling situation and invite his appraisal. Should she altogether leave this man? change her job? leave Carlisle and start again? have a child and bring it up on her own? He was let into the heart of her life; he appreciated the compliment and responded carefully.

That he, Edgar Crowther, should be visiting the flat of an alluring woman, talking to her in that overwhelmingly feminine room about affairs and illegitimate children and then, however disastrously, making love to her, was wickedly attractive.

In those first few weeks there was some calming of his turbulence because of Rosemary's self-absorption: she did not need him, he thought, uneasily aware of the ease this brought him; it was low, he knew well enough, to find excuses in what might be her pain; or, worse, her decision to save *him* from pain.

But she would not let him follow her. When he asked, as he did, often, what was wrong, she simply shook her head and smiled gently as if to say "Thank you for being so kind but I'll sort it out myself: don't worry: I can do it," and then Edgar would admire out of all proportion the inner resources which could carry such a burden and be silent in a way which was beyond him; and yet, this warm and chastening feeling would soon be overtaken by a fleeter, base reaction, a sulky feeling of resentment that she would not be open to him, a trivial, grudging sulkiness which was inexpungeable.

Another strain lay in the fact that he had not made sufficient provision for the success of his new job. He had saved up a little money while in the pub and so there was no immediate worry but he could see trouble if he was not lucky fairly soon. So many people did a little dealing on the side, in beasts and furniture, in fields and houses: the market was very depressed; there was not much cash around, and in these post-war years supply exceeded demand.

Most of those who did it full-time were tinkers or from tinker stock. Edgar liked them, liked their dark skins and colourful dress, their humour in a scarcely decipherable dialect, their cliquishness and solidity—their dogs, the trailing kids, the raucous, restless women. He had welcomed them into his pub and they liked him for that. Thurston was one of the places where gypsies and tinkers had long made their winter encampment.

They were hard men to beat at their own game. They traded between themselves; they could live off very little if times demanded: they travelled light. They had always been Edgar's secret heroes, though, and as a boy he had loved their gaudy clothes and caravans, the lurid tales about them and their independent scavenging among the bits and pieces of life which had seemed pleasure as much as work. His friendship with Scrunt, never broken and now revived, had been part of this.

It was not easy to make enough money at such a game. Edgar's contacts, thanks to the pub, were very wide; he had a foot in the agricultural community and good ideas about what could be valuable. But he did not see any way into the scrap business or the real junk trade; he had neither the taste nor the facilities. Besides, that market was hogged locally by a man with an iron on one leg who drove a pony and trap as if he were in a trotting race, John Willie Stewart. Mr Prince from Water Street kept an eye open for that sort of commerce, too, and further afield were the Bowmans. Kitchenware and pieces of furniture were cornered by Diddler and his son. Patchy and his friends worked the auctions. Suddenly every back alley in that riddled little town seemed to hold a rival.

Edgar's strength, his eye for a striking piece of stonework or a carving, his affection for stone troughs and such like, was not all that useful to him. Very few people appreciated the charm of those things just as no one wanted the mirrors and iron tables he took with him from the pub. When he went around he found in the old farmhouses that the women would beg him to take away some massive piece of furniture—a large Welsh dresser or a settee, sideboard or an oak chest, no charge—just to get the "great old thing" out of the house. These were what he loved and his discernment was good. But so few people were interested in buying; the trend was all for contemporary furniture, light and airy houses, small rooms; the heavy Victorian stuff and all it represented were thrown over. He could stack only a limited amount in the warehouse, but after that it meant passing up bargain on bargain. There was nothing to be done about it.

So he was forced back to cattle. He rented two more fields to extend his temporary grazing business and he set out to travel all the district over, covering scores of miles to make the small margin which he only just lived by.

What disarranged him most was the nature of the work. Since his marriage he had been regularly employed in a disciplined way and even though he had been his own boss in the pub, he had regular and expected demands.

Now he was a free agent. In theory he could get up whenever he liked, work the hours he chose, choose the route he preferred, experiment, change, bob and weave through the day. He would have denied it fiercely but in fact the liberty rather intimidated him. To build up a structure of life out of yourself which would occupy not one day but many, not one month but, prospectively, years seemed an impossible job, more restricting than anyone else's rulings. Then there was the strain of never knowing what would work and what would not. A journey over the border to Hawick, costing dear in petrol and taking the whole day, could result in no deal: three such days, consecutively, could be very bad.

In the factory, in the army of course, even in the pub, the job itself had been a waiting engine: the work was simply to take it up. It would always be there with its secure and comforting and known demands. But dealing was a daily hustle. Each morning you had to think of new ways, to unearth yet again the drive to take you out on a hunch. Of course there was a regular route he followed for the cattle, but this provided bare existence—and soon it became important to him to take more risks; the very stability of income derived from the swopping of beasts from auction to auction came to be a bind; the style demanded as much independence as possible and promised success only to those who so abandoned themselves.

Most daunting of all, however, was the nagging feeling of obligation he felt towards the very liberty he himself had reached out to claim. He had to live up to it, he said to himself, but how this was to be done he did not know. He was infuriated by the general assumption that because he was independent he must be rich and because he appeared free he must be claiming to be more powerful than his acquaintances who waited for him to prove it. Envy bred fear of envy and the assumption that he was on the road to a fortune was strangely hard to bear. He would take the easy way out by being unnecessarily extravagant.

He became erratic in his hours and developed the *hubris* of those who think they can toy with time. He began to dress casually and flamboyantly, like the tinker, with a silk scarf about his neck which horrified Sarah who regarded such a sign as something as bad as theft. He let his hair grow longer as the other dealers did and took to wearing his suit with waistcoats—the uniform of the dealers who clung onto them oblivious of the fact that almost everyone else of their age and in their financial class was changing to the simpler and more convenient two-piece suit. He drank more.

Edgar's warehouse was in his beloved Church Street, smack in the middle of the town in the quaintest street of all. The building was opposite the slaughterhouse and next to the West Cumberland Farmers Grain Store. The stench of blood and cattle feed was powerful and toxic, reminding him always of his time in the butching business and of the rich smells of his father's farm, the inescapable stench of his past, far away from the drag of his wife's ever-circling certainties.

# Chapter Thirty-Nine

The carnival was on the first Saturday in September and Eleanor had arranged to spend the day with Jean's youngest daughter. Edgar got up about half past nine, rich in his new sloth. Rosemary had his breakfast ready: she warmed the bread which he loved, finding in that simple touch a continued delight in his wife's distinctive quality. She had resisted her own hunger and waited for him. They ate in the quiet of the kitchen which had been so furnished that it combined the qualities of an old-fashioned parlour also. One of Lawrence's clocks patrolled the silence.

It was a sunny day, promising the first mellowness, promise of autumn, gold coming through the green. There was an apple tree in the garden and you could see the green fruit buoyant on the leafy boughs. Lawrence had helped her erect a small bird table and there was a linnet, a regular feeder.

In other back gardens you could sense the beginning of activity; not by the men, almost all of them were at work for the half day, but by their wives and children who were drawn into family enterprise on this day. It was one of Rosemary's smaller regrets that Edgar did not enjoy such joint labour. He would dig over the garden and keep it in order—but he did not like the work and made no secret of it. There was an old rose bush, though, which he had attacked the moment they had got the house and now the last large soft pillowy pink blooms were a great daily pleasure. She would go out and gaze on them for minutes on end and then reach out to touch, moved by the silken glaze under her fingers, feeling the perfect texture of tenderness brush all over her.

As he ate he tried to avoid her glance. She reproached herself for the intensity of her determination and could not understand why she felt so pressed. After all there was time: there was a lifetime. She was settled in the house now; as far as she could judge, Edgar was well into his work; Eleanor had taken to the change with the declared indifference which seemed to be her style for everything these days and infuriated her mother—but still, she was patently settled in. And she herself felt that she could once more engage the world, more seriously than she had ever done and more pleasurably, why not?

He finished and smiled at her and she was warmed. How sweet he was, in his waistcoat and his white shirt, sleeves rolled up to the elbow, brown forearms strong and irresistible, something prowling and dark about him which she had always loved and which had come back to him over the past few weeks. Or perhaps she had only just begun to notice it again—she did not know—it was so hard to remember the history of their love which went neither forward nor backward in her mind but now glowed and now faded like a cinder in the wind. He sat by the fire though the day was very mild and smoked a cigarette as he looked into the flames. Quickly she cleared the table and washed up there and then because untidiness in her or in the house enervated him. He could be so irritable that she was quite frightened. She smiled at her own nervousness and when Edgar glanced across at her he saw as so often that intelligent merriness which had once beguiled him but now irritated him by its exclusive and inward quality. He looked away and Rosemary understood that he was annoyed—she could not understand her volatility. She must control herself: why it was so urgent she could not clearly comprehend but she felt the urgency unmistakably and it threatened to topple her balance. She must control it. She had waited for this day for some weeks now. She wanted to make them open to each other again—she was aware of her own recent inaccessibility and now discovered that he too had retreated. She understood this and considered it fully justified; but it had gone on for long enough.

"I wondered if you would show me," she asked, "all those beautiful objects you keep talking about. Stacked away in your warehouse. It sounds like Aladdin's Cave. Will you take me there?"

This sweet and unexceptionable request set off such a fury in Edgar's mind in the moment's pause before his reply; he resented the phrase "beautiful objects" and despised the affectation which would not say "things"; he did not "keep talking about them"; the reference to "Aladdin's Cave" diminished his whole enterprise and put it on a level of unseriousness which

239

failed to appreciate the slog of it all; and yet she spoke of being taken there as on a state visit!

Such an instantaneous swarm of antipathies made him feel ashamed. For there she sat, ignorant of his cheating and innocent of everything but a good and positive desire to be loving: which he glimpsed just in time through the clouds of his irritability and guilt; but he could not please her. "I was thinking of going over Brampton way," he said, for some absurd superstition forced to keep a vestige of accuracy even in the most straightforward and unchallengeable lie; he was thinking of going to see Margaret—but Carlisle was on the road to Brampton and so what he said was not quite without a wafer of truth.

"But it's the carnival," she said. She had not anticipated his leaving the town on carnival day for as his addiction to the town grew so did his loyalty to all its pageantry. And Thurston carnivals were notable local events.

"I thought I might be back in time for the last part of that," he said.

"Please stay."

"What do you want?"

"Nothing—just—*us*."

Again, that simple "us" drove into his feelings like a nail. "What do you mean?"

"We haven't talked for such a long time."

"We never do anything else. I bet we've already talked to each other twice—no ten times as much as my mother and father ever did in their entire lives."

"But that's *nice*, isn't it?" She steadied herself against his vehemence, blaming herself that her retreat from him had doubtless helped to lay the basis for it; but he threatened her as he sat so close, so big, so open in his antagonism. "Isn't it?" she repeated, not to show fear.

"Sometimes I think it is, sometimes not. We seem so full of our-*selves*. What *we* do, what *we* want."

"Yes," Rosemary admitted, sad for a moment at the recognition, "but egotism is an affliction best fed. Then maybe it will be satisfied and turn elsewhere. It would be good to go elsewhere, I agree, to go out to the world; only there can you really forget yourself."

"There you go. We haven't been talking five minutes and

240

we're getting into deep water. Have a heart, Rosemary. Let me digest my breakfast at least."

She laughed but politely tried to do as he implied and switched immediately to chatter about Eleanor. Gossip about those he knew and loved was always the way to gain and keep Edgar's attention. Rosemary made it amusing. "Do you know we first met on this first Saturday in September twelve years ago?"

"Did we?" Edgar glanced up at her and saw clearly the strange young woman standing in that pit, urging on her timid uncle while the frightened animals threatened to crush them both. How gallant she had looked and, even then, this same lilt of delicious fun in her eyes!

"I'd seen you before then," he said but the surliness had gone from him. "Yes," he remembered. "Twelve, is it? Good God. Twelve years. Can you remember that day?"

"I'll never forget it. You were such a man! Bashing those beasts on the nose with your bare fists. I would never dare."

"There's very little would frighten you, Rosemary."

"Oh, I'm easily frightened. I pretend, that's all."

"I don't believe it," he insisted. "What does frighten you?"

"The thought that I could lose you," she said, sadly, "sometimes I have nightmares about that and I don't know what I'll do."

Edgar schooled himself to keep calm. "What makes you think about that?"

"Oh—I don't know . . . you are a lovely man, you know. Other women must see it too. And I know I often bore you."

"Don't say that."

"Why not? It's the truth."

This simple rejoinder decided him. "I'll stay," he said, "we'll go to the carnival. And I'll take you to the warehouse. But first I'll get that garden squared up."

He got up quickly and evaded her opening arms.

She let him go without the claim or the thanks of an embrace and ordered herself not to be so moved at such a small gesture on his part. Yet she shivered as if she had engineered a great achievement.

The morning was strong and fine. She *loved* to watch him work and busied herself in such a way that she could look out at him often. She found the house very easy to run to her own satisfaction but at such times of communion with Edgar she would understand and accept his largely unspoken but felt demand that she should work about the house. He, in the meantime, systematically and swiftly tidied and organized the garden. He was so deft and so strong. Just to watch him with a spade gave her pleasure—the movement was so graceful. Occasionally he would pause and rub at the stiffness in his bad knee but apart from that he seemed to need no rest, never to get out of breath. She still regretted the vegetable patch, though she had said no more about it; in the cottage in the war she had loved it, especially planting lettuce—but Edgar did not believe her when she told him: just as her liking for cleaning windows was dismissed as mere affectation.

She drifted about the house in a state of tender excitement. Sometimes from the front window she would see a child rush past in his carnival costume: a great number young and old dressed up for the grand procession which was led through Thurston by the town band and had been known to be three-quarters of a mile long. And Rosemary would imagine the child to be some foreign spirit released from another world to do mischief in this, like those waifish truants from Olympus; like Cupid. Having fastened on this idea she delighted in it and let it curl around her mind. Now and then she tried to settle to a book, but always she would be drawn back to glimpse Edgar, "her man" as she murmured to herself, made more cheerful by his own labour, visibly making things better in the garden. She felt full of almost helpless love for him as she gazed through the window—standing well back in the shadow so that he should not see her.

Rosemary had read recently that the three great subjects for a life's work were God, Culture and Sex, and this she remembered now, but, at this moment, she believed they were all subsumed in the simple and open love any man and woman could have for each other: in that unity all trinities were possible. Edgar reminded her a little of Levin, her hero in *Anna Karenina,* with his passionate alternation between the land and the mind: of course Edgar had none of Levin's religiosity or his scholarship but *mutatis mutandis* there was a comparison which was not silly; within Edgar's enclosed character existed possibilities which needed only light and air to bear him up to whatever height he cared to command, she thought: and she would release him. As she stood poised, watching him work in the golden morning sun, the sound of his spade only a soft pluck at her ears behind the

242

glass, the very shadow seemed to grow warmer and to feed this resolve and in the soil of the half-dark shadow the seed of her intention burst open: she would try again! She *would* find ways to take them both on this adventure which she was convinced was the highest gift a man could bestow on himself; though where it would lead to and how she would find the way she did not know.

So the morning passed and by the end of it Edgar felt restored. The garden was sorted out and tidy. While engaged on the work he had discovered in himself an appreciation of Rosemary's mood. Something was stirring in her and he wanted to respond to it: his resentment of her seemed intolerably unjust out here in the open air doing something simple and effective. If only he could come to an agreement with himself about the place in the world that Margaret should occupy.

In one way, even in such a short time, Margaret had helped his marriage, he would think. Unsatisfactory as his sexual encounters with Margaret were they provided an alternative to the increasing difficulty of any effective physical relationship with Rosemary. Knowing, though too embarrassed to admit it, that he wanted a lot of sex, Edgar had in Margaret a possibility, not a safety valve but a repository for fantasies otherwise threatening to overwhelm him; for the thickening of lusts in the imagination seemed to grow remorselessly. Whole days would pass when, at the end, he could look back on nothing much else but an ocean of dreamt desires, everything in life became sexual, people, things, thoughts, feelings, and he, the thirsty man, standing on the brink, almost mad enough to drink salt water. Margaret helped him as much as he helped her: and the mutual nature of the compact palliated the unpleasant taste of convenience.

Another way to look at it of course was that he was both avoiding present difficulties and compounding future troubles. For by dividing his attention he was not giving Rosemary the one thing above all which in some profound cave of his mind he knew that she most wanted: his undivided attention, love, will, body and soul. He could not give anyone that. Yet the feeling of failure remained. She stood above him in his mind, beckoning to a magnificent open prospect: he skulked in the valleys, mind locked in sick anger with himself. But there was a way. It was dangerous. He could send some of himself up to her and keep the other part out of it. Give to her what she most loved and valued, the "higher" side of his nature such as it was; and leave behind what in any case she feared or despised, he thought, the lurking ignorant instincts. The two women cut him in two and though such a neat division did not do justice to the temporizings and qualifications and cross-correspondences in the two relationships, yet the polarization was there and he did not deny it.

So he made an uncomfortable but workable alliance with his conscience and prepared for Rosemary's campaign, for as such, momentarily catching sight of her discreetly looking at him deep in the room away from the window, it appeared. Her decisiveness made him feel warm to her. She was no coward. The recklessness of her ambitions was one of her most marvellous qualities: if only he could hang on.

He put away the spade and the fork and saw a gang of youths dressed as cowboys walking self-consciously down the avenue. One of them was playing a ukelele and they were singing "It's a long way to Tipperary". His interest in the carnival suddenly quickened. Margaret would understand.

# Chapter Forty

After the meal she suggested a walk, gravely, and he hugged her as he accepted, so serious was her tone, so intent her expression to elude the look which might annoy him.

She had hoped to take him over towards the Roman Camp and then perhaps along the river through that winding little course which was so sensuous in her mind. But once in the road the pull of the crowd was too much for him—a few hearty greetings—a recognition—a wish not to miss—and they turned down— towards the town teeming with visitors and concentrated on this extraordinary popular jamboree, full of fun and invention.

Rosemary clung to his arm rather tightly. Crowds worried her. Edgar might stride through them like Moses through the Red Sea she thought, knowing all would part before him, but she did not have the same faith. All those people whose faces she knew but whose names were beyond her: all those intimate glances which relied on forgotten conversations in the pub; and the loud conviviality of the scene! The few months away from the pub had drained off her will to succeed in that sort of bustle and now she wanted to cultivate slow friendships, if any, and keep acquaintanceship at arm's length. Edgar enjoyed the numbers: the more the merrier. Rosemary endured it and thought of him in the garden in the morning, giving her mind to that.

Yet her sense of what was amusing and of what was ingenious, above all that part of her mind which responded so fully to any innocent gesture, was soon charmed by this carnival—the brass band, the children dressed up in fantastical costumes—the coarse merriment of the adults, the lorries with their staged displays, the music and the Morris Dancers—fifty girls in white dresses, bells on their handkerchiefs and around their ankles, making such a lovely sound. Rosemary vaguely recognized the woman who trained them—she too was a landlady; Rosemary envied the woman's composure.

Strangely, despite all Edgar's hail-fellow-well-mets, she

thought that he was not quite integral to this scene either. He loved it just as she could sift enjoyment from it in a different way, but she was glad to see that he was as cut off from the dancing centre of the event as she was and not surprised when he led her away up the alley beside The Lion and Lamb to the narrow twisting Church Street, in shadow, damp-feeling, suddenly away from the noise and the excitement which floated over the roof tops enticingly. She preferred it at this distance.

"It was grand, wasn't it?" he said.

"Yes." She welcomed the cool street, feeling that they were young again, she and Edgar, to be dodging the mass and seeking out a private pleasure as lovers do. "People are so clever and so full of fantasy. What do you think happens to that part of them at other times?"

"I don't know." It would never have occurred to him to ask such a question and yet he was instantly intrigued and he could have hugged her for bringing such gifts. "I mean, if anybody even gets out of line by half an inch on other days—if they wear a fancy pair of socks or a fresh tie—everybody makes their life a misery."

"It would be lovely to be gorgeous, wouldn't it?" she said, happily. "I remember when I saw those miniatures of Nicholas Hilliard's, I was reading about Francis Drake and Walter Raleigh and Richard Grenville and everyone seemed so very strong, tough as nuts, and so fierce, such men!—but they must have dressed like those men in Hilliard's paintings, I thought, with hair long and obviously attended to, and embroidered clothes, with ruffs and lace and jewellery, and legs like a Hollywood actress all exposed for show. I like contrasts."

"But you don't like the tinkers," he responded, shyly, pleading his own cause by proxy.

"I don't like *you* being like the tinkers, no."

"Why not?"

"Good gracious, man. If you want to look like a peacock, find a way of your own! That's all."

He enjoyed the reprimand. At this moment, Rosemary could say nothing wrong. The carnival had acted on him as a powerful and normative cleanser and corrective.

"Here we are."

Edgar opened the doors and stood back, proudly Rosemary noticed with a smile, to let her go in first.

246

It was most gloomy and she only just repressed a shiver.

"Is there no light?"

"There's a hurricane lamp. There. I'll light it. But I must say I prefer it in the half-dark like this, myself. It has a better feeling about it, I don't know."

"It reminds me . . ." she turned and smiled at him so lovingly that he felt himself able to relinquish all his deceit: her unstained affection could absolve him, he thought. He would tell her. "Exactly . . . *exactly*, of your stable, the first time you took me there, just after we'd met. The same feeling. O Edgar! You've become the man I fell in love with." To take the weight off her declaration, she lightened the tone of her voice and laughed, gently: but there was no doubting her sincerity.

"Oh—I thought I might have progressed a bit since then, Rosemary."

"No. You've come around to make a circle. That's the only progress for an honest man."

"Don't be so sure I'm honest."

"You are incapable of anything else."

"Don't be too sure," he repeated, grimly.

"But you are! Don't you see! Stick up for your virtues. You have such rare qualities and yet you are so modest about them that you're in danger of letting them die of neglect." She put her hands on his shoulders firmly and gazed sternly at him. "Be what you are—*then* you will be a great man!"

"Don't look at me like that." He pretended to embarrassment to conceal the deeper sense of inadequacy. "And I'll never be a Great Man: what nonsense you talk."

"But I don't." She knew he was flattered and that in some way he was convinced. "You'll never admit it of course with all your Northern stubbornness and pride."

"What d'you think of the stuff?"

"It's *you* I want to talk about. Not the '*stuff*'. *Stuff* indeed!"

"Look at it, Rosemary; I mean, that's what we came for, isn't it?"

"Did we?" Her teasing was so well-intentioned that his irritation at her manner was reprehensible, he knew: yet he felt that he wanted to keep her at arm's length, unhappy that he could think so about this woman who loved him so much. As always when he felt his instincts lock against her, he was confronted with the bewildering observation that she represented everything he most admired.

"Please look around, Rosemary, and take anything you want."

She nodded, suddenly and rather humbly obedient.

Edgar went to the door and looked up and down the deserted street, smoking, listening to the diminishing sound of the crowd and the band, waiting on Rosemary's verdict.

She smiled to herself frequently as she pottered through the immense pile of acquisitions. It all seemed so like Edgar! These splendid great wing armchairs fit for heavyweights; the dusty bronze statues which looked so powerful; the broad-beamed cabinets and cupboards—anything massive and dark. From floor to ceiling the place was crammed; and that, too, was very like him.

Though she tried, she could not give much of her attention to these cumbersome objects with her husband in attendance so near and the day such a rare one of liberty for both of them. But she took some time, for politeness' sake.

"Well?"

"You have so *much!*" she said, finding it difficult to express the enthusiasm she knew he wanted. "How did you manage to get so much in such a short time?"

"You don't like it."

"I think it's very impressive," she said, judiciously.

"I knew you wouldn't like it. Damn!"

"Tastes differ, that's all."

"I wish I'd never bought the bloody stuff."

"Do *you* like it?"

"What do you think? Of course I do."

"Well, nothing else matters! *I* don't matter. No one does except you. I like more delicate things, that's all, and smaller things. These are too imperial for me—they would bully me in some way. But you can tame them; so there you are."

"Nobody else likes them either." He laughed. "I'll stick to horses and cows."

"No!" As before she laid her hands urgently on his shoulder. "This, what you have in here, whatever *I* might think about it, is something very very important to you. It's how you want to express yourself. Don't you see? You *must* keep on with it. This is what makes your work worth all those boring trips you tell me about, when you're away all day and do no business at all."

"Smaller pieces, eh?" he said.

He went into the warehouse and clambered over the main pile to discover a lovely mirror, gilt, oval, with four candle-holders gracefully curling away from it. "How about this?" And even as she reached out to accept it he knew that she did not *really* like it. "O.K." He took it back and laid it on a mahogany dining-table which would unfold to accommodate a dozen sitters. "Let's forget all about it."

"I've never liked mirrors," she said, "but that *is* one of the prettiest I've seen."

"Out! Out!" He bumped her away with simulated fierceness and locked the large doors of the warehouse.

"You're like a gaoler," she said, "or a pirate hiding away his loot."

"Trust you to say something like that. A pirate or a gaoler. Some choice!"

The carnival was far away in the Park, but it could still be heard, the sound ullulating over the deserted town like a benediction.

"Let's go to the Camp," she suggested.

Edgar demurred, sensing the symmetry and not wanting to be gulled so easily. "You mean to take us to the spot we first met twelve years to the day!" he accused her, and she shrugged with a kind of helpless admission of happiness. "I would say that was a proposition, Mrs Crowther, and I'm afraid, as a married man, I must refuse it."

"O Edgar! *You* say then. I put myself entirely in your hands."

They walked along Longmoor and around Forester Falls to Speetgill, a wooded gully, quiet and rather removed, the claw of an ice age, a badger's paradise. Rosemary watched the leaves catch the sun: she could have gazed all day.

Now they were alone. Somewhere was the throbbing beat of a tractor. That was all. The birds dominated the air and Edgar distinguished their songs for her. She sat nun-like in her stillness, wanting to be pupil to him forever, Heloise to his Abelard, she thought—her favourite romance, her favourite hero, keenly remembering the first time he had impressed his knowledge of the natural world on her in that awkward trudge around Mr Bland's farm at Abbeytown. She kept the recollection to herself and restrained herself as he began to whistle in imitation of the birds. She was alertly aware of the fidgety nervousness which lay just under the thin skin of his sociability and preferred to enjoy present pleasures. It was so long since they had been so calmly together—always the pub or Eleanor or some disjointed obstacle of their own making. She wanted to go and dangle her feet in the narrow beck, they were hot from the two or three miles of road they had walked, but she held herself back even from that, afraid it might be too extravagant.

"A blackbird's the one I've always wanted to get right and never could," he said. "I knew a girl once who could do it perfectly—Cowper she was called, her people came from a long way down South. One day I was out, not far from here in Westward woods with the gun, I can't have been much more than a boy, and this blackie started up. It was such a sound—they used to be the prime singers, you know, in the old days—four and twenty blackbirds—it's a beautiful sound, there's no brake on it and nothing piped like linnets or too much like canaries. It's such a hearty sound if you can say that of a bird, better than the lark or the nightingale any time. So this blackie started—so loud and full I was rooted to the ground, I can tell you. It kept on and on and I thought it must be such a prize, this one. If only I could trap it, I thought, and tame it—my grandfather tamed one, it's not so hard. I started to look and walked about but the minute I did that it broke off. Then it would start up again. It seemed to be playing a game with me, as if it could see me and take its cue from me, a blackbird; I tell you, I was a bit worried. I played it crafty and pretended to go away. Then I tip-toed back. But I wasn't sharp enough and it was then I realized something was up because there was a laugh in it, you know what I mean?—I could hear a laugh in the sound and I thought some boy had been having me on.

"I had time to look and it was easy enough. He was bound to be up one of the trees in that patch, I thought—still believing it must be a boy—so it was just a matter of being thorough. But, you know, she almost got away. She must have slid down like a squirrel and if she hadn't stumbled and hurt her ankle I'd never've seen her to this day."

He stopped and Rosemary fought against the jealousy which threatened. He spoke of this girl in such a tone! So tender! How could he be so cruel!

"I suppose she was one of your hundred old girl friends that Thurston seems full of."

"No." He paused, still wrapt in the memory. He had wanted her—perhaps more than anyone before or since, but she had been one who would need much careful courting, demand the right to evasions and teasings and all the wiles of seductive virgins, light-hearted but bound fast by the law of chastity. "She left the district soon after."

"You sound disappointed." She laughed and heard the hollow sound. Why could she not hold her tongue?

"I was," he replied, finding much relief in this minor honesty. "I was."

"I can't whistle for toffee."

"O Rosemary, don't be silly." He was gentle and contrite and yet even here these qualities were clipped at their edge by the shadow of the knowledge his guilt brought him that his "honesty" was mere play: whereas Rosemary's clarity of spirit was unquestionable. Somehow his qualities seemed to bring him down more than his deficiencies: better, according to a morbid logic, to be bad if you were bad than to pretend to a goodness which would always be hypocritical. Stung by the contrast between his wife's purity and his own flawed character, he jumped to his feet. "I want a drink," he said, and without glancing at her he went down to the beck.

"I'm sorry," she called after him, bitterly regretting her lack of poise and yet still perturbed. "I'm sorry."

He appeared not to hear her but went down and knelt beside the clear water to drink. Rosemary took out a cigarette and something about his posture there at the foot of the grassy bank made her smile to herself: he looked a bit like a bull-calf with his bottom stuck up in the air! She drew deeply on the cigarette and girded up her mind: this was only the very beginning of her fight and she was not going to be put off, not even by her own instability.

"Could you bring some to me?" she called out. He looked round, almost balefully. "How am I supposed to do that?"

"Think of a way," she said. "See if you can."

Edgar checked the rage of anger which came out of nowhere, a tidal surge of opposition to this test. Who was she to give tests? But the overwhelming nature of the emotion set up its own reaction and again he chided himself for such antagonism in the face of such love.

Rosemary was thinking—did my mother and father go for

walks together? Did she, too, have to bring him to a way of life that was worth something? did he have to draw her on?—or were they the lucky ones who appear to make no effort? It was no good. It was no help. They might not even have been in love, she suspected, though this was too painful to dwell on. Who had she to turn to in her mind but that Self projected and idealized through reading and through thought? Sarah's existence was no guide: Edgar's mother could be no exemplar; Jean's entire matrix of life was totally foreign to her own. No. Only in attaining her own dream could she make a reality: the alternative was to be depressed or so utterly passive as to deny the plenary ordinances of nature. She would resist that with all her might.

He came towards her, slowly up the hill, his hands cupped before him, as delicately as if it were a chalice he bore, she thought, and in the moment she scrutinized him and found him wonderful. The worst enemy to her intuition was this capacity he had when least aware to melt all her feelings to a viscous of yearning: for he seemed so unattainably solid before her, the dark hair, the strong features, the powerful, steady step, the elegant but large hands, the manliness: his actual presence, the being that he was, excited a kind of envious longing which stirred in the affections and threatened to drown all her plans.

She dipped her head forwards as he held out his hands, in her head the taste of cool water already anticipated. "Oh! What's that? Oh!"

He grinned as she recoiled. "It won't hurt you! We call them cock-leggies."

The tiny fish scurried in the shallow pool between his palms. She examined it. "Put it back," she said, "it must be in a panic."

"They can't think."

"They can feel."

"That puts me in my place."

"I didn't mean to."

"Maybe not."

"But I didn't. No," as he turned away she clutched his arm and the action caused him to lose some of the water.

"Sorry. You—you must see, I am not your enemy, Edgar, truly I am not."

"I must get this fish back in water."

It was an excuse, and both of them knew it, but the excuse by standards mutually subscribed to was unexceptionable. He went down to the beck and threw in the fish and then, to Rosemary's delight, he once more cupped his hands and this time brought her a clear drink.

They came back by another road and as they entered the town were met by people returning from the carnival, those in fancy dress like survivors from some comic battle. There was a replete feeling which came off the people and it made Edgar annoyed that he had missed it all.

"What a lovely afternoon," said Rosemary when they were once more at the table they had sat down to twice already that day. "It was so gentle. And," her generosity was uncalculating, "you looked so solemn when you told the story about the black-bird. Like someone repeating an ancient myth. I shall never forget that." She poured out the tea.

"There's a carnival dance," he announced, abruptly. "We could go. Eleanor could go around to Lawrence's."

She hated local dances: their boisterousness which often resulted in what those attending considered to be tolerable violence—a fist-fight—frightened her.

"If you want to."

"You don't want."

"You know what I think, Edgar, but a carnival dance," she nodded, "that could be fun."

"It's all right. Forget it."

"I *will* go. I *want* to go."

He accepted her concession uneasily.

Eleanor returned full of secret pleasure in a day spent in a spoilt self-indulgence of ice-creams and lemonade which her mother would never have allowed her. She was not unhappy at the suggestion that she spend the night with Sarah and Lawrence.

Confined to the house as he was, Edgar resented everything about the neat, bare, isolated, compact place. Rosemary's wish for him made him unable to abandon her and go for a drink or simply stroll about the town which would be bubbling with life on the streets this warm early autumn evening, he could feel it; none of that seemed allowed to him: and he could understand neither how her constraint was enjoined nor why he complied with it.

When the time came to go down to the dance, he was sorry for his restlessness. It seemed unimportant, this traipsing down to

253

join a crowd. Rosemary's unspoken attitude permeated his own feelings about the matter and the house ceased to be a cell and became a snug lair with the wireless and the books, Eleanor away for the night, the chance to make love uninhibitedly.

"We needn't bother," he said.

"Oh no!" She sidestepped what she saw as his little test. "We're ready now."

"Do you really want to?"

"Now, Edgar. This was your idea but I'm going to love it. *Love* it," she repeated, loudly emphasizing the words, her attitude poised between irony and conviction.

They walked down to the Market Hall and on their way saw other couples of their own age strolling down to the town, the men in dark suits, the women in dresses. It was a cheerful dance, the carnival dance, and even the hard men, the local cowboys, would, usually, respect the geniality of the occasion.

The Hall was decorated with the bunting which had made the main streets of the town look like a rigged ship. Long lines of small flags, union jacks, the crosses of St George and St Andrew and St Patrick, flags of the Empire and flags of the allies, all looping across the hall while the nine-piece band played waltzes. There were children there, one or two, from the estate, still in their white and bells from the Morris dancing; and quite a few of the entrants had not bothered to change out of their costumes. They were dotted about the hall, actors who had strayed into the audience. All about the place was a general gaiety and much of the pleasure, for many, consisted not in the dancing nor in the music but in the many recognitions.

Edgar danced rather awkwardly: Rosemary also was no great shakes but whereas he went cautiously at it and kept well to the edge of the floor, Rosemary soon got swept up in the music and the atmosphere: she abandoned herself in a manner which Edgar found slightly unseemly. Others did not. Rosemary was well enough known to be included in the general good-will and though her aloofness might be held against her yet her presence was evidence to the contrary and she had enough common memories to be part of the rich undercurrent which charged the place.

It was a good dance. Edgar partnered one or two others; it would have been churlish and remarked on if he had stayed with his wife all evening; and when he saw Rosemary dancing with someone else, he felt a great spurt of love and pride.

Everyone but a few of the drunkest stood respectably still for the playing of the National Anthem. Some even sang the words.

It was still warm. There was a smell of the sea in the air and they strolled back calmly. Rosemary wanted no words and leaned her head on his shoulder as they walked, a habit he liked for she fitted there very well and he knew she adored his arm about her waist.

Taken all in all, he thought, it had been a good day. The itch to see Margaret had come on him more than once but he was glad he had managed to resist it and felt all the stronger for that: a blind loathing of his house had filled his gorge—God knew why —but that too had passed. His marriage was worth the effort she demanded, he was sure of it and in the certainty felt a great tenderness for his wife and himself. A challenge was being thrown down, that much he could divine. He would pick it up.

"One last look," she said when they had reached their house and she breathed in the night deeply, closing her eyes, taking into her imagination the stars, the warm wind, the smell of the sea, the indescribable certainty given her by Edgar's steadying arm around her waist against which she could lean forever, she thought; all this and the pleasant events of the day swirled slowly about her mind, turned in their course and rolled over the doubts and uncertainties until her entire body was suffused with that moment's progress of the night. She opened her eyes and looked at him and saw a dark, serious loving face which leaned down to kiss her gently on the lips. It was complete.

# Chapter Forty-One

Yet, for about the next two years they fought, locked together as animals and insects are locked together in love that you could easily mistake for the deadliest hatred. Neither was later able to trace a clear line through this time nor to describe it satisfactorily. Rosemary was convinced, whatever the pain, that it was worth the struggle and often enough she delighted in it for she saw new things and learned from it. Edgar did not enjoy the battle, he did not delight in the effort, he resented it and obstructed Rosemary's best wishes for him, only a sort of bone-pride in his own strength made him go on.

Rosemary made every action and thought accountable. Edgar squirmed. His life fed on the margins in the twilight between definite decisions and conclusions. Hers now could only be nourished by light and more light. She had come to a decision about the whole of life, what it was worth and what it demanded, and this decision she was going to implement, using the instruments of truth and patience. In the edition of La Fontaine which had been one of her mother's earlier gifts she had underlined the phrase "*Patience et longueur de temps vaut mieux que force et courage.*" She did not know where she was going although there was unquestionably a vision, a sense of perfection which drew her on.

Perhaps it came from her engagement with Edgar's inaccessible secret. He locked up Margaret in his conscience and lied and lied again though it was obvious to him that Rosemary *knew*. He denied her. But on the infallible beam of her truthfulness she picked up the disturbance. She gave him numerous opportunities to confess. I wouldn't mind you having a mistress, she would say, provided you told me about it. Men have these desires and you're a man: in France everybody goes to the brothel. But a deeply searing prohibition would hold him back. Physical infidelity is unimportant, she would say, who cares who sleeps with whom? These appendages have a right to lives of their own, arms and

256

legs to exercise, lungs to air, bellies to food, tongues to salt and sugar, and cocks to gratification. The occasional vulgarism almost caught him (she knew he liked her to be vulgar in private) but he braced himself against the fury of her searching and denied all implication. The strain it brought added to his own fiercening perplexity and restlessness.

She was baffled. The certainty of her own true knowledge was so clear and unambiguous; the pain alone proved its validity. He was betraying her, this husband; and it was important that he didn't get mixed up in deceits or guilt. She knew that in such a nature as Edgar's, shame could corrode all other affections and she was afraid of that, for just as he was her best friend so he could be her worst enemy. Yet he denied the implied charge. She risked a great deal to prise a confession out of him but he would not yield and at times she considered that she might be mistaken. But that would lead to madness.

In her jealousy for his complete attention she considered she might be discovering deceit in obstinacy: and she was aware that Edgar needed his stubborn resistance because so much of his life depended on it. To wear that away would be dangerous. Perhaps, she thought, the resistance she felt was the resistance of a man who was somewhat shocked by what she was saying and would not allow himself to admit the possibility because such an admission would impair his moral universe too grievously. He was a good man, Edgar, she kept reminding herself, a nice man, a kind man. Of course he dug in his heels—what else could she expect from such a man when confronted by such wild surmises on the nature of infidelity and French brothels? Thurston was light-years away from that. Here she was in no contact with the ease of the Mediterranean; harems were merely comical, mistresses wicked and dangerous; prostitutes unacknowledged. This community came from those Nordic clusters which had cabined themselves against the bitterness of nature by strict laws and masculine skills. Her urgings were foreign to him. That was it. Her foreignness came out in this anxiety and there was the nub of the matter: it was the foreignness which he resisted, the incomprehensible moral laxity which she presented as enlightenment, this was what troubled him. At times she would be satisfied with this line of reasoning. She could have hugged him.

She forced herself to believe his word and not her own feelings. He was true to her. But if something was not wrong with *him*, then it must be in *her*, the fault, the flaw; slowly she turned her forces onto herself, seeking the truth within.

Under the glare of her mind, Edgar almost cracked on many occasions. They would be sitting opposite each other in that front room, listening to the wireless or, more usually, himself doing some bookwork while she read, and then there would come on him, like the hand of God on the nape of his neck, a tremendous desire to shout out his crime. His brain would feel squeezed by the force of the wish but he never did speak out and later he thought that an even greater power within, his stubbornness which had prevented him, had been the healing power. For, again in retrospect (at the time everything was inchoate) he was convinced that the knowledge she sought would destroy her. That conviction came in the light of future actions which would have been otherwise had he done as she willed, however, and so there was no certainty and was his silence brave or cowardly? That tormented him.

The relationship with Margaret was under pressure. She was perfectly willing to give it all up, with regrets and sadness, but without causing or feeling much pain. This very looseness took the danger out of the connection as far as Edgar was concerned. He did not feel that there was a commitment worth the deep worry which the earnestness of Rosemary's enquiry insisted on.

He was finding it hard going in business, which did not help. It was clear now that he had come out of the pub and into the dealing business at precisely the wrong moment. Subsidies in farming were changing the character of that industry. It was rapidly becoming more organized, more efficient, more centralized, more accounted for, more mechanized, less and less fertile to the invasions of the local middlemen. As for his other main hope, the antique trade, that period at the beginning of the fifties was perhaps as bad as any time ever for someone who operated at Edgar's low financial level. The whole feeling of the working classes and the lower middle classes was to throw off the past and the great furnishings of Victoriana littered the attics and choked the salerooms and fed the fires even as the Empire they had dressed and matched fell away from the once-conquering island. Getting was easy; selling brought bare pickings to an independent entrepreneur, short commons.

Only by the most strenuous efforts could he make a living at all. But he had finally been caught by ambition or maybe by an inflated desire for security and he was determined to make more than a bare living. For the first time in his life he doubted his ability to cope with the future. It appeared a tremendous place where once it had seemed a snug come-uppance to the present. To subdue his fears he had to shore himself up and he found that he worked and schemed obsessionally. He was despairingly restless.

While admiring the plans, indeed lavishing on them compliments and insights far beyond Edgar's fairly modest expectations, Rosemary fundamentally considered him to be shallow, he thought, and nothing could dislodge that thought—neither praise nor proof. But there was an enormous amount to relish in her appreciation: it was an aspect of her character quite foreign to his background and past.

Most confusing of all, he admired her more and more. He did not have her single-mindedness, her fidelity, her total lack of fear for the world's opinion, her love of the strain essential in any human achievement. She was his superior in every way that mattered.

When he came back from a job she would be waiting for him. Her eyes which could be so brimful of love they looked unsullied by life, would fix him with an affectionate interrogative glance which contained most profoundly serious and fierce demands. What was his life worth, she seemed to ask. What was it for? What did it mean? What was its good? What was its vision? Where was its "credo"? Where was its soul? And to brazen out even the return of such a blaze of questions needed every inch of his nerve. Those eyes which seemed to come out of the lair like the eyes of the Tiger in the poem which Eleanor had once chanted to herself for days on end: "Tiger, Tiger Burning Bright." There seemed no alternative but to compete or to go under for in acceptance of her terms was the bottomless pit of her ideal.

Irritability became necessary armour: hateful because of its constriction, detestable because of the hurt it inflicted on both of them as she hurled her being against his, but he could not be without it and weeks on end seemed to drag by in this ignoble, dreary, dispirited and banal state of irritability.

He fought back by calling out all his qualities and there were times and days in this period when all seemed worth it, when they seemed to reach a new level of communion, when the world was packed with pleasures and delights. Such days. A walk: an evening reading: a visit to another part of the county: one brief rambling holiday in Yorkshire to the Abbeys of Riveaulx and Fountains. Never such days.

Yet even there was the trembling of fear and Edgar could not find its source. He had been afraid before in his life, and usually discovered why and dealt with it. But now the fear was of an entirely different kind and proportion. It was as if life itself were being carried perilously and might slip and be lost: the fear was the loss of balance.

Rosemary began to play a great deal of music to herself: she took up painting again, she did not resume her work at the library and Edgar neither pressed nor encouraged her to do so. Her chief joy was Berlioz and, increasingly, books to do with descriptions of the mind, whether popular philosophy or popular psychology.

Berlioz enthralled her. She had bought a gramophone at the church jumble sale during the war and she managed to acquire his *Symphonie Fantastique* and extracts from his *Requiem* which she played over and over again. She also rooted out a biography and was ravished by the romantic life, the tempestuous and unfulfilled loves, the passion for the beauty of Shakespeare. Berlioz became a great comfort. Edgar at first had felt his hackles rise: some curious false routing of his education had led him to identify classical music with the attitude of effortless dominance practised by those set up to rule over him and in detesting "their" music he could hit back, in an easy way but in a satisfying one. She sensed this and winkled it out of him and undid the harm. Nevertheless he could never succumb to it as he could to local songs or popular songs or, most of all, the marches played by the town's silver band. He was grateful though for her re-education and listened to the enormous sounds with respect. When she listened to music she was as alive as a newly caught fish struggling between finger and thumb.

He had always been a little vain—and it had been so lightly carried that it was a part of his character that offended no one; but now vanity swelled up and he began to think himself very handsome as Rosemary constantly told him he was. Perhaps the devotion, in their very different ways, of two such interesting women worked to loosen and bring forward the feminine part of his character. It was unusual to see it admitted to in a man, at that time and place, when "manliness" was so much prized; his dandyism sat on him like a late blossom; people were made rather uncomfortable by it, there was something rather silly about it, they thought.

His manners softened; he lost weight, he felt lighter and more poised: his accent lost its roughness; his opinion, which had always been quick and harsh, became more thoughtful, less adamant, more self-conscious.

He liked this new malleable self though he feared the danger which might come from its softness.

And all the time he lied and sweated with the effort. He would do anything to stop lying, he thought, except, by some hopeless perversity or divination about his survival, cancel out the cause of it. In his anger with himself he hit out savagely at Rosemary, confronting her with her past, with Wilfred of course, but even with those two squalid local affairs she had so honestly told him about. He had felt flattered by her truthfulness then. Now he used it against her.

Closer and closer together they came, tighter and tighter did their interdependence draw them. Such intense mutual absorption soon laid siege to the innermost citadels of their personalities. Once begun, Rosemary had to find out more and more about herself; to follow up every attitude and even reflex for its possible value as a clue to the unlocking of some part of herself which might be blocking a view of life unseen or clouding some aspect of the world which had to be seen clearly. If Edgar was *not* lying, then there was something wrong with *her* and she must find it. She forced Edgar back on himself, assuming that he too wanted to get to the root of their pain—for surely he must want that! On and on she would innocently go until rage would suddenly take possession of him like a venomous swarm of hornets loosed inside his skull clustered pendulously about the brain, stinging, jabbing, poison.

She went into her past and after scrutinizing her memories eventually concluded that her mother and father had hated each other; and into his past too, discovering much the same, calling him to give her evidence. The more he protested the more she smiled and talked on and though his mind screamed out in darkness at the sacrilege being done his mother he was forced to acquiesce in her analysis because she could tie him in knots.

It was after the weeks involving the unpicking of the "childish" love for his mother that he decided to call off his relationship with Margaret entirely and finally and without equivocation. There was a calm tense farewell one evening and he stepped out of the red velvet flat feeling that he had been granted his liberty and a free pardon.

And that night was one of the good times with Rosemary; he was absolved and she found a worthy lover.

But this uncovering of the past and more especially this admission of hatreds was the open invitation to the devil: who came to both of them with promises of ease. For if they could unearth those hatreds, those repressions and omissions then, it seemed to Rosemary, and only then, could they go forward. She was reading about the Renaissance in Italy at the time and was much impressed by the insistence of the old historians that in order to progress, the men of that time had to go back to their past, back to Greece before they could go on to Florence. Like all auto-didacts, she applied this new knowledge immediately to herself, transplanting it into a personal context without great difficulty. Once they had cleared up the past and in a sense re-built it for themselves, then the future would be clearly seen and could be firmly challenged.

It was a terrible struggle, though, for to admit what she wanted he had to think badly of what he was: and he feared that he might not be able to continue to function in the world if he undermined himself. This was one of the drives towards his changeableness, as if to defeat the enemy within.

But the saddest thing of all about this backward quest was that it took them farther apart, for while she was left flailing for air in the infancy of her terrors and departures and uprootings and treachery, he went back to a land which, however bestial, was warmly solid and present, full of the smells of the market and his father working with cattle; however much he unearthed of conflict and brutality, the past was solidly linked with what he inhabited now and his mother lived on to prove the tenacity of it.

She would not give up though, not even when she hurt herself badly in the clashes with Edgar which were becoming so frequent and so malignant.

They had begun to accuse each other. He accused her of leading such a sheltered and protected life that all her judgments were by that definition suspect: she did not know what work was, he said, she did not know what the world was like, all she'd done

262

was let herself be holed up among a lot of books in a library where everybody was on their best behaviour, a sort of butler, fetching and carrying as everyone desired, contending with neither struggle nor strain. She accused him of marrying her under false colours and trying to break her spirit by finding precisely the sort of world which would most upset her: but she had not let the pub upset her and so now he was leading a life which meant he could leave her at any hour of the day and return at any other hour unimpeachable—an impossible system on which to base any sort of domestic economy and yet she managed in ways he did not even notice. He was mean with the housekeeping and yet they ate well because she scrimped and because Lawrence would lend a hand and his mother if she did nothing else could at least see their plight in this quarter and was helpful with the welcome gift of a few surplus eggs or part of a chicken. Otherwise they would be eating scraps. Furthermore he was a coward. He had agreed to try this adventure with her but now he avoided all opportunities for talking, he beat her arguments down with bullying shouts, he ignored the fact that she wanted to work things out properly and needed a certain amount of leisure. He was unfair to her. He wanted her unusualness and yet he would not pay the very modest price in understanding. That, he would reply, was typical! To sit and talk about your own "unusualness"! She was no more unusual than any other woman in the town, not one of whom would subject him to this terrible grilling about what he did. She never asked him where he had been, she claimed, and he of course could have been anywhere and with anyone but she never once asked.

Perhaps it was her fidelity which was most intolerable to him; that and all her other qualities which now seemed to combine in his mind to make an almighty rack on which he was being pulled limb from limb.

Sometimes Rosemary would spend the whole day in a chair looking out of the window, scarcely moving, sore all over her nerves and her feelings from these terrible encounters which grew in intensity despite the regular relapses into forgiveness. She developed asthma and was put on a powerful course of pills. And for this illness, too, she could say, he blamed her despite his natural concern: she could see that under his kindly phrased questions and meekly repeated declarations of help there was resentment that he should be lumbered with a sick wife. This realization, the truth of which she did not question, added the wrong sort of urgency to her wish to improve her health and the asthma grew worse and, it appeared, another intractable element. If only he could see how much more whole he could be if he would face the wholeness in himself, she thought, face the bad and look at it, face the good and look at that, face the tenderness, face the violence: a man must not be a mole or an ostrich, she said, he had to seek for air and light and once finding it he had to take advantage of it and grow. Of course it was painful!

Edgar took to pain badly and resentfully. Whereas pain was part of life for Rosemary, to Edgar it was part of death; he avoided or ejected it as fast as possible. Her belief was that to absorb it was to grow stronger; pain was Edgar's enemy and though he let it in for the sake of her whom he loved, yet it was with the greatest possible apprehension.

Rosemary was stunned by what she had uncovered and unleashed in herself—such desolation and hurt—but her faith in why she had begun did not waver. Anyway, she would laugh to herself, there was no way to retreat; once Pandora's box had been opened there were no neat solutions.

Yes, sometimes she would laugh quietly as she sat alone in that little domestic fortress overlooking the town. Edgar begged her to move out and go into the middle of the town, to Church Street in a place near his warehouse, the street which snaked through the heart of Thurston and poked its alleyways into several covert archway exits: but she would not budge. She felt her position strong where she was and the easy communality of the town did not appeal to her at all. She would smile to herself, not quite knowing why but sensing that in some way or other she was flaunting her power, she was flying close to the sun, she was in uncharted waters. She wanted to be where she did not know. She wanted to feel strangeness like the feeling she had when in childhood Lawrence read her a poem or story in which the words evoked vast crystal caverns and underworlds with sapphires for stalagmites and magical figures on the mirror—frozen lakes: she wanted to feel her own being in an utterly singular conjunction with the world it found.

The music of Berlioz on some days would totally infuse her mind and she would close her eyes and see the stars themselves orchestrated and feel a cold thrill of meaning though there was nothing to grasp at; no stigmata to show to doubting Edgar.

It was Eleanor who drew the matter to a head about midway through the second year when Rosemary was labouring under asthma and Edgar was wearing himself to the bone both doing his usual jobs and also building with his own hands a house on his land: for that, he had decided, was where the money was. But the energy he put into it was cruel on himself and tore at him, ripping out and using up reserves that could have lasted part of a lifetime. He would accept help from no one in no way. If he came on something which he could not do he would go down to the council estate they were beginning to erect on the west side of the town and get himself a few days' casual labouring work until he found out how to do it.

Eleanor was finally no longer able to evade the effects of what had become a raging almost ceaseless quarrel, with Rosemary forever teasing Edgar into change and Edgar defending himself and returning the injury by heavy, often unfair and powerful rejoinders which thudded into his wife's unprotected mind. The girl saw her mother becoming more and more ill and at the same time increasingly happy, as if a terrible inner fire both consumed her and consummated some profound desire; she saw her father becoming thinner, more erratic, altogether more "nervous" and while she was attracted to this, he had ceased to be entirely her "daddy". She was a resilient child with the great security of a bounded town and Sarah and Lawrence to support her, but as puberty approached Sarah and Lawrence were of no use. They were so old now and so old-fashioned: Sarah with her unearthly habits of early rising and home baking and trudging down to the town for the dawn communion in the middle of the week: Lawrence with his clocks which seemed to spawn more parts than it would ever be possible to assemble and his notes which lay about in cardboard boxes never finally to be sorted and shaped to those books he had reserved for his retirement. The girl really loved the old pair and they were lucky in her appreciation of their ways for she delighted in the unique atmosphere which met her the moment she walked into that ancient silence, more than commonly silent despite the clocks, something sealed and accomplished in the small rooms. But as the restlessness of her body warned her of change and the end of childhood, she turned to her mother and her father and found herself in the middle of a battlefield.

At first she tried to ignore it as she had done so far: but soon it became impossible for her not to take sides and she swung, increasingly violently, from defending her mother to defending her father, from attacking one to attacking the other, to attacking both, to accepting both, to defending both. Her father's physical changes, with which it seemed he tried to counter his wife's attempts to pin him down and examine him and operate on him, baffled the daughter. Her mother's relentless pursuit of her father's reasons and motives began to spill over and she felt that she too was being diagnosed.

She contracted glandular fever and the illness dragged on. A period of physical growth coincided with the long convalescence and she emerged after about three months a different person, she thought, feeling uncomfortable in her body, taller, scraggy, awkward, listless and, for the first time in her life, horribly shy. When she returned to school she would break into tears at any harsh words; she played truant; she refused to go in the mornings.

Rosemary raged at Edgar who, she said, was culpably unable to control his temper in public, that is to say between the three of them; such a lack of control was contemptible, she charged him, childish, selfish, not like a man but then he was no man. If only he returned, she had shown the normal responses of a normal mother and been able to nurse the child in a normal way instead of pumping her full of ideas and neglecting the normal comforts such as cuddling and cossetting which all normal mothers gave to their normal children, then perhaps their child would not be drifting around in such torment. No! Rosemary would not have that. There was something fundamentally oppressive and bullish about him which trampled on feelings, bellowed down the murmurs of distinction and took a brute male pleasure in treading all over anything which moved.

Even their qualities contributed to make the quarrel grow: Rosemary's gaiety now lashed Edgar's mind like scorn; his energetic bursts of activity now seemed to her ludicrously unnecessary and quite disproportionate to the result. If only he would calm down, accept a more moderate external life, and look at the real riches he had in his own mind and in their joint possibilities.

Eleanor did not improve in this turbulence and Edgar suggested that she change school. She was at present at the girls' grammar school, but just on the edge of the town was a small Quaker school, largely a boarding school. Edgar knew some of the

teachers there. He had once spent some time in the place re-
decorating the classrooms, and he had been impressed by the
quiet, kindly air of the school. It was set in its own grounds, a
pleasant country house well converted, boys and girls boarded
there, Eleanor could stay overnight during the week or she could
be a day-girl, just as she wished. It would cost money but not
much and anyway that was the sort of challenge which appealed
to him at the moment: somehow or other he would get it. A
change would do her good. He could see her there in the peaceful
countryside, farmland all around, among the calm Quakers: he
had an overwhelming regard for her safety and felt it could be
secured there. When he confided the scheme to Rosemary it was
with all the trepidation of one who fears that a most precious
request will be rejected.

It was. Rosemary saw no reason at all to move Eleanor from
one school to another and every reason against it. At least she had
friends where she was: the teachers knew her and sympathized; it
would as likely as not increase her vulnerability to be dumped in
a different place and anyway she objected to public schools on
principle: most of all, though, it made no difference where you
were, Rosemary said, you carried your problems with you and
you had to fight them through.

Edgar was so full of sick anger at having to engage in such an
argument at all that he scarcely trusted himself to reply. Could
she not, for once, let something pass? Let a hunch be given air?
Had everything to be raked over this so-called reason which often
missed the main point? She could not imagine, of course, the
certainty of his feelings when he had passed by the school—
"seen" Eleanor there. Could she have felt the absolute
"rightness" of that image, then she would not be so stupidly
antagonistic. It was a fragile image but he was certain it was right.
Easy to destroy; and impossible to explain in the only way she
tolerated explanations—in rational dialectic. She should have
taken his suggestions on trust.

Rosemary would not budge and soon Eleanor cried to stay
where she was. So he could not even be of use to his own
daughter! Was that, too, part of the retribution come from his
deceit or was it the inevitable consequence of the unleashed confrontation between Rosemary and himself?

Pitilessly he began to find fault with her, and always he would
point it out. The safety barrier of silence was down. There was

nothing "natural" about her and nothing tidy. She dressed carelessly to the point of slovenliness which he hated and feared, reminders of the desperate and abject condition of some of his friends' mothers when he was a boy. Edgar pestered her about this and she took it to heart but basically she did not care how she looked and thought his concern a superficial and neurotic one which described *his* state of mind rather than her own. She told him so. Such back-firing logic, so easy for her to understand, made him writhe. If what he said about her was really about himself, and if, as she also pointed out, what he hated in others was what he found most disgusting in himself—then where was he, for God's sake? Was he not allowed to trust his own words or his own acts? Dimly he saw the light but it was soon extinguished by fear. They began to lose respect for the other's separate identity.

Though he had the freedom of the area and could range over it from the sea to the Scottish Borders, west to the Pennines and south into the Lakes, always returning to the maze of villages and settlements on the Solway plain and to Thurston, its natural centre; though he could choose his hours and to some extent his occupation, yet she held him tight in that sedate box he so detested on a rope as tough as an umbilical cord. He needed a mother, she said, all men looked for mothers in their wives: and she was not prepared to be his mother. Nor would she be his mistress.

His head ached with the confusions.

Sensing that her time was running out, Rosemary threw everything she had into convincing him that there was a better way, that exploration of all the possibilities of life through your own nature was the noblest imposition you could lay on yourself, that to seek out beauty was the only road to grace. She hounded him with what she believed were self-evident truths and hammered at what she saw, accurately enough as far as it went, as his obduracy which resulted from the silt of an ignorant and violent childhood and a vainglorious youth. What she promised him was something of the highest worth: to really care for life and to take it seriously.

To his credit—and she was generous with praise—he tried. He wanted to be different, that was certain. In the rage of argument which had lasted about two years now he had come to abhor the person he saw.

Though no blood flowed it was a barbaric contest, each side

adopting a thousand stratagems and disguises, locked in equal struggle, taking measures which had they been transferred onto the physical plane would have covered them in blood. They acted as if it were less important and less dangerous, an emotional and mental and spiritual duel, than any purely physical confrontation. That the body would be like the sea and cover up these wrecks. They ceased to acknowledge each other's separateness, and from then on they were at risk.

As the contest went on and revealed more and more levels of disagreement and darkness, a strange and weird twist of events occurred. They began to swop characteristics without knowing it and suddenly Rosemary would find herself shouting like an old farmer at Edgar and he would discover himself wilting before her, bereft of response. Or he would see that what she needed most of all was mothering and look out for her, tenderly, remembering the good days in his own childhood, and she would grow suddenly tractable to his will. Then there would be the collapse when all he most feared in his own nightmares was acted out before him by his wife who would assail him with ultimate questions of meaning and purpose and intent until he felt his brain turn into a single throb of terror. What truth could salve such fear?

Could the deceit he had practised have brought on all this? He never ceased to believe it might have done and so in a score of ways he would find his position undermined. But in retrospect once more he had to see that if it was not one secret it would have been another. What she most wanted was what was unattainable and there was no stopping her attempt.

The fiercer it grew the more full of lust he became and the cruder the images of satisfaction grew.

There had been times in his life when to live was to make love but even in the most hectic circumstances there had been some boundary to his desire. Now there seemed none. In his head he experienced almost every woman he saw. His appetite roared within him. He had never been as wild and the force of it appeared insatiable and slightly insane. He was after all, he would tell himself, a husband, a father, a decent enough citizen, a businessman of sorts, a domesticated man of sorts—rarely out at the pub now, no hobbies but other work. Yet inside his skull were unimaginable schemes and longings which unnerved him. What sort of man had he become to be saturated in such filth?

Yes, it was filth. He was sure of that. Everything in his education and in his personal construing of that education told him firmly that what he was thinking about was obscene. But he was obsessed and found pleasure there; pleasure.

Rosemary's body gave him little pleasure. Increasingly he felt that to make love to her at all was to abuse her. She did not make love with him but seemed to suffer him to take his pleasure. She did not like to be touched, indeed ridiculed his love of stroking her and told him that men, real men, had no need of that. Real men, she said, did it all with their penis. He knew he gave her little satisfaction and bitterly regretted this failure. And as their quarrel reached the very centre of their being he felt more and more that he was a hulk on her: that he straddled her like an unwanted lump of meat. That the whole thing was disgusting.

But he was absolutely determined not to be again unfaithful. The longings grew so powerful however that to contain them was beyond his powers and it was his wife he turned to, as he had to, for some ease. He could excuse himself by saying that he sought to awaken in her once again the easy common and interlocking desire which had originally sparked off their mutual attraction— there was some truth in this. He desperately needed the marriage to succeed because he saw no alternative. But the truth was more selfish and his experience with Rosemary had certainly taught him how to plumb that depth most speedily. The truth was in his terrible, unbearable need.

He was brutal and she allowed him to be, he hurt her and she allowed him to, meeting his sexual assault with a kind of fearful contempt which whipped him on to greater and greater desperation. According to all he had imbibed about sex (for he had been taught nothing; the custom at that time was to leave the young in total ignorance, often bewilder them by false and facile information, and outwardly affix to the sexual act a dangerous taboo) what he was doing was so very wrong that it was worse than sinful, almost criminal: and though Rosemary would convulse and quiver in some spasm of fulfilment, she too, he knew, regarded what he was doing as devilish and a sense of evil arose from their two bodies as strong as the smell of sweat.

Yet though he was heart-sick of himself and dreaded the mornings when he would have to look his wife in the face, he could only stop altogether: and then recommence.

As she had tried to drive through his mind to a light which she believed was there, so, perhaps, he tried to drive through her body to a peace which he hoped could be found. But the violence of the act, the pain it brought her, checked him, made him unsure of any end to be got by such means; and he was in total darkness.

Now all hell broke loose.

He imagined her dead. He imagined himself dead. He imagined his daughter dead. He saw himself as the perpetrator of all three crimes. He wanted them dead. The distance between mild disagreement and almost mad feelings of bloody revenge shortened daily and he felt he walked in fear of all their lives. There was destruction all about. He had dreams of detonating the home in which they lived so that every brick would explode into its least particle. He was suddenly struck with lurid and vivid pictures of maiming and butchery, happening to him, happening to others. There was an incubus on his brain now and it could not be torn out.

Rosemary knew his fears and waited, for she saw this as the final stage of their battle. She was very tired. She believed that insofar as anyone could have taken Edgar through his worst fears and shown him the possibilities in himself, she had attempted it. She saw herself as having teased him down from a safe molehill and gone with him through the valley of the shadow of death to where there would be a great height to be scaled. To this they would devote the remainder of their lives but now she must rest.

He would not let her rest of course but she knew (as she put it to herself) that at the end of the valley was the lair of the greatest dragon and now Edgar was engaging this beast and must slay it. It was the image of all he most feared and hated in himself, she saw that. She would sleep so that she could find nourishment to be ready for him when he came through. She was so tired: so white-faced; gaunt from the asthma and taking far too many pills; she was worried about Eleanor and often afraid that Edgar might actually break down and attack them all as he had already, twice, attacked the furniture in the place she loved so. But all would pass, she was sure: in some untouchable part of her being she was sure. He had a pureness which would not be denied and her call had always and solely been to that. She had read somewhere in Dostoevsky and noted it in her mind that when a man is preparing himself for a crime he first degrades himself spiritually: and this she believed to be exactly half true: for when a man degraded himself, as Edgar was doing, he could also be preparing himself for rebirth into a new life. Life was a birth and a re-birth. That was her trust. Meanwhile she endured and tried to pull back and leave him alone: but the new habits had bitten hard and even in loving moments she would find herself at cross-purposes with her real intent. "I love you, you fool," she would say, "you must understand that. Don't you see? Horrible man. Rely on that." But the teasing had lost all its fun and she could see that abuse seemed to him to be real: but she was too tired to change.

Edgar was now in a crisis. He had betrayed everything he had been bred to obey and now, in retribution, he knew the furies had been let into his mind. He would wake up often through the night and listen to the dull silence which surrounded the house, longing for the sounds of the country he had once woken to or the exciting though occasional sounds in the centre of the town which had glamorous interest still.

What a waste, what a waste, what a terrible waste. Next to him a marvellous woman who had racked herself to such a pitch that it threatened to make her an invalid. Why? In the next bedroom, the occasional sobs of a daughter who should have been sleeping happily, deeply, with her dreams tinted by wicked innocence and not drenched in the horror she reported most mornings. And himself; nothing to be said.

And tomorrow they would get up and something or other would begin again the quarrelling, whatever the incident it would not matter: the new skin of night would be ripped off and once again the sores would be seen. It had become a ritual and was in need of a sacrifice. Round and round they trailed and he no longer knew why.

Inside him, in his last redoubt, just out of reach of the infestation which ravaged the rest of his being, was that safe of self which he had never surrendered: where he kept the secret of Margaret; where he kept his escape from this life: where *he* was. Now even that was threatened. He could feel it. The ritual. The sacrifice. There was a terrible stillness about the world which seemed to be emptying all about him; he imagined a vacuum growing larger and larger with accelerating forces: and he feared he would soon scream without ceasing.

# V. A DEATH

# Chapter Forty-Two

All he wanted now was to be away from her. He was ashamed of his thoughts, horribly perturbed and afraid of what he might do. She held him in a vice.

Though he roamed about the Border counties more widely than ever, he was not free: there was an endless whirlpool in his mind which drew every sensation back to its focus in the dauntless, clasping mind of Rosemary.

It was on one of these far travels that he first encountered Jessie. He had gone across into the northernmost part of Northumberland, an area which, at this mid-century time, could claim to be as isolated and singular as any in the island; huge feudal estates of barren land patched with small independent tenacious hill farms supported on the backs of rural labourers who were as far from their twentieth-century inheritance as customary usage, total lack of alternative employment, and stubborn self-regard could make them.

From such a family came Jessie Kirk: her brothers and sisters had been scaled out over the countryside as fertilizer is scaled out over a field. She was not the youngest but it was she who had been kept at home by her father to look after "that side of it": her mother had died in giving birth to her tenth child when Jessie was five years old. It was this last-born, the youngest of all daughters, who was the pet lamb and it was her the father was waiting for; fattening her up with sweetest regard until she should be of age to look after him. At this fast-approaching time Jessie would be sent out to some farm to be hired as a help to the farmer's wife. Though the days of girls hired to do labouring in the fields had almost gone, plenty still went as rough servants to the wives of the hill farmers who prided themselves on such a distinction and convenience.

Her father knew about horses: he laboured now for a small farm but had once been a groom on the biggest estate in the district and was inclined to deal in a small way. Edgar found him useful and Mr Kirk—Edgar always used this polite address—Mr Kirk waited his chance to make a penny out of this "cocky young hawker" as he privately referred to him.

What Edgar sensed in Jessie was something entirely sympathetic to his nature, but shy, shy in the dark of the gloomy room, somehow screened from him; a shape only, he first remembered, and the whiteness of her inner arm he saw as she laid out bread and cakes between the two men on the table: such tender white flesh, he wanted to nuzzle it: and it was that, perhaps, which most strongly remained in his mind over the next two weeks. For much sooner than usual he returned to this place and took notice of the girl more carefully: but she was tired that day and her weariness rebuffed him.

Mr Kirk never asked about his personal life and Edgar did not say anything about his marriage. Moreover, the finger on which he should have worn his wedding ring had been damaged at the knuckle: he had chipped it with a chisel while working at his house and the carelessly attended wound had left a permanent lump there. The ring had had to be cut off. Fearfully, Rosemary had marked the circumstance down in her symbolic calendar. From the first Jessie thought he was free.

The distance between the next few visits lessened and even the dour, unhappy, work-twisted Mr Kirk was forced to conceive that it might be something other than the horses that brought the man around so frequently. But he did not like dealers and sent Jessie away to work. The youngest daughter was ready enough to run the place. So on his fifth visit, Edgar found her gone.

"It'll be Jessie you'll be looking for," said Mr Kirk, with just a glint of humour, after their customary tea this time served by the youngest daughter who cooed over her father like a dove.

"Yes. Yes, I was wondering where she'd gone."

"Women want nothing with hawker-men," the Calvinist labourer said. "She's where she has a good roof and her three meals a day. No hawker can promise a woman that much."

"I wasn't thinking of . . . *where* did she go?"

"I'm not going to tell you that," said her father. "She's safe and well enough set up. That'll have to do . . . Your tea'll get cold, Mr Crowther." He drank from his own large cup and stared straight ahead.

"Why won't you tell me where she is?"

"When you get yourself some daughters you'll remember that question as a foolish question."

"It won't be hard to find her."

Mr Kirk did not deign to reply and Edgar looked around to catch the merry glances of Margaret which was the disconcerting name of Jessie's youngest sister. At that moment a very faint alarm sounded in his mind, for Margaret's jolliness seemed the sensible way to deal with this beaten intolerant father, the only way to survive at length, and by contrast, Jessie's passivity, the docility which lapped in his mind so soothingly, appeared something very weak, the camouflage of despair rather than the self-contained pool of quietude. He was often to remember that moment, though it passed soon enough.

Margaret had given him enough of a hint and after making his departure, he stopped the car a few hundred yards away and strolled back along the narrow road. The girl came around a sharp corner and laughed before any word was said. It did him good just to look at her, so cheerful. He felt a fine gust of life come off her. The forceful father, he thought, happily, had nurtured if not a viper then certainly not the dove she disguised herself as.

After she had told him where her sister had gone to, they walked a while and in his state of abject emotional exhaustion, Edgar was soon aware that he could well be attracted to Margaret, too. No pretence. He was. The whole thing was ridiculous and intolerable but it would have been false to deny it. Her manner showed that she had picked up the pointedness of his interest and she dallied in the lane until they reached the car. She stroked the bonnet as if it had been a cat.

"I suppose you'll be taking our Jessie out in this all over the place, Mr Crowther."

She was far too young: indecently young. Only a few years older than Eleanor! But he had not the snap to be decisive.

"Will she want to come?"

"Who wouldn't want a ride in a motor car like this?" Still she stroked it: the gentle, steady, rhythmic gesture had a mesmeric effect on him. She looked up at him slyly. "Would you take *me*?"

The direct invitation almost brought Edgar to tears: he was so weak as a result of the struggle with Rosemary and so raw that the simple indication that he was wanted made him respond with a childish fervour which he had just the wit to choke back. "I have to get back," he said. "Besides, your father would have my scalp."

"He'll never know. He only sees what he wants to see. Anyway, he doesn't matter." She was utterly confident of her power to dominate the old man. He smiled.

"Why are you laughing?"

"I was thinking how different you are from your sister."

"Oh Jessie!" Margaret looked angrily at him. "Jessie's too soft."

"What did she say when he sent her off?"

"She would be too frightened to say anything." Margaret hesitated, and then, almost viciously, added, "He can't see which side his bread's buttered, the old fool! *She* should be the one stays at home. It would suit her. She wants nothing else."

"Oh I don't know." Edgar picked up the challenge. "You can never tell about somebody else."

She moved abruptly away from the car, looked about her and then gave way to a heavy, impatient sigh. "There's nothing goes on here. Nothing. It's so dead I could go mad."

Edgar thanked the instinct which had held him back from her: here was a restlessness would give him neither peace nor diversion. She was too full of herself to let anyone else in; the pose was coquetry and he guessed she was sulky now because her stratagems had not worked. "Where do you want to go?"

"London," she said: the word was expressed with such a wealth of longing and expectation that, still in the dangerous state of being pulled wherever a woman wanted, Edgar felt, quite crazily, that he might help her in some way.

"I expect you'll get there," he said: and she smiled at his interest.

"There's a dance," she said, "in the School Hall, in a fortnight's time; a fortnight on Friday." She looked at him roguishly, her temper restored once more at the prospect of the dance. "I expect I'll be able to persuade our Jessie to go. She'll take persuading."

"Will you?" His tone was so urgent that Margaret was turned from rival into confidante.

"It's as bad as that, is it?" She mocked him lightly.

"You will ask her?"

"If you give me a ride in your car."

278

They drove about a mile along the lane and then they drove back again, Edgar nervous, Margaret content to be silent in her victory.

Out of some inexplicable sense of symmetry, he decided to call on Margaret in Carlisle. He was losing his grip on the world and only such apparently meaningless gestures had resonance. She was not there. He was not disappointed. His mind seemed suspended, above the reality of his life past or present.

He arrived back at his own house rather calm, and on that evening they talked and lived with each other as they had done before the argument entered its serious phase. Indeed, as the evening wore on he could imagine that nothing had happened; that he had dreamed it all: or that this was firm land and the storm was past. He looked at Rosemary with a tenderness absent over the previous weeks. How terribly tired she looked; her fingernails bitten, the dress so carelessly untidy, exhaustion all about her.

In bed they made love and afterwards she fell asleep with her head resting on his arm. He waited until her breathing was very steady before drawing his arm away, but he could not be delicate enough for her and she woke up. Immediately, she was happy. She kissed him hard on the mouth, holding him fiercely. Then she turned from him and once more seemed to be asleep.

Edgar stared into the dark. That strong, loving kiss of hers had quite inexplicably filled him with revulsion and fear. For what reason could the spell of the healing evening be so violently and completely broken? Revulsion, yes; it was not too strong a word for what he had felt.

As if, again, according to a pattern—though Edgar was weary of Rosemary's patterns and longed to escape from the grip they appeared to exercise—Lawrence had a mild stroke the very next day. It was some way to insanity for Edgar to regard it as retribution for his lurch towards Jessie via her sister, but on reflecting on the news he did make just such a connection. A few days later, Lawrence had a more serious stroke and Rosemary's time began to be consumed by attendance on him. Stephen came up for a couple of days when the situation appeared criticial, but the old man held on and Stephen returned to Oxford where he was in his final year.

There was no hope for Lawrence but his body was tenacious and would not easily give in. Rosemary read to him and was rewarded by looks of the greatest devotion: he could speak only with the greatest difficulty. She was glad to be able to repay him in this way, to perform these last rites for one who had steadied her so much and, now she realized it fully and painfully, loved her so much. She could never have managed without him: she was sure of that.

He had been reading Anthony Trollope and she took up where he had left off; the embroidered bookmark neatly placed in chapter three of *Phineas Finn*.

They were good days, in their sad fashion, and Sarah was grateful: she had great difficulty staying with her brother for any great length of time, unnerved by seeing his frozen, twisted face, the inert limbs, the terrible trembling when he had to be fed or cleaned. Eleanor, too, was much upset by this and sought refuge with Edgar's mother. It was there she was often to be found from after school until dark, finding a solid centre in the country-woman's sure domestic round.

And, as if drawn by the command of some imperious lord whose power drove out all other fears and loyalties, Edgar waited for the days to pass until he could go to the dance in the hope of seeing Jessie.

# Chapter Forty-Three

It was the first time Edgar had been to a dance on his own since the war. All the way there in the car he brooded on his behaviour. It was in no way and by no standards right, normal, decent, acceptable or defensible. To carry it through would mean to change himself radically. Perhaps that was what sealed Rosemary's curiosity: perhaps she thought he would never deny his "true self" as she kept calling it and so she could brush aside the felt threat as mere sound and fury. Edgar could not do that, she would have whispered to herself. Marriage to him was as sacred as mother: the bond was like a birthplace: the contract was his life's blood. He would frighten her and make her anxious, and she, easily panicked, was open to all his scares: but in the end he could not be the man he was and break up the marriage. In her final despair this comfort never failed.

Yet she wanted and expected him to change radically. Why was he going? He was already regretting it, already working out how he could get back "home" for the night should Jessie not be there or things not turn out as he . . . as he what? Hoped or dared imagine? He imagined himself in Jessie's body as in an ocean, satiated.

But what was he doing? Amid the turmoil only a few things were clear. The unsettlement he felt when he lay with Rosemary now appeared to stretch back to the day of their marriage which appeared an act of will, not a consequence of desire: to bring in the demands of love was bound to disturb the situation either to pleasure or to pain. Each asked from the other what could not be given. Each now needed, it seemed, what could only be found elsewhere.

And the thought of Jessie gave him hope. He felt good, thinking of her: good—and with Rosemary now he was evil, he thought. But, he was honest as Rosemary would have been, his greed for life sprang up like a plantation of weeds and he wanted everything: everything.

This was not allowed. You had to make your choice, the inexorable injunctions of time and place reminded him, you could not have everything and you would be punished for trying. You would suffer for breaking the law of moderation and the customary usages of the age.

But he had already suffered and more than he would ever have thought possible. With someone else, to whom he would appear differently, both cause and consequences might disappear. To break the marriage knot needed something that he began to imagine to be boldness.

And underneath, pike pinions supporting him, were the savage convictions—that he could not go on with such a quarrelsome life; that he feared his own temper, his visions of destruction; that he was beginning to hate himself before Rosemary to an unacceptable extent; and that the first duty is to survive.

While above, beckoning, open to the sky, was the thought of Jessie.

He found it very difficult to walk into that strange dance-hall with his pink raffle ticket bought for two shillings and six pence, number 128, entitling him to a tea and a cake later on. He recognized one or two of the farmers there but made it plain he was in no need of companionship (though he was) wishing to stay alone, wishing he had never come. For in the cheerful well-lighted place, the floor shining from its afternoon chalking, the accordion band playing the old favourites with spirit, among the well-scrubbed local faces from the ages of sixteen to twenty, he felt like a thief. The word was not too strong. He felt that his sole intention was to do something wrong, an affront to all these good people whose warmth of communality he recognized from his own experience in Thurston, but who were closed to him here.

It was Margaret who saw him first and she came across trailing Jessie behind her; it could appear, as if it were she, the local princess (for she was easily the most obviously attractive young woman in the hall) whose good offices alone were bringing about the meeting. But a discerning look at Jessie would have seen, beneath the blush and shyness, a resolution which, the glance shifting to Edgar, would dare meet its match there. Margaret was soon requested to dance and whirled away: Jessie, too, was asked to dance and it was thought typical of her local reputation for strangeness that she should shake her head and send away the poor supplicant in shame. To Edgar it seemed as natural that she should want to stay with him as that he would want to stay with her. She earthed him.

They danced, together. She was light to hold, he noticed, surprisingly for such a woman whose movements appeared so firm and leisurely. To feel her body so close to his and their hands clasped, her breasts occasionally brushing against his chest, inspired him with a sensation he had forgotten since adolescence. People recognized their absorption with each other and left them alone.

They said very little that first night; it was clear that his apprehension of her had been returned. Each fed on the fact of the other's being there. Every ordinary reaction she had, every calm answer she made, every definite gesture and above all every tranquil yet sparkling look, bathed Edgar in a great saturation of peace.

Jessie, too, was in need, though her wants were so exactly met by Edgar's needs that her wounds were completely hidden: and hers was not the temperament to reveal them. But in truth she gave him peace because in him she found, as she thought, the solution to her life. She had weighed his glances and visits in the silence which preserved her sanity before that father who had clipped her wings so brutally, and she had decided that he loved her. This conclusion was gravely reached. She was still a virgin who had concealed her fears of men in the slowness of manner which her young sister found such a ready butt for her kittenish wit. Having decided that he loved her she released for him a great burden of desire and affection and longing which had always weighed on her and lately threatened to oppress her: by nature she was violently loving; by chance and circumstance every gesture in obedience to that impulse had been checked and battened down. To Edgar she could at last give everything.

While they danced he felt more and more the density of her lovingness, and out of his own miserable lust was born a vision of her as the woman with whom he could be whole. The music from the accordions and the violin, the soothing tread of the dancers on the springy floor as the whole room packed its way through an Olde Time Waltz, the feeling of dislocation coupled with the sensation of recognition (for though this was not Thurston it was a replica) made his senses drowsy with a powerful and intoxicating relief. She would take him for what he was, he could feel it in the steady strength of her arms, the quiet certainty of her steps, the firm unselfconsciousness of her breasts, the serious smile on her lovely oval face. For she grew lovelier as if his touch was the water to the cut stem of a flower: even as that evening went on she bloomed.

Margaret noticed it and commented on it with rude cheerfulness.

Jessie, equally, sank into the idea of what they were and could be together. She felt herself, physically, sinking; had to take care not to close her eyes or a slow suck of voluptuous darkness dragged her away from this firm self in the arms of this solid man. He was such a fine-looking man, she thought! Boys her own age, in so far as they had shown interest in her at all, had disappointed her: she was distressed by their clumsiness and fearful of the lives they promised. And Edgar would defeat her father when it came to it. She was sure of that. He told her that he loved her and felt certain it was the truth of the matter.

# Chapter Forty-Four

In the next few weeks, all the emotional and speculative part of his nature was submerged in Jessie, and the solid matter of his life came to rest entirely in the building of the house. He cut down on his dealing; he limited his runs. From dawn until dark, except when he took off to visit Jessie, he would be in his field working rapidly, fretfully, keen to tire himself out, pricked to urgency by an impulse he could not explain. One day, his plan was, the entire field would be a housing estate, and by that time he would have the capital to move to other things. Property though, he was convinced, would make him his fortune. All his other schemes were insubstantial compared with this fact: people were wanting more pleasant places to live in and those who could were saving money for that purpose. Sooner or later, a great number of people would want to own a new house. Edgar's plan was to be in business to meet that demand.

He was lucky in his site: planning permission had been given easily. Water and sewers were available because they had just recently cut across his field to serve a cluster of farms and cottages in the hamlet known, like the Camp, as Old Carlisle. Lighting had appeared to be a major problem but the new electrification of the countryside again dovetailed with his needs. Never had he had so much good fortune with a scheme. In his desire to finish it he broke his rule about doing it all alone, and Scrunt turned out to be both a useful "brickie" and a reliable source of supply for those odd accessories so often in demand in such a job. One of his brothers was a decent carpenter and in return for a suckling calf had fitted up door-frames throughout and was willing to do cupboards and help with the window-frames and the staircase. From his previous employment at the woodyard, Edgar drew many benefits and was able to "have now, pay later" on a number of crucial occasions. The bricks had come from Bobby Wilson, himself a builder and a genial, generous man who liked to see a fellow getting a start in life and had let him have the entire

285

complement for a small payment and a few weeks' labouring which Edgar willingly gave. His experience at Porter's garage, too, came in handy because through that connection he was able to arrange for pipes and fittings for the plumbing. It was the first time he had been so lucky and he held onto it.

Most of Rosemary's days were spent with Lawrence. When she was free she was tired or Edgar was out. She never went up to the house to see how it was getting on. Between them was a lull. Rosemary paid it little heed. What remained of her strength she gave to the man who had so carefully looked after her for so long, profoundly grateful to be lucky enough to return something of the gift.

It was in those weeks that Jessie and Edgar first made love. The memory of it was never to leave him and for the few days afterwards he felt that he had been given an infusion of something altogether rare and powerful. The firm tension of her skin under his hand, the sweet breasts, everywhere so white and smelling of health and cleanness. He had not trembled and neither had she; though he knew it was her first time. She pulled him deep inside herself and he felt the long impacted groan of happiness shoot through him from recesses he had thought no longer fathomable.

He could be happy! He could go through one, even two days without the fear that his skull would be crunched like balsa wood. He had found someone who liked him as he was. The relief made him dizzy.

It was impossible to conceal his pleasure or to deny his fulfilment although the one seemed to blaspheme the protracted pain of Lawrence's death and the other to mock the worn-out aspect of his wife.

And so Rosemary took note of it then began to observe it more closely and finally divined exactly its cause and the force of it: and she shuddered. She had not the heart for more fighting. She was so weary after a day with Lawrence that all she could do was to stumble about blindly into bed, her eyes sore from the intensive reading, her back stiff, the asthma churning about her lungs like a fatally clogged propellor: she could not find the energy to take care of her dress or her looks or even Edgar's clothes or, apart from barest essentials, his food. Eleanor, too, was blotted out from her view.

She was immersed in the idea and in the fact of Lawrence's

health. What made it doubly difficult was not only to see a friend, a relation, a near-father going so helplessly to death but also—and this she recognized clearly—her safest prop was being removed at the moment she could need it most. Sadly she acknowledged the selfishness but it would have been false not to have admitted it.

And what was false had to be rooted out. There was no quarter ever to be granted in that battle. Untruth was her enemy: and now it stood before her, in the shape of the strange husband she had come to adore; bold as brass and clam-tight.

Quail as her body might, her spirit never would flinch: she took it on.

Things began to correspond and coincide with ominous pointedness.

On the very day that Rosemary woke up to brace herself for a talk with Edgar in the evening, *he* decided to use that evening to carry out an unlonged-for conversation on his own conscience, and he was not there when she came back from Lawrence's.

Margaret usually got in from work just before six. He arrived at her flat about seven. It was still very light: summer was coming on fast. He stood and looked over Rickerby Park, following the River Eden as far as he could see it. A few couples strolled together on its banks. She opened the door cautiously. "I've been hoping you'd come," she said, nervously. "I'll get you a drink."

Edgar was dry-throated with apprehension but beneath it all calm, calm to the centre of him as he had been since that first love-making with Jessie, that act like a snowfall in his mind, utterly changing the landscape of his inner life. At all times the simple vision of her trusting oval face and the feel of himself plunged inside her gave to his senses both a feeling of freshness and an unfailing certainty.

"Well," said Margaret, "I reckon I'd better get it over with." She "took a slug" from her glass; once again he recognized the ancestry of her slightly theatrical gesture and yet again felt both pleased and a little disarmed to be involved in such a play. "I've been seeing him over the past few months. He's going to do it. We're leaving for the south at the end of July."

"Do what?"

So consumed was he by his own affairs that Edgar's reply was no more than a reflex. Who was she talking about?

Margaret did not reply.

"You've been seeing him?"

"Yes." She paused, but there was no feeling of hesitation: rather she was taking her time. "You told me very little about your life. Not that I asked. But still it was, very little." She smiled at him, scoring, he recognized, just as so often Rosemary scored.

"I'm glad you came. I was thinking I would have to write to you." She finished her drink and poured out another for herself. Edgar refused. He could not think what to say but gradually, as the implication dawned on him, a mixture of regret and relief settled inside him. Ceremoniously, he raised his glass. "Good luck."

"Thank you."

"Where will you go?"

"Oh—London to start with. Where most people go who're in a hurry to get lost, I guess. After that he'd like to consider the south-west. Devon or Cornwall. He seems to think we could build up a new life there. And the scenery's good, too." She drank. "I'll miss the scenery."

"I'm glad it's worked out for you."

"I knew you would be."

For the first time in their meeting, her eyes gripped his glance keenly and he felt himself to be exactly where he was and no other place. Jolted into the immediate present.

"What have *you* been doing?" she asked.

"Oh, this and that." He told her nothing of his own life; nothing that she had not learned at their first meeting.

Now the lie of omission seemed too large to repair. "How's your house?" Her smile was very gentle: suddenly.

Edgar found that he resented her having had this other affair, yet he saw that such an attitude was unutterably hypocritical.

He told her about the house. That day he had finally completed the roof with some tiles grudgingly given by his eldest brother from the roof of a long disused barn.

"You've been very kind," she said, powerfully, much later when the desultory conversation had soaked up all the gin and a bottle of scotch and some beer had been produced to replace it. Edgar noticed the new riches: the other man must be a steady drinker, too. He wished he had paid more attention to her description of him. But they were in a past so very distant.

"You're very kind." Perhaps he was too tired to be able to judge anything any more. The words reverberated inside his skull as if it were caverns large. And indeed, under the influence of the hard spirits, he felt no reason to object. Perhaps he was very kind, scattering the largesse of himself over whoever claimed it, really who knows? Anyone could eat off him. "You're very kind."

"What do you mean by that?"

"You've listened to a lot that no one else would have put up with. I'm grateful for that. Perhaps you saved my life." She sipped at her drink, still nervous.

"That's a bit strong."

"You never know."

He wanted to say nothing at all. A few birds were settling down in the garden outside. It was most sombrely silent. It was in the silence that his solution would be found: if only he could find the time to listen and the will to obey.

"You're looking very well," Margaret said. "Much better than when I first knew you. Much younger, too, which is rather disconcerting."

"You must have done me good."

"I'd like to think so."

He put down his glass and went across to kiss her. She returned the kiss willingly but when he indicated that she should stand and then go, as they had done often enough, to the bedroom, she resisted.

"What's wrong?' Dully delivered. What dykes had broken down? He did not know where whim or obligation or kindness or loyalty began and ended: nor, it seemed, could he separate them from the acts of lust. Will degenerated to wilfulness, instinct became mere whim.

"Not that," she said. "I feel, you see . . . I feel that he's committed himself now and so must I."

"Oh?" he paused. "Oh—I see. I understand. Yes."

Edgar backed away, bumping into a small table but just quick enough to steady it. He was indifferent, he thought, but when the implications of her remark percolated to that small part of his consciousness uncaptivated by narcissism and the locked survival-love he felt for Jessie, he was stung.

"*I* did it for *you*," he muttered. But said no more except, "I'll go. I must be going. I'm going."

"Are you fit enough to drive? Are you sure? I can make you some coffee."

He shook his head. He had not noticed how much he had

drunk. The last thing he wanted was for Margaret to make him some coffee.

For about half an hour he drove aimlessly along the road that would take him to Jessie—out to Hadrian's Wall where the line against the Barbarians had finally been drawn. But it was a fruitless gesture. All the time he knew he would have to turn the snout of the machine westwards.

What was he to do?

Each time he saw Jessie—and yet he had not seen her many times—he was confirmed in the strength of their union. She made him realize how weak he had become. She made him want to shout aloud Yes, Yes to his life. To copulate with her was affirmation; it sloughed off the clustering prohibitions and accreted miseries of his former life. He was neither omnipotent nor impotent with Jessie, neither Zeus nor a holy eunuch, not a failure and not a prize ram, neither a Greek God nor a Nordic invert—but himself, for what it amounted to, a body in the arms of another body with a woman who gave and took in equal quantities and wanted no more than that he should take what she was. In the heart of him, then, where, according to Rosemary, the greatest and most living truth always lay, in that core of being which made him know what he was, he loved Jessie and clung on for dear life. Yet in that love had kept her ignorant of his position as husband and father and just attempted to deceive her.

Aimlessly he drove along the straight Roman road, swooping up and down without deviation, barely inhabited land to north and south, a frontier, a conclusion, the end of a civilized world which had later yielded to the savages who rose up from the hollows and valleys of just such barely inhabited territory. The sound of the motor droned into his brain. He could have been alone in the world, he thought; he *was* alone between those women. He had hoped that Margaret would bridge them, somehow: there was no reason in the hope, nor much faith and less and less reliance on the impulse of the moment. This instinct locked him to Jessie: the effort to hold on to that instinctive rightness in the face of all the civilized forces which rose within him to subdue what they recognized as a savage act took all his strength.

Again and again he rehearsed it but there was no way out. Rosemary was established with her forces, Jessie with hers. If things were to change then he would have to act, he would have to be the mover. Margaret should have clarified things.

He stopped the car, wound down the window and looked out across to Hadrian's Wall, barely to be seen, an indistinct line of rubble on a mounded crest in the middle distance. Margaret should have acted on him in some way. By compounding the deceit, by sleeping with her despite a declared passion for Jessie and an apparently unassailable admiration and love for Rosemary, something would break, something must be revealed.

This notion, which Margaret's snub had helped him to understand, had the urgency of superstition. But nothing else in his make-up could help. Between them the two women took all sides of him and to them he gave as much as he could: only the irrational, unnatural, even magical pressure of superstition was free.

Sitting there, smoking, trying to work out a way through the impacted absolutes he felt his mind strain with it all: there had been some excitement in the "affair" with Margaret, some pleasure even in the lying, at first, an enlivening sense of danger. Now he was battened down.

He turned the car and swiftly drove back to Carlisle.

Margaret had changed and her welcoming smile was not for him. He said nothing.

"Come in." She turned and led him into her room as she had done so many times before. He clasped her around the hips, her back still towards him, and then drew his hands up onto her breasts.

"No."

Saying nothing he pressed her breasts fiercely into her body, feeling the jet of excitement rapidly ride up inside him. She struggled and twisted around; the buttons of her new blouse came open. "You've no right to do this."

As he kissed her his hands slithered rapaciously over her, pressing through the thin skirt and blouse, feeling the rub of one material against another. Her hands cupping his head, suddenly gripped his hair and pulled back his face from hers. "I don't want to, Edgar. Don't torment yourself like this. It has nothing to do with me. I don't want you. And you don't want me. It's not me—no, it's not me."

She stepped back, but he would not let her go; they tumbled clumsily onto the chair which had been "his". His hands were on her flesh now, and once more he answered her by forcing his mouth onto hers, straining, teeth, jaw, tongue. His hands rubbed smoothly and urgently and erotically on her and she slackened, submitted, only moaned when he tore at her clothes, sank deeply into his need and held, held fast as a final inhuman groan broke his silence.

They stayed interlocked: the doorbell rang loudly, three times: neither of them stirred, or looked at each other.

Eventually Margaret got up and left him. He heard her running a bath and went away, sickened.

But he had done something; he had heard his call answered in the moral void.

Instead of driving straight home he made for his new house. It was very nearly ready.

Striking matches one after the other without stopping, he walked the small area of the minute place he had constructed, touching the recently plastered walls tenderly as if rubbing a piece of sculpture: he let his feet spring, just a little, on the floorboards; he opened the windows and ran a finger-tip lightly over the even putty which secured the panes of glass.

Leaning out of the window he looked over to the hill. The moon seemed artificial, a perfect, slim crescent. "Fine Views," his advertisement would read, "In All Directions." In Thurston the church clock struck twelve. He had waited for that, wanting to hear the sounds at this distance. They came quite clearly over the fields; they did not sound real to him in his troubled state.

He saw no way now but to face up to Rosemary. She had caught onto his change, he could tell that. Part of his reluctance to return home now was the knowledge that she would certainly be waiting for him. It is possible to know people far too well, he thought, even those we love, and though he smiled to himself to be able to predict the course her action would take there was a much greater feeling of doom its enclosing inevitability.

But home was where he had to go first if he were to begin again.

# Chapter Forty-Five

The fire was out. Rosemary was splayed awkwardly in the arm-chair, her mouth half-open, one arm dangling almost to the floor, the other imprisoned between her side and the side of the seat. As he looked at her, he wondered what his life would be like if she were as dead as she appeared to be, and then he lost all hope that he could have such a thought.

She opened her eyes and in the moment before her focus cleared, he saw a look of terrible vulnerability. She smiled.

"Hello, sweetheart," she said, gaily, her mind fresh and wiped clean after the sleep. She held out her arms and when he moved into them she clasped and locked her fingers behind his neck as she used to do, wanting him to lift her up as he straightened himself. He obeyed and they stood body against body.

He remembered Margaret's betrayal. He remembered the smell of Jessie's hair.

"What's wrong?"

"Nothing."

Rosemary put her hands gently on his shoulders and fixed her eyes on his. If only he could evade that gaze! It searched out every stain and speck. He could not bear it. The demand for truth was relentless.

"I'll get you some tea," she said, energetically, "*you* build up the fire—you can always do it so beautifully and it takes me hours. We can talk things over. We must talk."

She went through to the kitchen and reluctantly he did as he had been bid. He did not want to talk. He did not want to face up to it. His obstinacy hardened like cement. He would not be talked out of what he felt.

The fire was going when she came back with the tray: she had managed not only to make tea but to cut some bread, butter it, lay it out elegantly on a plate, put some jam in a small dish, and complete the whole thing with a single rose which she had popped into a half-pint milk bottle. The total effect was touching and yet once more his resistance grew to smother the tenderness, growled at it like a monstrous hound stopping help coming to the caves he was to guard.

"I was looking at a reproduction of a painting by Cranach," Rosemary said, as she set up the table between them. "Here it is." He looked on the floor but did not feel inclined to pick up the book. "Judith and Lucretia," she said, "the murderess and the suicide. You rarely see passionate women in paintings—unless it's Mary Magdalene worshipping Christ."

She sat down and waited for a reaction, bright eager, generous with information, ready to subsume the entire problem in one of the cultural metaphors she so loved. But all Edgar could think of was those dreadful words—suicide; murder. He shook his head, brusquely, as if to shake out an object which had stuck onto his hair. The smudged prints of both women made them look, to his eyes, untouchable and mad.

"What *is* wrong? Tell me."

"Nothing."

"Tell me. Tell me. Please. You can be honest with me. You know I love you whatever you do."

"Nothing's wrong."

"Why do you go away from me? Why do you have to drink so much? Where do you go to?"

"Nowhere. Look—I've told you. I have to go all over the place."

"There isn't someone else, Edgar, sweet Edgar, is there? Is there? Tell me. Tell me quickly. Get it over with. Then we can talk about it."

"Of course there isn't. Why do you say that?"

"There is, isn't there. Don't lie. You're too good to lie."

"Don't say that! Nobody's too good to lie."

"True. I agree. But some lie badly, their soul can only tell the truth. They are the pure-hearted ones. You're like that. You're one of those."

"Oh, Rosemary. I wish you wouldn't say things like that. How do you know I'm pure-hearted and anyway, what does it mean?"

"You see—he blushes. How sweet! Only the pure in heart can blush. A blush is one of the few expressions that the body allows the soul to have. The soul's repertoire is very limited. It is like a prisoner in a dungeon who can only communicate by tapping the wall—and so ignorant fellows think the soul doesn't exist just as cruel people think the prisoners don't exist. But they *do*. We know that."

"I don't."

"Don't deny yourself, Edgar! Don't do that."

"Deny what?"

"You know what I mean." She lit a cigarette.

"No, I don't."

"You do. You know exactly what I mean, you old devil. But play your tricks if you must."

"I-do-not-know-what-you-mean."

"Tell me. O Edgar! Don't hurt me so much. Can't you see I'm in pain? Don't hurt me."

"I—Rosemary—what do you want me to say?"

"The truth."

"About what?"

"About everything. Love comes and goes, Edgar. It is beautiful and it is important. And sex—I'm no good at sex, I know. I used to be. But nowadays I get so desperate. I think you don't like me. Isn't that silly? But I *do* think that."

Neither could afford to allow a silence or a pause to develop: as if in such blankness might be revealed the abyss which would swallow them both.

"There's no need to think that."

"But I do. Then I say, he will come back. Skins change. Bodies decay. Blood is re-cycled. The main thing is truth. If we live by that we live well."

"Let's leave here, Rosemary. Let's go away! Let's go from Thurston—let's get out of Cumberland—altogether. England— all of it—let's go to Canada. Let's decide that, *now*. Let's go. Please." It was a chance.

"What a boy you are! Oh—I love you so much. How can anything be changed by going to Canada? What do people *do* in Canada?"

"I'm sure they manage."

"I'm sorry. I didn't mean to mock you. It's hard for me, you know, living with someone who doesn't appreciate my sense of humour. Maybe it isn't funny."

"Why not leave?"

"I like this place. And nothing is solved by running away. We all know that."

"Maybe—maybe not. Some things could be."

"What, for example?"

"Well. I'm known here. Everybody knows what to expect and they expect just that and no more and so I do just that and no more. I'm putting it badly but you're clever enough to see what I mean. And wherever I go in England it'll be the same. 'What've you done?' they'll ask, and I'll have to tell them and then they'll say, 'Oh, that means you're such-and-such a man.' But in Canada I can say 'I've just come to find out, that's it, to find out who I am. I've left my past behind.' Don't you see how much better that is?"

"You can never lose your past." She would not give up. "And you'd still have to do some sort of work. I can't remember what they do in Canada."

"It doesn't matter," he said.

"Lumberjacks! You'd make a very good lumberjack! I'd love to be married to a lumberjack!"

"You never take me seriously."

"On the contrary. I probably take you far too seriously for your good and for mine. Sometimes I think that my big mistake has been to take you seriously. But there we are. When we got married I didn't think of it as a light-hearted jaunt. I thought we were trying to do something important and would do it together. And I still think that, God-dammit!—whatever you say or do or are. We're not interested in making fortunes or having large houses or whatever—all those things are of little importance: the great triumph is to live well, to make something noble just out of the little that you have. And we have minds and consciences and souls, you have and I have: we must live by them."

"You make it sound such a strain."

"That's my fault. I'm sorry. It is a joy to me."

"I don't understand you."

"That's just another way of not facing up to the argument."

"I don't understand you."

"Understanding is painful. Learning is painful. Living is a painful business, Edgar—haven't you noticed?"

"Well it needn't be."

"It can't be anything else. And so we must make conquest over this pain. And Truth is the greatest victory."

"I don't want pain. I've had enough pain."

"You've hardly started."

"I've had enough! You talk as if you enjoyed it."

"I don't try to avoid it, that's all," her voice was becoming more flat as the tiredness shrouded her.

"Well I do. And I will. And if I have to run a mile with my tail between my legs I'll do it. I do not want pain. I prefer pleasure. I want happiness and not misery. Truth will have to take care of itself."

"That's the only thing it can never do."

"Well it can go to hell then."

"You don't mean that."

"Yes I do. I *do*!"

"That's sacrilege!" Rising in anger against his rejection of what was her creed, she threw away all precautions and boldly defended her beliefs. "Sacrilege! If you really think that then you must be mad. Without truth the whole thing is stupid, and ugly and utterly worthless. We *can't* abandon that! Not in the world and certainly not in our personal relationships. Once we do— then we lack all dignity and interest and we might as well become idiotically happy slaves. Of course it is painful, you man, you: yes! But who *cares*? It's glorious! That's the only thing that matters! Don't you see?"

"Yes. I see what you mean. I admire you for it. I do. But not for me. I'm not cut out for it."

"That's self-pity."

"All right." He waved his hand as if warding off a blow.

"That's self-indulgence."

"All *right*!"

"That's better." She laughed. "Now we're getting somewhere. So tell me. Tell me the truth. Is she blonde? Is she pretty? Just don't tell me *who* she is or I'll scratch her eyes out."

"I wish you wouldn't go on."

"I'm right, aren't I, Edgar? Please. I can't seem to make you understand. It will drive me crackers not to know the truth, don't you see? Years ago I could endure it because I did not know, *really* know, what life was about. But now I'm too tired for that pretence; and I'm too old as well. Seeing Lawrence dying has helped me to understand more clearly. He's given me so much, that man; even in his death he gives me much. I love him."

Edgar felt jealous but was incapable of explaining the meaning of this reaction or comprehending its importance. All he felt was that it was bad to feel jealous of a dying man and especially when his own actions made such a stance hypocritical. But the feeling existed.

Rosemary had become fixed on the thought of Lawrence and let all else slide out of her mind: Edgar had often seen this when she looked at something, a flower, a sunset, a leaf, a child, which caught her total attention; everything else would be forgotten. "Do you know what I think he said to me today? I'm almost sure he *did* say it—we have a way of communicating. He said 'If I have another stroke and it leaves my body totally paralysed and yet my brain functioning, would you please kill me?' I repeated it to him. And he nodded." Rosemary who had been looking straight ahead as if transfixed by the powerful memory of the scene, turned to Edgar and he saw that she was beginning to cry. "He nodded. So you see—that's what he wants. What am I to do?"

"You can't, can you. You just can't." Edgar was sure.

"But why should he be a vegetable? How can we be so cruel?"

"It'd be classified as murder."

"The Greeks took hemlock. This taboo against taking your own life or having someone take it for you when you're in no possible state ever to enjoy it again is just stupid Christian superstition at its worst."

"You mustn't do it, that's all."

"But imagine, Edgar. Your brain clear, active, hearing everything but not being able to speak, knowing all that is said but not being able to answer, not being able to act or ever to move. And having all your eating and excreting done for you—as if you were some monstrous imbecilic baby. Horrible! Horrible!"

Her crying brought relief to them both. When she had finished, he waited his moment and then returned to his urgent advice, carefully delivered. "Whatever he says, Rosemary, and however you feel, you-must-not-do-it. Now promise me you won't."

"I promised *him*. I promised I would."

"I accept that. What else could you do? But now you must promise *me*."

"But if I do—I shall have to break one of my promises."

"Dying people need comfort. If your words gave him that you did a good deed. But, I want that promise, Rosemary."

"It's his right."

"Maybe it is. But the law says you can't do it. Not even a

doctor can do it. And I agree. Nobody should have that right. Please promise."

"No . . . I shall have to see what happens to him. Sorry. I can't make two mutually contradictory promises. It would be absurd."

"You can't be God."

"I don't believe in God. Neither do you. So stop being sentimental."

"I'm going to bed. I'm tired."

"No you're not. You're annoyed."

"Have it your own way."

"Don't go, Edgar. Don't go. We haven't finished. Edgar. Don't go. I don't mind." She had grasped his wrists and was now staring intently into his eyes. "I don't mind. I love you and I don't mind. Where you put your stupid penis is not going to change what is basically true between us. So I don't mind. Do you understand that?" She tugged at him, fiercely, and he felt that a long fuse of panic was remorselessly burning its way towards their fate. "It-doesn't-count. Please. Oh please—understand *that*. Fucking does not count. Not really. Not really. So go. Do it. Be happy. Go. Don't deny it any more. Just tell me! *Tell me.*"

"There is no one else!" Edgar wrenched himself out of her grip with a violence quite disproportionate to the effort needed. "Leave me alone! Let me be. Just let me be!"

Shaking from the pressure on his conscience which now he imagined to be suppurating like a terribly infected appendix, bladder-like within the bone of his skull, he went across to the door and out of the room. The house shook as he ran up the stairs.

"I believe you," she called after him, sadly. "I do. Truly. I believe you. I wouldn't blame you if you had—but I believe you haven't. Forgive me. I'm tired. Lawrence is taking so much time. Forgive me. I believe you. I'll be up soon. I'll just wash these few things. You hate dirty dishes in the morning, don't you? Don't you? I believe you, Edgar. That's that. I must sort it out in my mind, that's all. That's all."

# Chapter Forty-Six

She would not let his pretence of sleeping obstruct her but bounded back into the argument intrepidly. The shiver which came off him when she got into bed she interpreted as an infantile-comic reaction and laughed to herself.

"You won't shake me off that easily, you old bugger."

"I want to sleep. I'm worn out." His back was towards her: he was huddled on the edge of the bed.

"No you're not. You're fed up with me. I understand."

"Goodnight."

"No. Edgar. Look at me. *Look* at me, Edgar. I want to tell you something very important."

"Please. I'm sick of talking."

"Just one thing."

Violently he turned to her, threateningly. "Leave—me—alone!"

"Why are you so angry?" The sudden sadness in her voice exacerbated him unbearably.

"I want to sleep, that's all."

"You're never tender to me now." Truly penitent for what she now thought of as her bullying of him earlier, she yearned for the very gentlest show of love.

"What do you want me to do?"

"Let's lie, could we? Just together. I would like you just to put your arm around me, that's all. Or without touching. Whatever you want. I'm sorry I pursued you. I need you, Edgar. Help me."

Her manner was now so subdued and beaten that, through the irritation, pity forced a way. He lay with her in his arms and with a grateful smile she nudged her body against his but his generosity did not go deeper than the gesture. His muscles were stiff as bones. In his head was the coarse grind of discontent.

What was the point of continuing when you could not love someone? That now presented itself painfully because he had Jessie with whom to compare her. It needed the utmost injection of will-power to stay in her arms. Yet he did. And tried his hardest to conceal his unspeakable aversion from her. The grimmest jest of all on the face of the skull of this love was that he could rest there only by virtue of the strength and peace he knew would later come from Jessie, whose skin opened to him like the waters of a clear lake, whose touches absorbed him.

"Make love to me, please."

The voice was so low, so plaintive, as utterly without pride as her previous thunderings had been full of it. Before he had been a little afraid of her, now he was afraid for her. The sound of the need was so immense; beneath the pitiful heap of words was a howl which curdled his blood.

Out of what feeling he did not know; out of guilt or tenderness or love or hate or conscience or remorse or habit or even pleasure: he did not know, but despite himself he made love. It was brief and wrenched his mind even in the resentful spasm of the body. The confusion was complete.

"You're so kind," she murmured, clustering around him even more tightly, "so good to me. I'll always love you, whatever you do. Whatever you do—you must know that."

"No. You can't love people *whatever* they do. No one can."

"I can."

And again he wanted to scream at her certainty, her arrogance and her impossibly splendid idealism. Although his mind ached, he clenched it against further thought and tried to sleep.

His dozing was interrupted by the awful sound of her asthma.

"I'm sorry," she said. "My pills are downstairs. Beside the clock."

He went and brought them for her with some water and stood over her until she had swallowed them. She handed him back the glass with the happy docility of a child. "You hate my being ill, don't you?"

"I wish you weren't, that's all."

"It upsets you though, doesn't it?"

"I don't like to see it, of course not."

"But it upsets you. You don't want your woman to be weak. It annoys you. Doesn't it? It's only natural."

She was right, but how could he admit it to himself, let alone her, and still preserve any decency between them? Her insights offered him the kind of illumination which can make blind as well as plain. To admit to such thoughts and feelings would be to release in himself the devils he had trained a lifetime to contain. Why did she feed them?

*Truth!*

She sat up against the two pillows she had backed behind her, the breath struggling through the poor strained tubes, the sound filling the room with strain and the undeniable evidence of battle and courage. She smiled at his worried face. "I'll be all right."

"Should I sleep downstairs?"

"No. I want my man beside me." Then her face clouded, in a moment, with annoyance. "There I go again being selfish. Of course you must go downstairs. No. *I'll* go downstairs. I won't sleep tonight. Yes. Don't you see? If you'll be so kind as to make up the fire, I could get myself pots of tea and read and be as snug as a bug. Please."

"It's so uncomfortable on the settee. I'd rather."

"No. No. You must sleep. You are tired. I can see that. You have to sleep. Let me, just . . ."

Edgar got out of bed once more and helped her up. She was so frail. He put the dressing-gown about her shoulders and then went downstairs with her. The fire was once more kindled, more easily, this time, the embering ashes strong enough to catch at the wood. He made her some tea and set it down nicely on a table beside her. He moved a lamp over for her to read by and brought down the eiderdown from their bed to supplement the rug she had taken.

"There," she said. "I'm so lucky. And it's so quiet! Leave me now. I'll be fine."

He kissed her on the cheek out of a felt respect and affection and that small positive feeling transferred itself to her immediately. The skin of her sensibility was gossamer. Only by the most elaborate defences did she survive at all: when she made herself open to someone, as she did to Edgar, she was permanently at risk: and also, because even here there was a balance, always available to the touch of pleasure and love.

"I don't know what I did to deserve you," she said.

Edgar had no possible way to meet that remark.

"You know what you said," she continued, "about going to Canada. I think you might be right. I've remembered—there's French Canada, isn't there? We could go there—and we would be equal, don't you see? And then there are those hundreds of miles of snow and ice—whiteness everywhere and huge forests. I think we could love Canada."

"Don't strain yourself, Rosemary. Just—read; rest. If you want me—call out. I'll hear."

"Lovely! 'Call out—I'll hear.' That could be our motto, couldn't it? I could embroider that on our crest. Our crest would be a black cockerel—an old English game-cock like those Harold Sowerby used to have. Beautiful, beautiful birds and yet—how savage!"

"Goodnight, Rosemary."

"I'll be all right. I'll read."

"Goodnight."

"I love you."

"Yes."

As soon as he had gone, she took up the Cranach reproduction and threw it on the fire—watching keenly until both the women were burned. He would appreciate that, she thought.

And until the morning she thought of him and strained to stop herself fleeing into panic. For she loved him now: indissolubly.

# Chapter Forty-Seven

Jessie had never imagined she could be so happy. Afraid that openness might imperil it, she hugged it tight and kept it from anyone. It was in her nature to be unconfiding but her father by threats and her sisters by pleas could generally invade such recesses of privacy as she had elected to define. Now she bent as much energy as she had—which was much—and all her guile— which was very little—to the problem and she succeeded. Margaret, the sister who saw her most often, had herself become attached to a man at the dance at which Jessie had first properly met Edgar; she was full of her romance and expected everyone else to share her preoccupation, or at the very least to reflect on it. Her own concerns dazzled her and Jessie's were not noticed.

Nor did her father sniff anything out. His daughters were known to him by their obedience and his recognition did not go very far beyond the scrupulous tabulation of their behaviour in his presence. Outside that they were free—to delight him, as Margaret did, by the wildness which was yet always on the leash of his rule, or to charm him as Jessie had never done because he could never be sure what she would be up to next. She was the child most like his wife, Jessie, and just as that woman's life had plagued him with doubts as to his own worth—his religious observances had never been able to match the dedication of her own—and her death had left him plagued with bodily demands bitterly insoluble, so Jessie could not give him satisfaction in himself. Her mysterious potency threatened his ordering of things: he suspected that under the meekness was a rage after anything and everything, extravagant, unbounded and ultimately uncontrollable.

In this he was right. He protected himself by exacting the usual rites and tributes and cutting himself off from her. The glow within, which, to any alert sympathizer, transformed everything about her, was seen by him as the glowing of a rebellion. He sidestepped this neatly, he thought, by the royal act of sending her fifteen miles from home to labour in the house of a man and woman who needed an all-purpose help.

Jessie had made various systems with which to cope with her life. She liked to read, for example, but the only book in the house was the Bible; and yet by burrowing, she had distinguished the power of the Book of Ruth, the beauty of Isaiah and the Song of Solomon. In her early youth she had chanted scraps of the great prose to herself until they had become incantations. She felt her lack of education to be a crippling disfigurement and shrank back from contact with anyone even of the least eloquence although she longed to be satiated with their words. Her body, too, was a burden but of a different kind for she knew it was full and desirable: she saw herself naked in the long mirror in her mother's room while her father and all the others were away at Sunday church and she stayed to see to the dinner: she looked at it lovingly; she could see its worth but she saw, too, the grabbing of women by her brothers, sensed the crudeness of their contact with her female acquaintances and locked her flesh against such invasions.

She lived inside herself, then, like the princess in the fairy tale entombed in the castle, unable to get out of it but by the intermission of true love. As such, as the liberator, had Edgar appeared to her. His talk was easy and interesting, different from her brothers his boldness before her father. She was ready for him and fell into his hands at a nod. Once he had declared himself then she could show her true colours and begin to be the woman she had longed to be for years. He made her someone she could love.

There was no point, it seemed to her, to play the games of tease and tarry her sisters and brothers described so vividly: her body was to be no obstacle course; no "favours", no forfeits. He could take whatever he wanted. His words, too, were too solemn to question as her sisters always declared they questioned their lovers; he spoke of "finding her", of loving her, of being completed in her, of discovering peace there, of wanting to spend a life with her and she did not stint in her responses.

It seemed in those few weeks as if the miracle had happened. She knew that she did not deserve it—enough of a Calvinist to retain some vestigial anxieties about the voluptuous carnal pleasures however hard she beat down the forest of prohibitions sown around her since childhood. But she welcomed it! Welcomed his body on hers, the ravishment, the tremulous pain, the sad repletion, that satiated and melancholy coda most of all, perhaps.

When there came, then, those few days on which she saw no sign of Edgar, and the days turned into a week and the week threatened to double, Jessie asked for a mid-week day off.

Rosemary's asthma had become much worse after that night: the work attached to looking after Rosemary and Eleanor and looking in on Lawrence besides attending to such business as there was and taking advantage of generous accidents to get on with the final touches at his bungalow, had left him no time for the long trips to Jessie's country. This omission worried him increasingly although the anxiety was allayed by the salve to his conscience which the simple business of helping those who needed it brought him.

He had no worries about Jessie's fidelity.

She walked a couple of miles and then took a bus to Hexham: from there she took a train to Carlisle and then sought out a bus to Thurston.

In Carlisle she felt very gauche seeing the smart turn-outs of the town women, and bought herself a fine new headscarf in green silk with beech leaves patterned on it.

She had not expected Thurston to be so big. Edgar had always given her the impression of a tight, snug little spot and she'd imagined it not much larger than a village. The bus left her on the pavements of a town.

It was a warm day and the warmth seemed to permeate the feeling she immediately had for the place. She had made out a simple plan of action and rehearsed it several times during the journey but now she stood irresolute, a little tired, wanting to take stock.

It seemed a quaint place. Opposite her was a broken wall, and in the gap sat an old man carving wooden knives: a few finished specimens were beside him. Behind him was the Fire Station. She saw blue street signs—Tickle's Lane, Plaskett Lane, Reed's Lane—the town seemed permeated with back-alleys which Jessie found friendly, cosy. She walked towards the shops and went into the Spotted Cow café and ice-cream shop attracted by the unusual name, the friendly blue and white painted front.

The proprietor, Mr Ismay, a man with pleasant brown eyes and a mournful moustache, served her with a generous wafer—

and then came outside to help her on her way, ignoring the three children who stood beside the ice-cream tub with their money burning a hole in their hands. Her enquiry for Edgar Crowther led to no compromising speculations in the mind of Mr Ismay; he was dealing, he thought, with a young woman who had a fancy for old-fashioned furniture, not common nowadays, but one he shared, against all this present-day trash, badly made, wouldn't last. He watched her on her way up the street and then turned to scold the children for making a noise. They would do without ice-cream, he said, if they could not behave.

Jessie was encouraged by her first contact with a native of Edgar's town and walked up the street in a leisurely manner, her anxieties unwrinkling in the drowsy mid-day, men lounging outside the pubs, a few women shopping, a mongrel waddling along the pavement; only the children ran; even the few cars seemed to potter through the place. The glances of the curious did not disconcert her as she had expected: the legitimacy of her claim and the excitement of this surprise visit gave her all the self-sufficiency she needed.

She turned into the arched way which was the entrance to Church Street and was chilled by the gloom of the place. No sun fed that twisty narrow street, and in it she felt less sure of herself. Afraid that someone might slip out of one of the many odd-shaped houses which opened directly onto the straitened way and confront her. She hurried and looked around rather wildly for the warehouse which Mr Ismay had so laboriously described.

But he had given her the wrong references, telling her it was on the left-hand side after the Photographer's-with-steps-going-up-the-outside: to the left she went and found herself in the slaughterhouse. The beast had been shot and hauled upon the pulley. She came just as the big belly was slit open and the innards tumbled out with a gleaming stink. Though country born and bred, she had never been able to overcome her squeamishness and the sight of the guts and intestines of the beast heaping up on the concrete floor while the sallow man in rubber boots and apron and gloves leaned in to scoop out more and more of the freshly dead animal's entrails startled and sickened her. She turned and ran out into Church Street where the chill once more gripped her: she could not go back the way she had come and quickly walked the other way, forcing her stomach to regulate its sick convulsion, whimpering slightly as her gullet expanded and contracted rapidly. She was sick on the corner leading to the church and looked around, tears stinging her eyes, to see if anyone had noticed. From down Church Street two old men advanced towards her. Looking for refuge, she went into the church.

It was calm, large, still, cool. She sat down and wiped the cold sweat from her brow. Parts of the wafer had been regurgitated and stuck between her teeth.

Harold Sowerby had seen her come in. In his retirement he had taken to doing even more for the church and on Fridays he cleaned the brass. He had become rather affected with age, the glass-cased life of bachelordom beginning to respond in unexpected ways to the pulses of dismay which came to him from within, cries of waste and loss, and the increased vivacity, as it appeared to him, of the outside world which seemed to pass him by. The church was more and more the ground on which he stood most firm and he loved to be there at unexpected times, to play the organ and walk about the chancel as if ordained. He watched Jessie very carefully and soon concluded that she was distressed.

Using his polishing of the sidesmen's brass-topped staves as an excuse, he worked his way up the nave until he was near enough to see that she was white-faced, upset and crying. Harold thought no more but moved into action: his long devotion to his mother and his ministrations to Rosemary, among others, had given him confidence in his talent to aid women in distress. He felt for them overwhelmingly and this poor shocked young woman's need could not be doubted.

"I'll get you some water," he said and almost trotted to the vestry and back, bobbing at the altar scarcely breaking his step.

Jessie drank gratefully. But the water seemed to threaten her devastated stomach and she had to tense herself against another lurch of sickness. Harold saw the poor woman's condition and knew what he should do.

"I'll get you something else," he said. "You'll be all right. Don't panic. Just try to take deep and regular breaths. Through your mouth if you have to. Deep and regular."

Once more he trotted down the nave, his apron flapping before him, solemn and excited by the idea which had risen into his mind. He would pour out a little altar wine for her: that would put new life into her, he thought. And of course he would tell the vicar all about it and excuse himself on two counts; firstly, it was his Christian duty to help those in distress and, secondly, as yet the wine was unconsecrated and indeed looked all-too-mundane in the wrapping provided by the ecclesiastical suppliers in Hexham. Nevertheless, excuses one or two no matter, it was a very bold stroke and Harold trembled as he poured out the small portion into a tumbler. He crossed himself.

He held the lip of the tumbler to her mouth. The poor woman was shivering; his sense of doing the right thing was confirmed. "Drink this," he said. "All of it. It'll do you good."

Jessie sucked at the wine and the action dislodged the irritating scraps of wafer which she managed to swallow together with the sweet but rather heavy drink.

"Do you feel better?"

She nodded.

"You must have had a shock, have you? Don't answer if it's too much trouble. No bones broke I hope?"

"No." Her voice reassured her. "No thank you."

"There you are. Deep breaths. Deep and regular."

She breathed as he instructed and a final, dreadful shiver passed through her, taking away the sickness. She felt very cold and desolate and enormously reluctant to press on with her quest.

"Where were you going?" he asked when she had begun to recover herself.

"I want to see Edgar Crowther."

"Oh." The name was still distasteful to Harold Sowerby. "You'll be wanting furniture, I suppose."

Jessie did not answer.

"He'll be at that house of his. No doubt of that. It's a long way to walk." Harold looked at his watch. "If you can wait for about ten minutes you'll be able to catch the Cockermouth bus just outside. Ask for the stop before Red Dial. Where you get off there's a gate just behind the bus-stop. Through that is his field. You'll see the little bungalow he's built—you can't miss it: it's an ugly little thing, quite out of character with the surroundings. I'll take that back if you've finished with it." She handed him the tumbler. "Are you from the Scottish side?"

She told him where she came from and he picked up a clue word in Northumberland to repeat what the vicar had said a fortnight previously about the Venerable Bede. Jessie listened gratefully to the paraphrase of the sermon; it took her mind off the horrible image of the slaughtered beast and gradually she felt herself becoming restored.

Harold escorted her to the bus-stop and watched it go until it turned the corner.

He found the green silk scarf on his way out at the end of the afternoon and decided that he would take it up to Edgar the following day. He could find out the name and address of the young woman and return it to her. It would, also, give him an excuse for making contact again with Edgar, about whom he had never ceased to have his suspicions.

# Chapter Forty-Eight

Eleanor had decided to help her father. Lawrence's illness gave her an unexpected resurgence of feeling for the companionship of her father and she knew that to volunteer to help him at the new house would be pleasant for both of them.

Rosemary did not like the new building and she had said so: in her heart of hearts, Eleanor agreed with her. But she found it much easier to pretend.

They had been there for about a couple of hours when Eleanor saw the stranger walking towards them across the field. It had been a good time; Edgar finishing off the papering in the front room, herself scrubbing the floors. He had been telling her about what Scrunt and himself once did together and she had loved the stories, gobbling them up like a child at bedtime.

Eleanor had gone outside to take some sun. It was so beautiful, looking over to the fells, the blue haze of the mountains, the emptiness before her.

The stranger walked quite slowly as if she were very tired, though she looked young, Eleanor could see that, and pretty.

"Dad," she spoke quietly. The window was open: he could hear easily enough. "Someone seems to be coming to see you."

"I'll just finish this strip. I won't be a minute," he replied. "Anybody we know?"

"No. Nobody."

Eleanor tried not to stare at the young woman but it was difficult not to as she came forward so deliberately, somehow dominating the scene by the very measured purposefulness of her slow walk, pausing momentarily once or twice to look around and take in the panorama. Eleanor felt, or so she swore afterwards, that the woman had something dreadful about her which forced you to look at her, draw your attention in some disturbing way, made it impossible for you not to stare.

Seeing the young girl whom even at a distance Jessie assumed to be a younger sister of Edgar's, or another relative, she was glad

311

to anticipate female company. For the reluctance to press her mission had grown and she waded through the overgrown grass as if the blades were swords and threatened to cut her in her tracks.

Edgar saw her just as she came within talking distance. He had looked out through the window suddenly drawn to discover the identity of the visitor.

Looking back, he remembered his efficient reaction with disgust. Rapidly he was out of the house and interposed himself between Eleanor and Jessie. He ordered Eleanor "home"— mentioning neither "Rosemary" nor "mother" nor giving her the time to call him "father" or "dad". It was a thoroughly successful operation. Eleanor walked away quickly, offended and puzzled but nothing irredeemable while Jessie stood before him, a little bewildered at his coolness but not alerted. He was still safe.

But reckoning on no luck, he took Jessie over to where his car was parked and drove her away from the town, into the fells, to a rarely frequented beauty spot near the village of Caldbeck.

It was a waterfall, the Howk, a gorge in a wood, glacially gouged out of the fell-side, and for a few hundred yards, on a small scale, spectacular and dangerous with only a slim wooden bridge as a crossing-point and that at the most perilous stretch where the water fell sheer over large ugly rocks which jutted out balefully through the spray.

Edgar took her across the frail bridge as he had bustled her into the car and led her a few hundred yards upstream until they came out of the dank gloom of the wood and onto an unexpected little pleateau, shaded, sunny, peaceful, with the river running fast but unobstructed by rocks and the noise from the Howk distant, like the sound of sea in a shell.

For a time they sat silently, not touching, not even looking at each other, while Edgar, suspended between one life and another, between one trust and another or between two lies, tried to see a way through. Feeling his mood foreign and cold, Jessie began to be afraid.

The man was thinking—This is it: one way or another in the next few moments my life will change utterly. He did not look at Jessie but could see her clearly in his mind's eye and such a feeling of rest and stay was in the image as sunk without hindrance to the roots of his mind, feeding them, calming, nourishing. He loved her; in so far as he was capable of telling his own mind, that was a fact.

But he had met her out of order. And in such a situation the tradition was clear: you cursed your bad luck and let the chance go by.

Edgar had been impressed by Rosemary's arguments on many matters but most of all by her fanatical and growing insistence on the nobility and supremacy of truth. In a similar situation, he had no doubt, she would tell the truth and shame the devil.

Partly, then, to return good for good or, another way, to pay her back in her own coin, he was inclined to be bold. There were other factors. It seemed to him that Jessie was more vulnerable than Rosemary: he could not believe that anyone who spoke as toughly and insisted on deeds as difficult as his wife would be unable to endure adversity. While Jessie, it seemed to Edgar, was entirely on his hands: to reject her might be to destroy her—there was that uneasy, undefined possibility.

And what would happen if he stayed with Rosemary? Most likely it would trundle on, the marriage, until he bumped into someone else. The thought of future infidelities appalled him. It was no way. He wanted to live with one woman.

It was so hard with Rosemary. What did she want? What was this bloody glory, this marvellous "truth"? He was embarrassed by it and ultimately, unimpressed. While the wilful defiance of the details of everyday reality was leading to a decline in his capacity to find satisfaction in anything. What it came down to was that she had an idea of life for herself and for him: but it was not *his* idea. He was prepared to admit, indeed, to proclaim to himself, that her idea was better, finer, perhaps even more accurate in its appreciation of his qualities: but he could not any longer live as someone else expected him to, even if it were in his own best interests.

Besides, he could not remove from his memory those moments of alarm and revulsion he had felt: there was no explaining that and no fighting that: except to lose.

What bound him to Rosemary were the conventional virtues of loyalty, responsibility; social respectability played its part and of course the future of Eleanor was critically important.

But what would her future be with parents who were forever at each other's throats? Where was social respectability in face of personal hypocrisy? And to what greater power could you be loyal and responsible, he could hear Rosemary say, than truth?

She would have to compromise, that was certain.

All this churning of pros and cons had, in various guises, chiefly as rapid sensations graphically illuminated by melodramatic cameos, passed through his mind since he had first met Jessie: now they spun faster and faster.

There was one way out. To do nothing. To continue with Jessie and to stay with Rosemary. To say nothing. To let it go on as it had developed and hope the ending would not be too awful. This was the coward's way, in Rosemary's language: he could hear her condemn it and dismiss it. Yet it did offer a chance for avoiding any critical moves: and they were worth avoiding. It meant carrying the load of lies further.

That was possible: he was not, he reflected, rather savagely, uneducated for the task.

So he made love and false talk to Jessie and then drove her back to the place where she worked. When he returned late at night he had excuses for Eleanor and apologies for Rosemary, who no longer knew what to believe; her own insights were so blandly contradicted so often. And that night he made love to Rosemary. Even when Harold Sowerby marched up to Highmoor the next day full of portent with the green scarf in a brown parcel nothing was given away. Edgar remembered the woman very clearly, he said, she had wanted him to go and value some furniture. He would send on the scarf by post.

# Chapter Forty-Nine

Rosemary stepped out of Lawrence's house uncertainly, as she always did these days, fully conscious of the fact that the next time she entered her childhood home she could find him dead. Still, though he failed steadily his strength was not used up. He had not, thank God, had another stroke. The weaker he got the more certain it became that the next would be the last.

She came out of the gate and peered up and down Longthwaite Road in an uncertain, short-sighted way, which made her look like a heron, Edgar had once told her, pecking the air for possibilities.

She stood for a while irresolute and then turned to go not home nor to the town but to see Edgar's mother, a visit she had planned to make for a long time. The two women saw each other now and then, at the shops or on the street but they were by no means friendly: at first each had found much to appreciate in the other. Now, time had eroded that respect. Edgar was living proof to his mother of a wife's neglect, so wild and clashed he looked. While to Rosemary, the search for the ultimate causes of Edgar's confusing behaviour led her directly to his mother who already, in the younger woman's mind, took a great deal of the blame for his difficulties. It was time that she confronted her, Rosemary thought.

She walked slowly, savouring the thin sun and taking care not to overstrain herself. The asthma was still bad: her lungs felt worn out.

Despite all that had happened, Rosemary had retained an undeniable innocence and youthfulness. She often smiled to herself— suddenly illuminated by a private recognition. In the quick glance of appreciation as someone passed, or at a snatch of overheard conversation, in the shape of a cloud or the movement of the branches of a tree she would discover pleasures and route them to that inner source of joy which never left her and was her greatest gift. So this walk, like every walk she ever took, was open to that influx of minor pleasures which make a mind rich.

Perhaps her most considerable achievement in the town was that over the years, quietly and without policy, particularly since her marriage, she had come to be regarded as a person who was particularly responsive to the injured and oppressed; as if her own pain gave her authority among them. This is not to say she sailed about the place like Lady Bountiful—she would have mocked such a woman: nor did she go out of her way to seek for those who needed help—she was no saint. But she always had time and more importantly she had both a proper sympathy and an imaginative way of proposing relief or even solutions. A woman she had talked to several times previously came up to her now and despite her preoccupations, Rosemary sat down on the bench beside the Show Field's gate to listen.

The woman thought that she was going mad but no one believed her. Her husband had begun to hit her for talking such nonsense: her doctor told her to pull herself together. Rosemary's opinion of doctors was very low (this comforted the woman) all they ever did, Rosemary said, with those who did not actually bare wounds was to tell them to pull themselves together—she hated the licensed ignorance of doctors. No one could see any signs of this poor woman's incipient madness: but that was only because she was devoting every grain of energy and guile and experience to get through the day without cracking up. One of her methods for self-preservation was to take a walk in the afternoon if she could get the time and hope, longingly, that she would meet Rosemary although when she did she was ashamed of her need and her strategy. Once Rosemary accepted to talk to her, however, there was no holding the woman back and the flow of misery was bottomless.

It took some nerve just to listen, for often Rosemary found the woman's circling fears and lurid horrors too near to her own. But she stuck it.

Terror. Panic. Neglect. Unbearable loneliness. Depression. Pain. Hopelessness.

When after almost an hour she could excuse herself from the woman's company, Rosemary walked on with much heavier steps. It was as if the woman had passed on the load. Sometimes the world seemed nothing but an open sore that would not cease to pick at itself.

She had to keep her mind clear now. It was important to resume her train of thought. She must not be tired.

She was in her early forties; Edgar in his late thirties—at a time when all their contemporaries appeared to have made the compromises and accommodations which lead on to a settled second half of life.

Why was she still as entangled as she had ever been?—worse—threatened by this indefinable feeling of doom which would neither reveal its face nor leave her in peace?

As ever she found comfort in analogy and strength in the past. Winding her way reluctantly though she could not precisely analyse the cause of the reluctance, along the twisting lanes to the Crowther's farm, she thought of herself as Ariadne. The daughter of Minos who had fallen in love with Theseus and gave him the thread so that he could extricate himself from the labyrinth after challenging the Minotaur—which he did, successfully, and came out to marry Ariadne, following the thread. "But then he abandoned her after she had helped him to live, he abandoned her," she said to herself walking slowly but resolutely along the Cumbrian country lane, hedges high in leaf, clouds light and grouped, smells rich and sweet. "He just left Ariadne. How could anyone do that?"

It grieved her that Theseus had done so. Her clear, defiant spirit saw neither cause nor justification for such an act. To have loved, to have been saved, to have been embraced in a marriage and then to have gone, just gone: it appalled her.

Yet what a man Theseus was! He was one of the Argonauts, he fought the centaurs, he attempted to rescue Proserpine from Hades: and in literature, too, he had been immortalized. But he should not have abandoned Ariadne, she insisted stubbornly: the rest could go to the devil. The Argonauts could sink, the centaurs could gallop all over the Greeks, Proserpine could rot in hell—all this was irrelevant to his primary duty which was to stay loyal to the woman who had loved him and saved him.

Slowly, in the dark of her ignorance which was not unknowing, Edgar grew more powerful, more important, more dangerous and more essential than ever before. In order to survive, she thought, she had to hack him away from some of his roots of strength, for the sake of both of them.

To be scrupulously honest with herself, she loved Theseus, too, and loved what he had done even after leaving Ariadne. "But it was fate with him," she said to herself, comforted. "He was an agent of gods. He had no choice. So in the end he was a puppet.

317

We can choose. Though they'll never call us heroes—we have the choice that really matters. We can choose to believe that this life is all there is and we can choose to distinguish between what is sufficient and what is necessary. And when we have chosen we must act on our choice and that calls for human qualities. Discovering these qualities and then attempting to live by them is the only heroic way now. Everything else is feeble."

Edgar had lost faith, she had concluded. It was like a sudden switch of climate between them. He was lazy. He was impatient with absolutes, he had neither the time to tease out any thought nor the will to accept that their problems were sympathetic to solution. In fact, and this was what chilled her most of all, he seemed set on a course of destructiveness; she could feel him drawing himself up for some terrible and irreparable act of vengeance against the hordes of foreign notions and injunctions with which she had beset him for so many years.

She thought she saw a way of heading that off.

At Mrs Crowther's she welcomed the offer of tea. The brother who had stayed on the farm was out doing the evening milking and the clearing up: they had the place to themselves. It had not changed much since her very first visit.

Rosemary used to like it, so solid, so enduring. Now it represented indomitable entrenchment. Mrs Crowther made the tea in the back kitchen, silently: neither woman was interested in trivialities. They engaged when they were settled and had paid brief tribute to the conventional courtesies.

"What was Edgar like," Rosemary began, rather desperately casual, "when he was a boy?"

Mrs Crowther nodded to herself: she had been right. The woman was after him. Her duty was to protect her son, that was clear; and all her answers were wary. "I can't remember much," she lied. "I expect he was a boy like all of them."

"He sometimes talks about his father," Rosemary said; and gritted herself to go on—it was the only way she knew. "I get the impression that he didn't really like him. His father used to hit him, didn't he?"

Mrs Crowther was outraged. Rosemary's statement flaunted confidences, and made a mockery of manners: besides attacking the two men she herself had most loved. But she had long prepared herself for something like this and held herself against outburst. "Fathers used to hit their boys in those days. Some still do. Nobody thought anything about it: and it's not like Edgar to whine."

"Oh, he didn't whine."

"I see."

"But," Rosemary went on, as the clock ticked their lives away and she relished the smell of stew which came from the kitchen and imagined Edgar in short pants hoisted up beside the high dining-table in this gloomy room to eat in silence, as he had told her he did. "Perhaps you could remember if ever he was very unhappy for a long time."

"They all had their ups and downs, Rosemary: everybody does. Dear me, I didn't keep a diary, you know. I had more to do."

"Yes. He tells me how hard you worked. He uses it to blame me for the easy life I have!" She laughed.

"I worked no harder than anybody else."

"But you were his mother." Rosemary laughed: it was nice after all to be talking to Edgar's mother, the woman who had borne him and nurtured him, for this woman accepted she was her son's wife and though she might not like it she would not conceive of that ever being altered: in the certainty Rosemary found unexpected relief. "I love it here," she said. "I see why Eleanor can't keep away."

"Since you bring the subject up," said Mrs Crowther, with apparent reluctance, "I've been wanting to ask you about Eleanor." Rosemary felt herself shrink from the anticipated criticism: she knew that Eleanor was being neglected but she had to get it right with Edgar first of all; after that there would be all the time in the world for her daughter. "From what I hear she's mixing with very low company."

"Pardon?" The muttered antique phrase "low company" jolted the younger woman into amusement.

"Dick Waters' boy—they call him The Duke for a nickname. She's been seen around with that gang. I've nothing against them. But it's no kind of crowd for somebody like Eleanor to be mixing with."

"The Duke! They have such nicknames in Thurston. It sounds as if she has good taste anyway!"

"He rides a motor-bike."

"Oh mother!" Sometimes Rosemary risked the word, through need or an urge to flatter: and always its resonance made her smart. "Riding a motor-bike doesn't make him a delinquent."

"I'll say no more. But she should be kept away from him. It's just storing up trouble."

"I'll deal with it when it comes." She took a deep breath. "I have enough with Edgar at the moment."

"Now that's none of my business, Rosemary. You've never welcomed advice and I would never stoop to interference." That sentence had been in the old woman's head for ages: polished almost daily as she had daily strived to reconcile herself to the sight and thought of her favourite in a troubled marriage.

"You've been very good," said Rosemary, sincerely. "But now I want help."

Mrs Crowther shook her head and fussed over the teapot, pouring herself a second cup although she never took a second cup, finding it almost impossible to contain the hundreds of thoughts and accusations, the slights and bruises and warnings which swarmed to the surface at the bidding of her daughter-in-law's straightforward appeal. "You can only help yourselves," she said, eventually. "That's the top and bottom of it."

"Why is he so cruel to me?" Rosemary let the tears come. "Why does he seem to hate me so much?"

"He doesn't hate you, Rosemary."

"It *feels* as if he does. He makes me feel he would prefer me dead. He could love me then."

"You can't say that. You are his wife."

"That's why he hates me. I bind him, I nag him, I ask him to look at himself seriously; I love him, mother, but everything I say seems to annoy him so much—whatever it is—the slightest thing."

"Yes, well. You've got across each other's nerves, that's plain. But then, everybody does, from time to time."

"Did you and your husband?"

"We wouldn't have been normal otherwise."

"And how did Edgar react at those times?"

"He would be upset, I suppose. You couldn't hide that sort of thing from him. The others seemed less bothered but then I've often thought since it was just because they didn't show it. Edgar showed it more."

"Yes. He's very sensitive, isn't he?"

The word was effeminate to Mrs Crowther and it embarrassed her. Yet she could not deny it.

"What I think," Rosemary went on, "is that he's behaving as if he hated himself. The thing is to discover why."

"You're always talking about people hating this and hating that. Nobody hates things, Rosemary. He's—I don't know what he is—but it doesn't help to talk about hating."

"Maybe you're right. I'm sure you're right! How stupid of me." She looked fulsomely at the older woman. "You are so much wiser than I am."

Again, Mrs Crowther wilted as if she had been heavily criticized.

"But what must I do to get him loving to me again?"

"He'll come round."

"Will he? Are you sure?"

The questions were so urgent that the older woman sloughed off her superficial and obstructive reactions; she saw the desperation and reached out. "Of course he will." She was sure of it. "What do you think is going to happen, anyway?"

"He will stay then." There was a fractured joyousness in the lilting tone of voice which stung Mrs Crowther's eyes.

"He can be terrible to live with," his mother agreed. "They all can. You must learn to ignore them and leave them alone."

"He'll stay. I'm so glad. You've made me very happy." Rosemary released her tension like a child releasing responsibility to an adult: and her face filled with the relief of dependent docility.

"What *can* he do?" Mrs Crowther's curiosity was stronger than her sense of caution. "He doesn't hit you, does he?"

"Oh no."

"He gives you your money."

"Yes. Yes—he's a little mean there. But I can understand that, from his childhood experiences. He keeps saying I ought to work for my living but I know he would hate it if I did. Edgar wants his woman at home."

"Anyway, with your asthma—he should have more sense. The trouble with Edgar is that he never took a real job. There was never anything good enough for him. And he'll suffer for it—he's suffering now."

"Do you think so? I disagree entirely. He'd hate a regular job. It would drive him barmy. I think he likes what he's doing."

"No." Mrs Crowther was quickly reverting to her former misgivings about her son's wisdom in his marriage. "I see him looking worn out and harrassed all the time. Dealing's all right for a bachelor."

"But he has such an opportunity!" Rosemary exclaimed, wildly, enraptured now by the security she felt come from Mrs Crowther and seeing all her perplexities fall away (how stupid she had been!) and Edgar emerge bright and clear. "When things settle down for him then he can concentrate on antiques and old statues and stones and the work he's always loved. He could have been a great archaeologist, Edgar, if he had had the education, or a great collector. He had the eye. All that he needed was the opportunity. He could have been a famous trader in antiquities," and for a moment in her mind's eye she saw desert camels and Eastern markets, ruined Parthenons and derelict Roman fortresses, the treasures of cathedrals and the furnishings of Empires: the daydream, brief as it was, refreshed her: she had thought herself dead to such loving and cathartic fantasies. "Marvellous!" she concluded.

"The way I look at it the man has a struggle to make a bare living," said his mother grimly.

"What's struggle?" Her sudden gaiety was beginning to offend the older woman. "Every great man has to struggle."

"I don't know about that."

"Was he such a fighter when he was a boy?"

"He got into his fair share of trouble."

"No. You misunderstand me. Did he fight—like he does now —*against* himself?"

"I don't follow you, Rosemary. You must remember that I'm not an educated woman."

Rosemary could not ignore the rebuff: but her new wave of excitement simply swamped over it. "Of course you are educated! It's just that the foolish world has decided to categorize these matters under labels that don't honour your sort of knowledge and wisdom. You know exactly what I mean, mother, to the last nuance." She paused. "I wish I didn't offend you."

"How can my own daughter in-law offend me?" Mrs Crowther's exasperation grew: the wistfulness confused her entirely.

"I'm sorry ... But, oh, there's so much I don't know about your son!"

"Goodness me, Rosemary! You're married to him. You know him as a man. All I can remember are a few of his antics as a boy.

And there was nothing different about him: nothing at all different." Here the old lady folded her arms across her bosom as if having dispensed once and for all with a necessary but unpleasant piece of business.

"But don't you see—it's the boy I want to know about. The child in us can explain so much."

"Now my head's starting to go round and round, Rosemary, and that's a fact. I can't be done with it."

"We always stay children. We only seem to grow in mind because we grow in our bodies but inside our heads there is a great deal from childhood which never goes away and influences us for evermore."

"I don't know about that."

"And don't you see? This is precisely what I *don't* know about my husband. There are things he does now which can have no other explanation than childhood. They must be traced to his childhood."

"I know nothing about that," and indeed the older woman was becoming distressed by the vehemence of her young visitor and shaken in some core of her being which she did not wish to be invaded and would defend tooth and claw.

"I should imagine he was a very charming little boy, wasn't he?" Rosemary enquired, slyly.

"Charming?"

"It would never be too difficult for him to get his own way."

"Over what?"

"Oh—anything. He loves you of course. He idolizes you."

Mrs Crowther was silent.

"Did he love his father?"

That was too much.

Mrs Crowther nodded, brusquely, but it was an acknowledgment, it was not impolite, and then she got up to begin clearing the table leaving Rosemary in no doubt that she had gone far too far.

Despite this, though, and the consequent embarrassment she felt, Rosemary was not too unhappy as she walked home, carefully, for it was growing cooler and her inclination to hurry threatened to bring on an attack of asthma; yet if she did not hurry she would get cold; she smiled at the fix.

She had achieved something. She had been soothed by the

older woman's utter certainty (it went without saying) that Edgar would never leave her.

That was her dread.

Everything else could be endured, she told herself: though she would never cease to look for true solutions. As long as he stayed with her.

When she reached home she found she was so worn out she could do nothing. Eleanor made them all boiled eggs for supper.

# Chapter Fifty

Edgar felt that he might be alone in the middle of an enormous ocean with such stillness and vastness all about him that everything that he was ached and ached ever more deeply for something to disturb the scene.

He was beginning to be giddy with the strain; in his own way he wanted to be just as concerned for the truth as she was. The failure was in his character, not in his thoughts. This double game had now nothing to justify it but the apprehension that worse might come were he to stop it or bring everything out into the open. He was fast becoming sickened with self-loathing, poisoned by it: he waited for something in himself to prompt him. The self-disgust was staining every thought. And, dangerously, horribly, there was pleasure in the tension and in the chaos. His former self was being eroded; Rosemary would have said, firmly, corrupted.

He did not visit Jessie for about ten days after her visit to Thurston, but after a few hours away from her he again realized without any doubt that his love for her was unfeigned; there was about it that tug of certainty which is the only guide. He wrote to tell her so.

This mid-day he came back from the bungalow after a hard morning. He was fencing off a garden area and he had run out of stakes. His credit everywhere was used up. Though he had got used to the idea of riding out storms and lulls in his freelancing life, he had not learnt to enjoy them and this time the weariness of mind and body contributed to a feeling of panic which he could not quite stifle: what if he could never finish his building? Or, having finished it, find no buyer? And be stuck with the place and the debts. How could he pay them off?

At such times as this his buoyancy drained quite away. He was assaulted with nightmare prospects of a destitute future.

Rosemary was surprised to see him. Usually these days he would make himself up a crude picnic of sandwiches and boiled eggs so that he could work throughout the day. But she made his unexpected mid-day return home into an occasion for delight and the meal was a pleasant affair.

After it he slumped heavily in his chair, a large, wing-backed Victorian piece. Somehow this chair had recently come to represent himself as—an object. In it he felt utterly empty of all sap or spunk or blood. He sat there, clamped by invisible straps, awaiting execution.

Swiftly, silently, mockingly deft, it seemed to him, Rosemary brought him tea, as his mother would have done and drew up a small table on which she placed it carefully. Then she sat opposite him bolt upright and waited.

"There's no more money," he said, urged on by her unspoken longing for conversation to plunge, heavily and inelegantly foursquare into the centre of one of his anxieties.

"For what? We live. We eat. We have shelter. We have books and thanks to you I have my music. We need so little." She spoke rapidly, eagerly.

"Yes. Yes. Yes. That isn't what I mean."

"Who needs money? I've often thought that the most irrelevant of all the great so-called truths—that money isn't the root of all evil. No one I admire writes of it at all."

"Then they must have *had* it." Reluctantly drawn to an engagement he had sought only to evade, Edgar, as he often did on such an occasion but now with a bitterness that ought to have warned but merely incited her, shifted to a reliance on the coarser side of his nature.

"Not at all. It was simply never a claim on their lives. And why do *we* need money?"

"I have to finish the house: you know, that ugly little bungalow you say spoils a nice field."

"Sell it as it is."

Now this was fair advice: but Edgar was utterly set on finishing it in the way he had intended. For a hundred reasons the notion of leaving it incomplete after the time and thought and work he had put into it could not be entertained. She would never understand that, he thought, unfairly.

"Sell it as it is," she repeated, happily. "Then you'll be rich."

"*Rich?*"

"I agree. We are rich as we are."

"We'll never be rich. Never. That has to go."

326

"Who cares?"

"I do. I want to be rich. I want to be a big fat rich man in a Rolls Royce with a big fat cigar."

"Nonsense!"

"You, of course, haven't a clue how money is made. You probably believe I find it under rhubarb leaves."

"Cabbage."

"It's not funny. I live with a woman whose idea of the world is about as real as a fairy's."

"I don't believe in fairies." Her facetiousness was desperate now.

"Have you any idea what I have to do to make sure we can live even as we do now?"

"Oh come on, Edgar, you enjoy it. You like taking risks."

"No I don't. I'm tired of it."

"That will pass."

"I wish I was as sure as you are."

"You are," she asserted. "You are."

"I'm sure of nothing! Nothing at all! All I'm sure of is that I—am—sick. Sick! Sick! Sick! Don't you understand?"

"No you're not. You're tired and confused and in pain—like people are when they are being reborn. But you are holding on. I'm so proud of you. You will be such a man!"

The silence which followed seemed to cleave to the bottom of Edgar's heart. And in that terrible silence the decision was made. "There *is* somebody else," he said, his voice raw as if the room were full of sawdust: a terrible clutch of hoarseness in his throat. "You're right."

In her scream was both agony and triumph but the former soon prevailed and she leapt across to him, flailing helplessly, her feeble arms against his solid supine figure. She crumpled before him with sobs and gasps of pain.

He found that he was stroking her hair.

It was strange that it was spoken. There was no relief; nor was there any shame. He had scoured himself already. Rosemary's sobbing was racked as she fought to control it and then saw it caught up with an attack of asthma. The dreadful wheezing convulsion which shook her brought him to his senses. How could he stand by when she was in such trouble?

He got up, lifted her gently from the floor, placed her in his chair and then went to fetch her pills and a glass of water. But

327

despite her distress she waved him away: "want to"—"myself"—
"a minute": she gasped out the words at such cost that he could
not argue. Sometimes, according to a system of her own, it was
better to fight the attack of asthma and let it take its course rather
than slug it with drugs. This meant the most melodramatic
heavings and sibilant sighings from her. She grasped his hand
tightly and held onto it fiercely as if she were biting on a strip of
leather while undergoing an operation without benefit of
anaesthetic.

Her face was blotched with the tears and the effort to stop
them and the force of the asthma. Edgar was still not used to it:
the sound was awe-inspiring: the terrible lunge for air and the
noise of it being sucked in as through a score of leaky tubes: then
the groan as the air was released, a throaty raw animal groan
which seemed to come from a deep and ineradicable source of
misery. She looked at him, tears flowing, fixing his gaze with such
an intensity that he felt he was being forced to contest it rather
than return it. He held his own; it was both the least and the best
he could do.

Gradually her attack subsided. She did not let go of his hand.
Gradually she overcame. The lungs cleared. The breathing grew
quieter. Soon it was no more than a little strained. She looked
utterly exhausted: but her eyes shone. "Thank you," she said,
gripping his hand even harder. "It must have been very difficult
for you to say that. You are a brave man."

Edgar shook his head: any concern for his feelings seemed to
him to be totally irrelevant and shameful. How could she do that?
He marvelled, yet again, at this extraordinary wife.

"We must be calm," she said and then the intent look
crumpled into sorrow and she howled, nuzzling his hand against
her cheek, crying her heart out. "Why did you have to? Oh,
Edgar, Edgar. Why?"

Though he forbade himself to give any indication of it, Edgar
too felt like crying. For this was the end not only of his deceit but
of her dream of himself, a dream which he had been proud to
have inspired however great a burden it later became. And it was
the end of their marriage.

Once more she imposed her will on her feelings and the crying
came to an énd. "Kiss me," she asked, looking at him with a face
pathetically swollen and red. "I feel so horribly rejected. Kiss
me."

He kissed her and she gripped him tightly around the neck, holding on to him for dear life.

He extricated himself gently and indeed felt a great wave of tenderness come over him. She was so fragile: if only she had accepted that. "We have to decide what to do," he said.

"Decide?"

"It can wait." He paused. "No—I want to decide. Now."

"I forgive you. No. Don't look away. Look at me, you old rascal! I forgive you." This was said most earnestly. "You must never forget that. Nor this. I love you. My love for you is unimpaired. You have hurt my feelings and you have broken a trust but you have not broken my heart and you have not done anything fatal. You have taken a mistress, that's all. Whoever the creature might be she is no threat to *me*. I would like you to give her up, of course, but even that can be talked over. There is no rush. There is nothing to decide."

Edgar tried to find the strength: she could wrap him up so effectively, so lovingly it seemed; he was the stone to her paper. But his say had to be said. He could not count on contriving such another opportunity. "I love her. I'm sorry. Believe me, I'm sorry. But I love her."

"Of course you do." There was steel in Rosemary's tone now: she would not let him go. "Of course you think you do. You must. You are a loving man. I wouldn't expect your mistress to be a casual pick-up."

"I think. If you love. If you love someone then you should live with them."

"You love Eleanor. Don't you? And you still love me after a fashion. I'll wait until the rest of your love comes back to me. I can wait." He must not see the crippling effort she was making: he must not see.

Edgar felt the panic which had been building for months on end now begin to rush into his throat. She was right, of course. In every way. "You would say that loving people meant you want to live with them?" he asked, obstinately.

"I would?"

"You believe in people acting truly. Doing—you know, what they must."

"What you must do depends on the circumstances. In this case you have a wife and child."

"But it's no good, Rosemary: the way we live is no good."

"You'd find exactly the same problems living with another woman and having her child. Your difficulties are to do as much with the situation as with me. More, I'd say. And anyway, Edgar, all that is changing; can't you feel it? We're coming through. You can't just throw it away. It's work. We've been trying to make a relationship *work*. Don't you see?"

"I've had it, though, Rosemary. We'll never get on. It's too painful."

"There must be pain. There is nothing worth a damn possible without it."

"You're right. I'm sure you're right. But I've had enough."

He wanted to talk no more: already he could see that she was set for a talk which could last out the day and into the night as far as she was concerned. Her stamina was prodigious. He moved away: he must see Jessie, at that very instant, urgently.

"Edgar."

"Yes?"

"Don't leave me."

"I'll be back later."

"I don't mean that. I mean, don't leave me. No one can love you as much as I do. No one knows you as much as I do. We need you, Edgar, your daughter and your wife."

How, he asked himself later and hopelessly, how on earth could he be irritated with such a small thing as her vocabulary at a time such as that? But the drama of the last sentence, as of many others, did unquestionably infuriate him out of all proportion.

When he had gone Rosemary shivered violently and then made herself a hot drink and sat down to concentrate on her reactions and her plans. Every so often, though, despite her attempts at control, that violent shiver stole over her and she was afraid.

# Chapter Fifty-One

Edgar was now in a territory where he had no guide or example for his actions and no standard or comparison for his feelings. The sensation of wild solitariness made him determined to keep his head. Very little made sense.

There was no sense in Rosemary's acceptance of his confession in such a way: true she had been unhappy, but she ought to have berated him, he thought, and he was worried that she had not done so. There was no sense in his leaving her after delivering such an awful blow to her and racing over the moors to Northumberland to see Jessie except that there was a feeling of urgency so strongly felt as to be irresistible: he had to tell Jessie too and so keep whatever balance it was held him sane. There was no sense in thinking about a future because it yielded nothing: no more was the past a blessing, for it contradicted all he was doing. What he had learned and what he had come to believe in had been thrown to the winds. He had never felt so alone, so surrounded as with a duct of cool air which isolated him. In Carlisle he stopped for a few drinks—quick gins—and even considered going up to see Margaret again. That strange, even eerie whim was resisted but still he felt open to anything.

The dominating pressure in his mind was the overwhelming urge to leave things as they were and stay with Rosemary. Every consideration he could think of pressed him to do this. Everything he respected in himself pointed that way. Her need was obvious; Eleanor's need was equally obvious. His own needs had been so generously served by this woman even if he could find cause for dissension in the physical contact. Yet the message of the flesh was powerful. He did not want to resist it, to miss this chance; he did not dare.

Once back in the car and pointed towards Jessie's place, he could allow himself to be flooded with an extraordinary release of happiness. This had been repressed or diverted or concealed for too long: the thought of Jessie made him full of enormous joy and now that his lie was admitted, now that, though shaken, he felt the beginnings of decency attainable once more, he could feed this feeling and let it roar!

It was glorious! Blow, blow the horn on the straight and empty road! She was mag-nif-i-cent! Blow, blow the horn! Her lips received his like soft wax. Inside her was the certainty which outreached any idea of truth. Blow, blow, blow the horn!

Across the high Roman road the car went, sounding its way as by bugles. Edgar felt that his existence was entirely, utterly and without any doubt in the grip of the present: it was extraordinarily exhilarating. Guilt was waiting like the straitjacket, remorse like the cell and regret like the blade of the guillotine, but all were stayed by the natural force of his love for this woman and his total belief that in his love was sanity and happiness and the consummation of pleasure to be found nowhere else. Go, go, go, he told himself: the moment is all there is.

Stripped, then, of the layers of past and future which wrap around most people except at such times of drama, and indifferent to the lateral connections which exist to hold a man in his place in the multiple grids of society, Edgar's mind felt as if a raw hard wind were whipping through it, raking out all the wrinkles of complexity and reducing his life to a simplicity which was both shocking and wonderful.

At a pub near the Wall called Twice Brewed he stopped again. But the bar was closed. He was checked by this, wanting more alcohol to celebrate this mood which must be kept up. But the licensing laws were unyielding.

Jessie was not in but the woman knew Edgar by now and she showed him into the old-fashioned parlour to wait. There was a chill about her attitude quite new: full of his own tensions, he picked it up but could not analyse it.

The parlour was a much smarter version of his mother's best room and he waited, idly looking into a book, quite unable to allow the prose to grapple with him.

The gin seemed to trickle around and about his brain and that calmed him down.

When Jessie came in, she entered silently and impassively. Edgar got up to embrace her but she avoided him and he sat down a little angry even though he understood her reluctance to be compromised in her place of work.

It was awkward in the foreign and formal room. To his consternation, Edgar found himself remembering the recent exchange with Rosemary. Vividly, in his mind's eye, he saw her blotched, bewildered face: it made him flinch, shake his head abruptly as if stung, dip into the possible and horrible consequences.

"What is it?" Jessie was sitting far from the window, in the dusky part of the room: in that light, her creamy skin made her seem very vulnerable. He scarcely knew her, he thought.

"Nothing. How are you?"

"Well enough." She hesitated. "What have you come to tell me?" Her voice was very soft.

"Who said I'd come to tell you anything?"

"I hope you have." The tension in her rejoinder once more wrenched him back to the scene earlier that same afternoon: he had to separate them.

"Yes, I have."

"Tell me."

She waited: and between them rolled a powerful wave of sorrow. This was the last time they would know each other in the way they had come to find and to love each other: this was the end of that first affection which to her had appeared flawless and to Edgar, endlessly healing. "You must know it already . . . I'm a married man. And I have a daughter."

Jessie nodded and held herself against her feelings. She had learned a few days before: the gossip had had an incontrovertible ring to it. There was nothing she could find to say.

"I should have told you earlier." He waited: and then had to go on, pausing hopefully at the end of almost every sentence. "I wanted to. No I didn't. I deliberately didn't. I wanted us to be as if we were free to meet as we did. That's the truth, Jessie. I wanted us to be free."

"But you weren't."

"No."

She did not trust herself to say anything and waited. Her silence drew out Edgar's thoughts till then kept hidden even from himself under the easing lubricant of a self-deceit which no longer answered.

"We had our time anyway," he said. "Do you think I should have told you?"

"I don't know."

"Do you want me to leave you now?"

"No. I don't."

That straightforward and negatively expressed affirmation fed his fear.

He spoke without thought and yet the words were from the heart of the matter. "I want you to come to Thurston with me."

She stiffened, almost bridled, and firmly shook her head.

"We can live in the new house I've built—it's almost ready—ready enough."

He paused: his lips were dry but the simple action of licking them seemed to be too obtrusive. There were a number of supporting reasons which came to mind to justify his request: that his means would not allow him to keep up another household, that he needed to be near Eleanor; that his work—essential for them all—was focused on Thurston: but all this was neither here nor there. Jessie needed to be won; the truth was the only serious weapon.

"If you don't come," he spoke with difficulty, aware of the tremulous ground he had to cover to make his violent and immoral suggestion acceptable; reaching into himself for explanations which were better unspoken and yet needed the affirmation of language, needed that final proof. "If you don't come," he repeated, "then I won't be able to hold out. And I don't know what will happen."

Jessie steadied herself. "If you don't know—you're better off staying as you are. Aren't you?"

He acknowledged this, but knew for certain that however incontrovertible her common sense or common humanity, it had to be breached if there were to be any future. "I won't stay as I am." He paused. "It's all changed now. She knows there is—you; someone else. It's changed."

"I couldn't live in the same place or even near it. You know that."

"We have to. Don't you see? We have to."

Jessie realized that he meant to have his way and appreciated the consequences. Yet everything in her which had risen to condemn his recently discovered infidelity now reared up to kick out at this dreadful suggestion. Her training held and she waited in silence.

"I can't run away from Rosemary. She couldn't stand that. She'll want me to be open. This sounds—I don't know—in a way. We have got to live together in Thurston because it's what she wants and I have to give her that. I owe her that. And besides I have to be near her to help her over it—but that isn't as important as this other thing."

They sat, formally addressing each other in the tranquil twilight, strained to find a way.

"You mean if you don't face up to her you'll never be able to be—able to be free of her? Is that it?"

"Yes." Edgar spoke eagerly, clutching at the help. "Yes—yes. But—there's that *other* thing: she's a woman who must face everything, you see. Nothing is to be hidden: I think her way now. I believe that now. She's right. And this must not be hidden. If it is—then—everything's hopeless, hopeless altogether."

The desperation in his voice cut to the quick of Jessie's love so lately untroubled, so lately whole and unblemished. She thought on that. "What if I don't come with you?" she whispered.

He groaned. "Then I don't know what will happen. God only knows what will happen."

Jessie's pale face grew even whiter in the dusk which surrounded it like a dark encroaching circle. "If you want me to, I will," she replied, eventually.

His spirit lurched dangerously that she should so straightforwardly take him at his word: yet again the lack of complication and contradiction unsettled him—but unsettled him to make him glad.

"It would be painful to stay around here anyway," she added. "My father knows all about you."

"Oh? What did he say?"

"He says I'm never to go back home. And if he catches you he'll horsewhip you."

"He knows his own mind." Edgar laughed at the thought. "Like you." Then he realized how difficult it was for her. "Are you?—Well you must be upset by it."

"I can understand his attitude," she said, calmly. "He nearly killed one of my brothers for making a girl pregnant even though he was going to marry her and did marry her. He wouldn't go to the wedding and hasn't spoken to him since. He won't even have him spoken of in the house."

Peace and quiet: these were what Jessie epitomized; even now, in the middle of a terrible period of discovery and alarms and rejections. She was shaken but she was not disturbed: yet he did not know the price she was paying for her apparent placidity, the price she made herself pay. The even outer surface, for its unbroken appearance, scooped out painfully hoarded resources now sacrificed to keep the line firm. Jessie would not afford herself the consequences of plunging into her own confusion sensing that it was Edgar's actions that were to be the guide. She loved him greatly and he needed her.

"Yes." Jessie said the one word conclusively and with great effort now, bravely: she was extremely tired by the shock and strain of the past few days, and her attempt to be fair to Edgar and, equally, to herself, was taking too much out of her.

"It will be horrible." Edgar repeated, uneasily. "God knows what Thurston people will say to it. Let alone our friends and hers." He was appalled at the prospect. "But what's the alternative?"

"We could part," she whispered.

Seeing her distress he went across to her and held her closely against him, knowing that the physical contact would help her as it did him. She was so solid against him, neither clinging nor pulling nor utterly limp—all of which Rosemary could be—all of which unnerved him.

Yes. Despite what had to come it was Jessie he could live with. Rosemary's union with him was over. The wonder was it had taken place at all.

He locked the door of the parlour and quietly made love to Jessie, without contraception, wanting her to let him give her a child. They made love silently in the dark, formal room.

# Chapter Fifty-Two

That same evening Edgar drove Jessie back to Thurston with him. He took her to the bungalow, made several quick trips between the warehouse and his new home and by about ten o'clock they were hastily organized. The couple Jessie worked for had worriedly lent them sheets and blankets and some cutlery and crockery, the essentials necessary for the preliminary period of camping. He was glad to reach the bare bungalow, so empty, stripped for a new start. The heavy Victorian furniture from the warehouse, unlikely he would have thought to fit the modern angularity of his design, actually graced the place extraordinarily well: and even the makeshift arrangement of those first few hours gave him an aesthetic satisfaction which he had never gained from his former uncluttered home.

The time came to tell Rosemary what he had done and what he intended. Although he was aware that it was a cowardly thing to do he went to The Lion and Lamb and had three large gins.

So he told her, with that raw alcoholic spirit informing the brutality of his soft-spoken words. She neither raged nor collapsed but waved her hand at him, a helpless reflex action, fending off the evil dart and giving him a fine reason for departing.

And further to plunder what was left of his conscience, he laughed and played that night with Jessie on a mattress on the bare floor, gambolled with her as if they had been a pair of spring lambs. This was proof, final and unequivocal, he thought, that he had no shame.

He woke up the next morning poised between fear and exhilaration. Jessie was still asleep and he looked carefully at her face. She slept with her mouth half-open: it rather distorted her features and made her nose appear larger than he had previously thought. In the morning light the paleness of her skin had a pink texture which was deepest on the lips. On her left shoulder-blade was a large, faintly brown patch of skin, a birth-mark, like a straw-

337

berry patch. He had seen it before but in this pure morning light it worried him. He had an urge to brush it off: then he kissed it.

There were none of the usual morning sounds: no Rosemary downstairs making weak tea to combat the first asthma of the morning; no Eleanor scrambling to do her homework before going to school, no chat from outside, Mr Tate breathing fiery Methodist goodwill on the day, Mr Allison already at his garden, the milkman at the bottom of the avenue, the early schoolchildren chattering down from the flats which had been hacked out of the great mansion. He was released from all that, all the gentle suburban intoxicants which unhappily had given him so little nourishment.

Instead, outside, to the south, was an unbroken view to the fells. He went outside in his trousers and a singlet only and felt some of the giddiness he had felt as a boy on balmy summer mornings such as this: he had a distinct and, for him, rare visual memory of himself as a teenager, dressed thus, in "long trousers" (his brother's) and a singlet, going out to get the horses ready for his father—one chore he had loved, never ceasing to enjoy that first breath of rich, stinking, stable air, his fingers longing to touch the tensile skin, his face to feel the nuzzle of the friendly old shire horses. That had been happiness! And now happiness was inside the ugly structure he had raised with his own hands: with Jessie there he found no pain in acknowledging the place's ugliness. Jessie liked it, she said, both the building which she praised as being ingenious and convenient and the location which she blessed for being detached and lonely.

But when he turned to look north to Thurston, seeing the small incongruous green dome on top of the tower of Highmoor Mansion and the churches below, then there were other memories, all laden with the weight of his crime.

He had to prepare for the worst. His action would be violently condemned and he expected no less. It was part of the price he wanted to be made to pay; part of the reality, the "truth of the matter" which Rosemary would have wanted him to face up to. He believed in what she stood for now, although he had not the spirit for defiance. Rosemary had that sort of spirit. His would be an obstinate perseverance.

Their first morning hours together passed with such slowness that it seemed a new reckoning of time had been born. He walked

338

across to the nearest farm to get some milk: he said he had forgotten his bait and the woman gave him some bread and cheese and a couple of apples. This was their breakfast and they ate it sitting in the sun, their backs against the rough red-brick walls, their faces flooded with the heat. Every crumb was eaten up.

It was an enchanted morning, wonderful and terrible at the same time, imprisoned in that paradox for the last time: after this it would be one or the other, they would alternate or altogether fade, but never again could there be this tremulous double-feeling which they shared. Little was said: the sun strengthened and beat into their skin.

Eventually, when the sun was over the hills and Edgar once more felt hunger, he had to go to the town. There were stores to get, more furniture from the warehouse, and Rosemary to be seen—she would need to see him and he would make himself available.

An indescribable dream-time was how he remembered those few hours spun out like a glistening web when everything seemed in the balance and yet everything was settled; for beneath the callous calm was that simple deepest tranquillity of all, knowing that he could rest in this woman Jessie. Maybe she would leave him, maybe the strain would be too great: but what he was about to fight for was peace.

# Chapter Fifty-Three

Rosemary had decided on her plan of action that first night and she stuck to it for a long time—longer, she later thought, than she ought to have done: but then again she would blame herself for not sticking to it for long enough.

Her analysis was clear. Edgar, she reckoned, had been much more upset by the internal, struggles of the past couple of years than she had anticipated. She had seen him whimpering with pain all the more devastating to him because it came from a source unknown (though *she* could identify it, she believed, taking thought); she had seen him the victim of ridiculous obsessions and manias such as the powerful and quite irrational, even violent dislike he had taken to their unexceptionable home—as if it were of the smallest importance where you lived or in what conditions, she thought. He had, in fact, she concluded (and there was a dossier of evidence in her mind because Edgar to some extent had become her chief study) become a child again in order to grow into the different man both of them wanted him to be and in the process she, Rosemary, his wife, had been forced to act as his mother would have acted. Her reading in psychology, limited though it was, made her certain that this was so. She had become his "mother": and of course, now he was a man, he wanted to throw off the mother.

"That was the risk I took," she said to herself. "That was always the risk I took. Once he appreciates it, there will be no problem. No. He's a good man and a fair man. I'll point this out to him, I'll explain it all—I'll show him how true it is—and then we'll see. Because he loves me. I know that. And I love him. That is all that matters."

In a most peculiar way, she could even be thrilled by the incipient struggle, perverse though that seemed to her saner self. She saw it, though, as the apotheosis of their life and in her dauntless moments welcomed it.

But there were times when she was pitched into a grief so

steep, she feared that she would never pull herself out of it.

Not so much at first, though. Then she fairly bristled with concentration. Her mind had never been so fully extended, rapidly scanning her own past history and that of Edgar, landing on salient points, seeing patterns where before there had been none, weaving an ever more complicated scheme of attack. Then he would come to see her, as he did every day, and the longed-for, loved sight of him would bring about a bitter collapse. "You're not a man," she would accuse him, hard-eyed, utterly unhappy and determined, it seemed, to make herself even more miserable. "A man would have an affair and leave it at that. He wouldn't make himself and his wife the scandal of the town in this ridiculous way. Why couldn't you keep quiet about it?"

"You say tell the truth."

"Truth! You've never told the truth in your life. You're too weak to hold it. It's a pretence, that's all, a smack in the face for your mother and me and the whole town. Just because you can't achieve the importance you want by legitimate means, you adopt this sensational method. It's so childish! Calling attention to yourself. No; don't you dare leave me. Wait until I'm finished! That would be typical of you to run away in the middle. You've never been able to bear anything. Coward!"

He would stay and be abused, feeling that she was right, holding onto the secret sense of his ultimate power to go away as to a lifeline.

Even in her scorn for him was something wonderful, he thought. She was like a paper rose which unfolds in water: any problem brought to her mind was seized on and petalled with her intelligence. She accused him of failings which astonished him but when he said, All right, all right, if that's the way you feel isn't it better that I go away? she would instantly retract all she had said. Usually his returns were less honourable and less subtle. He accused her of idleness, frigidity, selfishness, being untidy, careless with Eleanor—the dam had broken: he accused her of all he feared and hated in himself, in her, in them, in his life and in the world. She was in the way of the deluge, that was all, and took the flood. He was demonstrably and lamentably unfair; just as her attitude was breathtakingly splendid, he thought.

For, fundamentally, she believed that he was testing her to discover new liberties and must be allowed and even encouraged to do it. Insofar as she had the strength to pursue this principle, she did so. It was very clear to her and she explained it clearly to Edgar, thus releasing him from a great deal of entangling thought and braking guilt. At one and the same time she honoured what he was doing, made it easier for him and made it much, much more difficult for herself.

"You must choose," she said, having prepared herself for his daily visit carefully and nervously, paying attention to matters like clothes and hair-style which had so little interested her before, "you must choose your own life and ignore all those who must be telling you to behave as *they* behave. Your beloved Thurston is no more than a petit-bourgeois-dominated place and that sort of morality is only for the conformists. You are braver than that. You want to fly your own path. I admire that."

Crazily, she cheered him up and strengthened him immensely because he was very far from thinking that Thurston did not matter. The scandal weighed heavily on him and he moved about the place surreptitiously. Yet he was prepared to endure it and spent the little energy he had equally between making sure—by sign and token—that Rosemary was not denied and that Jessie was not reviled.

People were terribly curious; he could see their snouts lift as he came near, he thought. All the more so because the couple had led such a glamorous life; the small pretty cottage on the hill with all its little effects so enviably well contrived; the successful plunge into the whirl of business; finally, respectability for Rosemary and adventure for Edgar. And with all this there had been something very self-contained about the pair, not secretive so much as untouchable; it was by a queer wild justice that all their affairs should now be so widely known. Rumours about Jessie's magnetism and the sensual depths reached in the unfurnished bungalow grew darker every day. Friends of Sarah and Lawrence tried to keep it in proportion and sickle down the weeds but it was impossible to resist speculation. Rosemary's aloof poise during the first months only fed the fury. Did she approve? Or worse, did she not care? Or, worst of all, was she trying to get him back?

Despite the discoveries of Edgar's action, there was nothing clear-cut about it. Rosemary would still refer to "my husband" in the course of an ordinary chat, for all the world as if he were back home with his feet up in front of the fire. Which, amazingly, was where he could be, often enough, because, so they said (and they were well-informed) he dropped in every day and stayed an hour or so and pottered around just as before. He neglected the garden but then he never had been keen.

It was Sarah and Eleanor who suffered visibly the most from the scandal. Had not Sarah been sustained by her brother's need of her, she might have succumbed to the most alarming degree because the entire episode was proof of her worst fears and an affront to the appearance she had cultivated with much care and sacrifice. Her sense of what was respectable was central to her sense of her own being and this scandal with its squalid ramifications—tales of wildness on the Border, rumours of illegitimate children and violent abduction—was like a virus on her soul. Her sense of charity towards her brother was, thankfully, a powerful antidote.

Eleanor's cure was to seek solitude. Outside the knowledge of her parents, she had developed an elaborate, vivid and intense life of her own in the town; a life which was beginning to move forward powerfully in a sensual and intellectual harmony which (surprising to all but one of her teachers who had despaired of the flashes of unusual talent so soon effaced by desultory indifference) promised a life of possible riches. She had survived the virulence of her parents' antagonisms. She had ridden the whirlwinds of their never-ending coupling: she had coped with all that and steadied herself to take on life on her own terms. The prospect was exciting both to herself and to the one or two who had an inkling of what she could achieve. Now, in the glare of this shameful scandal, she lowered herself down deep into solitude as if she were in a bell jar.

Jessie kept her thoughts to herself. She did not shop in Thurston but got most of her supplies from the small general stores at Red Dial. Delivery vans brought the rest and it was the drivers of these patient vehicles who were the messengers between the town and the fancy-woman. Soon the burden of their report was a statement on how the pregnancy of the new woman was developing. They liked her, these drivers, found her manners easy and pleasant, her sense of conversation and values much as their own, much closer to comprehension than the strange dazzlings of Rosemary: though she was not, of course, and never would be the "lady" that Rosemary could be called. Often in a single afternoon those drivers with their small vans stuffed full of fruit and vegetables, meat or pastries, would visit

343

both the women within an hour. Then there was food for talk and for comparison! Rosemary was getting thinner as Jessie grew more pregnant; that provided an uneasy laugh. Jessie's skin grew darker, as Rosemary looked ever paler. The married woman grew more and more tense ("full of nerves"); the scarlet woman (there were those among the elderly who could still use that ancient description confidently) grew calmer. Jessie was ever concrete and particular in all her dealings, a careful housekeeper: Rosemary's buying was erratic, dashing, ill-planned, over-eager. These drivers, on the few occasions they talked to each other, sensed a growing sympathy among themselves for both women and an insoluble problem in divining what was going to happen.

In one respect the town was right. The ugly new house was the place of great sensual pleasures. Edgar was besotted with Jessie's sex and she could easily take all he had to give. Before they had lived together he had found making love to her something which restored him: now it was a drive to pleasure of a kind and power which he had avoided in his years with Rosemary. She had refined his tastes in all things. Now, crazy with thirst for what he totally believed to be the only quality of experience which could sustain him, he let his lust for her surge over him like a giant wave and he wallowed in it. The imprisoned self which had survived for so many years in opposition now came out of his crevice and like the genie released from the bottle the wonder was how it had ever been confined to such a small space. He took on the world of sexual satiety with brutish satisfaction.

Further and further he went from Rosemary and she saw him go with pain which would have been insupportable but for two things: her belief in the accuracy of her vision; and the fact that Edgar would still say he loved her.

To him the words meant one or all of several things. They were a blind acknowledgment of the truth that once you have really loved then you will always find love: they were a poor expression of his gratitude and admiration; they were a token of his astonishment that still, as she grew weaker and the asthma became chronic, she would receive him as if he had been the truest of lovers and herself the most cherished of ladies and make him feel like a lord while pouring stewed tea into the large willow-patterned cups; the words expressed what he knew she wanted to hear and his culpable soft-heartedness wanted her to enjoy this benefit though a harder self told him it was doing her no good at all. For of course she took the words to mean one thing only: that he would come back.

Oh what a dream that was, and how she nurtured it! As her body began to waste from the rack of the asthma, the lack of sleep, the carelessness about health and appearance except at the hour of Edgar's expected visit, when she would leap into a bonnier self at great cost to all her sense of tragedy and propriety and decency, as the flesh began to fail her, what she felt and thought grew and intensified and flamed inside her until her eyes were liquid with a flame of such beauty that Edgar found it unendurable. He could not hope to meet her gaze.

Often he would try to qualify the words as she drew them from him but there was no going back on what she took and grasped as a declaration of the most profound truth and promise and—who knows? he would feel as he trudged away from a luminous hour in her company, she could be right.

For Edgar's sense of right and wrong had been smashed in the conventional sense but the formless gropings his bared emotions made reached only to the tactile "*rightness*" of Jessie: she was the beginning and the end of his journey into the jungle of self and it took him all his strength to hold the territory he had gained. Other possibilities were always present: he had neither the energy nor the capacity to deny them, though when it came to taking action what he always did was to hold onto Jessie more stubbornly and more tightly than ever.

He soon found things to criticize in his new love: every bit as many as in the old. The move was from quicksilver to quartz. He missed the play of Rosemary's mind as keenly as a man with salt in his imagination misses the sea: but where there was that glory there was also danger and finally he came to one of the saddest evasions of all: that his wife would be better off without him.

Badly needing a confidant, he was surprised until he reflected on it to discover that Scrunt fitted the part. For Scrunt had kept up his friendship with both Rosemary and Edgar, not being the jealous mate of the same age that some of Edgar's friends had suffered from, and above all he treated the matter most seriously, taking his cue from his younger friend whose intense concentration on it he appreciated: Edgar was not, he thought, someone to get upset and in such a mess for nothing. Many evenings passed with the two of them working at the house or in the field and Scrunt listening to the nervous declarations of the younger man.

345

"You see, I can love her but I can't live with her any more. Does that make any sense? Does it? I mean it doesn't really, I can see that. I can see it gets you nowhere at all but that's always what I come back to. She's twice what I am, more, ten times what I'll ever be. I can't understand why I can't go back. Whenever I see her, we talk, she's lovely, she makes me laugh, she makes me think, she makes me feel better than I've any right to feel. I mean what can I want out of life if I don't want her? What more is there?"

But even as he uttered the rhetoric he knew with certainty that his reaction to Rosemary had fear in it, nerve and skin: he could never confess that.

It was made clear to him that Lawrence wanted to see him and he went in trepidation. It was a miserable interview. The old man could only make sounds through one corner of his mouth and the words came out scarcely distinguishable through spittle and saliva. His eyes, which had widened sorrowfully after the stroke, fixed themselves dolefully on the younger man and Edgar listened in silence to what could only be a plea to return to Rosemary. Lawrence soon sensed that he was having little effect: the man was being polite and even sympathetic but he was intransigent. Then an urgency came into the half-rigid old body which began to shake fearfully as he tried to express his forebodings. Edgar called out for Sarah and she came and without a glance or a word at the visitor made it clear that his time was up.

Outside that house Edgar remembered how, so long ago, he had delivered the stone head, the present wrapped in paper. Rosemary had rediscovered it recently and placed it prominently in their living-room, glancing at it with shy significance, now and again, when he went to see her. For a while he hovered about the front door, self-consciously swinging in the balance, but his steps took him past his old place and out towards the new.

Jessie was getting darker-skinned now as the curve of the belly arched further outwards. And as the approaching birth was bringing up tints from the blood so also from her mind which deepened the lustre of her character. She, too, was lonely. Margaret had managed one brief visit: the people she had been hired with had come twice—but Edgar did not like them, he could not bear the feeling of complicity; they had not mistaken his attitude and kept away. Her father did not write nor would he

346

ever come to her, she was certain of that. But in some way much of her life had prepared her for this rejection and she found her own long-imagined fears had furnished her with defences. Inside her womb was the life that mattered.

She tried not to think about Rosemary. Edgar spoke of her—not often but often enough. Sometimes Jessie saw him in a grotesque posture she remembered from one of her brothers' comic books: the blotched picture of a man standing legs apart, arms outstretched, each hand and leg being pulled with great violence, one by gorillas the other by white men. As the comic strip had progressed the tug of war had become fiercer until, finally, the man had been ripped in two. Though this was from a crudely drawn cartoon in a cheap book, its perfect appropriateness to the essence of her nightmare made Jessie wince as with physical pain whenever she pictured it.

She concentrated on organizing the garden. It was simply a part of the field rather clumsily fenced off. Slowly but methodically she dug it over, planted potatoes, saved for saplings, planned it, sought large stones for a rockery, had Scrunt help her lay a path, devoted herself to it in the many hours she was alone.

These were very many because Edgar soon found that he would have to do something dramatic to fill out his earnings. He acted quickly and effectively. There was a new road being built between Penrith and Carlisle and labour, chiefly Irish, was well paid—provided you worked every daylight hour. He did that, often putting in fourteen or fifteen hours and then driving back to make sure that Jessie did not spend the night alone. She was afraid of that. Scrunt took over the residual dealing business which Edgar would occasionally firm up by taking off a weekday and working flat out to keep in business. In a lucky streak now, he had a few sales of the Victorian furniture to two young couples, teachers who were converting farm cottages for themselves. That helped. But the main flow of cash came from his work as a labourer on the roads and the six months he was employed there was the hardest stretch of muscular labour he had ever undertaken. The first few weeks threatened to cripple him for life, he had thought.

And here too was scope for his plunge into coarseness. The obscenities came as regularly as the swing of the pick; and the fights and sordid scuffles between men whose only strength would have been to have sunk individual differences and fought side by side. For despite the glamorous cash payments (by local labouring standards) the conditions of the work and the totally unprotected nature of the employment exacted the historic toll. On those drizzling winter days, inadequately clothed or equipped or fed, the men stored up debilities which would knot their bodies way before the three-score years and ten. The loud shouting was often not much more than a scream of anger tuned to resemble human speech out of a final pride in manhood which was soon driven to find proofs in everything. Edgar survived.

The fatigue was welcome as drink was welcome. He could not give himself the luxury of gin now and drank mild and bitter, the mixture smacking exactly right on his palate after the brawny exertion.

Caught by the need for money, Jessie wanted to do the hundred and one things of which she was well capable but in the end she took in washing from an orphanage called Greenhill which stood in its own grounds about half a mile away. This helped a little.

Rosemary, too, caught the fever and decided to return to the library. But her doctor advised against it and anyway, to her amused chagrin, she discovered that the qualifications were no longer what once they had been. She would have to take a re-entry examination and this she prepared for, spasmodically, breathlessly assuring Edgar that it would soon be all right, she would soon be able to work. Her attitude annoyed him and yet once again he could see no reason for his irritation. She was making a great effort: she was doing what she thought he wanted and as usual she was right—it was what he wanted; she was noble and heroic but he could only feel meanly irritated.

In those months, Rosemary read more greedily than ever before in her life, particularly poetry, philosophy, mythology and psychology: everything pointed in one direction. Whether she was the Lady of Shalott or the Oedipal Mother, whether her latest infusion came from Jung or Frazer, she saw every single thing in terms of Edgar and herself. He was the hunter, the prince, the sailor, the warrior, the witch-doctor, the noble man, the high priest, the free spirit, the man of the earth, the overman, the force of nature, the child of circumstance, the man of his times, the reality principle, the way, the libido, the flesh to her spirit, the blood to her water, the id to her ego, the alpha and the omega and she was attendant, trapped forever in her own unchallenged and unchallengeable belief in the sanctity of the struggle for liberty, greater and greater liberty, through the recognition and comprehension of truth.

More and more abstract her life became until days passed in banded groups rather like the flotillas of cloud in the sky, slowly skimming over the surface of her mind while deep within she fought to maintain her principles, to control her instincts and most of all to quell her awful terrors. The starved monsters of childhood and infancy were at large, loose in the cusp of her brain, waiting to pounce on the life she had succeeded in keeping from them.

She began to paint again, whirls of colour, vortices, fathomless, figureless, clamant. And Edgar calmly said he quite liked them.

The subject of money seemed to be preoccupying him more and more insistently and he would talk about his lack of it; he would bargain with her over what she needed to live on; though he was earning good wages he became even more mean. His former flashes of generosity which she had loved were gone. She dreaded these talks about money in which she had no interest—which seemed a banal and destructive intrusion into the serious argument which, so she hoped, was being resolved between them. But she forgave him this vulgarity.

She had learned that Jessie was pregnant and following that information had spiralled into a state of despair which Edgar alone could and did coax her away from. But to lift her he had to tell her that he loved her.

Winter passed and spring brought no relief to her whose mind was now a circular library of memory and vision forever whirling about in her mind. Fearing for the effect of this awful strain, Sarah took Eleanor into her own house despite Lawrence's condition. The long-drawn-out last period of the old man's life had changed the way in which his illness was regarded and he was looked on now as an habitual invalid. The urgency was gone but Rosemary thought—though she banished the thought for fear of its tempting vanity—that he was hanging on only to try to be an influence for the good on Edgar and she thanked him with all her heart, for if anyone could penetrate the stubborn will to deny her which she now saw rooted deep in her husband, it was this gentle old man. But Edgar, in cowardly fashion she sadly observed, avoided him.

He did not want contrary advice.

349

A conclusion being forced on her weary, weary mind, one which she fought both because of her love and because of her fear, but one which could not be evaded, was that Edgar was destructive. He was after some sort of revenge. For what, she could not imagine beyond acknowledging that by helping him to a second birth she had necessarily incurred his wrath. But could he not see that she had deliberately and openly taken that risk for him? Oh, the fool, the fool! Could he not see that he was as he was because of her?

She feared his revenge.

Relinquishing her faith in her ability to cope with reality alone she saw him often that spring, about Easter when he gave up the job on the roads as Jessie's time drew near and the chance to deal briskly came as it always did in that season; she saw him when he came to see her as if she were seeing him for the last time. She spent much of the day in bed now. The house was dirty and that annoyed him; the asthma had almost struck her down. He would sit on the edge of the bed and talk about whatever she wanted and she would force herself, thrust out something she knew would amuse him from the very heart of herself, from that part most needed to nourish her own health and sanity, ignoring the fact that by so helping him she was weakening herself in every possible way, offering it gaily and without a second thought to the man she had decided she loved above all with a love she believed was worth her life. And now she saw him, as she thought, in his splendour! How well he was!

Fit from the hard work, lean, hard and tanned; reflective from the burden she appreciated that he carried; careful to help and comfort her, he appeared the very make and mould of her ideal, there, before her, undeniable, fired, she concluded, in the crucible of truest experience. She took his hands and kissed his fingers and then released them to respect his embarrassment; once, very slowly and strangely, she passed her hand all over his face as a blind person does. This was the man she wanted to live with, yes, this was he.

Invariably he would leave her and she would shudder with a sob too deep for any sound but a small animal whimper, a note of sorrow that pierced her heart.

For her plan, her clear, clean, honest, honourable plan; her ideal, splendid, courageous plan, had failed. He lacked the faith she had hoped for and now it was almost done.

After long and troubled debate, weighing up all manner of factors and considering Jessie's feelings more carefully and coolly than would be thought possible, she decided to risk all her remaining strength on a meeting with this woman who had taken away her life, this woman she had never even seen.

She prepared herself scrupulously, in mind and in her sick body and then, at mid-day, when the woman would be most likely to be alone, she set out on her journey.

# Chapter Fifty-Four

Jessie knew who it was as soon as she saw her come in through the gate over the other side of the field and she watched, spellbound, as she stood as if calmly admiring the view.

The walk had been most tiring and Rosemary fought hard to get her breathing under control. She did not want her illness to give her a false advantage of this other woman. Moreover, in a strange way she was happy: the view was so beautiful, it was Edgar's field, her husband's field; they had met very near the spot where that bungalow stood, where that pregnant woman watched.

Rosemary's apparent calm aroused fears in Jessie which no amount of belligerence could have animated. The sense of wrong-doing and of sin which had been avoided by the traditionally cruel simple expedient of avoiding contact with the one who had been wronged, had now no place to hide. On this grey spring day, clouds dark and even, moving slowly from the sea to the hills, remorselessly shepherded by a cool wind, there, before her, was the woman whose family she had violated and there was no escape. Her self-confidence left her and as Rosemary turned to come slowly across towards her, Jessie thought that that pace, too, like the clouds, like the justice of God, was remorseless. She could only stand and stare.

The first thing she noticed was how beautiful Edgar's wife looked, how distinguished and elegant—too thin but then she had been ill and slimness suited her. Jessie felt very rough in the boots and apron she wore for gardening. She rubbed her hands in a handkerchief in which she had twisted some mints as comforters during her work. She felt the large belly as an obtrusive offence.

"I'm Mrs Crowther," said Rosemary, quietly, "Edgar's wife. You're Jessie, aren't you?"

"Yes." Jessie's throat was so dry that the word almost stuck there. "Yes," she repeated and swallowed.

Rosemary looked at her intently, almost greedily, taking in the younger woman's health and solidity. Her fears were justified; Edgar had sought out no playmate but someone with whom he could establish a life-long existence. She quenched the flames of panic which spurted inside her. "I would like a cup of tea," she said. "Would you be so kind as to make one for me?"

Jessie nodded and turned to go inside the house. Rosemary followed slowly, her eyes restlessly searching and assessing. "He's done more work to her garden than ever he did to mine," she observed, grimly; the area of garden was large and Jessie's daily efforts throughout the winter were just now beginning to show results. Rosemary could appreciate the work that had gone into it and thought of her own scruffy patch which she had attempted to tidy and mow only the previous day. The effort had been beyond her and the lawnmower was still stuck at the bottom of the garden, grass entangled around the blunt blades. Here she saw shrubs planted, young trees, daffodils and tulips and a small forsythia, a neat vegetable garden, paths marked out prettily by stones, lines and criss-crossed furrows everywhere. The calmness and orderliness brought a surge of desperate weariness to her head which she struggled to resist.

Jessie was very scared when she heard the woman come slowly into her room. She concentrated on making the tea but there was so little to do. She had to stand and wait.

Thankfully, Rosemary sat down on a rather hard Victorian chair. It was upholstered in green and looked moss-coloured in the dull afternoon light. "This furniture looks very well here," she said as Jessie brought in the tea on a tray, setting it down on a small table expertly and unfussily as she had so often done for her father and for Edgar. "I always thought it would be too heavy but it looks very attractive. I prefer lighter pieces myself, though, don't you?"

Jessie handed her the tea. Then took her own and with great reluctance retreated to find a seat on the sofa. She did not want this talk: she was defenceless before this woman: she felt gross. With difficulty she forced herself into the sofa which was too low for her: usually she sat on the chair which Rosemary had taken.

"When is it due?"

"In about a fortnight, they say."

"They can never quite tell. How could they?" Rosemary laughed at some private reflection and Jessie felt chastened. "You

look very well. Are they frightening you with any of their pretentious jargon?"

"I have too much iron," said Jessie, rather sulkily.

"No one can have too much iron, surely! From what I
remember, babies positively gorge themselves on it. It was a great
surprise to discover that one had these mineral deposits inside,
don't you think. One suddenly felt a great deal more valuable."

Jessie smiled. Rosemary was encouraged by this polite
response, taking it for sympathy; and any indication of that
quality from whatever source was ointment to her inflamed spirit.
"In the end I thought of myself as a little self-sustaining econo-
mic unit—don't you remember? the things they used to write
about in the war? I had the milk coming from these glandular
pastures slung across my chest and the heat generated by a form
of internal combustion which was rather clumsily dependent on
lengths of intestine like a sausage factory but there it was: and the
minerals, the iron . . ." She broke off and looked fixedly and
pitifully at Jessie.

"Leave him," she whispered in a tone which brought a chill to
Jessie's flesh. "Leave him," she repeated.

Rosemary willed the other woman's acquiescence, trying to
convince her by force of psychic influence that the pain she was
causing and would continue to promote was not worth even the
greatest pleasure she could expect. Rosemary would not stoop to
what she would have considered the blackmail of invoking
Eleanor, the marriage bond, respectability, or Edgar's future with
two families to support; she spurned the conventional methods
and went as she thought to the core. Would this woman be made
to see that pleasure, however rich it might seem, was no more
than a transient explosion of emotions, a burning of past and
present which would surely die for lack of sustenance? The sus-
taining qualities of life and the noblest were, and would ever be,
the appreciation of beauty and the search for truth. And these she
could give to Edgar, her husband.

She did not even cast her own pain, her humiliation and her
dread onto the scales, wanting the woman to be as relieved of that
weight as she had ensured Edgar would be. In so far as it was
within her power, she wanted the three of them to be free.

"I love him," she said. "I need him, too, but I love him. And
he loves me, I think. This—chaos—will pass. He drinks a lot
now; I can tell. He never needed to. This is an indication."

Jessie had to struggle against a feeling of being immersed: it was as if the woman were enclosing her, suffocating her. "He doesn't drink all that much, does he?" The poor reply stumbled out slowly.

As she spoke she had a disturbing sensation of hollowness, a new and alarming sensation which threatened her.

"Yes." Rosemary looked past Jessie, her eyes keenly staring out of the window: she did not want to menace the younger woman. She was already aware of her ability to overcome this younger woman, aware that in some way she could crush her and aware also that it was her intense desire to do so. She craved to destroy the rival before her and yet, as always, she thought the matter over, decided on the principle of politeness and on the superiority of free unpressured choice and forced herself to obey her reason, choking back the emotion which rose in fury and diverting much-needed energy to the strange labour of saving her rival from her own worst feelings. It was an act of great courage, superlatively honourable, and self-denying to a dangerous degree.

"Have you ever thought," Rosemary began, carefully, scrupulous as ever, "that it would be a good idea to let him live on his own for a while? To think things over on his own."

"I suppose he would if he wanted to."

Jessie wanted her to go away. The will to be in the same room as Edgar's wife was not in her. She felt ashamed and deeply perturbed by the whole thing. This calmness! This discussion! It made no sense. She was beginning to tremble and wondered desperately how she could control it.

"No. Edgar doesn't know what he wants. Perhaps I shouldn't say that. You must think he knows *exactly*, of course you must! But don't you think, perhaps, he ought to be alone for a while?"

"I don't know."

"Of course he hates being alone. He's terribly dependent. His mother saw to that."

Not understanding, Jessie clutched the underside of the sofa with both hands, unseen, and gripped as tightly as she could. The weight of her belly was increasingly in her mind and yet she did not want to think about it.

"She spoilt him of course. He was the little lord. Freud writes somewhere that when a boy has conquered his mother he can conquer the world. We shouldn't let them. Domination is every bit as dependent as slavery. Neither counts. We must have all knowledge and all freedom."

Rosemary turned to her, strained beyond reason by this unyielding woman's reticence: she gave her one look, one only, one which expressed the loathing, the terror and the violence of her feelings. Jessie felt as if she had been stabbed. Her fingernails pressed into the chair; the child inside her seemed to lurch suddenly and, aware of herself, Jessie had the extraordinary feeling that the unborn baby had also been hurt. She wanted to shout at this woman to go away, to go away! Her own carefully repressed feelings, her evasions and justifications were released by that look, Pandora's box was opened, the demons came out.

Then Rosemary blushed at her loss of control and her display of hateful feelings, immediately wanting to apologize: but that would have been understandably interpreted as hypocritical and the subsequent disentangling not worth the candle. "You look very well," she said. "Who is your doctor?"

"Dr Dolan."

"Oh! He was mine too."

The memory of her own pregnancy overcame her: these days her mind presented no barrier at all to the past and it swirled about her on the flood. She remembered the weight, now so sweet in retrospect, new smells which had come off herself, the feeling of earthiness, legs so widely planted on the ground: she had loved to rest her fingertips on the stretched skin and wait for the kicks and nudges from the womb. An utterly crazy impulse made her want, more than that, made her *long* to stroke Jessie's belly at this very moment, feel the taut silken flesh, feel the life within. For a few moments the thought was like a pulse inside her skull and would not be soothed. To stroke this woman's life-filled flesh. She half-closed her eyes to concentrate and drive it off.

Sensing the switch away from her, Jessie used the moment to regain some poise: she heaved herself to her feet, the mental effort every bit as difficult as the physical; she had been so sunk into herself that the contact between her thoughts and her movements had almost been lost. She smoothed down her skirt over her front and Rosemary glanced at the action, glutinously. "Let me help you wash up," she said.

"No. It's nothing."

"I can help."

"It's nothing."

The quivering sense of life which had passed through Rosemary at the impossible quixotic thought of them working together went as quickly as it had come. Jessie took the tray and left her alone.

Alone, Rosemary sank instantly into a slough of depression. Within these walls he betrayed her hourly. He sat here and—what did they talk about? But she could not allow herself contempt for Jessie. No. Here was the unanswerable evidence of his rejection.

Oh God: that fact was such a terrible weight. It threatened to crush her skull, she thought, as flies to wanton boys. She must go to her house. Home was no more. House. She must go while she could go. She too had to wrench herself out of thought to get onto her feet. She must hurry. She could feel the tide of misery rising, rushing up the channels of her mind. Before long she would be inundated with nostalgia and regret and inconsolable misery. She had to be alone or that luxuriance of grief would overwhelm her.

Her farewell was muttered but it was not rude. Soon she was walking across the field, holding down her hurt with all her might, taking yet more risks with her body as she drove it across the land, his land, at a pace which laid up future stress.

The spring day was cold now and her optimistic dress inadequate. The wind came from the town. It cut at her and buffeted her. Inside her mind a multitude of conversations began, conversations with Edgar, with Wilfred, with Eleanor, conversations with her mother, with her father, with Lawrence, with herself, conversations in which she accused, conversations in which she apologized, conversations where she laid blame, conversations where she craved pity, hectoring conversations, whispering, declamatory, conspiratorial conversations; those mirrored voices which had been so long under the crust of consciousness now burst through and cascaded into her mind dry and cracked with fear and waiting, until the din of words made up a cacophony inside the bone of skull, a sound which rose as on a single note, with the strain in her body from the walking thankfully pushing out thought, becoming, as at last she approached her house, a dirge, a singing pain, a dreadful wailing. The sound trickled through her lips as she went the last few yards along the avenue, an inhuman keening.

The stairs to her bedroom were so steep. Where was Edgar?

357

Unseen, she could throw off all pride. He should be with his wife. She crawled up slowly on her hands and knees, the rough cord staircarpet leaving marks on the skin. Oh where was her husband? The keening strengthened until she lay on the bed where it came out as a moan of agony, low, ugly, guttural, shivering, so badly hurt, her knees drawn up for warmth and comfort, her eyes wide open staring at the brown hard-backed chair on which Edgar used to throw his clothes before coming to bed. Could he not feel her need?

Out of all that was being said inside the aching mind out of the Babel one of the most persistent sounds was an address to Edgar. In the comfortless silence of the austere bedroom the ullulation arose like the voice of mourning from ancient times.

"She'll never love you as I do. You know that. I know you know that. I can remember from your face—you can't fool me, nobody knows that face better than I do, you can't hide it. You've turned to her but I am the one who loves you best. Can't you see? I know it was hard and complicated with me but that's all right, isn't it? You're a brave enough man. I know the sex thing was not much good after a while. It used to be. You must remember that. I went to see the marriage guidance people in Carlisle. Yes. It came to that. A horrible office, horrible, hateful green walls that seemed to glisten with misery, hateful! The man said had *I* ever made love to *you*? I thought my whole life had been that. But he meant all the tricks. Do you need them? I'll learn them if you want them. But they are only tricks, Edgar, and you know it as well as I do. Sex is very important. I have had only what you have spared for months now and it is almost driving me crazy—your charity isn't enough. But there are a great number of things more important—there are and whatever you say or feel I know that that is true. Freud is only right up to a point. There is beauty and there is truth and those are the important facts of life. I miss you—I wonder if you have any idea how cold a single bed is after sleeping with a man for twelve years. Just that: the loneliness of the spirit I am used to: the loneliness of the flesh is unbearable. But I will not give in. I will not take a lover. I will not abuse myself or you. You would hate that. I know you would.

"Most of all what I want to say is how I've come to love you. Don't look away. Look at me—please—do my eyes disgust you? Why do you look like that? Listen. Come on, you old bugger, I know you love me—you say you do and I believe you. You don't

358

*like* me much at the moment: you prefer to fuck that country girl, your mother, but it's me you love. And I love you. You're such a man now, Edgar, you're so full of feelings and wildness: you can just touch me and I feel a charge of life coming instantly into my body. Oh, you've behaved like a bastard but that isn't important. You had to be independent. I understand. And maybe you had to be cruel too and evil, and mean, though I blame you for that a little—it's been a silly worry for me—money is *not* important, not at all, not once you have eaten a meal and gained a roof; it's like sex, the one for the personal world the other for the public world—it is a concrete metaphor representing much greater things. To show our love we fuck but in itself the act proves very little: it expresses a thousand things—with tarts or friends or even enemies, it's just a physical function after all. Love includes it but only insofar as it includes a great number of other functions and qualities. Money, too, is merely a representation: that is why it hurts me when you talk about it because we know the world better than that. Your cows and your antiques and your stones *are* value: your field is value: money is just a matter of exchange. The value of things and properties which *is* important, I can understand that though I must confess I can't feel it, but I understand you. I know I am overprotected about such matters. To discern and discriminate in such real values, which is what you *do* with your working life, is to be employed on something very interesting and critically important. It is like love, such proper valuation. But sex and money are merely the crude little flags indicating where the treasures are buried. Most people snatch the flags and run away. But we tried to dig, Edgar, didn't we? We did. We did. We tried to find the treasure and you were so strong! I was hard on you because I was up to my ears in confusions and uncertainties but now I can see how strong you were. And how horribly difficult it must have been for you because I was used to the company of my mind. You were frightened of it. You had lived in the external world where you were bold, you were a king. I might have been harsh on you: I could have helped you about sex; I'm sorry about that.

"But don't you see what we've achieved? Don't you? Look at yourself, even in the poor mirror of glass and see who you have become. You're a man. You've been in purgatory and you have survived. In every way now you are a man.

"And you know it and you love me and yet you leave me here.

I must wait. I understand. I have seen her. She must have the child and she needs help. I, too, God knows, need help, Edgar, but I won't press you, I won't lay claim. You are free. You know how I long for you and Eleanor longs for you and you long for us. I know that you understand it all: all, all, all.

"Yet—you might not return. It needs faith and I can see also how trapped you are. Ashamed, too, this small town's shame hurts you. You look coarser. You swear much more. You drink too much. You have nothing to say. You have subsided like a sullen beast in its lair. You pretend to ignore all my feelings. All my help is disregarded, any sacrifice taken entirely for granted. Sometimes I fear you might be too selfish to return. Or that you might be destructive.

"That is the worst thought. That when you come out of your cave you will be so mad with pain that you will want to destroy your past. You think it will release you but it will not. How can I warn you? Such a destruction is to bind yourself forever to what you have lost in a grip which age will tighten like the sun tightens a wet rope. It is no way. To kill me in yourself and yourself in me is no way. Believe me, Edgar. You will make only an abyss in your life and then be drawn down into it, down and down like Orpheus on his second visit to Hades when there was nothing and no one to be found. Believe me, Edgar. I want to help you. I want us to live. I want us to live. I want us to live. Please. Oh, please."

# Chapter Fifty-Five

During this time, as he watched Jessie's form distend as relentlessly as Rosemary's argument swelled to meet the force of his pull away from her—himself the moon to her ocean—Edgar was isolated and became cold, like the moon, and in some ways made himself dead. He could not respond to the demands except by continuing to trudge obstinately along the path to which he had committed himself. He was fixed there, the pressure of pull and counter-pull only adding to his fear. It was enough to get through a day. To think of Rosemary's future was not possible for him: it would have meant imagining his own part in it and that was too difficult. He could only take the days as they came, visit her as often as he could, be as helpful as she asked. And yet he realized that perhaps his attentions had precisely the opposite effects to those he intended. She would accuse him of hanging on to her, of not letting her free to search for someone else, of using her, bleeding her, confusing her and, always, of hurting her. But if he did not go to see her she would complain and be upset. Similarly with Jessie, he could not imagine the future, could not "see" the baby, could not imagine the three of them, man, woman and child in the security, in the settlement which in his mind enclosed that family grouping. Yet the child would soon come.

He did not seek advice, knowing that there would be only criticisms of his course and unable to bear the thought of them: he had enough to do to hold the position he had arrived at. That it was "wrong" and extraordinarily difficult made him no less convinced. It would have been much easier (earlier) to have stayed with Rosemary. Now he was suspended between the two women, each of whom claimed more from him as the weeks passed.

In Jessie he still found the release and satisfaction of sex though that was temporarily threatened as the birth drew nearer: and with Rosemary he still had niggling but bitter arguments about money. These things colonized his life until they appeared sole powers within him: the one insatiate, the other miserly: a spendthrift and a hoarder, consumed now to give everything, not to withhold everything. In all ways he was fixed.

Neither of the women mentioned their meeting to him.

Rosemary had expected Jessie to tell him and had feared his reaction; she had even prepared a list of excuses and, in that diminishing area in which enjoyment could still be discovered, looked forward to the fight. She yearned for solid matter between them. Her fantasies had now the quality of hallucinations and her lurid solitary imaginings did her little but harm, she knew: and yet they could be her only comforter. She thought to protect Eleanor by telling her no lies but only the sparest details. When Edgar did not bring up the subject she did not specifically conclude that Jessie had not passed on the information: her first fear was of a conspiracy. Then she gave her husband credit for respecting her feelings. Then blame for ignoring them. Then elaborate theories were painstakingly constructed only to be blown up by one of those fierce jabs of realism which she administered to herself whenever the spin of unreality became too fast. For it was all a nightmare now.

No, Jessie had not said anything. It had taken all her energy to contain herself after Rosemary's visit. She wanted to run away.

Edgar came home, strained and rather sullen, complained that things were dull (compared, Jessie thought, to life with Rosemary) and that he was bored (that, she, Jessie thought, was boring). He fell asleep soon after supper and she watched him, intently, the head awkwardly flopped to one side as if the neck were broken, the nostrils distended so that she could see the hairs, the breathing heavy and deep. A trickle of saliva creeping out of the corner of his half-open mouth. Later, in bed, he wanted to make love to her, and resented her resistance, although he knew she was right. Sometimes she thought that he would forever find cause for conflict. Jessie took the night silence for comforter and tried to interpret her position which so far had rested in the love she and Edgar had for each other, considering such a bond justified even the breaking of an older bond. Now as she lay beside the unconscious body of her exhausted lover, the simple truth disappeared into a labyrinth. Love as in mind and body she had known it, the certain physical conjunction, now seemed inadequate: it could not cope with the complexities Rosemary's visit had raised. And Edgar, too, she believed, knew this. His passion fed more and more on a discreditable obstinacy. He could make no move because all he could do was more hurt: she saw that and knew that she was the only one of them who could act now.

In the days following Rosemary's visit, Jessie gnawed at what she should do, with the desperation of a trapped fox which will bite off its own leg rather than be caught.

But the solution would not come. The simplest—that she should go, run away, vanish as if she had never been, was utterly impossible because of the expected child. The chains were inside her. And anything less would not be enough.

What happened, though, took her completely by surprise, for instead of being caught up in this dilemma which was at least sympathetic to consideration, she was diverted from it into an area where fear and superstition were so fiercely planted and so resistant to reason that she felt herself sucked into an irresistible whirlpool. For she began to imagine that her child would be born dead or deformed. More: she "saw" the child, still bloody from the womb, there, before her, struck down for her sins. This image, once entered, would not leave her mind but lurked about it ever set to attack her peace.

This too she kept from Edgar. He noticed her increased nervousness, he saw the whiteness of her cheeks, the circles under her eyes, and advised her to take more fresh air, to rest, he could do whatever housework was necessary, he said. He could call on no one else. His mother, formally on Rosemary's side but in fact aloof from the battle, frozen by the unconventionality of it all into an attitude of endurance, could not bring herself to the new house.

Jessie saw the effort in his kindness and could not accept it. Effort, strain, will, those essential parts of the vaulting necessary to extend most civilized structures including relationships were only proof to Jessie that the spontaneous, living feelings which Edgar and herself had thought strong enough were not so in fact. He was forcing himself to love her, she thought and this deduction began to drive her frantic.

She had deep reserves of calm, Jessie, and she stayed herself for almost a week after Rosemary's visit, ready though she was at every blow in the womb to run away from it all. The kicking was not unusual, the doctor said, it proved the baby was alive and well, that was all, but her time was very nearly on her and she must come to him every day now and let him know the moment any regular pains began.

The image of the punished child became a leech on her brain and she could not pluck it off.

A day came which was exceptionally hot—a fine high summer's day when the inside of the house was unbearable and she felt herself too restless to sit about outside. Nor could she walk anywhere at all now in the immediate neighbourhood; for Rosemary's visit had opened and deepened the sense of shame and she heard accusations ringing Thurston, attacking her from out of the thin air.

She caught a bus to Caldbeck where Edgar had once taken her, she remembered, with puzzled pleasure for something had not been quite right, but it was a lonely spot, and there was water.

Yet when she came to the waterfall, after a heavy trudge up the road from the village she was made afraid by its terrible cold force. She stood on the narrow wooden bridge which vibrated from the pressure and looked down at the cruel rocks which smashed the water into a million glinting drops, and she experienced a deep chill, striking through, it seemed, to her blood. It was cold above the water. The sun which had stifled her in the bus and wearied her on the walk up the road was forgotten now in the gorge, tree-veined, glacial. The fall of the pounding water transfixed her gaze and she held on tightly to the ricketty railing bemused by the cold which clarified possibilities in a terrible way and by the thunderous noise which was strangely soothing.

It would be very easy to fall in.

The child struggled inside her and she stood back, horrified at the train of her own thoughts. She hurried across the bridge—up to the peaceful glade where Edgar had taken her.

Here the sun was full and rich, the grass warm, the noise still soothing but heavy-leafed beeches in her vision now as she lay back and saw small lamb-playful clouds replacing the steep fall of water and the black rocks. She tried to look at the sun in order to have the black spots when she closed her eyes: the aimless irritation distracted her.

It was a lonely spot. The heat this mid-afternoon time was hazy in the trees. The grass felt so warm as she let her fingers trail through it: the river was shaded by some willows nearby and on the top glitter of their leaves she could see scores of tiny flies dancing about. The drone of bees, the ceaseless boom from the waterfall: she tried to forget the terrible thought on the bridge—not an impulse; it had not come to that—and to will herself to drive out the terrors about the unborn child. But her will, unless informed by instinctual need, was not strong and the dreams which followed were full of fear and distress: she groaned aloud and, panting, broke the sleep once or twice to notice the sun sinking behind the trees, the shadows growing longer but the grass still warm as her fingers clutched at it and once more she was claimed by her guilt. It was a heaving painfulness in the mind she felt; a regular throb of cramp, it seemed, in her skull.

When finally she woke the sun had gone and the grass was cool. She felt her brow: a layer of cold sweat was there to be wiped away by her hand which was trembling. She waited a moment, horrified and then the pains began again. There was no doubting them now—regular, strong pulsations as the doctor had said, forcing her to gasp for breath. She tried to remember how she should breathe.

God! It was almost like a convulsion. She felt her thighs widening in preparation, the flesh opening to let the child out. She moaned until the pains were past and then, after she had recovered herself, tried to work out a plan. She gathered her strength to get up but even as she had finally prepared herself the pains came on her once more, harder this time and faster so that she was splayed on the ground, her fingers digging into the cold soil, her head tensely swinging from side to side.

Still no sound above a low moan. A deep modesty schooled her to keep the trouble to herself.

This time she took longer to recover herself. The sweat ran down her face and body: the flesh palpitated. She forced herself to think carefully.

There was no doubt that she was in labour. This was an unfrequented spot. Her best chances were screaming or trying to reach the village. Screaming would do little good—though better here than closer to the waterfall—and despite everything, while she had strength, while she had her faculties she was embarrassed to scream for help, preferring to get herself out of a situation she was responsible for. She managed to get to her feet. A mere twenty yards further on, she was forced once more to lie down and let the birth-pangs drive through her. This time they were so strong that instead of being able to gather her strength and get up, a more powerful demand pressed her to semi-consciousness, somewhere between a light sleep and a spell of fainting. When she woke she felt clear-headed: when she tried to move she was much much weaker.

She crawled on her hands and knees, her belly brushing the ground, down towards the bridge across the waterfall, into the clammy coolness of the Howk. At the bridge after a long pause she pulled herself upright and walked as if walking a tightrope. The cold from the thundering water struck her with the deepest terror of all but by steadying herself with the rail she managed to pass across the narrow wooden planks.

What faced her now was formidable—an extremely steep climb up steps very roughly and unevenly hacked out of the side of the gorge, often using tree roots for stepping stones. She paused and took her time.

Finally she began to climb. Even at the first step she knew it would be impossible but she urged herself on with the thought of the easy field at the top which reached out to a road: once there she could somehow attract attention. She went up six or seven of the steps, each one a risk, and then she had to stop: her trembling threatened to bring on another fainting fit and she could not risk that now—the child was to be born.

Jessie turned from the staircase of roots and got herself to a small patch of grass, fairly level. She cleaned it as best she could.

The better to efface her pregnancy, she had brought a light summer raincoat, and this she spread carefully on the ground so that when she lay down it stretched from the small of her back to her ankles. She lodged her feet against the firm trunks of two young trees and their resilient strength gave her some comfort. She tore off her underclothes carefully to prepare swaddling clothes for the child. They were not enough: she ripped off her dress from the waist. Then she waited as the heat left the day and a chill began to come from the ground. She could scream as loudly as she would; the waterfall drowned every sound.

Edgar found her about two in the morning. He had at first thought that she had taken off on a longer walk than usual and been delayed; then he had imagined she had made for her former employers, remembering now her paleness and silences the previous week. A fast drive across country had led to nothing but a growing panic. It was after ten when he got back to Thurston and difficult to raise people who might know anything. Finally, well after midnight, he had gone to Rosemary who had told him to think of any special places they had been together, somewhere important and, her word, romantic for both of them, somewhere, she persisted, herself afraid now and fearing her own responsibility for what might have happened, where there were good memories.

He drove straight to the Howk, alone.

The child had caught a severe cold and by the time he reached the Cumberland Infirmary in Carlisle there was a delirious fever upon it. The two of them sat in the jolted back of the old car, covered with Edgar's jacket, their flesh, mother and child, caked with blood, Jessie, who had kissed Edgar so tenderly on seeing him, crooning to her baby without ceasing. It was a girl.

She died a few hours later and Jessie stayed in the hospital for a fortnight. They did not even allow her to attend the funeral and that small white coffin went into the earth attended only by Edgar and his mother. A few days later, Lawrence died, and his large, eloquent town burial took place solemnly, a worthy testament to his decent and devoted life.

When they had all gone, Rosemary came back with some lilies. She divided them into three portions, placing one on the grave of the man who had been so quietly loving to her for so long; the second beside her mother's cross and the last on the tiny mound marking the coffin of Jessie's child. It was by this place she stood longest, while the tears came to her helpless eyes, inconsolable.

Inside her head went a song from childhood, perhaps even her mother had taught it to her; round and round without ceasing, the last few lines:

> Ma chandelle est morte
> Je n'ai plus de feu
> Ouvre-moi ta porte
> Pour l'amour de Dieu.

It was finished.

Before her last action, though, she would once more and finally try words. She wrote compulsively now, her firm, rather severe-looking handwriting loosening to sprawled loops across the small pages of the exercise books she had taken from Eleanor's room. Now and then would be drawings, diagrams, illustrations or fierce doodles giving the pages a look of some experimenter's note-

367

books. Most of her life went with these drawings and writings.

The house was horribly neglected, so disordered and unattended that Edgar on his increasingly rare visits had to force himself to regard it as a pose: it could be tidied up in half a day if she tried, he would think, and be angry at the miserable confusion which stared him in the face. Once again there was something foreign about the mess which both unnerved him and gave him liberty: for what he did not understand he could not help.

Eleanor came regularly like a visitor but now spent most of her time with Sarah who had broken down after her brother's death and clung to the girl pathetically and obsessively. Seeing the older woman's need, Rosemary let her daughter go though she sadly missed her. Just to have another body in the house was so important; but Eleanor must make her free choice and Rosemary did not blame her for moving away out of the line of fire. For such it still was as far as Rosemary was concerned: all her thoughts and talk and hopes were based on the relationship past present and to come, with Edgar.

Even Jean's ordinariness was no use now: her friend tried, but she could not break into the looped despair of the woman who saw herself abandoned cruelly. Worse, Jean perceived that her cheerfulness, her children, her health, her happiness, her success in life pained her old friend, raked at the roots of jealousy, and this was doubly distressing for both of them. In the end Jean obeyed the signals of mute despair which came from the eyes once so intense with life; and left her alone.

Everyone, Rosemary reflected, left her alone. Throughout her life, everyone had found an excellent reason for leaving her alone.

But she would find courage in the solitude; aching from loneliness of the flesh she sank deeply into the spirit now and hovered over the school exercise books night after night, sleeping and doing the essentials during the day, bent over the paper before the fire like someone trying to cast a spell. As indeed she was. She called up from some store in her mind, and from her unconscious, those forces of symmetry and coincidence of destiny and charm which were once imagined to devise the world of events, and tried, tried, tried as she sipped her black sugarless coffee and smoked the filtered cigarettes, to conjure up her love, to cause the phoenix to be reborn, to bring him back.

"In the beginning man must have lived in fear," she wrote. "In the cave, in the forests, in the swamps. For thousands of years there must have been fear and that is in us now like the mineral layers under the ground, deep and rich veins of fear which can be bared at a scratch of the surface. The only great relief was death. A death was a triumph over fear and not even birth was such a victory. Violence could kill the fear: love was violent. Love is necessary for that, above all, to kill the dark.

"When man learned other things, when he found fire and agriculture then he began to become the man we know today. Fire and agriculture were all he needed. The rest is just an extension. And with these two great gifts he saw a new world: he saw there was joy as well as fear and beauty as well as ugliness and the greatest men saw that all these opposites were one and the truth lay in harmony. Harmony was the truth. And failing that there would always be fear.

"It is fear which is at my throat now. I recognize it, I can smell it, it sickens me, I am frightened of everything, there is too much of the world in my gullet, I need love to kill it, I need to be dead and re-born and die once more. Only Edgar, only you can do that for me now.

"But you can scent the fear. I see your nostrils sniff like a dog on a trail and it excites you. You smile at the challenge. You can afford to. You are covered in sex.

"Men must have covered themselves in sex before going out to hunt. They must have smeared it all over them. Themselves and the women. That is what those tom-tom dances are for. The beat of the tom-tom is the heart-beat and that is the rhythm of coitus. The seed, the sperm, would be like a silken net, protecting like a gladiator's net in the arena, like a spider's web to trap the barren enemies. Sex or blood: but in the beginning, sex.

"You are glorying in sex. I know now that I have let this part of my life go because I concentrated on your mind and our domestic love and because I was always afraid of you. You hurt me Edgar; your hands were rough; you were impatient with me, and in your body I felt a tremor of revulsion which alarmed me with antagonism.

"But I can love you now. *I* can cover you in sex. I can give you the seed, the ointment for battle.

"Of course you must leave me if you must. You are free. You have made me unable to be free but that is probably my own fault. We are all free. That is the greatest illumination from the fire: that is the greatest gain from the agriculture. The rest is

369

piddling. Even sex is just another way of *piddling*. Because without the love which kills fear it is mere enjoyment and will wither. Love needs fear and sex needs both otherwise it is acrobatics in a sperm lavatory!"

At this point Edgar laughed aloud. What a woman! She had left the notes deliberately for him to find and he had read them as naturally as he had always read anything she had written or anything which had been written to her. She had left him alone ostensibly to go and pick some flowers—she was so nervous of him now that his longed-for visits threw her into an all but uncontrollable panic and she could not, literally, face him.

He read on. She wrote of his magnificence and of the great possibilities they had: she knew, she wrote, that it was a question of faith now and she relied on his strength to find the faith. The rats were after him, she wrote, in the town, but he would ignore that. What did that mean or imply, he wondered, offended.

Then she began to write about their relationship, analysing, explaining, carefully taking it to pieces and putting it together again scrupulously. She was right: there were still possibilities and what she was prepared to tolerate and endure astounded him. But he grew increasingly exasperated, fearful, fretful, and when she came into their house, flowers in her arms, her eyes shining with love, her face almost gaunt from the strain of her effort, he could have screamed. He had to ignore her.

On his way back to Jessie he discovered a note which she must have slipped into his pocket. It read:

Dearest,
Please come back to us. Please. We love you. We need you. Please. Please. R.

A splinter of fear drove into his will and paralysed it, "It is only your indifference which I truly fear," she was writing. "Only if you pretend I do not exist can our love—which is still there, still there, still—only if you pretend that I do not exist, only if I do not exist, only I do not exist I do not; I do love you, Edgar, please, please, exist, exist."

# Chapter Fifty-Six

There was one last attempt she could make and, taking the little
that remained of strength and all her courage and boldness, she
made it. A few days after Lawrence's funeral, and after that
sterile encounter with Edgar, seeing Eleanor well settled with
Sarah for their mutual comfort, she went to London.

The impact of the city was so much greater than she remembered it even though it was little busier in those early fifties than
it had been in the few years before the 1939 war. There was no
one to meet her this time though she remembered every look and
pause at the barrier.

She took a taxi out to Kew.

When she got out of it the opulence of a summer even these
few miles south overcame her with a nostalgia whose roots
reached even farther south. The land around and about the
Botanical Gardens had been full of orchards and many fruit trees
had been kept in the grounds of the large Victorian and
Edwardian houses such as the one Wilfred still lived in with his
new wife, his mother and Stephen. His father had died some
years before.

She breathed in the heavily sweetened air and soon found the
proper source of the intoxication. It was the roses. Past high
summer now, the roses were opening out and never had she seen
so many in private gardens; large and luxuriant bushes, rare and
exotic varieties, primary colours, delicate tints, before and behind
every house there were scores of roses, hundreds in some as they
clambered up trellising over the front of the houses, climbing up
to balconies and bedroom windows. She smiled with great
pleasure at the sight and the effect.

Wilfred came out of the house and carried in her case—the
same one (would he notice?) the very same as she had brought
—more than twenty years before. A gift from Harold Sowerby.

Although she had sent a hasty postcard which had just arrived
that morning, Wilfred behaved as if her visit had been long-

planned and surely prepared for. His mother was truly delighted to see her, remembering with great affection the young woman so quivering with life who had entranced them all so much before. She was, however, as she said later to her son, so shocked at Rosemary's appearance that she would have had the very greatest difficulty in recognizing her.

As soon as she saw Wilfred's wife, Rosemary's plan (if it could be described in so solid a word) collapsed and she felt deeply ashamed of herself. Though she knew Wilfred had eventually remarried, in her tormented and upset condition she had allowed herself to think this did not essentially matter. Now she was introduced to this pleasant, calm, rather plain woman she was immeasurably thankful that she had never posted the impassioned and elaborate letter she had written to Wilfred: the postcard, substituted at the last moment, had not said anything which could not be decently said.

They had heard of Lawrence's death—Stephen had wanted to get up to the funeral but there was an interview for a job which he had to attend having won through to the short list in the face of "stiff competition", his grandmother explained proudly. It was assumed she had come to get over the shock and the strain of it, knowing how devotedly she had nursed him in his last months. They had no inkling of the break-up of her marriage and enquired kindly after Edgar: she replied as if all was well between them, each lie a further cut at herself.

A few aeroplanes went over during the night bound for Heathrow airport and she used this as the excuse when asked why she looked so tired in the morning. Mrs Lewis, too, had insomnia and she promised Rosemary some of her sleeping pills that evening.

The next two days did succeed in slowing her down a little. Her mind would function almost normally, more brittle than usual and also more brilliant—but this was only in the company of Mrs Lewis or Wilfred and his wife. Alone, the thoughts and images coursed through the sore and swollen mind like the deluge. Only by virtue of her extraordinary will-power and her determination to maintain the standard of manners expected from her could she dam up this waterfall, seek out of her past the character they would recognize and revert to it. This was the final strain.

On the third night she got her wish by accident. Wilfred's wife went to her parents' home because of her father's sudden but not serious illness: Mrs Lewis retired early. Wilfred and Rosemary were left alone in the gracious high-ceilinged drawing-room, books, pictures, one or two elegant pieces of furniture. Only occasional aircraft spoiled the peace and she was sorely tempted to draw symbolic conclusions with reference to their talk the previous time, about Icarus and flight: but these aeroplanes had come to mock all such silent preoccupations and she denied herself the pleasure of such personal correspondence.

"Would you like a drink?"

"Please."

"Are you sure? I mean—you've been taking such a lot of pills —none of my business, of course."

"I'd like a whisky—no, a gin." She wanted to complete even that circle: Edgar's drink would be his remembrance. "Gin," she repeated. "And something to go with it."

"I believe we have some bottles of tonic, somewhere, yes. God knows, they might have been here since Christmas. I'm the only one who drinks at all regularly and I rather like whisky. That do for you?" He held up a glass, standing across from her at the other end of the room, like an auctioneer, she thought crazily, holding up a priceless object before calling on the bidding to begin. She nodded. He brought it over and then returned to the table to pour himself a whisky.

Rosemary observed him.

He was a little fat, which surprised her because she associated everything about him with the lean, austere principles which, she was sure, governed his life. But he had quite unmistakably the beginnings of a double chin. He dressed conventionally for his type and time—sports jacket, checked shirt, stout shoes, silk handkerchief stuffed in his breast pocket—a hundred university lecturers in England could have worn his clothes without their wives noticing the difference. To Rosemary the way he dressed appeared to combine ease and elegance in a very individual and satisfactory manner. No one in Thurston looked like that: even if they wore similar items, there would be a formality which would produce an entirely different effect.

She was forced to concentrate on such superficialities, as she thought then, because, so far, it had been extremely difficult for her to penetrate the mask of affability which Wilfred unblinkingly presented. She had speculated, of course, pessimistically and ravenously, but she still retained enough hold on her good

373

sense to appreciate that she had not yet discovered the man he was now.

"Shall we listen to some music?"

She did not want to: she had to talk: that was her lifeline.

"As you like."

"I've just bought a new recording of the Brandenburg Concerto." He held it up for her to see.

Rosemary nodded and watched him put it on his large gramophone. He walked back beating time with his free hand and sprawled in the wing armchair with an air of such careless joviality as made her wince. How could she ever have expected him to have remained her counterpart? He was further away from her now even than Edgar. They listened in silence except for the occasional grunt of pleasure from Wilfred, who continued to demonstrate his love for the piece by drubbing time with his fingers on his knee.

"Another drink?"

"Yes. Yes, I like it. I never used to."

"Tastes change." Wilfred yawned as he went across to pour more drinks: he did not even bother to apologize.

The concerto came to an end and the gramophone switched itself off.

"What are you working on at the moment?" she asked, risking the reproof for such awkwardness.

"Oh nothing important. Boring really. Attempting to make sense out of a man called Claudel."

"Claudel?"

"You won't know him. Nobody does except those of us who are paid to. Still—somebody's got to read the poor bastard."

"What does he write about?"

"Rosemary, life is too short. Believe me . . ." He stirred himself sufficiently to register her disappointment. "I'll give you one of his books in the morning. You might like him."

Something stirred in his memory, the enthusiasm Rosemary had expressed for Dorothy Wordsworth and how ideal it was to be called to serve a great poet as Dorothy had served William. Yes, he remembered clearly now: he had been touched to think she had seen him as a poet. How much more then would she be moved if he told her about Claudel who had worked in Provence, her birthplace, and been supported once again by a loving, sacrificing sister; and this time for a work whose philosophical obses-

374

sion would match even Rosemary's appetite. He considered whether he ought to tell her all this: it would delight her, he knew, but he was afraid of the consequences. She would take it to be such a symbolic, significant proof of profundities he did not want to know about.

"What about that marvellous book *you* were going to write?"

"Which one was that?"

"Oh, I can't remember clearly. You were so secretive about it—you wanted to keep it to yourself for fear of losing it—I can understand that—it was magnificent, that's all I remember; and it was about all the great things, all the important things—it was to be a splendid book."

Moved by the intensity of her recollection and the devotion so clearly contained in it, he tried to put aside the friendly second skin of light-hearted cynicism, and though he was tired and wary of the passion so naked before him, he tried his best. "I'm afraid that went the way of all flesh," he said. "But Claudel is a good subject. It takes me to Provence in the vacations—that's something to thank him for."

"Provence?" And the yearning in her speaking of the word threatened to pierce his fat soul—but it was too much to take on and he again yawned as he replied. "Romans, Greeks, Charlemagne, Aix, Popes, Avignon, Crusaders, Kings, Dukes—all great builders, palaces, castles, churches, hot sun, little pillaging, olive trees, a marvellous region, lavender, wine, sunflowers, painters, poets, red roofs, red earth—O God, please don't cry. Rosemary—what—Rosemary—please—don't cry."

She shook her head to reassure him but could not stop the course of tears: she bit her bottom lip very savagely to keep herself from blurting out what he already knew, that her mother had died there and there her father had lived with herself his child.

It would mean nothing to Wilfred and she did not want to upset him. She took the offer of another gin gratefully and washed down the two sleeping pills with it.

In the morning she woke up late and knew the abyss. She had nowhere to go.

Obeying Mrs Lewis' kindly call, she got up: eating her well-cooked food, she took her breakfast; following her thoughtful suggestion she went out, down the road and through the Victoria Gate into the rich and sumptuous Botanical Gardens, walking

375

right across them, past the lake not pausing to look at the rare ducks and swans, onto the tow-path where she turned left to go up the Thames to Richmond.

She walked very slowly, her body still drugged and numb except when a start of asthma strained it into tiring activity. In her head now was a circular band of singing, high-pitched like the sound of a saw; and a multitude of thoughts and images swirled endlessly within that banded loop. Not noticing the trees, the boats, the pretty bridges, the elegant houses, she went past Richmond Promenade and then she stopped where the river swings sharply north. It was on this stretch that Wilfred had taken her in the boat that day and, she glanced up and behind her, yes, on the hill was the terrace where, she had hoped, they would eventually discover a house in which to live.

A compulsive sense of symmetry made her will herself to go up that steep hill, through the lavishly terraced gardens, up, with many a pause to catch her breath, to the place she had fixed on with such unfulfilled passionate hope those years ago.

She came out where there is a telescope on a swivel which schoolboys sweep across the Thames valley, imagining themselves little Nelsons scanning the ocean for Napoleon. It was not being used and she rested against it, not wanting to sit down for fear she should become too settled to be able to get up again; a foolish fear but one which prevented her taking a rest.

As she stood there, a large and impressive cortege drew up quietly outside one of the very tall white houses which stand on the very crest of the hill. Drawn as if into a mirror, she walked across to the road and watched.

There were about a dozen vehicles, large, an old-fashioned black hearse followed by huge black cars highly polished, all, every one, surmounted by a thick layer of flowers. Other traffic had been stopped for the while along that stretch of road.

Out of the house, which she could see above the roofs of the cars because the steps to the front door went high above street level, came, first a dignfied man in full mourning dress, black silk top hat, nimble and authoritative, leading the way. Following him was a small rather frail woman on the arm of a young man; both white-faced, both in full mourning, both dazed by their sudden exposure to the sun.

The cars moved along one by one, conducted by the nimble man in the black silk hat as the full party came out of the house.

Rosemary saw it all through her pain, trapped before it like Narcissus by his reflection. Unable to move.

Of all that pounded her poor mind now and threatened it nothing was more simple or more pressing than the clear "sight" she retained of her father the last time she had seen him when, as a little girl, he had taken her for a walk along the road from Lawrence's house and tried to explain about the war. She saw him young, loving, full of expectant battles and glory, his face made ideally handsome by her memory, his presence and words strong and all comforting. "You will be beautiful," he had said. "You will be a beautiful woman like your mother—I can see that already. And I want you to do one thing only for me. Will you? Will you promise even before I ask it?" She *had* promised him, eagerly, longingly. "Always tell the truth, Rosemary," he said. "*Always!*"

And then she heard French. At first she was not sure but there could be no doubt. One or two of the mourners were speaking French. That finished her: her grief overwhelmed her: inside her mind was the sickening shudder of its charge too heavy to bear.

Grief for all those she had loved and lost, for all those who had not loved her and those who could not love her, this grief fell upon her, bursting the last banks of hope and sense and she turned to run, run, down the hill, down to the water, collapsing on the tow-path, dead to the world as the last cars drew away and the corpse was carried to its grave.

> The One remains, the many change and pass;
> Heaven's light forever shines, Earth's shadows fly;
> Life, like a dome of many-coloured glass,
> Stains the white radiance of Eternity,
> Until Death tramples it to fragments.—Die,
> If thou wouldst be with that which thou dost seek!
> Follow, where all is fled!—Rome's azure sky,
> Flowers, ruins, statues, music, words, are weak,
> The glory they transfuse with fitting truth to speak.

# VI. ROSEMARY

About five years later at the end of a summer afternoon a small black Ford, driven most tentatively by a grey-haired woman who seemed to peep through her spectacles at the quiet country road before her, left Thurston in the direction of the fells, heading for a hamlet called Ullaby. Though the hair was completely grey, the skin was most youthfully fresh, the face slim and full of a sense of amusement which mocked the aged crown. Rosemary's long illness had left her unlike herself.

She was extremely apprehensive of this visit and so she drove with extra care, all but switching off the engine at a crossroads. It was the first time she had dared to go to visit Jessie and Edgar. In the hospital she had decided that when she was well she would face them together: it would somehow atone.

Rosemary had suffered a great deal and survived in the end by good fortune. Her convalescence had been helped and cheered by Sarah—who was grateful for the opportunity to repay this forever strange woman's devotion to her brother, and by Eleanor, who found relief in being able to be a help and repair something. Eleanor had grown intensely close to her invalid mother and had chosen to go to a college nearby so as to be on hand.

Rosemary's plans were laid and she was set fair to realize them. The library in Thurston needed a part-time librarian and the woman who held the job had agreed not to retire until Rosemary was fit to take it on. The library was only open a couple of hours a day: housed in the Quaker Meeting Hall, its atmosphere of plainness, openness and thoughtfulness was very soothing to someone whose emotions had been so violently disrupted. Together with the money Edgar allowed her it was enough. She needed very little. She would begin to paint again, she hoped—she had done a good many sketches at the hospital and received encouraging praise from a local artist who made it his business to visit the long-term patients in his spare time. She had her paints and her sketching pads: he had given her two canvases. She would read. And Beethoven had become a new passion: the last quartets sounded in her head whenever she willed them to. She would lead a chaste life.

Occasionally she had the dizzy sensation that she did not exist: that she had passed through one band of reality and entered a zone of spirits. Wordsworth's lines of mourning on his dead, unattainable Lucy would be as an epitaph in her mind.

> No motion has she now, no force;
>  She neither hears nor sees;
> Rolled round in earth's diurnal course,
>  With rocks, and stones, and trees.

Already the effect of chastity and tranquillity seemed to have transfigured her: people would have to look twice to be sure it was her. The combination of very grey hair and apple-taut, blooming skin was unusual, even disconcerting. But once they caught her glance they could be sure: for the eyes which, when alone were always full of puzzled melancholy would sparkle with irony whenever they met another's gaze.

To her great surprise she found she was highly thought of in the town and much cherished: and already those few troubled spirits who had found such relief in pouring out their pain to her had sought her out. She was glad they did and honestly welcomed them.

She crossed Red Dial, headed towards Caldbeck then turned off and made for Ullaby, this isolated fell farming spot which lay on the northern flank of the fells below Skiddaw. Edgar's cottage was on the snow-line.

His time had been hard. Remorse, guilt and the relentless feeling of shame and scandal besieged him all about. He had left the town to give Jessie and himself at least some chance, finding this small old cottage and barn in a neglected state of disrepair and discovering some sort of nullifying satisfaction in over-working to put it in order. Now it was beautiful and Jessie found necessary occupation there. She had made for herself a lovely small garden stocked with old English flowers where birds came regularly and she could enjoy endless employment.

Sometimes, in the ferocity of his self-accusation, Edgar either to himself or—his temper had broken forever—before Jessie herself would bitterly regret the loss of Rosemary, grieving the loss of her wit, her cosseting of his mind, her life full of surprises. He would feel a lesser, a duller and a worse man without her: and those morbid reflections made him despair.

He loved Jessie and she him although the baby's death and Rosemary's dramatic and long-drawn-out illness had blighted both their lives. Both of them had grown very much older in their looks and in their reactions to life. They kept to themselves in this isolated cottage although Edgar put a bold face on it in his business dealings and there were many who said he was a hard-faced bastard who did not give a damn. Look, see how he laughed! He gnawed on his pain in secret and drank steadily, always spirits now.

Having sold the bungalow at a profit he had instantly begun another with the help of a couple of labourers: luck at last came his way and he discovered a bank manager who understood the soundness of his plan and was prepared to give him businesslike loans. An estate of bungalows was rising above the Roman camp. Edgar was on the way to being a rich enough man by local standards.

By now, of course, such an achievement seemed small. He missed the soaring of spirits and of mind which he had had with Rosemary, for better or for worse, and yet, earthed in Jessie, he would school his remorse and tell himself he was a fortunate man.

Jessie might have suffered most of all but she said the least. She was still only his common-law wife and made no move to urge him to legalize her position; knowing that talk of a divorce would unsettle Rosemary, Edgar waited. It was no great matter, he thought. In the small community about that hamlet, even there, Jessie had met with some of the cruelty which had never been far from the surface of many who had brushed against her in Thurston. But she had found two good friends: the wife of a young farmer setting out for himself on fifty acres he had scraped to rent by a dozen years of intensive labouring; and a spinster, an odd eccentric with five Yorkshire terriers who had a little cottage further down and a small private income which she supple-

mented by doing book reviews for a popular magazine on anything to do with animals or gardening: she had also written
several unsuccessful romantic novels. Jessie counted herself
blessed with these two.

When Rosemary arrived, Jessie was at the bottom of the fruit
garden, weeding the blackcurrant patch. She saw who it was and
stood quite still, alarmed enough to feel her heartbeat quicken.
Edgar came out of the cottage where he had been doing his
books: the two of them went back in together, glancing down
towards Jessie but not beckoning to her. In accordance with her
own laws, Jessie let them be and got on with what she was doing.

"It's beautiful," Rosemary said, glancing avidly about the oak-
beamed room. "Lovely! What I've always wanted." She clasped
her hands together silently. "Lovely," she repeated with a slight
catch in her voice. He nodded, dry-throated, wondering what was
in store—excited and delighted to see her so near him and so full
of life, the dazzling face and the hair silver in the dark interior
giving her the luminescence of an apparition. "And all the furniture fits so well—you always had good taste."

"You're very welcome here," he said, standing, as she was, and
tense, as she was.

"I only wanted to pop in," she said. "I made up my mind to. It
seemed as if we were so like enemies otherwise. I want nothing
from you, Edgar: don't worry."

"I see."

"Don't be scared, Edgar. I never bit you yet, did I?"

"You're looking well, Rosemary. I'm very pleased to see it."

"You were very kind to me."

"Don't say that."

"Why not? You were. You were very kind."

"*Please* ... Would you like a cup of tea?" He hesitated. "I
could make you one myself."

"That would be nice but no, I think, your, your Jessie would
be hurt, wouldn't she?"

"She could join us. But anyway she won't mind."

"I thought I could take you both on but I find I can't. Please
forgive me. Perhaps another time. You know—I'd like to walk up
that fell behind your cottage. It's quite famous."

"They all are."

"Oh Edgar. You never change!" She paused. "It's a dream
cottage, isn't it?"

384

They went out of the back door and into the lane which led up to the fell top. He pointed out the best way to go. "Stick to that wall," he said. "George Marrs keeps his bull on that fellside and it's no good."

"No good?"

He smiled at the tone of her enquiry for her voice slightly mimicked his gruff warning. "A bit frisky," he said, and smiled again.

"You saved me once from mad bulls." she said, "don't you remember?"

He nodded and she turned to go. For a moment he watched her, elegantly walking away from him, with rather uncertain steps on the rutted track. Remorse was now set in him, as fixed as the alcohol in his blood—both would have to be endured. He watched her until she was almost at the top of the first hillock which dipped down to a hollow quaintly named the Humble Jumble: then hopelessly he turned to join Jessie, feeling he had neglected her.

Conscious that Edgar was watching her, Rosemary walked as firmly as she could, looking about her only casually, restraining the rapid intensities of glance which nowadays characterized all her country walks. High above, sounding only as a purring note, was a silver aeroplane: like a free spirit, she thought. That was how such a beautiful sight would have appeared to the prehistoric man whose tumulus crowned this ancient hill—a silver soul, forever sailing in the heavens. Then she saw that the moon had already risen, its pale wafered crescent clear in the sky before her: behind her the sun was setting but she did not look back for fear Edgar would be troubled by it. She concentrated on the bracken which ran up the fell like a smouldering fire and this drew her up too until she came to the first ridge.

There, out of some ocean within her which she had thought dried out for all time, came a spring of fierce, illogical, inexplicable love, for herself, for her daughter, for her friends and for Edgar. Most of all for Edgar who once had loved her and been so loved and would always be inspirited in her life. She turned to wave to him, but he had gone.

Turning once more she made towards the next ridge and her exaltation grew stronger. The cool air, the sky, the hills, her breath, her body, this was the beginning, this was what there was and for this—all thanks. To whoever or whatever had made it, to fate or accident or into the void she wanted to give her thanks. For the will and the happiness. But for the pain, too, even that, and the loss, much thanks; for this terrible illumination between the dark before birth and the dark after death, all thanks.

She stopped and stood quite still and looked all about her. At the drystone wall, a modest but tenacious monument to man; at the sheep and horses and cattle; and, up the fell, at bracken, scree and rock and tumulus and then the clouds, those countless ever-changing clouds tinted in so many subtle tones, silent messengers between earth and water. And from all that she looked on, Rosemary felt a deep and tender pleasure fill her eyes: the salt was on her lips and she tasted it, as she held on tightly to the glory of the moment, full of life.

# A PLACE IN ENGLAND

## MELVYN BRAGG

For some time now Melvyn Bragg has been hailed as one of Britain's most talented young novelists — and A PLACE IN ENGLAND goes some way towards proving the point. Set in the years before and during World War II, it is an invigorating and exciting story of one man's attempt to pull himself up by the bootlaces from the degradation of working for others and into a position of some independence. That independence, however, is something hard won and bitterly kept; and the struggle for its achievement makes Joseph Talentire (whose father, John, was the hero of THE HIRED MAN) one of the most interesting of characters to appear in a modern British novel.

'Melvyn Bragg's latest novel places him solidly in the main tradition of English fiction, with an honourable ancestry through such disparate figures as Wells and Hardy, Dickens and Jane Austen to Henry Fielding'
*Tribune*

CORONET BOOKS

# JOSH LAWTON

## MELVYN BRAGG

From one of Britain's most talented young novelists, here is a book that will appeal to many people on many different planes. At once a love story and a tragedy it charts the quiet career of a young Cumbrian — Josh Lawton — who falls in love, marries, fathers a child and is then betrayed. Moving with deftness from scene to scene and character to character, the book ends in a tragedy that is both powerful and salutary — both a warning against simplicity and a cry for its presence in everything. And throughout, one of the strongest of 'characters' remains the landscape against which the various plots are played out — the Cumberland that Melvyn Bragg knows so well and describes so evocatively.

'Every scene is clear, every character immediately recognisable ... It is a brilliant try at producing a pastoral tragedy, certainly Mr. Bragg's best book'
*The Daily Telegraph*

**CORONET BOOKS**

# THE NERVE

## MELVYN BRAGG

"Uncommonly high talent"

Norman Shrapnel
*The Guardian*

'Bragg is a graceful and confident writer'
*The Observer*

'Since his first novel, Mr. Bragg's talent has grown until he has now achieved utter truthfulness'
*Sunday Telegraph*

'Mr. Bragg is — or seems — an effortless writer. He never strains, for effect, simply achieves it'
*The Sunday Times*

**CORONET BOOKS**

# MORE FICTION FROM CORONET

### MELVYN BRAGG
☐ 19853 2   A Place In England          50p
☐ 19852 4   Josh Lawton              40p
☐ 19991 1   The Nerve                75p

### R. F. DELDERFIELD
*A Horseman Riding By*
☐ 04360 1   Book 1 — Long Summer Day   80p
☐ 04361 X   Book 2 — Post Of Honour     60p
☐ 12971 9   Book 3 — The Green Gauntlet   50p

*To Serve Them All My Days*
☐ 17599 0   Book 1 — Late Spring        40p
☐ 16709 2   Book 2 — The Headmaster    40p

☐ 15623 6   God Is An Englishman      80p
☐ 16225 2   Theirs Was The Kingdom    95p

*All these books are available at your local bookshop or newsagent, or can be ordered direct from the publisher. Just tick the titles you want and fill in the form below.*

Prices and availability subject to change without notice.

............................................................................................................................

**CORONET BOOKS**, P.O. Box 11, Falmouth, Cornwall.
Please send cheque or postal order, and allow the following for postage and packing:

U.K. — One book 18p plus 8p per copy for each additional book ordered, up to a maximum of 66p.
B.F.P.O. and EIRE — 18p for the first book plus 8p per copy for the next 6 books, thereafter 3p per book.
OTHER OVERSEAS CUSTOMERS — 20p for the first book and 10p per copy for each additional book.

Name ...................................................................................................................

Address ...............................................................................................................

............................................................................................................................